FOR A
QUEEN'S LOVE

FOR A
QUEEN'S LOVE

The Stories of the Royal Wives of Philip II

JEAN PLAIDY

THREE
RIVERS
PRESS

Copyright © 1954, 1971 by Jean Plaidy

Excerpt from *A Favorite of the Queen*, copyright © 1955 by Jean Plaidy.

Published in the United States by Three Rivers Press, an imprint of the
Crown Publishing Group, a division of Random House, Inc., New York.

www.crownpublishing.com

Three Rivers Press and the Tugboat design are registered trademarks of
Random House, Inc.

Originally published in hardcover in Great Britain as *The Spanish
Bridegroom* by Robert Hale Limited, London, in 1954, and in hardcover
in the United States by G. P. Putnam's Sons, New York, in 1971.

This book contains an excerpt from the forthcoming Three Rivers Press
reprint of *A Favorite of the Queen* by Jean Plaidy, which was originally
published as *Gay Lord Robert* by Robert Hale Limited, London, in 1955.
This excerpt has been set for this edition only and may not reflect the
final content of the forthcoming edition.

Library of Congress Cataloging-in-Publication Data
Plaidy, Jean, 1906–1993.
[Spanish bridegroom]
For a queen's love : the stories of the royal wives of Philip II /
By Jean Plaidy. — 1st trade pbk. ed.
p. cm. — (A novel of the Tudors)
Originally published: The Spanish bridegroom : G. P. Putnam's Sons,
1971.
I. Philip II, King of Spain, 1527–1598—Fiction. 2. Great Britain—
Kings and rulers—Fiction. I. Title.
PR6015.I3S63 2010
823'.912—dc22
2009022659

ISBN 978-0-307-34622-3

Printed in the United States of America

Design by Maria Elias

1 3 5 7 9 10. 8 6 4 2

First Three Rivers Press Edition

Contents

Author's Note

I feel it is necessary to add a brief explanatory note when writing of Philip of Spain, whose character has given rise to so much controversy.

From the extensive research which I undertook before writing this book, it would appear that two different men are being dealt with, so diverse and opposite are the appraisals of him. One is a conscientious lover of duty, a worthy husband, and a devoted father; the other is a cold-blooded monster, completely devoid of human feeling, without charm, gloomy, morose, and moreover guilty of several murders including those of a wife and son.

I quote examples which come from two contemporaries: The French Ambassador, who witnessed his farewell to his dying wife, Elisabeth, said that her death was "enough to break the heart of so good a husband as the King was to her." But William of Orange, on the other hand, charged Philip not only with the murder of his son Carlos, but of this same wife Elisabeth, which crime he declared the King committed because he wished to marry his niece Anne of Austria, the richest heiress in the world.

I have come to the conclusion that the various judgments of Philip's character have been greatly influenced in each case by the religion of the chronicler; and it has been my aim to clear my mind of prejudice, to cut away religious bias, and to discover the real man.

I acknowledge the invaluable help I have had in this from many sources, the chief of which I detail below:

The Spanish Calendar of Letters and State Papers: English Affairs of the
Reign of Elizabeth. Edited by Martin A. S. Hume, FR Hist S.

History of the Reign of Philip II, King of Spain. William H. Prescott.

Spain, Its Greatness and Decay (1479–1788). Cambridge Historical
Series. By Martin A. S. Hume. Revived by Edward Armstrong.

Philip II of Spain. Martin A. S. Hume.

The Spanish Inquisition. Janet Gordon.

Spain. Henry Dwight Sedgwick.

The Dream of Philip. Edgar Maass.

Queens of Old Spain. Martin A. S. Hume.

Cardinal Ximenes and the Making of Spain. Reginald Merton.

Lives of the Queens of England. Agnes Strickland.

King, Queen, Jack. Milton Waldman.

The Pleasures of the Torture Chamber. John Swain.

Two English Queens and Philip. Martin A. S. Hume.

British History. John Wade.

J.P.

MARIA
MANOELA

ONE

Crowds had gathered early in the *Plaza Mayor* of the city of Valladolid on that May day. Peasants had come in from the slopes and valleys of the Sierra de Guadarrama, and wandering gypsies from as far south as Toledo. There were many vagabonds and beggars looking for easy pickings; they were sure they would find these in plenty, for all true Spaniards who could make the journey on this day would wish to be in the ancient capital of Castile.

In the shadow of San Pablo they stood, but it was not the beautiful façade with its memories of Torquemada that interested them; nor could the exquisite traceries and canopies of San Gregorio attract them at such a time. They chattered, breathing onion-tainted odors at one another, but they did not notice such odors, which were as common as the heat of the sun at noon, the smell of goats, or that of the blood of bulls.

"How long?" was the frequently uttered question. "Surely her time is at hand. Will it be a son, think you? A prince for Spain?"

They hoped so, for then the great bells of San Pablo and Santa Maria la Antigua would ring out; there would be rejoicing in the town; the best bulls would be brought forth, and there would be processions bright with the purple and gold of royalty. There would be free wine for the people. Girls with flowers in their hair would dance—Castilians, Andalusians, and luscious gypsy girls. There would be feasting and merry-making throughout the country. That was what the birth of a prince would mean. So eagerly the people waited, asking one another: "How long?"

In the mansion of Don Bernardino de Pimentel, which was but a stone's throw from the Church of San Pablo, a young man of twenty-seven sat alone in one of the great rooms. The room was dark and sparsely furnished, but the walls were hung with tapestry, some of which had been worked by Queen Isabella during her pregnancy.

The man stared moodily before him, his hands on his knees, his prominent lower lip jutting out as he stroked the hair on his chin. He was straining his ears for the cry of a child: he did not wish to go into his wife's chamber until he heard it. There would be women everywhere—his wife's attendants, and the ladies of the court, as well as those who had come to assist at the birth. It was too important a moment for him to be there, for to these people he was a legend. He was the greatest monarch in the world; he was hard and ruthless, and men and women trembled before him. Now he felt as he did before a great battle—strong, unconquerable, ready to efface himself if necessary for the sake of victory. He, Charles the First of Spain and the Fifth of Germany, would not disturb those women at their all-important task, any more than he would disturb his soldiers in the process of ravishing a town they had won.

He knew how to act, and what was more important, when to act. He was not the most feared man in Christendom for nothing.

He prayed now for a son—a prince, another such as himself, a great ruler who would combine the lusty strength of a Hapsburg with the subtlety of a Spaniard. He himself was all Flemish. He had been born in Flanders, and this land of dark, fierce-tempered people often seemed an alien land to him although he was its king. An accomplished linguist, able to converse in dialect with the subjects of his wide Empire, he spoke Castilian as a foreigner speaks it. He had inherited his love of good food from his Hapsburg ancestors; his fair, florid face was Hapsburg. He had great physical energy which he enjoyed expending on war, jousts, and plump German women.

He was, nevertheless, too clever to deceive himself. There were times when moods of melancholy would envelop him. Then he would remember his mother, Queen Juana, who lived out a poor mad existence in the Alcázar of Tordesillas, refusing to change her filthy rags, letting her gray hair hang in verminous strands (unless the fancy took her to have it dressed with jewels), screaming that she would kill her faithless husband (who had been dead more than twenty years) unless he would give up his six newest mistresses. She had been called a witch; the Holy Inquisition would have taken her long ago and have put her to torture and death by the flames, but for the fact that she was the mother of the Emperor.

The mother of the Emperor a raving lunatic! Such thoughts must bring with them considerable uneasiness when, in a nearby apartment, that Emperor's son was about to be born.

Moreover, the Emperor's wife, Isabella, was his first cousin, and she came from the same tainted stock. Could the child escape its heritage? Could it be bodily strong and mentally strong?

The Emperor felt the need to pray.

"*Shut out the* light. Shut out the light," cried the woman in the bed.

Doña Leonor de Mascarenhas leaned over the bed.

"No light comes through the window, dearest Highness. All light is shut out."

Leonor, plump and Portuguese, lifted the Queen's heavy dark hair out of her eyes before she returned to her stool at the side of the bed.

"It must be soon now, your Highness. It must be soon."

Queen Isabella nodded. It must be soon. This agony could not long endure. Her lips moved: "Grant me a prince. Let me delight my lord with a prince . . . a prince who will live in health to please him."

This was more than the bearing of a child; she knew it well. This was to be the child—the boy—whom his father wished to rule the world. Never had she been allowed to forget her great destiny. As the daughter of Emanuel the Great of Portugal, descended from great Ferdinand and even greater Isabella the Catholic, it was meant that she should marry the man who, through his father, Philip of Austria, would inherit the German dominions of Austria, Milan, Burgundy, Holland,

and the Netherlands; this wide inheritance, together with the Spanish crown, which came through the Emperor's mother, mad Queen Juana, would, it was hoped, fall to the child as yet unborn.

Isabella was a bride of a year only, but there had been times, during her married life, when she had seen her burly husband lapse into deep melancholy. Then she had shuddered, remembering his mother; and she had wondered—but secretly—whether in the fanatical fervor of the great Isabella herself—Charles's grandmother and mother of mad Juana—there had not been a seed of that which, fertilized in Juana, had grown to a lusty plant entwining itself about her brain and strangling her reason. For if Great Isabella had welded Spain together, she had also, with the help of her husband Ferdinand and the Holy Monk Torquemada, set in motion that mighty organization that brought out the sweat of all who dreaded its domination. Under Isabella the Inquisition had grown from a dwarf to a monster. New tortures had been invented, and from these none could feel entirely safe.

But such thoughts must not be hers at such a time.

The pain came and she could think of nothing but that. Tightly she pressed her lips together. She would not cry out; she dared not. Should the ruler of the world enter it to the sound of his mother's anguish!

Leonor, large and comfortable, was leaning over her again.

"Highness . . . you should not restrain yourself. It is bad for you. Cry out. There is none but your ladies and those who love you who can hear."

The long slender fingers closed about Leonor's wrist.

"There, there, dearest Highness. There . . . there . . ."

Isabella said: "I will die, but I will not wail. Shall my son come into the world to the sound of his mother's protesting cries? There must only be welcome for him."

"He'll not hear them, Highness. He'll be fighting for his breath. He'll not remember it against you. Cry out. It relieves the pain. It makes it easier, dearest lady."

But the lips were tightly pressed together; the sweat ran down her face, but still she did not utter a cry. And the first that was heard in that apartment was the cry of the child.

Leonor took the baby in her arms, exulting, while Isabella lay back exhausted, yet contented. She had done her duty. She had given a boy to Spain.

The bells rang out. The people crowded into the streets. In the churches praises and thanks were chanted. All Spain was rejoicing in the birth of a male heir. They were bringing bulls into the town, for there must be bulls when any event was celebrated. On the way to the bull-ring, many would be trampled to death in the narrow alleys—relics of the Moorish occupation. Already bulls were struggling in the artificial lake, the water of which was tinged with the stain of blood, for men in boats and others swimming were prodding the bulls with daggers, goading them to fury; this was a new kind of bull-fight, a prelude to the great occasion. Girls with flowers in their hair were dancing the old dances, kicking up their tattered skirts, exposing their shapely yet dirty limbs. There would be much lovemaking under the stars tonight; beside the *Puerta* they would lie—in the Plaza itself—fighting for a flask of wine or a gypsy girl. Knives flashed; voices were raised. There was laughter; there were screams of anger; and all in honor of the new Prince.

Into the center of this revelry the rider came. He was stained and weary from a long journey; only his desire to be first with the news had given him the spirit and courage to ride so far and so fast in so short a time. Through the gates of the city he had ridden, right into the market square. He was making for the Palace, but the people had stopped him.

"What news? What news?"

"I seek the Emperor. If you detain me, it is at your peril."

But these were the lawless ones, the robbers from the sierras, the beggars, the gypsies; they cared little for the Emperor's wrath. They drew their knives and demanded news as they would have demanded a man's purse when they faced him in a narrow mountain pass.

And when the news was told, they fell back; they crossed themselves—even the wildest of them—and they turned their eyes to the sky for a sign of vengeance. Silence had fallen over the alleys and court-yards.

"Holy Mother of God!" murmured the revellers. "What now? What an omen is this! God will be revenged. Holy Virgin, have mercy on us."

Here was calamity, for shortly before the royal Prince was making his way into the world, Imperial soldiers had been sacking the City of Rome.

Surely the saints, surely the Holy Mother, surely God Himself would never forgive the outrage.

𝒯𝒽𝑒 𝐸𝑚𝑝𝑒𝑟𝑜𝑟 𝒞𝒽𝒶𝓇𝓁𝑒𝓈 heard the news with horror. Hastily he crossed himself. He threatened to sentence the messenger to death in a cauldron of cold water slowly brought to the boil over a wood fire if the news should prove false. The messenger could only bow his head, tear his hair, and protest his innocence of any mischievous intent.

"I speak the truth, Imperial Highness. I have witnessed such sights with mine own eyes."

"At such a time!" groaned the Emperor. "At such a time!"

He was accustomed to misfortune; but had there ever been such misfortune as this? The Holy City sacked, the holy virgin nuns dragged into the squares of Rome and publicly raped; and all the drink-crazed soldiers had been starving until they scaled the walls of the city under the command of that fool the Connétable de Bourbon. And Bourbon, who had rebelled against his sovereign lord, the King of France, was an ally of the King of Spain. Hence it would be said that these soldiers, who were guilty of surely one of the worst times in history, were Impe-rial troops.

"At such a time!" repeated the Emperor. "My son just born . . . my country celebrating his birth . . . and now, instead of banners of scarlet and gold, we must plunge our city into sack-cloth and ashes. Let this not be made known. We must keep this secret."

But already he had heard the sound of wailing in the streets. He strode to the window and saw the people standing about, looking up at the sky, waiting for a sign from Heaven that the wrath of God was about to fall upon the land.

Charles dismissed the bearer of the dire news. He would be alone.

And when he was alone, he smiled slyly. The Pope had escaped to Castle Angelo and so saved his life. He was a prisoner there. There let him remain . . . the Emperor's prisoner. In the greatest disaster—any soldier knew—there was often brightness to be found. The Holy City had been desecrated by Imperial troops and the displeasure of Heaven would be directed against Spain just when that land had thought itself blessed by the birth of a prince. Alas! that was a great misfortune. But it must be remembered that the Pope was virtually a prisoner of the Emperor, and that was not such a bad thing. The wily Medici Pope had given Charles much anxiety; well now it would be the turn of Master Clement to feel anxiety on account of Charles. Henry of England was urging Pope Clement to grant him a divorce from Catharine of Aragon; and Catharine of Aragon was Charles's aunt. He believed that Clement would have granted the divorce in order to placate Henry; but now he would be obliged to reflect deeply. He must ask himself how he dared humiliate the aunt of a man whose captive he was.

Charles laughed his loud Hapsburg laugh. But he was sober almost at once. Melancholy was never far off these days; in the midst of pleasure and triumph it would overtake him.

Wily Clement was his prisoner, but the Holy City was desecrated, and many would mention his name—although he had had no part in it—when the Sack of Rome was recalled.

"Holy Mother of God," he prayed as fervently as any in the streets below, "let this not prove an evil omen to my son."

When the Queen heard, she had the child brought to her and held him fast in her arms.

Leonor, watching her with frightened eyes, made the sign of the cross. Her lips moved. "Holy Virgin, intercede for us. Let not the wrath of God fall on this newborn child. Strike not through him, Holy Virgin, Holy Mother of God."

She rocked to and fro on her stool, weeping for this evil thing, which had fallen on Rome.

Queen Isabella touched the baby's fair head and prayed. The baby cried for his milk. He was small and delicate, and everyone was now looking at him with trepidation. Any day the wrath of God would strike, and how could God strike more effectively than through the Prince?

But the weeks passed and the baby began to thrive; and now it was said in the streets of Valladolid that God did not intend after all to avenge the Sack of Rome on little Philip of Spain.

*T*he little boy with the fair hair and the pale blue eyes looked wonderingly into the dark face of the handsome woman on whose lap he sat. He loved her—loved the warm comfort of her plump breasts, the kisses and caresses which she showered on him. He loved to be rocked in her arms, to smell the scent of her—wine, onion-flavored food, and the perfume of her body mingling with the perfume she used to disguise them.

Secretly he loved her better than anyone—better than his mother, better than his little sister, the Princess Maria. His mother continually impressed upon him the need to be brave and strong; but to Leonor he was not so much Prince Philip, the heir to Spain and the Empire, as the baby boy. When with her he could suck his thumb in comfort; he could cry against her breasts; he could tell her that he was afraid of the solemn-faced men who came to look at him and talk of the greatness of Spain, and the part he would have to play in keeping it great; he could show her the bruise on his leg, the cut on his finger, and she would cluck and tut-tut and kiss to make it better. She would call him her brave little baby; and if he shed tears that would be a secret between them, because the rest of the world must believe that the Prince of Spain could never be so childish as to cry.

It was Leonor who made it possible for him to be the possessor of two personalities. Alone with her he was Little Philip, however grave and silent he was in the presence of the grandees. He was two years old, not yet breeched, still a baby, yet a Prince.

Lately he had grown jealous. Leonor loved him, but there was another. He saw Leonor's eyes soften when she held the new baby in her lap; she would laugh with pleasure when she held up her hand and the little Maria grasped her finger. "You love her most!" Philip would accuse her. But then her eyes would flash and she would swear by the saints that that was not so. "Never . . . never shall I be guilty of treason to my Prince of Spain."

"But," the little boy replied to that, "I do not wish to be *your* Prince, Leonor. I wish to be your Philip."

Then Leonor took him into her arms and kissed him tenderly. What thoughts went on behind those pale blue eyes? she wondered. They had feared his brain might not be strong; but it was. It was calm and capable of reasoning, if it was a little slow. All the delicacy was in his little body.

"Maria," she explained, "is but a baby, and women such as I am love little babies. They do something to us. Our hearts turn over to see their helplessness. Thus it was when you were a baby; now you are my prince as well."

And as she watched the children, Leonor compared them one with the other. Maria already showed her temperament. She was gay while her brother was solemn. Maria was a Hapsburg. There would be little to fear from Maria. But Philip . . . he was another matter. His gravity might please his mother and the statesmen about him, but Leonor thought it unnatural. She would have liked to see him laugh more often, not to think first: May I laugh? Is anyone watching? That was not natural in one so young.

Yes. Leonor spoke truthfully when she said she loved her Prince the better. She felt that though he was a boy and heir to half the world, he was the one who needed her love and, as Leonor herself had said, it was helpless ones whom women such as she was must love.

She sat with her arm about the Prince while she held his sister in the other and she told him of the April day more than a year ago when the great *Cortes* of Madrid had paid homage to him. He listened, attentive and grave, because however many times he heard her tell of this, it always seemed to be the first time.

"It was to you they paid homage . . . to you . . . my little one. I was so proud. I stood there and the tears flowed down my cheeks. *My* little one, and all the great men bowing before him, kissing his baby hand . . . the little fingers that had curled about mine. They all swore that he was their Prince and that when he grew to manhood they would follow him to the ends of the Earth and they would serve him with their lives."

"Did they then?" said the grave little boy. " 'Tis a pity, Leonor, that I did not hear them."

"You! You just blinked at them as though you did not think so much of them, for all their fine words."

"And did I cry, Leonor?"

"Not you! Though you were tired out with it all, and there was a jeweled pin tormenting you. I found it later. But did you cry? Not you. You remembered that your great father would not have liked to see you cry."

"And he was there, was he not, Leonor?"

"He was there, great and mighty, looking at you as though he cared more for you than all his kingdoms and his riches."

"And my mother?"

"She too."

"They love me dearly, Leonor."

"They do, my little one. And the people in the streets, they love you too. You should have heard the shouts. But you did hear them, of course."

"Did I, Leonor?"

"Yes, you did; and you did not cry. You lay there looking about you with those solemn blue eyes . . . a regular little prince."

"What did the people say, Leonor?"

" 'Long live the Prince. Long live Philip.' They then lighted bonfires in the streets, and they brought forth the best bulls. There was dancing and such goings-on in the bullring as never before. There was tilting with reeds, and such merriment . . . All that night and the next day, and the next night and the next and the next, the feasting went on. And it was all for you."

"They love me, do they not, Leonor?"

"They do, my love."

"But they love me as the Prince, Leonor. You love me as your Philip."

He put his arms about her neck and kept his head on her breast, for he did not wish her to read his thoughts. It was good to be a prince; but the best thing in the world was to be Leonor's little Philip.

His mother loved him too; but he wished that he did not know so much; he wished that he did not know she loved him so much partly because he had been born a boy, because he had not died—as everyone had expected—and because every time she looked at him she remembered that she had done her duty to her lord and to her country. Yet he felt that part of her love was his because he was her little boy.

She never petted him as Leonor did. Always when he saw her he must kneel before her and kiss the hem of her robe. He must remember ceremony before love.

Often she talked to him of his great duties.

"Never forget that you are a prince of Spain. Even if you have brothers, *you* will still be the heir to the crown. *You* must be more like your father than any."

"Why do I never see my father, your Highness?" he asked.

"Because he is far away. Your father is not only the King of Spain; he is Emperor of almost the whole of the world. That means that he cannot stay long in one place. He must roam the Empire, defending it."

"Why does my father own half the world, your Highness?"

"Because he inherited it . . . as you will. It came to him through his father and mother; and his father was called Philip as you are."

The boy liked that. He wanted to know more of this Philip.

"He was called Philip the Handsome because he was beautiful. He was fair and many loved him. Your grandmother loved him very dearly . . ."

Isabella's face altered when she spoke of Mad Juana, and Philip missed little. He had heard voices other than his mother's change when his grandmother was mentioned. He wished to know more about the mystery which surrounded her, the Queen who had brought the crown of Spain to his father. But Philip did not ask the question point blank.

He already knew that if he wished to take people off their guard it was better to approach a subject by devious means.

"And Philip the Handsome died, did he not?"

"He died long ago."

"And my grandmother . . . did she die too?"

There was the faintest hesitation, which the boy was not slow to notice. "Yes; she is dead, my son."

For dead she was, thought Isabella, dead to the world, living her strange existence in the Alcázar of Tordesillas, surrounded by those who were really her keepers, frenziedly gay at times, at others lost in the depth of her melancholy.

The little boy looked into his mother's face. One day he would discover more of this strange grandmother whose name seemed to have such an effect on everyone who heard it.

"Tell me of my father and his wars," he said.

She was eager to tell, for she knew that his father wished him to learn quickly all that was happening on the continent of Europe.

"Your father has many enemies, my son, for when a king and an emperor is rich in his rightful possessions there are many to envy him. Through his father—Philip, your namesake—he inherited Austria, and that means that he is continually at war with the German Princes who seek to take his lands from him. Through your grandfather, your father inherited the Duchy of Burgundy as well as Milan; and in France there is a wicked king who wishes to take these from him. So, as well as the German Princes, you father has to fight this wicked French King."

"But my father *always* wins."

"Your father *always* wins."

The little brow was puckered. "Why does he not kill the wicked French King and the German Princes? Then he would not have to fight them, and could be here with us."

"Once he caught the French King and brought him to Madrid. But kings do not kill kings. They make treaties. Your father sought to make peace with the French King so that all might be well between them; but the French King did not keep his word, and when your father released him, he went back to France and his little sons became your father's prisoners."

Isabella smiled at her son's eagerness to hear more of these French Princes. "Yes," she went on; "little Francis and little Henry came to be your father's prisoners in place of their father."

"Your Highness," cried Philip, betraying a little of his excitement, "if my father had been the prisoner of the King of France, would he not have taken him to France and should I not have had to go in his place?"

This was one of the moments when he betrayed his youth and his folly. His mother was looking at him in astonishment.

"Your father could never be the prisoner of anyone. Your father is the greatest ruler in the world."

The little boy blushed a deep pink. It was so easy to make mistakes. Now he could ask no more about the little French boys who had been his father's prisoners. But he knew that his Aunt Eleonore had become their stepmother. He wondered if they asked their stepmother— who was his father's sister—about *their* father.

His mother said, softening as she saw his dismay: "There is not only the King of France to plague your father; there is also the wicked King of England."

He nodded. He had heard of that King. His father distrusted the King of England, who was making a lot of trouble by being unkind to Philip's great-aunt, Queen Catharine.

"One day, my son, all these tasks will fall to your lot. One day you will have to face them as your father does now."

He knew it. Always the talk came back to that. It was the recurring theme. Already, although he was not yet three years old, he must begin his preparations. Yet he could not understand why, if his father always won, he did not put an end to the strife. Why did he not kill all his enemies and thus win everlasting peace? Philip was silent; there was so much to learn.

"Now I will tell you a story," said his mother. "Once upon a time there was a wicked man. He was a monk, and so he should have been a good man. But the Devil made him his own, and, with this monk, decided to destroy God's Holy Catholic Church. Do you know the name of that monk, Philip?"

This was the oft-told tale. This was his nursery legend. He knew the story of the wickedest man in the world, so he answered promptly: "Martin Luther."

She was pleased with him. "And what did he make throughout the world?"

He could scarcely pronounce the word; but he knew it and he would be able to say it for his father when he came: "Heretics."

She took his face between her hands. "Yes, my son, this wicked monk has gone about the world preaching evil until it has spread through Germany, Holland . . . the Netherlands. The poor, simple people there listen to the bad man and they believe what he says to be the truth. One day it will be your task to fight these heretics. You will have to drive them from the world as your great-grandfather and great-grandmother drove the Infidels from Granada. They must not be allowed to live, because living, they spread their evil. You will drive them from the face of the Earth. You will have the might of your father to help you, all the might of the Holy Inquisition."

He smiled, but he was tired. There was too much talk of what he would have to do in the future; he wanted to do something pleasant *now*. He wanted to play, but there was no one to play with, except his little sister Maria, and how could such a solemn boy play with a baby?

So patiently he listened while his mother continued to talk of the great tasks that lay ahead of him.

He was four years old—a baby no longer.

They had talked to him very seriously before they made the journey to Avila.

"Remember," said his mother, "that all eyes will be fixed upon you. This is a solemn occasion. As you ride through the city the people will shout your name; they will be thinking: There is the Prince. There is the boy born to be King and Emperor. You must show no fear. You must show nothing but calmness . . . dignity and pride in your rank. How I wish your father could be here."

Father, King, and Emperor. They were just names to the boy. He did not remember ever seeing the man. He visualized a giant, towering above all others, dressed in garments that dazzled the eyes—brave, beautiful, strong...the greatest man in the world. The thought of his father frightened him, for continually he was told that he must grow like him. How could he? He was not big enough—even for his age. He was inclined to be breathless. He was not clever enough; he asked a great many questions, but they were often the wrong questions.

He wished that he was more like his sister, who was now three years old. She laughed aloud without thought, never asking herself: Is it right for me to laugh? Everyone loved her. They shook their heads over her high spirits, for she too had her destiny prepared for her. If she knew, she did not care. She continued to laugh and play and charm those about her. "She's all Hapsburg!" people said. "She's her grandfather all over again." Her grandfather was that Philip the Handsome, the husband of the grandmother whose name was spoken in whispers, the mysterious grandmother of whom Philip could discover very little.

"Leonor," he said, "why must I go to Avila?"

"Because you are to be breeched, my love."

"I am to wear the clothes of a man. Well, why cannot I do that here?"

"Ah, my Philip. It is because you are a prince. You have to forget you are a little boy now. You have to be the people's Philip for a while. They wish to see you. They wish to say, 'He is growing up, our little Prince. He is not a baby anymore.' And they want to see the breeching done. They will be content with nothing less."

He shivered. He hated ceremonies. He was afraid when he rode through the town on his little mule and the people stared at him and shouted his name. He was always afraid that they would be displeased with him, that they would catch him laughing or see a tear in his eye. If they did and they gossiped about it, he would be disgraced for ever.

It was summer when they set out on the journey south from Valladolid.

On his mule, whose saddle was richly jeweled, rode Philip; about him was the bodyguard of soldiers and holy monks with the nobles of the court who were not fighting with his father in the Imperial dominions. In litters hung with rich cloth rode the Queen and her ladies;

among these was Leonor, with little Maria on her lap. Oh, to be a girl and not the heir of Spain! thought Philip. That was an ignoble thought, and he would have to confess, among his other sins, that it had come to him. But how could he help wishing it as he rode past the peasants' hovels, and the ragged people came out to look at them with strange expressions in their glittering eyes! Sometimes he felt that they were preparing to snatch his saddle from under him because they were hungry and the sight of so much riches maddened them. He felt frightened, which was wrong, for a prince must not be afraid. He felt sorry for them, which was wrong, for a prince must feel nothing but the need to preserve the dignity of his high office.

Beside him rode a boy considerably older than himself, a dark-eyed, sleek-haired Portuguese boy. Philip was drawn toward this boy because there was a look of merriment in his eyes and a dignity, which did not change when he met the Prince's gaze. He was courteous, yet not obsequious. Philip asked his name.

"It is Ruy Gomez da Silva, Highness."

He was all Portuguese; Philip knew that. "Keep riding beside me," said Philip.

Ruy Gomez said: "Your Highness is gracious." And his eyes seemed to say that it was something of a joke that a little boy of four years old should be Highness to one of his great age and wisdom.

He did look wise. How old was he? wondered Philip. Thirteen possibly, or even fourteen. A great age, that seemed; and a good age too, for he was not so old that he was a man, yet he was free from the bewilderment of babyhood, which still hung about Philip. Ruy was at the age when he had cut his way through the maze of youth and was not too old to remember the difficulties of one still struggling through it.

"Look!" said Philip. "Look at the blue hills in the distance."

"They are several miles away yet, Highness. When we reach them we shall know our journey is almost at an end."

Philip looked shyly at the boy; he wanted to ask what those hills were, but he must not expose his ignorance to a subject.

Ruy read his thoughts as, it seemed to Philip afterward, he did so often.

"Those are the Sierra de Guadarrama, my Prince."

"Yes," said Philip hastily. "Yes."

"They seem to recede as we approach them," said the bold boy. "Many things seem like that, your Highness."

How was that? Philip wondered. How could things seem farther away when they grew nearer. He would not ask. He must remember that a prince does not expose his ignorance to a subject. He turned away with a hint of haughtiness, but when he looked quickly back, the black eyes smiled into his.

Avila was built on a plateau, and as they climbed toward it the inhabitants came out to welcome them. Ahead rode the standard-bearers and the procession was a dazzling one to a people unaccustomed to splendor, but all eyes were on the four-year-old boy who, tired out with his journey, his little limbs stiff through the long hours in the saddle, longing for the soft lap of Doña Leonor, sat straight, bowing his head now and then in acknowledgment of the welcome, never for one instant letting any of them guess that he was weary and more than a little frightened.

The court rested in Avila before the great ceremony was due to take place, and during that time Philip's friendship with Ruy Gomez da Silva began.

Never in Philip's four years had he known such an interesting companion. Ruy was a clever diplomatist; he took charge of the Prince, while he never gave the slightest sign that he knew he was doing so.

And what tales he had to tell! They were such tales that Leonor had never heard. When they returned to the quiet of the palace in Valladolid it would be Philip who would entertain Leonor with his stories of the wonders of the world. He wondered if he might ask if Ruy could stay with him in Valladolid. He was desolate at the thought of losing him, though he would not show his grief if a parting were necessary; but how he prayed that this would not be so! Perhaps he could offer a prayer at the tomb of Torquemada or by the urn that contained the arm of St. Thomas Aquinas. Perhaps he could go to the Church of

San Vicente and pray to that saint, and if he thought of the horrible death that had befallen him, and if he suffered in thought that which San Vicente had suffered in actuality, the saint might listen and intercede for him.

In the meantime, here was Ruy attending the Prince, which the Queen and Leonor allowed, being glad that this should be so, for they had much to concern them. Maria, being so high-spirited, encroached on Leonor's time; and the Queen had many self-imposed tasks to perform. She must let the people see her; she must visit the tombs of saints and martyrs; she must distribute alms to the beggars who cried out at the gates of the palace, exposing their sores while they wailed of their misfortunes, as she must to the water-carriers who called out a blessing on her as they forced their mules through the narrow streets.

So Ruy would come to the Prince's apartment and bathe his feet and dress him; and all the time he talked, and his conversation was as colorful as he himself was.

"Did you see the great boulders on the road as we came along, Highness?"

"Yes," said his Highness. "I did."

"Did you know what they were?"

"Boulders," said the Prince calmly, but he was excited. Nothing was as it seemed, according to Ruy.

"So it would seem," said Ruy, coming closer, making his gleaming eyes long, bringing his face close to that of the Prince so that the little boy's heart began to beat fast with expectation. "But they are the tears of Christ." Ruy drew back to watch the effect of these words, but Philip was impassive, waiting. "He lived in Spain . . . here in Avila. He wandered among the plains and mountains of Spain, and when He saw this poor land . . . so dry that nothing would grow, He wept bitterly and when his tears fell on the barren land they turned into boulders."

"If they had turned into a river," said the grave little Prince, "that would have been better. For what good are the boulders but to make the way more difficult?"

Ruy burst out laughing, but he did not tell Philip why he laughed.

Philip wondered whether to command him to tell, but though he was a prince, he knew the etiquette between friends. Even a Prince could not command a friend.

"It may be, Highness," went on Ruy, "that Christ did not pass this way, for surely if He had, He would not have added to the difficulties of this land."

"We will pray for a miracle," said Philip. "It would be good to turn the boulders into water. Perhaps my father could do it."

Sometimes they talked of the Cid. Philip had not heard of that hero before; there had only been one hero in his life: his father.

"What!" cried Ruy. "Your Highness does not know of the Cid!" The black eyes gleamed. If the Emperor was a hero to his son, the Cid was an even greater hero to Ruy.

Ruy smiled and said: "We have the same name. He was Ruy Diaz de Bivar, *el mio Cid Campeador*. His real name was Rodrigo but he was called Ruy . . . as I am. And 'Cid,' that is an Arabic name which means Lord—the Champion Lord. He freed Spain from the Infidel."

Philip's brow was puckered. "My great-grandfather and my great-grandmother did that," he said haughtily.

"Indeed yes," said Ruy hastily. "But the Cid was the first to rise against them with any success. He lived long ago . . . long before great Ferdinand and Isabella."

"How long before?"

"Hundreds of years . . . two hundred at least; and there was fighting all that time; and when your great-grandfather and your great-grandmother married they united Castile and Aragon; and that was the beginning of good times for our country."

That was better. That was history as Philip knew it. But Ruy had many tales to tell of the Cid. He told of the hero's love for the beautiful Doña Ximena, and how the Cid had had to fight a duel for her before he won her; he told of how she loved him and how broken-hearted she was when he must tear himself from her to fight the Infidel. From Ruy, Philip learned her prayer:

"Tu que atodos guias, vala myo Cid el Campeador."

It was a prayer he might well say for his father. "Thou, who guardest all men, guard my lord and champion." But his father did not need such prayers, since even the Cid could not have been so important in the eyes of God as the Emperor Charles.

Now Ruy was telling him of the Cid's cleverness, how, wishing to raise money to pay his soldiers, he, with the help of his squire, filled coffers with sand and nails; these he showed to the Jews, telling them that they contained treasures he had won from the Moors, and proffered them as security for a loan. The Prince listened gravely. It seemed to him that sand and nails could not be worth very much, but he did not say so, as Maria would have done; he remained silent, waiting.

And the foolish Jews lent the money without opening the coffers which were heavily sealed. They dared not open them, for they knew that the Cid would be angry if they doubted his word. So ... he got the money and the Jews got the coffers full of worthless sand and nails.

Philip had to question this. He cried: "But ... how could the Cid keep the money when he had given nothing for it?"

"He rode away with their money, and it was too late to do anything about that when the coffers were opened."

"But that is stealing," pronounced the Prince. "And it is forbidden to steal."

The merry black eyes were opened very wide. "I see I forgot to explain to your Highness. These were *Jews* ... and Jews are infidels."

"They are ... heretics?" said Philip uncertainly.

"Infidels and heretics, your Highness ... one and the same. Burn them all ... torture them and send them to the flames.... That is the verdict of Holy Church."

Philip dropped his eyes. All was well. The Cid's honor was saved. He had stolen; but it was only from Jews.

Yet it did not say in the Scriptures: "Thou shalt not steal ... except from Jews, infidels, and heretics." He wondered why. Perhaps one day he would find out.

Ruy slipped Philip's shirt over his head. When the little boy was naked he seemed stripped of his dignity. His body was so small and white. He guessed that Ruy's was big and strong and brown. He felt that he was a very small boy without his clothes.

He said: "I wish that you could help me to dress with my new clothes. I wish I did not have to undress with so many people looking on."

"That," said Ruy, "is one of the penalties of being a prince who will one day be a king."

"But to stand there . . . naked before them all."

Ruy laughed his merry laugh. "Think nothing of it, Highness. It is no more than standing before me. There will merely be several hundred pairs of eyes upon you instead of one."

"But . . ." began Philip.

"You will not be afraid," soothed Ruy. "And when you wear the clothes of a man, you will have taken the first step toward becoming a man."

Philip was silent. He thought of the Cid, fighting for the lady he wished to marry, cheating the Jews with his coffers full of worthless sand. He supposed it was given to some, like the Cid, to do great and glorious deeds, and to others to be quiet and grave and clever enough to hide their fears and their joys, to learn to become, not what they wished to be, but what others had decided they must be.

At last there came that hot day when they set out for the ceremony.

The Queen, with her son and little daughter, rode in state to the Cloister of St. Anne. About them were the soldiers of the King's Guard, without whom the little Prince was never allowed to travel beyond the palace. The holy monks and nobles made up the procession, and all was pomp and ceremony of the most solemn kind.

Along the route the people had gathered. Philip was aware once more of thousands of eyes upon him. He felt smaller than he did in the privacy of his own apartments; he longed to be grown up, and as tall and strong as Ruy.

But Ruy was riding close to him. That gave him courage. He did not turn his head to look at his friend, but he was aware of him. He recalled his encouraging words: "Do not be afraid. There will be just several hundred pairs of eyes instead of one."

The procession, this time led by the Queen, had reached the gates of the Cloister. There it halted, and one of the nuns, who had been waiting at the gate, said in a loud voice, which could be heard by the stragglers on the edge of the crowd: "Who would enter in?"

Leonor answered for the Queen. "It is Doña Isabella, Queen and Empress, with her offspring, Philip and Maria."

The nun immediately made a deep obeisance and signed for the gates to be flung wide open.

How cold it was inside the Cloister! Philip dreaded the moment when he would be stripped of his clothes. If he felt cold he must not give the slightest sign. When he was stripped he must not shiver, for if he did, all would see, and what would they think of the one who was destined to rule them if they looked on a poor, shivering baby?

The Abbess had come forward to greet the Queen, and when the Prince was presented to her, she knelt before him so that her cold gray eyes beneath her hood were level with his.

They went along to the great hall where food was laid out for them, and the Queen sat at the head of the table with Philip on her right hand. Maria, who sat next to Leonor, did not realize the solemnity of the occasion.

"Philip!" she called. "Look at me!"

But he did not look at her. He gave no sign that he had heard her. How could he, heir to half the world, allow himself even to notice the frivolity of a careless child who, it seemed, would never understand Spanish dignity and Spanish solemnity. Leonor was smiling indulgently. They would all be saying: "Ah, but she is a Hapsburg. What can one expect?" Yet why should he not also be a Hapsburg? He had the same father and mother as Maria. But a prince who would one day be a king of Spain must be Spanish in every way. His father was a Hapsburg, but the people of Spain wanted a Spaniard to rule over them. Philip had no choice. He had to be a quiet, solemn little Spaniard. Philip of Spain must be what others wished him to be.

But in any case he would have been quiet on this day because he was frightened. This was his first big public ceremony, and it was devised for him. If there had been no Philip, there would have been no gathering of solemn people. He must not fail to play his part in the manner that was expected.

The meal was over and they left the table. His mother had taken him by the hand and was leading him through the cold corridors. He had become intensely aware of the cold; that was because he knew that soon they would take his clothes from him. He would shiver. He knew he would shiver; he would shiver with cold and fright. They would despise him and . . . his father would hear of it.

They had entered the chapel—surely the coldest in the world. Now he must stand on a dais. His mother had left him and he stood alone. The nuns came forward. He did not like their black, flowing garments; their cold, pale faces seemed to leer at him from their hideous cowls; they were like creatures from a nightmare.

His teeth began to chatter. He prayed to the Holy Virgin, to the saints, and to the Cid: "Help me to be like the Cid . . . like my father."

The nuns laid their cold hands upon him; deftly they stripped him of his clothes; they took everything from him, even his shift. There he stood, with all those eyes upon him, a naked little boy, with the whitest of bodies, which in itself was somehow shameful among these brown-skinned people.

He knew that somewhere among the watching crowd was Leonor; and the impulse came to him to look for her, to run to her and to cry against her breast, begging her to take him away from all these people and give him back his clothes.

He lowered his pale eyes and looked at his toes. None would guess how hard he was fighting to hold back his tears, to prevent the frail body from showing, by its shivering, how frightened he was.

The moments of nakedness could not last forever, although it seemed to the little boy that they would never end. But at last the cold hands were laid upon him and clothes were being slipped over his head. He was turned this way and that. The tight hose were put on his legs and he was forced into the breeches—the kind worn by men. Now came the black velvet jacket and the feather-decorated *biretta*. He watched the nuns' white fingers fix the jewel-encrusted dagger in his belt. He was tired with so much standing and he found it difficult to stand straight and still as he had been told he must.

And now that he was dressed the ceremony was not over. The noblemen and monks had come to the dais, and one of them began to enumerate his titles in a very loud voice. Philip had not known that there were so many. He tried to remember them, for he expected it was very wrong not to know them all. He discovered that not only was he heir to half the old world, but also to the new one. So many possessions and the tight new clothes were almost more than he could bear.

Then his eyes caught the face of his new friend, Ruy Gomez. Ruy smiled at him. Philip did not return the smile. He gave his friend a solemn stare, but he was happier suddenly.

He listened to the protestations of loyalty; he accepted the homage; he looked with indifference, as he had been taught to do, from the swathed figures of the Dominican monks to the helmeted soldiers of the guard. He might be Don Philip the Prince of Spain; but he was also the friend of Ruy Gomez da Silva; he was still Leonor's little Philip.

Philip never forgot the day his father returned. That was the end of childhood.

He had changed considerably from that frightened little boy of four who had stood naked before the grandees and ladies of the court, the monks, the nuns, and the soldiers in the Cloister of St. Anne.

He was less delicate, though still small for his age; his hair was yellow now, but his eyes were still the same pale shade of blue. He was quiet, dignified, and if he was not brilliant, he was intelligent; the most unusual of his characteristics was his astonishing self-control.

Friendship with Ruy Gomez had continued. Philip liked to have the boy in attendance, and if at times he wondered whether Ruy's affection for him was tempered by the knowledge that he would one day be the King, and a king's friendship could be a profitable one, Philip did not hold that against him.

Each day the importance of his position was impressed on Philip anew. When his father's letters arrived, they were read to him. Charles wished his son to follow the course of his campaigns in Europe; and

Philip, always docile, always obedient had listened when he was expected to listen, and absorbed as much as he could. He could speak no other language than Castilian; he had not distinguished himself in any branch of learning; but he could discuss his father's campaigns as intelligently as though he had taken part in them.

And it was at this stage that Charles found an opportunity to break away from his military life and visit his family.

Philip stood in the great hall waiting to receive his father. He was clad in black velvet according to the fashion, but he wore a blue feather in his *biretta*—chosen by Leonor because she said it made his eyes look more blue.

Philip was aware of the anxiety all about him. He knew that his mother wished he were a few inches taller, and that the blue feather was meant to add that extra blue to his eyes so that they did not seem weak. All those about him were apprehensive as to the effect of the Prince on his father, the Emperor.

Then came the sound of heralds, the clatter of horses' hooves and the cries of welcome; and into the hall stepped the hero, the legend, Charles the Fifth of Germany, Charles the First of Spain.

Their eyes met—father's and son's.

Charles saw a little boy—a very little boy—and his heart leaped with compassion and tenderness. He whispered to himself: "So that's my Philip. Holy Mother of God, give him a good life."

Philip had looked at the god and taken in as much as he could before making his obeisance. He saw a heavy man who seemed large more on account of his girth than his height. There was yellow hair, not unlike Philip's, a yellow beard, a broad forehead, and a large, aquiline nose. His eyes were bluer than Philip's; his face was criss-crossed with many lines etched, not only by anxieties, but by wind and sun of Germany, Italy, and Flanders as well as Spain. His aspect would have been benign but for the heavy, jutting jaw, which implied that ruthlessness and cruelty would not be lacking if the occasion demanded it.

To Philip he seemed to fit the picture of his imagination. There was power in the man and it emanated from him.

Charles had eyes for no one but the boy.

"My son!" he cried. "My son Philip!"

Then he strode forward and, as the boy would have remained kneeling, he cried: "Come, let me look at you. So you are my son, eh? You are Philip?"

Then he laughed loudly—for he was after all a Hapsburg, and if he wished he would defy Spanish ceremony—and embraced the boy, and held him fast against him as though he would never let him go.

At length he released him, and the Queen came forward with Maria. Maria, who was six, was old enough for decorum, but she showed none. She threw her arms about her father's neck and refused to let go when commanded by her mother. Over her fair curly head the Emperor's eyes met the solemn ones of his son and he smiled with approval, for he saw in this boy one who would be loved by the people of this alien land.

Throughout the town there was feasting and revelry at that time. Philip heard the continuous shouting of the people in the streets; and later he must stand on a balcony beside his father while the people cried out their loyalty; and when they declared that they could not see the Prince, his father lifted him on to his shoulders while the people cheered more wildly.

There was a great banquet, and while his father laughed and talked with the great ladies and gentlemen of the court, Philip was aware that he was the one whom his father constantly watched. Philip was quiet; he spoke only when spoken to.

When his attendants had put him to bed, his father came into the apartment. He stood by the bed looking down on his son.

"Tomorrow," he said, "we will talk. We have much to say to each other."

Philip immediately rose, for he knew it was wrong that he should lie down while his father stood, but Charles gently pushed him back on to the bed, saying: "No ceremony. We are alone. There are times when we may be just father and son. They have made a Spanish Don of you, I see."

"It was not what you wished, Sire?"

Charles stooped and pressed the boy's shoulder, noting how thin it was. "I am well pleased," he said. "Sleep now. Tomorrow we shall have much to say to each other, you and I."

Charles was delighted with his son's knowledge of his campaigns in the dominions. He saw at once that although Philip might not be a brilliant scholar his sharp intelligence would doubtless stand him in better stead.

Already Charles was growing tired of his military career. He told Philip so. "There are many times when I long for my home and my family. Grow up quickly, my son, for my armies need a younger man to command them. Affairs of state too can be settled the better by fresh minds."

When he took the boy on his knee Philip was at first shocked by such familiarity, but when they were alone Charles laughed at his solemnity.

"It is not always necessary to stand on ceremony, my son. Throw off the restraint when we are alone. Be yourself. Laugh. Drink. Enjoy good food. Good food ... good wine ... those are the real pleasures of life, and there is nothing to compare with them. Others besides great rulers can enjoy them; but that does not mean that great rulers should not also do so. Would I could live at ease with my family. I would like to see many brothers and sisters growing up with you and Maria. But when a man is always abroad how can he get children ... legitimate children? It is impossible. And when an Emperor has such a son as you, he feels his first duty is to hold his dominions together. Duty! It is the bane of a ruler's life. Oh, I sigh sometimes for freedom. Do you know what I would do, little son, if I had the free will to choose? Nay, you cannot guess. Become a monk, I think; give myself to prayer, keeping my soul safe for God, and saving the souls of others—for it is an easy thing for a wandering soldier to commit sins. Ah, you have a great task before you. I see great days ahead for Spain. We have made of it an industrial land. Who would have thought that possible? Think of Spain ... the whole of Spain ... Andalusia ... Aragon ... New Castile ... Old Castile ... all Spain. Think of the barren tablelands, the rocky, impassable sierras, the rushing rivers. Think of that. Or are you too young? You stand there looking so wise. Is it real wisdom, little son, or is it that you know when to hold your tongue? But perhaps that shows the greatest wisdom of all. You have learned to be silent. You will say: 'But, my father, you have not this gift.' " Charles burst into loud laughter. "No, I have it not. And how can I be silent when I meet my son . . . my *Don Felipe, Principe d'Espagne?* I have thought often of these meetings. I have thought of what I would say to you. I want your way to be easy. I want you to profit from the mistakes your father has made."

"You have made no mistakes, Sire."

That made him laugh more loudly. "So they told you that, did they? Bravo! But you are too wise to listen to such tales. A great task is yours, and you will do it better if you read the thoughts behind men's words, the meaning behind their smiles. I have had many defeats in my life, many disasters. I have made many mistakes, and you will not profit from them if you look the other way and call them victories. Oh yes, before the people we talk of victory, but alone together we will speak the truth. You understand?"

"I do, your Highness."

"Then call me *Father.* I like that word better on your lips. Philip, my son, my little one, grow up quickly. I need your help."

As Philip gazed into his father's face an extraordinary revelation came to him. This Emperor who talked of defeat seemed a greater hero than the faultless image which had been put constantly before him. This Emperor's struggles seemed more noble than the easy victories of that other.

"Yes," went on the Emperor; "we have made this into an industrial country. People from the valleys of the Elbro and the Douro, from the Tagus and the Guadalquivir leave their unfertile land and come to the towns. In Seville the best silk in the world is being made; from Toledo come the finest blades. Wool and cloth are being sent to our colonies. You see what great good our adventures did for Spain when they brought new lands under our domination, for it is *our* silks, *our* wools, *our* wine, and *our* grain that are sent to our colonies. We will allow no others to send it. The New World . . . Mexico and Peru is ours, and for that we must thank our adventurers. A country's greatness is measured not only by its native soil but by rich new lands that it has gathered to it; its foster-children are as important as its own, not only for the treasure they bring—the gold, the precious jewels, and the slaves—but for the commerce. You understand that?"

"Yes, Father."

"Then your task will be to extend our Empire and to lose nothing that we hold, for there will be others eager to seize it. Fight to the death any who stand in your way . . . as I have fought France, England, and the German Princes."

"Yes, Father."

"And there is another enemy whom you must fight more relentlessly than any, for on that fight depends the salvation of Christendom. Do you know who that enemy is?"

Philip had the answer ready. "It is the heretic."

The Emperor became a different man when he spoke of the heretic. The blue eyes lost their laughter and the jutting jaw showed how cruel he could be.

"The Holy Inquisition will join the fight with the *chevalet*, with the pulleys, with the red-hot pincers, with the wheel and the flames. It is your sacred duty to destroy them wherever you find them. If you hesitate to do so, you will destroy your own soul."

"Yes, Father."

"You must learn more of the holy work of your great-grandmother, she who is called Isabella the Catholic. You must learn how she worked with the holy monk, Tomás de Torquemada. You must learn more of the most sacred and holy Inquisition."

"I have learned much of these, Father."

"Then that is well. You cannot learn too much. You cannot hunt the heretic too zealously. And when you have found him, his torture cannot be too prolonged, his death too painful."

"No, Father."

"Now, my son, there is one thing that gives me some alarm. You have learned some of your lessons well, but in other matters you are not as learned as some of the Princes of Europe. You must speak French fluently, for who knows, one day I may find a French bride for you. Now, it would not be entirely necessary for you to speak with your bride in her own language, but it would not be amiss. Then you should understand Latin. You must speak Italian, German . . . Holy Mother of God, you must be able to speak with all your subjects. Nay, do not look downcast. The fault is not yours. You have not been given the tutors so to teach you. That shall be remedied without delay." The Emperor grasped his son's arm. "I should like to feel a little more flesh on these arms. I should like to see you shoot up faster. You sit a mule adequately, but a mule could not carry the Prince of Spain into battle. I should like to see you master a fiery steed. We must find a mount worthy of the Prince of Spain. We must find tutors. Have we not half the world in which to find them? You say little, my son. 'Yes, Father.' 'No, Father.' You are solemn for your years. Never mind. That is how I would have it. You will do well. I prophesy greatness for you. Go now, and later we will talk again."

Philip bowed with dignity and left his father. He was excited by the interview, yet filled with apprehension at the thought of the future.

𝒟on 𝒥uan de Zuñiga surveyed his pupil with some dismay. He had been courteous enough when the Emperor had brought them together; he had bowed with the ceremony Philip expected; he had walked at a respectful distance behind the Prince when they went into the stables; but as soon as they were there his manner changed.

The big man leaned forward and felt the Prince's arm.

"Your Highness will have to develop his muscles."

"If I wish to, I shall," answered Philip haughtily.

"If you wish to ride a horse and learn to fence, you will, your Highness," was the grim rejoinder.

Some princes would have lifted their whips and struck a servant for such familiarity; but Philip hesitated. His anger was cold. He would wait.

"Now mount," said Don Juan.

The man had been Commendador Mayor of Castile and he had spent much of his time at court, so he should have known how to address a prince. The Emperor could not know what an insolent creature he was or he would not have entrusted him with this task. Philip ignored the command. He stood very still, and only the heightened pink of his cheeks showed his anger.

"Well?" said the intrepid Don Juan. "Did your Highness not hear?"

"I could not believe that you addressed me," said Philip. "I am not accustomed to being addressed as though I am a serving-boy."

"Then I crave your Highness's pardon. It will, I fear, delay your Highness's tuition if your Highness must be addressed by all your titles on all occasions. What if your Highness's life should be in danger? Say the horse bolted? Must I crave your gracious permission to act before I aid you? Must I say, 'Your Highness, I fear your horse has bolted. Have I your most gracious permission to . . .'?"

"Enough!" cried Philip. "My father has chosen you to teach me to ride as he thinks I should, to fence and to acquire those tricks that will enable me to take part in tilts and tourneys. For that reason I will allow you to teach me. But I will not endure your impertinence, and if there is more of it I shall ask my father to find me a new teacher, and the old one shall not go unpunished."

"Your Highness has spoken."

During the riding lesson the Prince's anger was increased, though none would have guessed it as he sat his horse.

"Heels down. Back straight. Grip with your knees. Do you want a tumble?" Was that the way to speak to the heir of half the world?

"Saved you that time! A pretty pass if I had returned the Prince to his family with a broken nose, eh?"

Philip did not reply; but he had made up his mind.

And when the lesson was over the man had the effrontery to say: "Your Highness needs much practice. Why, you sit your horse like a bag of grain."

As soon as he was alone with his father, Philip said: "Father, I must have a new teacher."

"A new teacher! Why, Zuñiga is the best horseman in Spain. He's a master fencer too. There could not be a better teacher for you."

"But I cannot endure his insolence. He spoke to me as though I were . . . any boy learning to ride. He said I sat my horse like a sack of grain."

Charles drew his son to him so that Philip could smell the garlic on his breath. "You were a boy learning to ride this morning, my son; and a prince learning to ride must learn all the tricks that any boy must learn. I saw you ride into the stables, and, Philip, you did look like a sack of grain."

The boy did not speak, but his usually pale cheeks were fiery red. He felt that he would die of shame.

The restraint of the boy never failed to astonish Charles. He softened as he said: "Listen to me, my son. If Zuñiga were to flatter you and be only solicitous of ministering to your wishes, he would be like the rest of the court, and you would have one the less near you to tell you the truth—and a worse thing cannot happen to any man, old or young; but most of all to the young, for their want of experience does not enable them to discern truth from error. You are a wise boy and I rejoice in your wisdom. Do not be downcast. You have had a riding lesson this morning, but you have had too an even more valuable lesson. You have learned it well, I know."

Charles was right. Philip had learned yet another lesson, and he knew that it was more important than the management of horses.

In a room of his own house in Salamanca, the Prince sat at a table listening to the voice of his tutor, the learned Dr. Juan Martinez Pedernales. Pedernales—which meant "flint"—was not a name likely to endear its owner to his pupils, so the professor had somewhat ingeniously latinized it, as so many learned men like to latinize their names, and so was always known as "Dr. Siliceo."

He was fat, fond of good living, preferring to teach in comfort. It was, therefore, great good fortune to have been selected by the Emperor and his wife to tutor their son. What a change from teaching the poor boys of the University, who loved learning so much that they starved for it, begged for it, and came shivering with cold into the University of Salamanca, digesting knowledge in place of the food they could not afford to buy!

To this great seat of learning had come the Prince, riding in state to the town in the valley not far from the Portuguese border. Salamanca was one of the most notable centers of learning in the world, so that it was inevitable that Philip should be sent there. He could not, of course, be allowed to mix with the poor students or even the rich students. He had his own house in the town, with a full complement of attendants and guards.

With him had come his young cousin, Maximilian, who would one day marry Maria, Philip's sister, and return with her to Vienna. There was also the Prince's beloved friend, whom he was delighted to have with him—Ruy Gomez da Silva. These two boys took their lessons with Philip, and these lessons were made easy by Dr. Siliceo. In competition with these two boys—although Ruy was so much older and in any case by far the cleverest—Philip was always the one to be especially commended. The doctor made it his pleasure to see that Philip always knew the answers he was called upon to give; he never failed to compliment his royal pupil on his astuteness, his grasp of a problem or a translation.

The weak blue eyes would regard the doctor solemnly, and there would be no sign of pleasure in the pale face. Philip hid his thoughts, which were: But for Zuñiga's treatment of me and my father's comments on it, I verily believe I should imagine I am cleverer than Ruy and Max in spite of some evidence to the contrary. How right my father was! A prince, and especially one who is to be king, should be more ready to believe those who say harsh things of him than those who applaud.

Yet in his grave manner he accepted the compliments of Dr Siliceo, for he understood that in the scholar's mind there was the ever-present reminder that one day this pupil of his would rule Spain; and, even while knowing this, Philip could not help preferring Siliceo to Zuñiga, who was still instructing him in physical exercise. This might have been because physical exercise did not greatly appeal to him and he found it easier to apply himself with keenness to learning than to fencing or the hunt.

History—and in particular the history of Spain—enchanted him. When he rode out incognito with Ruy and Max, as he liked to do, he would gaze with awe at the landscape, at the distant sierras—and they

seemed ever-present, near or far, in whatever part of Spain he happened
to be—and think of the times when the Romans had dominated the
country, of the coming of the Visgoths; and chiefly he pondered on the
great Mohammedan conquest. Then he would feel a fierceness rising
within him, for everywhere in the country the influence of the Infidel
was apparent. The name of his great-grandmother, Isabella the Catholic, was frequently mentioned; and as he sat there at the table, pale and
impassive, inwardly he was swearing an oath, pledging himself to drive
the heretics from the world as Isabella had driven the infidels from
Granada.

The voice of Dr. Siliceo rose and fell in that quiet room as he
spoke of the past.

"Spain was broken. Her children were exiled or dead. Her noble
language was lost, and in the mountains and the plains was heard an alien
tongue. Blackamoors were in command, and the slaughter was great.
None was left to mourn save those women who had been taken as slaves
to the foul Infidel."

Philip clenched his hands, but he did not speak. He knew that the
expulsion of the Moors had not been effected until nearly eight hundred years had elapsed. Everywhere in Spain was the mark of the Moor
to bring humiliating reminders. Only the mountainous regions of the
north and the northwest had escaped, but everywhere else it seemed
the Moors lived on—in the buildings, in the customs and habits of the
people, in the shape of a face and the slant of a pair of eyes. Arabs and
Berbers had left their mark forever on the land of Spain.

The Cid had been a great hero, but it was not until the coming of
Ferdinand and Isabella nearly four hundred years later that Spain had
been freed, for that pair had conquered the Moorish stronghold of
Granada itself. Isabella and Ferdinand had grown rich, and Spain had
grown rich, and under them the dwarf Inquisition had grown to a
monster.

Philip was stung into speech suddenly. He said: "And now we have
the heretic. We will attack them as we have attacked the Moor and
the Jew."

Ruy looked at him with a faint smile curving his lips. He knew his friend well; he knew that beneath the grave calm a fierce spirit burned. It would be amusing to watch the great Siliceo pander to the Prince's ideas.

Maximilian, thinking of the chase which he longed to join, smiled too. Now, he thought, the old man can marvel at the cleverness of our Prince. Let him. It means no questions for me to answer, and who cares about the Moors and Moriscos, the Jews and the Berbers nowadays? What does the past matter when there is the future before us? Let them talk, Maximilian would sit dreaming, not of the past, but of the forest . . . the boar hunt and himself leading the chase.

"Your royal Highness has found the root of the matter as usual. Now we have the heretic! And we must drive him from the Earth with all the strength we once used against the Infidel."

"We have the Inquisition to help us," said Philip.

"And for that we must thank your Highness's great-grandfather and great-grandmother."

Ruy listened to them. He thought of the members of the Inquisition, the monks in their black robes with the masks of anonymity over the faces. They came to a man's house at midnight when all was quiet, and knocked at the door. They were admitted by trembling servants, for there was not a man or woman in Spain who did not know the *alguazils*—those familiars of the Inquisition—when they saw them. The victim would be dragged from his bed; he would be gagged with the Inquisition's terrible gag—an instrument that had been made in the shape of a pear when shut, but which was put into the mouth and made as big as desired by means of a screw. This was the first taste of torture to come. And through the night the victim was taken to the underground prisons of the Inquisition.

Ruy broke out in a sweat as he thought of it. During the last years he had come to hate cruelty. He was no coward, but he would not dare to state his views. What good could he do by stating them? He did not like the methods of the Inquisition. He did not like men who came by night and worked in the dark. Moreover, the victims of the Inquisition were often the rich, for when a man was condemned his goods were confiscated and taken by the Holy Office.

Now he listened to the impassioned words of Siliceo and the Prince's grave questions and answers.

Was it true, this history which they were teaching Philip? Had Isabella and Ferdinand been as devoted to the good of Spain as Dr. Siliceo implied? The Jews were the cleverest traders in Spain; and when they were condemned to death, the confiscation of their lands and goods had enriched the Catholic monarchs. But was it so wise to take the results of industry and destroy the source?

Such thoughts were dangerous, and Ruy was glad when the session was over. It ended as usual with the compliments of Dr. Siliceo to his Royal Highness.

After that it was time for the Prince's fencing lesson. When Ruy was helping him to dress for this he smiled, and Philip demanded to know the reason why. Great was the intimacy between them, so Ruy told the Prince that he was thinking that he would not be so softly treated by Zuñiga as he was by Siliceo.

"Indeed not," said Philip. "Zuñiga says what he means, but Siliceo what he thinks it behooves him to mean."

Ruy thought how astonishing the Prince could be. While he was gravely accepting Siliceo's praise, he knew it for gross flattery; and while with equal imperturbability he accepted the blunt words of Zuñiga, he knew them for truth.

A strange boy, this Philip. Young as he was, he made it difficult for others to read the thoughts behind his pale eyes; and as he grew older it would be even more difficult.

Ruy was tempted to go on: "And Dr. Siliceo's assessment of the past, your Highness, do you feel that to be as tempered as his assessment of your aptitude for learning?"

Philip said slowly: "I doubt not that he flatters my ancestors as he flatters me. But one thing there is of which we can be certain: There are heretics in the world . . . even in Spain . . . and we must not rest until we have destroyed them." The pale eyes had turned to a deeper shade of blue, which was due to the sudden bright color in the Prince's cheeks.

"Your Highness has read the works of this Martin Luther?"

Philip looked at Ruy in horror. "Read the words of Martin Luther! But that in itself is a sin."

"A sin, of a surety," said Ruy quickly. "But can you judge the man's teachings if you have read nothing of them?"

"This is a jest in bad taste," retorted Philip haughtily.

Ruy saw him in a new light. Here was the shadow of the man-to-be seen passing across the face of the boy . . . a ghost from the future. The calm, clear mind would never be calm nor clear on this subject. Ruy must remember that.

"In great bad taste, your Royal Highness; and for it I crave your pardon."

Philip smiled as he rarely smiled. He loved this Portuguese boy and because of that he would forgive him much.

"You love to jest," he said. "I know that." His eyes were a little stern as he added: "It is well that you make such jests only before me and not in the presence of others."

"But I have no wish to jest in the presence of others."

Philip gave one of his rare laughs. This was his true friend, and he had few true friends; he was quite aware, in spite of all the adulation he received, that he did not easily inspire affection.

"I shall be late for the fencing lesson," he said, "and that will put Master Zuñiga into a bad mood to begin with. But Ruy, before I go, I will tell you this: While we were talking with Siliceo I made a vow. I determined that in the centuries to come the world should remember Philip of Spain for his services to Christ. I will establish the true religion throughout the world. That is my dream. It shall come true . . . so help me God."

Ruy knelt and kissed his hand, but Philip hastily snatched it away. He was moved, and he was always embarrassed when he feared he might show his feelings.

He hurried to the fencing lesson, dreaming glorious dreams of the future.

Left alone, Ruy pondered. To be remembered for his services to Christ. But who should say which was the best way of serving Christ? Ruy tried to shut out of his mind his own picture of the grim torture chambers of the Inquisition, of the *autos-da-fé*, of mangled bodies in that yellow garment of shame, the *sanbenito*, with the flames scorching them while their cries of agony rose up to Heaven. He heard the voices of Dominicans chanting as they watched the flames; he saw their eyes gleaming through their masks. "In the service of God . . . in the service of Christ . . ." they chanted. Yet those martyrs, while the flames licked their bodies, had been known to cry: "I die in Christ. I die for the glory of God."

Ruy's dream of the future was different from Philip's, and Ruy was thoughtful, for he knew that the threads of his life were inextricably woven with those of the boy who had just left him.

We are both dreamers, he pondered. We are both dreaming our different dreams.

Leonor had a new baby to nurse on her lap. Philip, with amusement, could watch her clucking over the child as once she had clucked over him; once he must have looked very like his sister Juana.

This child was the sequel of the Emperor's visit, and before Charles left Spain there was yet another baby; this time the child was a boy.

Philip knew that the birth of his brother made him a little less important in the eyes of Spain. If he should become still more delicate, they would not be quite so anxious now.

Often he would steal into the nursery and look at the little boy in the cradle, imagining him, instead of himself, growing up, listening to the Emperor telling him of the dominions he would one day inherit.

The Emperor had returned to his dominions abroad, where his presence was urgently needed because of the menace of the Kings of France and England, and the spreading Lutheranism among the German Princes.

It was a year or so after his departure when Philip, on entering the nursery one day, found his little brother lying on the floor in a strange position. He thought at first that the child was playing some game.

"Get up," he cried. "You will hurt yourself if you kick like that."

Bending over the child, Philip saw that his face was distorted; his eyes rolled, showing the whites so that he looked grotesquely unlike himself. It was clear that he did not know his brother. He had bitten his tongue, and there was blood and foam at the side of his mouth and dribbling down his chin. A spasm seemed to pass through his body; he kicked furiously and lashed out with his arms. As Philip watched in horror, the little body became quite rigid and the breathing seemed to stop. Then the boy's legs began to jerk spasmodically; he started to breathe again; his face became bloated and he was gasping for his breath.

Philip called out in horror and Leonor came running in. She took one look at the child and crossed herself.

"We must do something," cried Philip. "What ails him?"

"Stand back!" cried Leonor. "The devils within him might leap out . . . and into you. That is what these evil-wishers would like. Stand back, I say."

"But he will injure himself. Look, Leonor. How can we help him?"

"We can do nothing but pray . . . pray the saints to help us fight this evil. I have seen him thus before. It passes. The evil spirits tire within him . . . and they let him rest. But each time he grows weaker. Go! I beg of you, go . . . lest they leave him and enter you . . . which is what they are trying to do."

Philip, obedient as ever, went to his own apartments.

Ruy was there, and Philip was glad of that. He sank on to a stool and told Ruy what he had seen.

"There are people here who wish me ill, who wish my family ill. Some witch has cast a spell upon my brother."

Ruy said nothing for a while. He was thinking that they would soon begin to look for the ill-wisher. Their eyes would fall upon some person . . . someone whom they wished to accuse. That person would be taken before the Inquisition, his body—or hers—broken in the torture chambers until a confession was extorted. But the explanation was simple. Ruy knew it. Not far away in the Alcázar of Tordesillas was a mad woman; and could madness be passed on just as the color of the eyes and the hair was passed on? Philip had his father's yellow hair and blue eyes. Why should not Philip's brother have inherited his grandmother's madness?

"What are you thinking, Ruy?"

Ruy spoke boldly. "It might be that someone has not put a spell upon him. He might have been born with this weakness."

It was impossible to know what was behind the mild blue eyes, but the Prince was waiting for his friend to continue.

"He is not strong," went on Ruy. "There are sicknesses of the mind as well as of the body. Sometimes the body wastes away, sometimes the mind. It might have nothing to do with witchcraft."

"Why should my brother be born with weakness? My father is strong, is he not? My mother also is strong."

"Yes, but . . ."

Philip knew. He had heard gossip about his grandmother. He knew now that she was not dead. He knew that there was a secret about her that was kept from him. He would not admit to Ruy that he did not know the nature of that secret.

He tried a shot in the dark. "You think of my grandmother?"

The shot hit its mark. Ruy bowed his head.

Philip tried to curb his curiosity. It would not become a prince to ask questions, concerning his own family, of a subject. But now he felt the shadow of his grandmother closer to him.

And when, a few weeks later, his brother died, it seemed closer than ever before.

THREE

Philip was twelve years old when his father, recently returned to Spain, broached the subject of marriage.

"You are twelve, my son. A fair age for a prince. We must get you a wife."

Philip murmured his thanks. None would have guessed his apprehension. The duties of a prince were numerous. Now the burden of possessing a wife was to be added to them.

"I have a fine match for you," said the Emperor.

Philip waited. There had been other matches that had come to nothing. That was how it was with the suggested matches of princes. Everything depended on politics, on war and peace. Events might throw him a lovely young girl or a woman three times his age; whichever came, he must accept her. That was part of his duty.

So he waited in trepidation for his father's next words.

It was typical of the Emperor that he should produce a map of their country. Thus were brides chosen for such as Philip.

"Now here is our country. Here is Navarre, which we conquered and added to our realm. You see how it borders on Old Castile. Now here are the Pyrenees Mountains, and on the other side of them is a continuation of Navarre, which is at the moment a dependency of France. How much more satisfactory it would be if the entire territory of Navarre belonged to Spain! But the conquest was not completed. There is a King of Navarre, as you know, living on the other side of the mountains—a vassal of King Francis. Now, this King Henry of Navarre has a daughter who will one day inherit his kingdom, for he has no sons, and is unlikely to have them."

"She is to be my wife, Father?"

"That is so. You do not seem pleased."

"I was rather surprised, Father. A daughter of such a small state to mate with Spain?"

The Emperor laid a hand on his son's shoulder. "You do well to wonder, my son. I will explain. Navarre is a small kingdom. It is not worth very much . . . in itself. But, Philip, it is the key to France. Give me a foothold in my enemy's territory and I verily believe that before long we may add the kingdom of France to our Empire."

"I see, Father." He was longing to ask about the girl. He tried to remember all he had ever heard of Jeanne d'Albret. He must show no eagerness, no desire to investigate the human side of this marriage. That was unimportant to Spain; therefore it must be unimportant to him.

The Emperor said: "You are indeed fortunate. Your bride might have been an old woman. She might have been a widow. She might have been four times your age. But no! She is a young girl of twelve . . . your own age. She is a high-spirited, handsome creature, Francis's own niece, the daughter of his beloved sister and that sly old fox Henry of Navarre. I'll tell you something, Philip. Francis is against the match. Of course he is against the match. He may be fond of dallying with his poets and his painters and his women in their mirrored baths, but he's no fool. He does not want me to have one foot on what he considers to be his land. He would like to get back our Spanish Navarre, I doubt not. You can depend upon it, that is a dream of his. I'll tell you something else: I am in secret negotiations with Henry of Navarre for his daughter. Yes; but at the moment Francis keeps her a close prisoner at Plessis-les-Tours. Yet her father longs for the marriage with Spain. And who would not? Why, my son, you are the greatest catch in the world. There is not a father who would not rejoice to unite his daughter with us. Nor a mother . . . except, of course, Henry's wife, Marguerite, who thinks only of her brother's wishes. They are like lovers, Francis and

Marguerite, and some say that the bond between them is actually closer than that of brother and sister. Nor would I be unwilling to believe aught of the King of France."

"And the girl . . . Jeanne," said Philip, "what does she think of the match?"

"She is eager. You can be sure of that. She, a humble daughter of Navarre, to be the Queen of Spain!"

"I would I could see a picture of her."

"You shall. I'll ask her father for it."

"And the marriage . . . when would it take place?"

"As soon as the arrangements can be made. You are a man. You are twelve years old. Why should you wait, eh?" The Emperor looked down into the grave face of the boy. "Now that I am home, you and I will meet every day. We will talk of state matters. You must learn something of the difficulties of governing an empire. You must learn how to choose your counselors; how to use them so as to prevent their using you. They will try all sorts of means. They will flatter you. They will try to tempt you through women. There is much I shall have to say to you, my son."

Philip nodded gravely. He was thinking: I am a man now. I am to have a wife.

He thought of her continually. He believed he was rather childish when he was alone. He talked to her sometimes, but not aloud. He would have felt deeply ashamed if any had heard him.

"Jeanne," he said, "little Jeanne." For, in his thoughts she was little; she was smaller than he was. It was a sore point that so many of his age were bigger. "Little Jeanne, you must not be afraid of the ceremonies and the grandees and the importance of all this. I know that you are but heiress to a small kingdom, and now you are a princess of Spain—to be its Queen one day—but do not be afraid, Jeanne. I will look after you."

She would be dark, he thought, in contrast with his own fairness. Her skin would be soft, and she would be gentle and loving, so that when they were alone together they could say anything to each other. He could love her as frankly as, when he was a baby, he had loved Leonor.

Rides through the palace grounds or in the surrounding country had a new interest. He imagined Jeanne beside him. He seemed to grow taller; he was bolder. Don Zuñiga was pleased with him; he scored victories in the tiltyard, and he sat his horse with more grace and firmness than he ever had before. It was true that his thoughts wandered during lessons, but as Dr. Siliceo had decided that the Prince could do no wrong, that was unimportant.

Jeanne! Little Jeanne! He was impatient for her. He thought of protecting her by day and loving her by night.

In the quiet of his bed, he said to her: "If I should seem cold, do not believe that I am. I am by nature cold, it is true . . . but that is for others, not for you. Sometimes I do not think I am really cold. It is just that there is so much for a prince to endure, and he must not show his feelings. With you, you see, I am loving and warm."

For strange, exalted weeks, Philip was in love with little Jeanne of Navarre whom he had never seen.

Then one day the dream was shattered.

The Emperor was in a fury. He was storming about the palace, and anyone who had good sense kept out of his way. The Emperor's rages were terrible. He sent for his son. The boy stood fearful before him, but carefully hiding his fear.

"That rogue!" cried Charles. "That cheat Francis! Do you know what he has done? He has taken your bride from you. He has married the girl to Guillaume de la Marck. He is laughing at us . . . snapping his fingers at us. He has cheated her father. He has lured the Duke of Clèves—this Guillaume de la Marck—from his allegiance to me by a bride who is a bribe from Navarre?"

"But, Father," cried Philip, for once forgetting his calm, for love was something which he had not yet learned to control, and even if he had been in love with a phantom Jeanne, he had been in love, "we cannot let this happen. We must lead an army to Paris. We must carry her off."

"But, my son, she is already married. The girl was forced against her will. Ah, she had spirit, that Jeanne. She would have been a good Queen of Spain. She protested . . . defying her uncle . . . defying her mother. She was beaten to within an inch of her life, I hear. But Francis had his way. He has married her to that scoundrel of Clèves. Master Guillaume shall rue the day, for I'll not rest till I have him on his knees."

"They . . . they beat her!" cried Philip.

"Until they were afraid they would kill her with their whips. And what good would a corpse be to Francis or to Clèves? The girl had not a chance against them. But they'll regret it. They *shall* regret it. Holy Mother! I'll set out at once. I'll take up arms against this upstart prince. He shall wish he had never been born to snap his fingers at me and side with my enemy."

So the Emperor left Spain on a campaign of vengeance while Philip mourned the loved one whom he had never seen.

He dreamed of his Jeanne, beautiful and weak without her Philip to protect her. He wept in the quietness of his room as he seemed to feel the whips on his own soft body.

Jeanne! Poor little Jeanne! How brave she was. She had written her protests and taken them to the Cathedral, where she had read them to the bishops. She had defied her uncle, the King of France, until they had beaten her almost to death.

This sorrow was something he could not hide. But Ruy, his confidant and friend, seemed to understand. Ruy had some comfort to offer; he introduced Philip to women.

Could nothing happen singly? Must he lose not only the girl who was to have been his wife, but his mother also?

Queen Isabella was lying in her bed, and all the ceremonies which accompanied the dying of a Queen were now being performed. Leonor sat in the death-chamber, rocking to and fro in her misery. Philip must stand by the bedside impassively hiding his grief, as became the heir of Spain.

Isabella was not sorry to go. She looked at her son and felt proud of him. She had nothing with which to reproach herself. As a beautiful princess, she had come from Portugal thirteen years before—with a dowry as attractive as her person—to marry her cousin, the Emperor Charles. The marriage had not only brought riches to Spain, but friendship between Portugal and that country. They had been happy—she and Charles—and if the Emperor had been guilty of certain infidelities, that was natural enough, since he was forced to spend so much time away from her. He had always behaved with the utmost dignity and decorum when in his own court; and she must rejoice when she contemplated the fate of those two French Queens, wives of Francis, who had allowed their court to be ruled by his two chief mistresses, first Madame de Chateaubriand, then Madame d'Etampes; and even more so would she rejoice when she recalled the fate which had befallen Queen Anne Boleyn of England.

So she felt hers to have been a happy life because she had done her duty. This pale boy with the serious face was her gift to her husband; she had two sprightly daughters also. It was true that two other boys she had borne had not lived; but Charles had his heir in Philip.

She had been popular in Spain; she had made many pilgrimages throughout the country; she had led a life of piety and usefulness; she had given alms to the poor and supported the Holy Inquisition; she had worked diligently at the beautiful tapestry that would proclaim her patience and her industry to the world long after she was dead.

She would be happy to leave this life, and she knew that her time for departure was fast approaching.

Now her attention was caught by the slight figure kneeling at her bedside. There were no tears on his face, yet she knew that he was grieving. Was he thinking of the days when, as a small boy, he had played with the jeweled crucifix that had hung about her neck? She remembered that she had been jealous of his fondness for Leonor; but now she could be glad of Leonor's devotion. Leonor would be a mother to him, and, in spite of his dignity, he was still a boy. She wanted to protect him, to stay alive a little longer. She wanted to talk to her husband about Philip. Perhaps she was being foolish, perhaps her mind was wandering a little, but she wanted to say something like this: "Do not burden him too soon. Do not make a king of him before he has been a young man." When he had been a boy they had tried to make a man of him; when he had been a baby they had made of him a boy. He was like a delicate hot-house flower, forced, always forced to be older, wiser than his years allowed.

She struggled up from her pillows as she tried to say her husband's name. "Charles . . . Charles . . ." she wanted to say, "he is but a child yet. Let him play. Let him learn to laugh and be happy. Do not make a king of him yet . . ."

Someone was putting a cup to her parched lips. "This is what your Highness is asking for . . ."

She shook her head and held out her hand to the boy. He took it, but as she smiled at him he seemed to fade before her eyes.

"Philip . . ." she tried to say, "be happy . . . be *young*."

But he could not tell what she was trying to say to him. He stood stiff, fighting the tears, aware of black-clad men in the chamber whose eyes would be upon him. He must resist the impulse to fling himself upon her, to remind her that she was his mother and that he was only a little boy after all.

But there was too much ceremonial, too many solemn faces, too many important men to remind him that she was no ordinary mother; she was Isabella, Queen and Empress, and he was the most important boy in the world because it was hoped that one day he would rule all of it.

It was Philip who must lead the procession. His father had decided that this should be so. Charles had shut himself up in the monastery at Toledo, and there, with the monks, he was praying for the soul of Isabella while the cortège journeyed slowly across Spain to Granada that Isabella might be laid to rest beside great Ferdinand and Isabella, who were her own and Charles's grandparents.

Philip's eyes were hurt by the glare of the sun, for it was hot May and the way through the foothills of the sierras and across the arid plain was tedious. As they passed through the towns he saw black cloth hanging from windows; everywhere was the black of mourning. There were black-robed monks and the hearse was covered in black cloth; the soldiers wore black feathers in their helmets; and among the black shone the silver crucifixes.

Southward rode the solemn procession; it crossed the Tagus by means of the bridge of Puerta del Sol; it wended its way from the valley of the Guadiana, through the foothills of the Sierra Morena to the valley of the Guadalquivir. Peasants watched them as they passed; they wept for good Queen Isabella, saying prayers for the salvation of her soul. Philip was interested in the subjects of that kingdom, which would one day be his; he saw farmers, tanned by the sun, bent by long hours of toil in their unfertile land, pausing now to watch the cortège pass; there were girls leaving the clothes they were washing in the streams to kneel by the roadside. Muleteers stopped beating their starving animals to look and mutter a prayer for the departed Queen. There were gypsy girls who refused to be solemn and smiled on him as though they did not know he was the Prince of Spain. He saw beggars who looked wistfully at the jewels in his clothes; he noticed the speculative glances of would-be robbers.

And into Granada at last they came—that city where every stone seemed to have been laid by an Infidel. In the Capilla Real, they set down the coffin of Isabella. There she lay beside the great sarcophagus adorned with alabaster images of Ferdinand and that other Isabella.

It was a solemn moment. None realized this more than Philip. He thought of his great-grandmother Isabella, who had defeated the last Moorish King, the great Boabdil himself, and had forced thousands of Moors to become Christians on pain of death.

He knelt on the tiles; he listened to the chanting voices about him as the last funeral rites were performed. He thought of his father who was praying for his mother's soul with the monks of Toledo; and he thought of the mother whom he would never see again.

The Emperor had insisted that Philip should undertake the journey to Granada without his company; Philip knew this meant that any childhood that might have been his was lost forever.

Life could not be all solemnity, and the Emperor did not wish that it should be. Yet he insisted that Philip should spend hours with him each day learning statecraft.

"I am growing old," said Charles, "but I care not, for soon you will be ready to take over my burdens."

Those were happy moments for Philip, but he was always disturbed lest he might not give the right answers to his father's questions. He looked to the future with apprehension; he was afraid that when his time came he would be unable to make the right decisions.

His father watched him with quizzical eyes. He was intelligent, this Philip, but slow; he was afraid of choosing the wrong course; his decisions would be laboriously made; there was no flash of genius there. Philip would never have brilliant inspirations.

Yet, steadiness was a good quality, the Emperor reminded himself. An unswerving sense of duty was even better.

Again and again Charles warned Philip of the gentlemen of the court, the grandees and the statesmen. "Trust them not. Never act on the advice of *one* of them. Listen to what all have to say, and weigh their words. They are full of hypocrisy. They will utter fine words because you are a prince and they seek your favors. They are greedy. They look for advancement. Listen to their counsel but . . . decide for yourself."

Philip listened eagerly. His desire not to disappoint touched the Emperor. On the whole, thought Charles, I am well pleased with this son of mine.

And when he left Spain once more, although Philip was only sixteen, he appointed him Regent, entrusting him with secrets that he would disclose to no other. He was to be *guided* in all things by the councillors whom Charles had chosen, but he, himself, was to make final decisions.

It was a test and, as it turned out, he came through it with honor.

He was indeed a man and, Charles decided, it was time he had a wife.

He was still the same sentimental youth who had loved Jeanne of Navarre. Now he loved another, and he prayed that this time he might not be thwarted.

He had her picture; he carried it beneath his doublet in a silver locket. She was a dark-haired, dark-eyed girl with a soft mouth in a face as round as a baby's. It was the bewildered childishness of her that made him know he would love her.

He had been mistaken in Jeanne of Navarre. She was a fiery girl of great spirit who would never have needed his protection as this baby-faced Maria Manoela would.

Twenty times a day he sought to be alone that he might look at the miniature. He must be young sometimes; he could not always think of matters of state. If he could not be a careless boy, he *could* be a lover, he could be a husband, for that was expected of him.

"Maria Manoela." He murmured it to her picture. He said it before he went to sleep and when he awoke in the morning. "Do not be afraid, little Maria Manoela. These solemn-faced people can do us no harm. We will laugh at them when we are alone together. We shall be the happiest King and Queen Spain has ever known."

He would tell her how he might have married Marguerite, daughter of the King of France, how he was allowed to choose between them, how he had looked at Maria Manoela's pictures and begged that she might be his wife.

There were times when fears would intrude on these pleasant thoughts. The blood-tie between them was strong, for Maria Manoela was not only his first cousin through his father, but through his mother also. Some members of the court had said that the relationship was too close. They whispered Juana's name—Juana, his mysterious grandmother. They spoke of the two little brothers who had been possessed by devils (for the second had died in the same manner as that one whom Philip had found writhing on the nursery floor). It was a strange thing, some said, that Juana should have been possessed and that these two children should have been also. They asked one another how God would view the proposed marriage between such close relations.

"The Pope will grant a dispensation," was the answer to that. "The Emperor will see that he dares do no other."

Philip trembled as he thought of all the marriages that had been arranged for him. How could he be sure that his little Maria Manoela would be allowed to come?

So the pleasant anticipation was tinged with apprehension.

𝒯𝒽𝑒 𝒫𝓇𝒾𝓂𝒶𝓉𝑒, 𝒞𝒶𝓇𝒹𝒾𝓃𝒶𝓁 Tabera of Toledo, brought the news to Valladolid from the Pope.

How difficult it was for a young lover to be calm, to sit on his state chair surrounded by the grandees and members of the council waiting while all the ceremonies took place, when he wanted to shout at them: "Well, what news? What says the Pope? Has he dared defy my father? Is she to come or am I to be disappointed again? I will have my Maria Manoela. I will."

But he sat still, and only the white knuckles just visible against the pale skin of his hands showed his eagerness.

The great men would not be hurried. Philip looked from the Primate to the Duke of Alba, who was one of those against whom his father had warned him. "He is ambitious, sanctimonious, and hypocritical," Charles had said. "He will try to tempt you by whatever means he has. But remember that he is a grandee. Do not let him have any share in the interior government of your kingdom. Make use of him in foreign affairs and in war. Those are his fields, and in them he is the best man we have." Now, looking at Alba's sly, aristocratic face, Philip thought: But this is not a matter of war, and if you try to prevent my marriage with Maria Manoela, Don Fernando Alvarez de Toledo, Duke of Alba, I'll not allow it.

But it seemed that Alba was in favor of the marriage.

"Militarily," he said to the council, "it is ideal. The peninsula of Spain and Portugal must stand as one country, and every tie which binds our two states together is for the benefit of both."

Philip could smile realizing that Alba saw everything from the military angle.

That other councillor, Granvelle, whom Charles had brought to Spain from Holland, and who was now one of his chief advisers, supported Alba. "Spain and Portugal should stand together," he said. "Nothing could be better for Spain."

Then Cardinal Tabera rose. He bowed to Philip and spoke the words which the Prince had been waiting to hear.

"The Holy Father has decided to grant your Highness his formal dispensation for the marriage between your Highness and your first cousin, Maria Manoela . . ."

Philip heard no more.

He longed to open his doublet, to bring out the locket and gaze at the bewildered face of his Maria Manoela, whom he was going to make the happiest Queen of Spain.

All through September Philip waited impatiently. Disguised, he would ride out with his friend Ruy and his cousin Maximilian. It was the duty of a ruler, he believed, to go unknown among his subjects. How could he properly see them through the traditional haze of ceremony that surrounded a ruler?

He watched the gathering of the grapes and the making of the wine; once he had to fly for his life from robbers whom he encountered on a mountain path when he had ridden too far from home, too heavily disguised. Such adventures did not excite him as they did Ruy or Max. He preferred the successes he scored with his councillors, for he was once more Regent, since his father was again away from Spain. He knew that his father delighted to leave him in charge of the kingdom and that he sought to press more and more responsibility upon him. Every day came long dispatches from the Emperor: he was entrusting Philip with every secret, insisting that Philip should know every move that was made. And the reason? As Philip approached maturity, so Charles stepped nearer and nearer to the life of seclusion that he craved.

Philip was proud of his father's trust, but how he longed—and particularly at this time—for a carefree life!

"When will she come?" he demanded impatiently of Ruy; and impatience was something Ruy had never seen him display before. "Do you think that even now they will make some excuse to keep her from me?"

"Can you love her when you have not seen her?" wondered Ruy.

"Is it not my duty to love her?"

"So it is duty, the need to marry young and provide heirs for the kingdom, that makes you yearn for her presence? So that is the reason for your Highness's eagerness?"

Philip half-turned to his friend. But not even to Ruy could he explain his true feelings.

Toward the end of October news came that the Infanta Maria

Manoela had left her native land in great pomp and with such lavish display that the eyes of all who beheld it were dazzled.

Philip scarcely slept during the nights of waiting. He longed to act without thought of ceremony and tradition! He wished he could have ridden out to meet her like some hero of old. He pictured himself inches taller than he was, dark and handsome as Ruy, covered in glory as was the Duke of Alba, as romantic as the Cid himself.

If he could have ridden thus he would not have made himself known to her at first; he would have impressed her with his chivalry, his virtues. . . . He would have been an unknown knight to rescue her from robbers, tilting in her honor, making her love him for himself . . . Philip . . . not the Prince of Spain.

Was this the essence of his dream? Was it merely to make Philip loved for his own sake? What a selfish, egotistical dream that was! And yet it was what he longed for. The love of Leonor was the only love that he could feel was completely disinterested. His father loved him for the duties he would take over; his mother had loved him because he was the son whom it was her duty to give to the royal house. Alba, Granvelle, Tabera, Medina Sidonia—all those men who had sworn to serve him with their lives—did not care for *him*; they gave their allegiance to the heir of Spain. Which of these people would love him constantly whatever he became? Only Leonor. And she made him impatient because she continued to treat him as a baby.

There was no one who could give him the love he needed—except Maria Manoela.

He longed for her; he wanted to tell her of all the trials that beset him, to make known to her the Philip whom none other—not even Ruy or Leonor—could know. That was why he longed for Maria Manoela.

He dreamed of her; he would wake with her name on his lips. And now that she was on her way to him, soon the dream would become a reality. No longer would he have to whisper "Maria Manoela" to the air; she would be beside him; he would put his arms about her, and his love would be tender because of her baby mouth and her bewildered eyes.

Meanwhile he must act, not as a lovesick young man, but as the Re-

gent of Spain. To abandon ceremony in this matter would be an unfor-
givable breach of that etiquette so dear to all Spanish hearts.

To meet the procession from Lisbon he sent an embassy to the
frontiers of Spain and Portugal. At its head was the Duke of Medina
Sidonia, the Guzman chief, the richest of all the nobles in Andalusia. In
the Duke's retinue would be slaves from the Indies who would proclaim
the extent of Spanish conquest; the members of his household would
be clad in the most splendid costumes; as for the Duke himself, the very
mules which carried his litter would be shod with gold. The Portuguese—and Maria Manoela among them—must realize the riches
and power of the Spaniards.

Philip was a little uneasy thinking of the Infanta's first glimpse of
the grandees of Spain. What would be her reactions when she compared himself with these handsome men? It was true that his entourage
would be more magnificent than the Duke's, his clothes more rich. But
could such magnificence, such fine clothes, make up for a shortness of
stature? If she were expecting a young man as handsome as Ruy Gomez,
would she be disappointed with her pale Prince?

He would make her love him. He would throw aside restraint; for her
he would be a different person from the Philip any had known before.

After all, he was not yet seventeen, and he still had time in which
to grow.

How could he wait for the formal meeting? He *must* see her; he must
have a glimpse of her before she saw him. He must have that advantage.

Ruy seemed to read his thoughts, for he said with a hint of mis-
chief in his eyes: "I know what I should be tempted to do were I in your
place."

Philip raised his eyebrows.

Ruy continued: "Ride out . . . disguised . . . mingle with the
crowds . . . take my first look at my bride before she met me formally."

Only the heightening of his color betrayed his excitement.

"I will consider that," said Philip.

Among the crowds that had gathered in the streets of Salamanca
to see the entry of the Infanta from Portugal was a young man in the

company of six others. He was a fair-haired pale-faced nobleman in a slouched velvet hat well pulled down over his face. Beside him was a dark, lithe man with merry eyes.

They saw the meeting between the Portuguese procession and the Spanish professors of the University of Salamanca. They saw the *regidores* and the judges in crimson velvet and white shoes—a splash of color against the somber academic robes of the rectors and the professors. Guarding the procession rode the soldiers in their brilliant uniforms; and the shouts of the people mingled with the triumphant music.

Through the gates of the city went the procession on its way to the palace of the Duke of Alba, where the Infanta would pass the night.

Philip's heart leaped with delight when he saw his bride, for she was all that he had imagined she would be. She was exactly like the pretty picture he carried in his locket. There she sat on her mule, which was covered with rich brocade; her saddle was of silver and her dress of cloth of silver on which flowers had been embroidered in gold thread. Her Castilian cape was of purple velvet and on that had been worked flowers in gold thread. Her lovely dark hair fell about her shoulders; her hat, decorated with a great plume, which drooped gracefully to one side of her face, was of the same purple velvet, gold-embroidered, as her cape.

But what did he care for these gaudy accoutrements! He looked at the thick, dark hair, at the plump little face beneath the feather-decorated hat, at the wide eyes and the rounded cheeks. This was his Maria Manoela whom he loved. He could see that she was frightened—frightened of all the pomp of Spain, which must match that of Portugal. There she was, his dear little cousin as yet, his wife to be.

He wanted to cry out: "Oh Maria . . . Maria Manoela, do not be afraid. I am here to protect you."

Then he wondered whether, much as she feared all these people, she feared her husband more.

If only he could have gone to her, pushed aside all these people. If only he could have said: "I will dismiss all these people and we will ride away together!"

The heroes of old might have done such things, but not the modern Prince of Spain.

He wondered what she had heard of him. Was it something to frighten her? Could it be that she had not liked his picture as he had liked hers? For a moment his restraint all but deserted him. This was, after all, the most important day he had yet lived through. There was his wife-to-be, and here he was, in the crowd, looking on like any humble sightseer. He all but pushed his way through the crowd to go to her.

But lifetime habits were too strong.

He remained perfectly still, his face impassive, his eyes fixed on the glittering young girl, as the bridle of her mule was taken by Don Luis Sarmiento, who had recently been Ambassador to Portugal. Now Don Luis was leading her under the brilliant canopy where she would receive the homage of the city magistrates.

All eyes were upon her, and not one of those attendants guessed that in that assembly was the Prince himself.

"Long live the Infanta!" shouted the people.

And if he did not shout as loudly as some, none spoke those words more fervently than Philip, her future husband.

He stood beside her, weighed down with splendor, while the Duke and Duchess of Alba, his sponsors, hovered close, and the Archbishop of Toledo performed the nuptial ceremony.

All Salamanca was *en fête*. The streets were filled with people, and the merrymaking would continue for days. From all over the country came the great noblemen to attend the wedding and the banquets and tourneys which would follow. The students from the University were given free meals to celebrate the marriage, for Philip, in his silent observation, had discovered what would please his subjects most; the people of the town were to be given the best bulls for their entertainment, and the finest matadors were coming from all corners of Spain to perform in Salamanca on the occasion of the Prince's wedding.

And, standing before the Archbishop, Philip was aware of nothing but his bride's covert glances. Her hand trembled in his. It was the first time she had seen him, for etiquette insisted that they should not see each other until the wedding day.

How he longed to reassure her! Poor little Maria Manoela! She was a few months younger than he was, and he was only sixteen. As he stood close to her he realized how young she was. She was a child, which was what he had never been allowed to be.

He had heard that she had wept bitterly in her apartments in the palace of the Duke of Alba; she had cried for her mother and her home in Portugal. She had admitted that she was afraid of her cousin Philip, for she had heard that he never laughed—and at home in Lisbon she and her family had laughed very much.

"But," said Philip's informant, "we made the Infanta laugh, your Highness. She could not help it when the Duke's comic dwarf did his tricks for her. And she was amused with the Duke's monkeys. She laughed so much at their antics that she forgot your royal Highness."

He would tell her that she would not long need dwarfs and monkeys to cheer her. Soon he would show her that she had nothing to fear.

He wanted to press her hand, but he did not do so. He had been rehearsed in the solemn ceremony, and he was accustomed to doing exactly what was required of him. He was also afraid that if he did anything unexpected she might turn those wondering eyes upon him and ask what he meant. That would be embarrassing under the solemn eyes of the Duke and Duchess.

The ceremony was long. The little bride was fatigued. The bridegroom saw the sheen of tears in her eyes.

He could not contain his thoughts then. He whispered: "It will not be long now." He had intended his voice to sound soft and comforting, but instead it seemed harsh. That was due to emotion, but how was she to know that! She would remember that she had heard how stern he was, how he never laughed. She flushed, concluding that in showing her tiredness she had been at fault.

Now she kept her eyes firmly fixed before her, and he knew that she was longing for her home in Lisbon.

After the ceremony was concluded the banquets and the entertainments began.

Would they never be alone? he wondered.

He did have a few words with her, whispered words, for how could he say what was in his heart, with all those people looking on?

"We are cousins," he said.

"Yes."

"And now . . . we are married."

"Yes."

She was straining to give the right answers. He is very serious, they had told her. Already, in spite of his youth—he is only a few months older than yourself—he has governed Spain in his father's absence.

He knew that she was looking for some significance behind his words. How could he say to her, "I want to hear your pretty voice. I want to watch your pretty lips . . ."?

But there was time. They had the whole of their lives before them. They danced together in the house of Christóbal Juarez.

"The Spanish manner is different from the Portuguese," he said.

"I . . . I crave your Highness's pardon. I . . . I shall quickly learn the Spanish ways."

He wanted to say: "Yes . . . yes. But I like the Portuguese way. I like it because it is yours . . ."

But he could not say those words, and he wondered whether he would ever be able to tell her what he felt.

But there was time.

He said: "We have all our lives together."

But again he sensed the fear in her. Did she think even that remark was a reproach?

Now they were truly married.

She was a little less frightened. He had not said all that he had meant to. He was too shy. It was, he had discovered, not possible to guard the feelings for sixteen years and then let them fly freely and naturally. They were like birds that had never learned to fly; and because their wings had been clipped they would never fly high and free.

Haltingly he had made love to her.

"You must not be frightened, Maria Manoela," he had told her. "It . . . is expected of us."

She seemed grateful for his gentleness. But she had expected that. Doubtless she had heard many stories of him. They would have said to her while she cried in her Lisbon home and begged them not to send her to Spain: "He will not be unkind. He is cold and stern, but never violent."

She was ready to laugh—though not with him. She liked to lie on her couch with her attendants about her, eating sweet-meats while they talked of their home in Lisbon; she liked to watch the dwarfs; she liked to hear the Indian slaves speak in their strange language. Such things amused her.

But when Philip appeared she would be subdued, although she did not shiver when he caressed her, as she had at first. She grew plumper and complacent.

Once he said to her, after he had previously rehearsed the speech: "It is a good thing for a Prince to find that he can love the wife who has been chosen for him." And she gave him great joy by laughing in her childish way and putting her arms about his neck, saying: "It is even better for a Princess to find that she loves the Prince they have chosen for her."

Her words and gestures were so delightful that he wished to continue with such a happy conversation.

"Then you love me, Maria Manoela?"

"It is my duty to love you."

"But apart from the duty?"

She laughed, showing her pretty teeth. "I was so frightened. They said that you did not laugh. And you do not much. But you are so kind to me and . . . I do not fret for Lisbon now."

He must remember that she was still a child, even though the difference in their ages was so slight. She had not discussed matters of state with a great Emperor; she had never had to listen to the discourse of generals, archbishops, and statesmen.

He thought of the home in which she must have been the petted daughter. Little petting had come his way—except from Leonor. That was all to the good, for petting did not help a prince or a princess to face what it was necessary to face. What if this little girl had fallen into hands other than his? His cousin Maximilian would have been impatient with her childishness. What would the Emperor, who was so vigorous, have thought of her? Philip thought of the French King who would not bother to hide the mistresses he preferred; he thought of the lusty man in that far-off island kingdom, who had beheaded yet another wife. She was not so unfortunate, this little Maria Manoela, to have fallen to Philip of Spain.

"I want you to be happy," he said. "I want you to love . . ." But it was difficult to talk of love. He finished lamely: ". . . to love Spain."

One day, he thought, I shall tell her everything that is in my mind. There is time yet, for we have the whole of our lives before us.

But he could not dally with his wife for long. He was the Regent of Spain, for even such an important event as the wedding of his son could not keep Charles from his exploits abroad.

The Prince must return to Valladolid and state matters. So the long journey north began.

Now there were state duties to absorb him. Every day he must read his father's dispatches and attend the meeting of the council; there were many problems to be solved, and such problems could never be settled quickly by one of Philip's temperament.

And all the time he longed to be with his bride. Constantly he wished that they could ride off alone together, not as Infante and Infanta of Spain, but just as Philip and Maria Manoela, two ordinary, simple people. How happy that would have made him! Was he, like his father, longing to cast off his responsibilities? He would have denied it. He told himself that he merely wished to be alone with her for a time, to learn to speak to her freely, not to couch his thoughts in solemn words, not to be afraid of showing excitement and the tenderness she aroused in him.

Could he not for a few short months be a lover instead of a statesman? Perhaps when his father returned he could explain his feelings to him. No! While he was alone he could imagine himself explaining but when he tried to do so he could never speak but in the calmest terms, in tones unsuited to the passions about which he wished to speak.

He imagined his father's loud laughter if he tried to tell him. "You have your nights with her. We do not intend to disturb that, you know. The sooner she gives you a family the better. You cannot start too soon. The country needs heirs."

He would have shrunk from his father's laughter. He would never be able to say: This love of mine is an ideal love. It is a state of companionship and understanding, not merely of physical love. That is but a part. She is my wife, and one day we will rule Spain together as Ferdinand and Isabella ruled. But I want more than that, Father. I want her to love me . . . me . . . Philip . . . not the Prince I am, not the King I shall one day be. I want to be tender to her so that she will come to me when she is afraid; I want her never to be afraid of me, and I want us to be happy as few people know happiness; and I think that because she is young, and because I am her husband and love her so much, I can build up that affection between us—strong and firm, so that it will make us happy all the days of our lives. But I must have time now to be with her. Now is the time to make her understand.

But how could he ever say such a thing to his father? The Emperor had been fond of his wife, but that had not prevented his having mistresses all over the world. Charles did not understand the ideal relationship which Philip sought.

It is because I am so much alone, thought Philip. I have been apart from others. But that is no longer so. There are two of us now and we must grow close together. We must be loving, tender, and faithful, my Maria Manoela and I.

They were riding the few miles from Valladolid to Tordesillas. They were going to visit Philip's grandmother because tradition demanded it; she was that Queen Juana who was also the grandmother of Maria Manoela.

Maria Manoela was frightened. She had heard tales of Mad Juana.

Philip wondered what his wife had heard, remembering how, in his childhood, he had been aware of the mysteries which surrounded his grandmother. He would have liked to ask her, but he could not. Doubtless some garrulous attendant had chattered with another in the Lisbon palace, and the madness of a queen—and that Queen a near relation of them both—would be an unseemly subject. Her madness, her captivity, her most embarrassing conduct were all matters that should never be mentioned.

Maria Manoela looked very pretty today, and he thought how charming she was with that bewildered and fearful look upon her. Thus she had looked when she had first come to Spain—like a trapped animal, wondering what was in store for her. He felt that when she was troubled, he loved her more deeply, more tenderly than when she was laughing and gay—although she was never so gay with him as she was with the pretty young girls whom she had brought with her. Sometimes, unknown to her, he had listened to her laughter. She could not believe that the important young man whom she saw at state functions could ever be the warm-hearted lover he longed to be. That cold young Prince was always between them; even Philip could not escape from him. When he tried to tell her of his love, that other Philip would be there, restraining him. He could only comfort himself by believing that it would not always be thus.

She would begin to understand him soon. She would cease to be a fearful child who could crow with delight over the antics of a dwarf. She would grow into a woman, and then she would understand. He longed for that day.

He could not take his eyes from her without a great effort. Her lovely black hair was combed high and her coif was decorated with rich jewels which she had brought with her. Her velvet dress billowed over the rich trappings of her mule. He must turn from her to bow his head in the acknowledgment of the greetings of water-carriers, muleteers, and gypsies who stood along the road staring at them as they passed. These people cheered him loudly and with affection. As a young bridegroom he was a romantic figure; and his little bride was such an enchanting sight.

"The saints preserve our Prince!" they cried. And some murmured: "Give him long life. He looks delicate. 'Tis a pity he has not his wife's healthy looks."

Courteously he acknowledged their greetings, but he gave no sign that he heard their words.

Philip and Maria Manoela rode on to that palace, which was in reality a prison.

Maria Manoela could not prevent herself from shivering as they rode into the courtyard. She would have been terrified had she been alone. She had heard that her grandmother was a witch who consorted with devils, for it was true that she had railed against Holy Church and the Inquisition. But for the fact that she belonged to the royal house, the Inquisition would have taken her before this.

"Is she truly a witch?" she whispered.

Philip answered: "All will be well." His voice was harsh with tenderness, and she turned from him. He wanted to tell her that he would be beside her, that she would have nothing to fear, but they were surrounded by attendants and this was not the time.

Maria Manoela wanted to ask Philip to turn back, but she dared not. She was never sure of him. Sometimes he seemed kind, but at others he was so stern. He frightened her. "He is always right," she had told one of her ladies. "I am frightened of people who are always right. Sins . . . nice venial sins are so comforting." And that was true, she thought now. Eating too many sweetmeats, not concentrating during Mass, passing on scandalous tidbits, not always confessing the more private faults . . . those were the little sins committed by everybody—except Philip. He was apart. That was why he was frightening. Still, she would be glad of his presence when she had to kneel before the old lady; she would pray then that her grandmother would not touch her. It was said that the touch of a witch was enough to lay a spell upon you. The thought of a witch, perhaps . . . no wonder she was shivering.

Philip whispered: "You are afraid." And he knew even as he spoke that the words sounded more like a reproach than the comfort he intended to convey.

"What . . . will she do to us?"

"Give us her blessing."

"Will she . . . touch us?"

"She will hardly be able to give us her blessing without doing so." And he thought: Little one, *I* shall be there. I shall be with you.

They had entered the palace now. They were walking through long, tiled corridors; their footsteps echoed through the gloomy halls. Maria Manoela moved closer to Philip; and he thought: She turns to me when she is afraid. Gradually she will come to trust me . . . to love me . . .

Now they were about to enter the presence of the mad woman of the Tordesillas Alcázar.

As one of the guards of the door knelt before Philip he said: "Your royal Highness, this is one of her Highness's good days."

Philip nodded. The doors were thrown open. A herald sounded a fanfare.

"Their royal Highnesses, Prince Philip and the Princess Maria Manoela."

They went forward together.

Maria Manoela was trembling; she was more frightened than she had been when she had said good-bye to her family in Lisbon, more frightened than when she had been left alone for the first time with her husband, for she believed herself to be in the presence of a witch.

The room was hung with black velvet which shut out most of the light. The air was filled with the smell of decaying food. Candles burned in their silver candlesticks.

Now that Maria Manoela's eyes had grown accustomed to the gloom she saw that dishes of food were lying about on the floor; they had clearly been there for a long time. It was one of Queen Juana's fancies that she should eat her food on the floor like a dog and that the dishes should be left until she commanded that they be removed.

In a high chair sat Queen Juana, daughter of Queen Isabella the Catholic and Ferdinand. Her face was unwashed; her hair hung in greasy strands about her shoulders; her robe of rich velvet was torn and stained; through its rents it was possible to see her dirty skin.

She peered at the young pair who were approaching.

"Who's this?" she cried.

A man who had been standing by her chair bowed and answered: "It is his Highness your grandson, Prince Philip, and with him is his bride, the Princess Maria Manoela."

"Philip!" she cried. "So it's Philip."

She began to laugh and her voice echoed uncannily in the strange room.

The attendant said: "Your *grandson*, Prince Philip, Highness."

She took the man by his sleeve and laughed up into his face. "You think I do not know this Philip. I know this one. He is my grandson. Go. Leave me. I wish to be alone with my children."

Maria Manoela, who was kneeling before her with Philip at her side, began to tremble so violently that Juana noticed this. "What ails the girl?" she cried. Maria Manoela gasped aloud as the skinny hand seized her shoulder and she felt the sharp nails in her skin.

"Nothing ails her," said Philip. "She is overcome by your majesty."

Juana laughed and released the Princess.

"She is overcome by my majesty!" She turned to the attendant. "Did you hear that? But what do you here? Did I not tell you I would be alone with my children?"

The man looked at Philip, who signed for him to go. In a few seconds the Prince and Princess were alone with the mad Queen.

"Do not kneel now." Her voice was quiet and quavering. "Do not kneel to poor Juana. Philip . . . oh, Philip, are you like that other Philip? Are you like *my* Philip . . . he who, they tell me, is dead? But he is not dead. He comes here. He comes often. He rises from his coffin and he comes to me . . . She trembles still . . . that child. She is overcome by my majesty. That is what this Philip tells me. He knows how to say the words which appeal . . . which appease. He is rightly named . . . Philip! My Philip would come to me after he had spent the night with one of them . . . fat Flemish women. They were the sort he liked . . . fat, ugly strumpets. He would come to my apartments, fresh from his love, and he would say: 'You're the prettiest woman in Flanders . . . or Ghent . . . or wherever we were. There's none can compare with my Queen Juana . . .' Philip. Philip." The cackling laughter broke out again.

Philip said: "Grandmother, we have come, my wife and I, to ask your blessing."

"Why do you come to me . . . to me? . . . Who cares for poor Juana now? . . . When they wanted me mad, they made me mad . . . and when they wanted me sane ... I was sane. That was my father and my husband ... between them they used me ... mad ... sane ... mad ... sane ... What's it to be today?"

"Grandmother, this is my bride, Maria Manoela ..."

"She's plump and pretty ... and she's your bride. What is your name, boy? What did you say?"

"I am Philip ..."

"Philip. Philip." She peered about the room. "He will not come out today. It is because you are here. He is hiding behind the curtains. It is a pity. I should have liked you to see him. Philip ... Philip the Handsome ... the prettiest man in Zeeland ... or Flanders ... or Spain ... wherever we were. I did not tell him that. There were too many to tell him. Child ... child ... come here, child."

Maria Manoela hung back, but Philip pushed her gently forward and Juana took her by the wrist. Suddenly Maria Manoela felt her chin grasped by the bony hand.

"Plump and pretty. As he liked them ... But dark. He liked them fair. You are looking for him ... you sly creature. Yes you are. Take her away. I'll not have women here. Can you see him? He comes in and laughs at me. They have tried to take him from me. He was in his coffin, but I kept him with me ... and when it was night and all had left me I would look into the coffin and he would talk to me ... laugh at me ... boast about his women. He is so beautiful. I wanted to die when he was with the others ... and when he came back I forgave him all ... I was mad for him ... sane for him ... And you ... you with your plump, pretty face have come to look for him ..." The mad eyes were wild with sudden fury. Philip put an arm about Maria Manoela and drew her away. She caught her breath in a sobbing gasp and hastily she crossed herself.

"Nay, nay," said Philip in his calm, clear voice. "Maria Manoela is my bride. Your husband is dead, dear Grandmother. It is many years since he died, and now we come to ask your blessing on our union."

Juana lay back in her chair and the tears began to run down her cheeks. "Is it true, then? Is he dead? Is there no longer life in his beautiful body?"

"Grandmother, it is true. He is dead."

The mirthless laughter rang out. "Come here. Come closer . . . both of you. He is dead, they say. That is what they say. But I will tell you a secret. He is here now . . . here in this room. He is laughing at us . . . He is kissing the fat Flemish women in the tapestry. One day I set it on fire. That'll spoil his game, I said. And it did." She glared at Maria Manoela. "Who is this girl?"

"My wife, Grandmother. Your granddaughter, Maria Manoela. Your daughter's daughter."

"My daughter's daughter. What daughter was that?"

"Your daughter Katharine, Grandmother, she who married into Portugal."

"Katharine . . . Katharine . . . sweet little Katharine . . ." Juana began to weep again. "They took her from me. I kept her here . . . in this palace close to me. She was so pretty . . . but they said I dressed her in dirty rags and I never let her go abroad. I dared not. I was afraid they would take her from me. Sweet little Katharine. I had a window made for her so that she could look from it . . . and I had children come and play that she might watch them . . . But I would not let her leave me . . . Did your mother speak of me, my child?"

"Y-yes, Grandmother," stammered Maria Manoela. "She spoke of you."

"Did she tell you how they came and took her from me? . . . It was my son Charles . . . my son, the Emperor . . . who is but a Prince and only rules because I am shut away. While I live I am the Queen . . . I am the true ruler of Spain."

Philip said sternly: "Grandmother, you were speaking of your daughter Katharine."

"My daughter Katharine . . . my sweet sweet Katharine. Charles my son had men come by night. They cut a hole in the wall of her chamber . . . at dead of night they came . . . and they took her away from me . . . my Katharine . . . my sweet little daughter." Her tears ceased abruptly and she began to laugh. "But they brought her back. They had to." She was sad again. "But I had lost my Katharine . . . They would not let me keep her to myself . . . There were tutors for her . . . She must be brought up like an Infanta, they said, not like the child of a mad woman . . . Mad . . . Sane . . . I was mad then. Thus it has always been. Mad . . . Sane . . . And which is it today?"

"Grandmother, I implore you, give us your blessing," pleaded Philip.

"Come close to me that I may see you. Is he good to you, this husband, eh?"

"He . . . is good to me."

"But you are newly wed. Wait . . . wait. Wait till he deceives you. Once I thought I was the happiest woman in the world. It was on that first night. He was lusty and golden-haired. He was a Hapsburg. He said: 'Do not be afraid, my sweet Juana. You will not regret that they have married you to me.' I did not know then that he would be making love to other women . . . the next night . . . the next day . . . any hour of the day . . . any hour of the night."

"Grandmother!" said Philip coldly; but his coldness could not touch her; she was back in a past which was more real to her than this dirty room with its candles and black hangings. Instead of the young bride and groom, she saw another pair—herself and another Philip. She lived in that moment the agonies of jealousy from which she had never allowed herself to escape. She saw that Flemish woman with the big breasts and thighs—the woman to whom he had been faithful for two whole weeks, which was surely a record for him. What had she, that woman? How was she different from others? How had she kept fickle Philip faithful for two whole weeks? Her strength, like Samson's, was in her beautiful hair. Never was there such hair—not before, not since. It was like gold in the sunshine and it rippled about her feet.

Juana began to laugh suddenly. She saw it so clearly: The woman standing before her, her hands bound behind her back. Juana mouthed the words: "Bring the barber in." She shrieked with helpless laughter for she was seeing the woman standing blankly horrified while her beautiful hair fell about the floor. Then she had her stripped and put in a cupboard, and she had been helpless with laughter when Philip came in.

She began to shout: "There is your beauty. Do you not long for her? Can you wait, then? Do not take any notice of me. When did you ever? She is there ... waiting for you as she has waited countless times before. Shameless hussy! Naked she has been, often enough for you ... but to be thus before the Queen ..."

Juana covered her face with her hands and rocked back and forth with her laughter.

"I beg of you ..." began the real Philip.

She was recalled to the present. She said: "And when he saw who she was, he turned on me and he struck me across the mouth. I fell back ... but then I flew at him. I scratched him and bit him. But I was happy, my children, because I loved him so much that I hated him ... and I hated him so much that it was the second best pleasure in the world to fight with him."

Her wild laughter had brought two men-at-arms to the door of the apartment. They stood motionless. The life of the heir and his wife must not be jeopardized, and Mad Juana, though so old, was strong when the moods of violence were upon her.

"What do you do there?" she called.

The men bowed. One of them said: "We thought we heard your Highness call."

Philip said quickly: "Stay there. Her Majesty was about to give us her blessing." He turned to Maria Manoela. "Come. Kneel," he said firmly.

They knelt, and it seemed that something in the calm manner of young Philip soothed the old woman.

"My blessing on you both," she said, laying her hands on their heads. "Philip ... my blessing on you. May this child be fruitful ... and bear many sons as handsome as *my* Philip ... and many daughters who have a better life than I have had."

Maria Manoela was gripping Philip's hand. He gave her a quick look of reassurance. "Rise now," he whispered.

Juana was speaking quietly now. "As handsome as my Philip," she repeated. "He put me away that he might spend more time with his women. If this Philip treats you thus ... come to me, child. Come to me. I will teach you how to deal with harlots ..."

"We thank you for your blessing, Grandmother," said Philip. "We will now depart."

"First you shall hear music," she cried. She waved a hand to the men at the door. "You . . . slave . . . bring in the musicians. Let them play merry tunes for the Prince and the Princess."

She insisted that the young pair sit on stools beside her while the musicians played. Juana sat dreamily tapping her fingers on the arms of her chair. She would have music which had been played when she was young and first married to her handsome Philip, in the days when she was a highly-strung girl, before she had gone violently mad through her love for the husband who had been chosen for her, through her jealousy of his many mistresses.

She called to Maria Manoela to come closer. She called her "Katharine!" She pointed out the dancers in that room in which none danced. Once she tottered to her feet. "I will kill her. Yes . . . you . . . No use hiding there in the hangings. I can see you. I will plunge a knife into those thick white thighs. When they are stained with blood, mayhap he will turn shuddering from them . . . perhaps when you are lying lifeless with your silly eyes staring at death and your red mouth gaping, he will turn shuddering from you and come to his lawful wife . . ."

The musicians played on. They were accustomed to such scenes.

Philip's eyes met those of Maria Manoela. Please . . . please . . . said hers. Could we not go? I can bear no more.

Then Philip remembered that he was the Regent of Spain in the absence of his father, and, standing up, he imperiously waved to the musicians to stop. They obeyed at once.

"We must leave you now, Grandmother," he said.

"Nay," she cried. "Nay . . ."

But all his cold haughtiness was with him now. "I fear so. Our thanks for the entertainment and your blessing. We will come again before long. Come, Maria Manoela."

The girl rose hastily and stood beside him. He was aware, amid all the strangeness, that she stood as close to him as she could. Philip took Maria Manoela's hand in his.

Juana said piteously: "Have I said too much, then? . . . Have I said wild things? . . . Have I talked of love and lust, then? It reminded me . . .

A young bride and her groom. I was a young bride once with a groom ... the handsomest in the world ..."

"We shall meet again soon," said Philip firmly, and he walked purposefully toward the door.

Juana called after them: "So you would leave me, eh? You would go to your women. 'Twill not always be thus. You have lost your limp, Philip. You have grown young and I am old ... old. Life is cruel to women ..."

They heard her shrieking laughter as they went through the corridors.

The sentries and the guards bowed low before them; and in the courtyard the young pair mounted their mules, and their attendants gathered about them as they rode back to Valladolid.

Philip never forgot the night that followed. Maria Manoela had a nightmare and awoke in terror, crying out that Mad Juana was hiding behind the tapestry and that she was about to set fire to it.

Philip comforted her.

"Nothing can harm you while I am here," he said.

She clung to him, forgetting her fear of him in her fear of the shadows.

She put her plump arms about his neck and said: "Do not let me see her again. She frightens me so."

Philip found joy in comforting her, speaking to her with more tenderness than he had ever before been able to show.

"Nothing shall ever frighten you again, my little one. Philip is here ... here to protect you."

And that night their child was conceived.

The news was received with great rejoicing throughout Spain. In all the churches there were prayers that the child might be a boy.

Leonor cosseted the mother-to-be, making her lie down for hours during the day, which Maria Manoela was quite happy to do.

The young husband was alternately proud and fearful, though he allowed none to guess how proud, how fearful. He thought of Maria Manoela continually, longing for her to be safely delivered as he had never longed for anything else.

State matters weighed heavily upon him. Charles was anxiously urging him to raise money for fresh campaigns. "If our subjects are not liberal with us," he wrote, "I know not how we shall fare."

When the *Cortes* met there was a good deal of grumbling. Spaniards
were beginning to understand that out of their very might grew misfortune. Better to be a small country, it was said, having plenty for its
needs, than a far-flung Empire with its constant demands. There was
even some murmuring against the Emperor himself, who was after all
half foreign. Philip did not know how they would have emerged from
their difficulties but for the handsome dowry which had come with
Maria Manoela from Portugal.

He was doubly grateful to her; she was his country's salvation and
his own; and it seemed to him then, in a flash of unusual intuition, that
his personal fortunes would always be linked with those of his country.
Maria Manoela, while her dowry brought the answer to his country's
needs, with her person satisfied all that he had wanted since he was a
boy. One day he would be able to explain this to her. She would cease to
be such a child when she became a mother.

He allowed himself to dream of their future with their children
around them and the love he desired growing stronger and stronger
as the years passed. He would mold her to his way of thought; he
would make of her the perfect wife whom a man of his temperament
needed so much. To her alone would he show himself; she should
know the real Philip who was quite different from the man whom his
father and those about him had created for the benefit of Spain and the
Empire.

He spent as much time with her as he could spare from his duties.
He fancied, though, that she was still a little fearful of him.

Sometimes he would see a bewildered look in her eyes when she
contemplated the future.

"The women of our family have difficult labor," she said on one
occasion.

He wanted to tell her of his thoughts of her, of how she would not
suffer more than he did. Instead he said: "You shall have the best doctors in the world."

She shrank a little, fancying there was a reproach in those words. She should be thinking of nothing at this moment but the fact that she was to bear the heir of Spain.

"Your mother was very brave when you were born," she said slowly. "Leonor told me. She did not once cry out. I . . . I am afraid I may not be as . . . brave as your mother was."

"You will be brave," he said; and although he meant it to be a compliment, it sounded like a command.

"What if it is a girl? Will you . . . hate me then?"

"I . . . I would never hate you."

"But . . . it is so necessary that the child should be a boy."

He let his hand rest on her for a moment. "You must not fret."

"No. That is bad for the child, Leonor says."

"And . . . for you too. If it is a girl . . . then we must not be sad. For, Maria Manoela, we have the rest of our lives before us."

She said: "We are not very old, are we. But I hear the King of England cut off his wife's head because she had a girl instead of a boy."

"He cut off her head because he wanted another wife," said Philip.

"And you . . . ?"

Now was the moment for uttering all those tender words which he had meant to say to her so many times. And all he could say was: "I . . . I should never want another, Maria Manoela."

She was satisfied; but he was not. He had spoken without the warmth he wished to convey. He had spoken as though to be satisfied with his wife was one of his duties as the Prince of Spain.

She had turned to her sweetmeats. He watched her pleasure in them. Perhaps she was thinking she was fortunate indeed. They might have married her to a husband who would have cut off her head if she did not have a boy. Instead, she had this strange, aloof young man, who was kind to her because it was the duty of a husband to be kind.

The baby was born in July.

Bells were set ringing throughout Spain and a messenger was sent to the Emperor with the news. Maria Manoela had given birth to a boy.

Leonor held the baby in her arms. She showed Philip a red, wrinkled face, a small head covered with black down. "A boy!" she cried. "A son for Spain!"

"But . . . the Princess?" said Philip.

"Tired, Highness. Exhausted. She is in need of rest."

"Leonor . . . all is well?"

Leonor smiled tenderly. She loved him the more because he forgot that as the Prince of Spain his first thoughts should be of the boy, and gave them to his wife.

"Let her rest a while, dear Highness. That is best for her."

"Leonor!" He caught her hand and gripped it so tightly that she winced with the pain. "I ask you . . . all is well?"

"All is well indeed. How do you think a woman feels when she has had a baby? She wants to rest . . . rest . . ."

He dropped her hand.

"I will look at her now," he said. "Do not fear that I shall disturb her. But I must see for myself that all is well."

So he went to her bedside. There she lay, her dark hair spread about the pillows, her dark lashes seeming darker because of the un-usual pallor of her skin; she did not look like little Maria Manoela. She had grown up since he had last seen her. She had become a mother. Gently he touched her damp cheek with his lips and, muttering a prayer, hurried from the room.

Leonor came to him as he paced the apartment.

"Has she not awakened yet?" he asked.

"It was an exhausting labor, Highness."

"But . . . so long. Others are not like this."

"A first child is always more difficult."

"Leonor, what is it? Tell me."

"Nothing . . . nothing. Your Highness distresses himself without cause."

"Oh, Leonor, I wish I could think so."

"Philip . . . little Highness . . . this is not like you."

"You too, Leonor? You too do not know what I am like."

"Philip, dear one, I understand."

"Then . . . tell me."

"What can I tell? It is a first child . . . It is always difficult."

"You have said that before, Leonor. All is well, you say. Yet your eyes say something different."

"Nay, little one. It is the anxiety which makes you think so."

"Is it, then? She is so young, Leonor . . . and we have been together such a short time. I had plans . . . for I thought we should have our whole lives together."

"And so you shall, my precious one."

"You treat me now as though I am a child. Thus it was when I was small and you knew a child's tragedy was pending."

"You must not think the worst, dear one."

"Leonor . . . do not try to hide the truth from me. I am no longer a child, you know."

"Do you love her so much?" He was silent and she went on: "You did not show it."

Then he began to laugh mirthlessly as Leonor had never heard him laugh before, and it seemed to her that his laughter was more heart-rending than sad words.

The tears ran down her cheeks and, because she could not control them, she ran, with a complete absence of ceremony, from the room.

Send the doctors! cried Philip. "I must see the doctors."

They came and stood before him, their heads bowed, their hands clasped together.

"Something is not . . . as it should be," he said.

"Your Highness, the Princess is resting. She needs rest after a difficult labor. The little Prince, Don Carlos, thrives, your Highness . . ."

"It is of the Princess that I wish to speak. Tell me the truth." Philip was astonished by the calmness of his voice; he had thought it must betray the agony within him.

They kept their respectful attitudes.

"The Princess suffers from natural exhaustion, your Highness."

Philip sighed. He was obsessed by agonizing thoughts. *They are telling me what they know I wish to hear. My father said all men would* do that. They seek to please me, not to give me the truth. The truth! What is the truth?

He was afraid that he would break down before these men, and he was enough himself to remember that he must not do that.

He dismissed them.

He sat by her bed. No one else was in the room, for he had sent them all away. Two days had passed, yet she lay there still and strange—remote, like another person.

He knelt by the bed and took her hand.

"Maria Manoela," he begged. "Look at me. Do you not know me?"

Her eyes were turned toward him—those dark eyes of wonderful beauty—but he knew that she did not see him.

"Dearest," he whispered, "you must get well. I cannot lose you now. That must not happen. Maria . . . Maria Manoela, I love you. Did you not know it? It was so difficult to speak of. In the apartments of our grandmother you turned to me . . . you turned to me when you were so much afraid. That made me happy. In the night . . . when the nightmares came . . . you turned to me. You put your dear arms about me and clung to me . . . to me . . . to Philip—not the Prince to whom they pay so much homage . . . but to Philip, your husband who loves you. I have planned so much for us . . . so much happiness. You and I together in a secret world of our own. Outside I seem cold and strict. I guard my feelings. It is necessary, my love, for that is the man they have made of me. I have to be a great ruler, as my father is, but I want to be happy too. I want to be happy with you. I will make you love me, Maria . . . Maria Manoela. I shall be tender to you . . . true to you. You must live, my dearest. You must live for me."

He stopped speaking and looked at her tired, blank face. He saw the irony of this. Now he had said all that was in his heart . . . now . . . when she could not hear him. She lay limp, with the fever consuming her; and she did not know who this young man was who spoke to her so earnestly, whose eyes pleaded so desperately.

But at last she spoke, and he bent over her to catch her words.

"I . . . am . . . so thirsty. Please . . . please . . . bring me lemons."

He called to the attendants.

"Lemons! At once! The Princess is asking for them."

Leonor came running in to him. She threw herself into his arms.

"The saints be praised. She has asked for lemons. Our prayers are being answered. This is a sign." Then she tore herself away from him; she began giving instructions. She held the cup of juice to the lips of Maria Manoela, and she was praying all the time while the tears ran down her cheeks.

Philip waited. He had told her of his feelings for her. Soon he would speak those words again, and this time she would hear.

The court was mourning her. Poor little Maria Manoela—so young to die. She was just seventeen. She was just beginning life. It was tragic, and the Prince had lost his calmness and control.

He would see no one. He shut himself into his apartment. He lay on his bed and stared up at the canopy saying nothing, just alone with his misery.

There was anxiety for his health.

Leonor said: "He will recover. He knows too well what is expected of him. Leave him alone awhile . . . just for a little while with his grief. Let him at least have a short while to mourn as other men may mourn."

"He will recover," said the courtiers, the councillors, the grandees, and the statesmen. "He will remember that we have a child . . . a boy child . . . a future King of Spain. He will understand soon that the tragedy is not so great as he now thinks it. Don Carlos flourishes. It is not easy to get sons, but it is a simple matter to find brides for great princes."

None knew this better than the Prince himself; but what consolation was it to a broken-hearted husband?

MARY
TUDOR

Entering the house of Isabel Osorio, Philip gave no sign of the anxiety he was feeling. Many knew of his love for his mistress, but he always behaved with the utmost discretion. Isabel did not come to court; he visited her whenever possible; and she lived in her house like any dignified Spanish matron.

He was anxious now because Isabel was in childbed. It would not be the first child she had borne him, but he could not escape the horror which came to him at such times.

He would always remember Maria Manoela. When she had died four years ago he himself had longed for death until he realized what an evil longing that was. He had shut himself away in a monastery and after much fasting and prayer he had come to the conclusion that only his faith could help him to live the life which had been ordained for him. He had clung to faith as the heretics clung to the crucifix when the flames consumed their bodies. He remembered that any trouble sent to him came through the will of God, and that to rail against misfortune was to rail against God.

He had decided that never again must he love a human being more than his faith. He had spent much time with priests, and the belief had come to him that it was his destiny not to look for happiness, but to purge his country of the heretic. In that must he find his greatest joy. He believed that it was his duty to inflict the cruellest suffering on heretics, not only because that was what his faith demanded of him, but for their good also. How many might he not turn from their evil ways with enough application of the rack, the wheel, and red-hot pincers?

And if that were not possible, if the Devil had their souls so firmly in his possession, then was it not a good thing to prepare them for eternal torment? Members of the Inquisition had applauded his fervor. He was with them as his great father had never been. When Philip was eventually on the throne, they doubted not that the Holy Office would flourish as it had in the days of the great Isabella and Torquemada.

Isabel's house was large and comfortable, yet it lacked that magnificence which might have proclaimed it to be the residence of a Prince's mistress. He found great pleasure in entering this house, for to him it was home. He went swiftly through the door which opened on to the *plazuela* and through the great hall, where a servant was throwing lavender on the *brasero*. This servant immediately fell to her knees when she saw him, but Philip, deeply conscious of the dignity due to his rank, did not give her a glance. Another servant appeared from the *estrado* at the end of the hall; she also knelt, and he ignored her as he had the other.

He mounted the staircase. He found that he was praying softly under his breath: "Holy Mother of God, let it be over . . . let it be over . . ."

He was asking that he might never again be called upon to lose a beloved woman as he had lost Maria Manoela. "Holy Mother . . . Holy Mother . . . let all be safely over . . ."

Often he had wished that he might marry Isabel; that was clearly quite impossible. He was so fond of her; she had been the only one who could comfort him when he had lost Maria Manoela. She was so calm that she brought him back to calmness; she understood him as Maria Manoela never had. She had become the wife and the mistress he needed at such a time; and he loved her devotedly.

He had sent Leonor to the house that she might be with Isabel at this time. That was the most he could give her, he knew. And Leonor, knowing all that Isabel had done for her Philip, was glad to go.

How fortunate he was in Isabel! He would never cease to be grateful for her. She conducted their relationship in that manner which she knew would please him best. When the Prince came to this house he was no longer the Prince; he was a nobleman visiting his mistress. No. He was a husband returning to his wife after an enforced absence.

As he reached Isabel's room, Leonor came hurrying out to him.

He gave her his hand and she bent over it. He saw that she was smiling. So all was well.

"Well, Leonor?"

"A beautiful boy."

"That is good. And . . . his mother?"

"Well too, Highness. She is tired, but I doubt not she would sleep better after a glimpse of you."

How different this was from that other childbirth four years ago! He should have understood then; he should have been prepared.

As he entered the apartment, the women about the bed fell back. He did not look at them. His eyes went at once to the woman in the bed. She was very beautiful, although the signs of her ordeal were still upon her. He took her hand and kissed it.

"My dearest, I am relieved that it is over."

"And pleased with the result, my Prince?"

"Pleased indeed. Another boy."

Leonor was at his elbow. "A *beautiful* boy, if you please."

"A beautiful boy," repeated Philip, allowing himself to smile.

Isabel smiled. He wished then that he was not the Prince of the Asturias, that he might marry her and live with her, see her each day, laugh with her more than he could now permit himself to do, discuss all the domestic problems as humble people did.

Leonor tiptoed out and left them together.

When she had gone, he said: "And you, my love? That is what matters most."

"I am well, Philip, and I feel strong and happy now that I have seen you. It was good of you to come."

"If only . . ." he began; he stopped and shrugged his shoulders. It was wrong even to wish that his destiny had not been thrust upon him. She smiled, understanding him as she always understood him. He remembered afresh how in the days of his great grief, when he was cold and aloof, she had known how to comfort him . . . she alone.

"We have been very happy for three years," she reminded him. "We shall be happy for many more."

"No matter what happens," he agreed, "I shall always love you."

He meant that if ever he had to make a marriage for state reasons she must not think he had ceased to love her even if it should be necessary for them to give up their life together. He would remember her always as the rock to which he had clung when his grief on the death of Maria Manoela had threatened to submerge him; she was the woman, a little older than himself, to whom he could in their privacy be something of the man he might have been if he had been allowed to grow naturally, if he had not been bound by rigid, iron casings which had forced him to grow in a certain mold.

"I am glad the child is a boy," she said. "You will see his brother before you go?"

"I will," said Philip. "And I should go now, my dearest—though I have no wish to do so—for I see that you are tired and should be resting. I but came to assure myself that you had come safely through. Now . . . to rest."

He smoothed the coverlet with the tenderness of a mother; he was like a devoted yet restrained husband, Isabel thought. He had been thus, even in the early days of their relationship. He had amused her then with his solemnity, and the more solemn he became, the more tender she felt toward him, for oddly enough, in her opinion, it made him seem younger than others of his age.

He insisted that she close her eyes before he went out of the room. He stood by the door watching her. The experience of being alone in a room without attendants never failed to stimulate him; and in this room he had known some of the happiest moments of his life because during them he had imagined himself to be an ordinary husband and father.

He went briskly out into the corridor, where Leonor was waiting for him.

"She sleeps, Highness?"

"I have commanded her to rest."

"Your Highness is pleased, I see. Then come to the nursery and see the little one's brother."

Leonor walked with him to the nursery, where a beautiful boy of not quite three was sprawling on cushions, Moorish fashion, on the floor playing with colored balls. His nurse bowed and retired when she saw the Prince.

"Papa!" cried the boy and rising and running to Philip, he clasped him about the knees. Philip stood still until the door closed on the nurse; then he picked up the boy.

"And how is my son Garcia today?"

The boy put his hands on Philip's lips and Philip wanted to hold him against him and kiss the smooth brown cheek. He glanced at Leonor before gratifying this wish.

"Hello, Papa," said the boy. "Garcia is well."

"And pleased to see me, eh?"

The boy smiled, while his chubby hand went to the jewel at Philip's throat.

"You like that, eh, my little one?"

The boy nodded and tried to pull it off.

"Methinks you are more pleased with that jewel than with your Papa."

"Nay, nay," said Leonor. "He loves best to see his Papa. Do you not, Garcia?"

The boy had charming ways and his answer was to release the jewel and to put his arms about his father's neck and make a soft, gurgling noise which was meant to express affection.

"You must show your Papa your beautiful toys, Garcia, my precious one," said Leonor.

The boy wriggled and Philip set him down. Philip watched him as he ran about, noting his sturdy limbs, the look of health, the eyes which were neither blue nor brown, but a mixture of Philip's blue ones and Isabel's black ones. How he loved this child! How happy he would be if he might throw himself onto the floor and become absorbed in the things which delighted the boy!

"He is growing clever," said Leonor. She went to a table and took up a book. "Here, Garcia. Now let us show Papa how we can read the little words. What is this now?"

The boy dimpled with great charm. "*El niño*," he said, and pointed to himself.

"So you are the little one, you are the little baby?" asked Philip.

"Yes, Papa. Garcia is *el niño* now. But I will tell you something. May I, Leonor? It is a secret."

"You may tell Papa, I am sure," said Leonor.

"I am to have a brother or a sister. Then I shall not be the little one. Then I shall be the big one."

Then Philip, aware of an intense emotion, took the jewel from his throat and gave it to the boy.

"Pretty!" he said, and he laughed with delight.

But Leonor took it from him as he would have put it into his mouth. She clucked her tongue and looked from Philip to Garcia with her own peculiar brand of indulgence.

"To give a baby such a thing! Why, he might swallow it. It is to look at, precious one, but not to eat. Leonor will put it away, and when you are a big one instead of a little one, you will remember that your father gave it to you, and you will wish to keep it forever."

The child was looking at his father now. Philip stooped to pick him up. He held him against him in such a way that neither Leonor nor the child should see his emotion.

Philip could never shirk a duty. After an hour spent in that nursery with Garcia he must return to the palace and visit his legitimate son, the child of his brief union with Maria Manoela. These visits were becoming, alas!, more of a duty than a pleasure.

He went to the apartments that were occupied by the little Prince.

Carlos was nearly two years older than Garcia, and Philip never looked at Carlos without wishing that it was Garcia who was his eldest son, Garcia whose place was here at the palace.

They were prepared for him in the royal nursery when he arrived. Perhaps they knew that he had just left the house of Isabel Osorio and that he had spent an hour with her son.

As Philip entered the apartment he heard Carlos's screaming. So they had warned him that his father was approaching; they had tried to comb his wild hair, to tidy his garments, to impress upon the boy the need to be on his best behavior.

Philip stood coldly surveying the scene. The two nurses were perturbed, desperately trying to quiet Carlos; the heralds and the courtiers
were uncomfortable; Carlos had turned to peer over his shoulder and
scowl at his father.

Philip said: "Leave me with my son."

"No!" cried Carlos. "Do not go."

He ran after them, but they had left quickly shutting the door after
them. Carlos went to the door, but he was not big enough to open it, so
he pounded on it with his fists, working himself into a rage.

"Come here, Carlos," said Philip.

The boy ignored his father and continued to kick the door.

Philip strode across the room, and picking up Carlos, brought him
to the chair, where he sat holding the boy.

Carlos was now silent. He glared at his father with his wild black
eyes.

"Why do you behave thus?" demanded Philip.

Carlos did not answer.

"Is it becoming for a prince to treat his father thus?"

Carlos's lower lip stuck out angrily. Philip looked at the big head
that seemed enormous on the poor, stunted body; he noticed how the
hair grew low on his forehead, almost reaching the eyebrows, the slight
hump on the back, the left leg which was not quite as long as the right,
the weak, full lips, the pallor of the skin; and all the time he was com-
paring Carlos with the boy whom he had just left. Why had God given
him one handsome and intelligent son, and another—the heir to the
throne—like Carlos? How had he and Maria Manoela produced a child
like this one? He thought suddenly of the apartments of Juana with the
food strewn about the room; he recalled the wild laughter which incon-
gruously rose above the music and made the mad scene more unforget-
tably horrible. Whenever he looked at this boy he was reminded of
Juana—his grandmother and Maria Manoela's.

"Carlos," he said severely, "you are growing up now."

Carlos continued to scowl at him.

"One day you will be a king. Kings do not kick and scream."

"Then they are silly," muttered Carlos.

"Why do you say that, Carlos?"

"Because when this little one kicks he gets what he kicks and screams for."

"Then you shall do so no longer."

Carlos's scowl became almost a smile. If he was not clever, he was cunning. Philip thought of Dr Siliceo, who had always been so ready to please him. There would be others as eager to please this little Prince.

"Kings have their duties," said Philip. "They must set an example to the people. If they behave badly their subjects will not love them."

Carlos was considering this, and it was obvious from the expression on his face that he did not care that people should love him; he only cared that they should give him what he wanted.

"Your grandfather," said Philip, "is a great Emperor."

"This little one shall be a great Emperor," said Carlos.

"You will not if you do not behave in a manner such as will please the people. You will have to do your duty and learn your lessons. How are you getting on with your reading?"

"Don't like it."

"Have you not learned your letters yet?"

"Don't like," said Carlos with finality.

"But you must try to like them."

Carlos's scowl-smile deepened. "Won't do," he said; and he laughed suddenly, doubtless recalling his latest tantrum when his nurses had tried to enforce his father's wishes.

"Do you not want to be a learned man when you grow up?"

Carlos considered this in his sly, secret way. He was thinking, Philip knew, that he could very well get what he wanted in his present state of ignorance. Kicking, screaming himself into a passion so that his attendants and nurses feared for his health, was, he was cunning enough to know, more effective in getting him what he wanted than anything he could learn from books.

"If you would be quieter, more gentle, do as you are told and learn your lessons, I should be able to love you," said Philip gently.

Carlos's indifference to his father's regard was in his answer: "His Aunt Juana loves him."

Juana! That name again. The reminder was at times more alarming than at others.

Philip put the boy down and, going to the door, asked the guard who stood outside to bring the Princess Juana to him.

Carlos had limped to the door, hoping to make his escape, but Philip held him firmly by the shoulder. Carlos looked at his father's hand as he contemplated digging his teeth into it; but he was not insensible to his father's power and the fear he inspired in others. Carlos, for all his wildness, was not a coward, but at the same time he was aware that a boy of four cannot easily pit himself against a man. So he contented himself with scowling, and allowed himself to be brought back to the chair.

"Why do you want to run away, my son?"

Carlos wriggled, but would not answer.

"Are you not pleased that your father should visit you?"

Carlos continued to stare at the hands which held him, and kept his face turned away from his father's.

At that moment Philip's young sister Juana entered. She was a quiet girl, with a serious expression, a little afraid now, as she always had been, of her brother. She came to him and knelt.

"Juana . . . Juana . . ." cried Carlos.

Philip told her to rise, and she stood up, looking timidly at him.

"You are with the boy more than anyone," said Philip.

"Yes, your Highness."

"Juana . . . Juana . . ." The boy was fighting free of his father's grasp, and Philip let him go. Carlos ran to his aunt, and, half laughing, half crying, he flung his arms about her knees.

"Make him stop that," said Philip.

"Carlos, dearest baby, be silent. You must not act thus before your father. Little one . . . little one . . . all is well."

Carlos kept his face hidden against her skirt. "He hurt the little one, Juana. He hurt el niño. He would not let Juana's little one go with the others. He kept him here."

"Hush. Hush. You must not cry before your father."

"Little one will cry. He will stamp and cry."

Little one! *El niño.* It was too reminiscent. Why had he punished himself by coming direct from one to the other? If he had waited, the contrast would have seemed less vivid.

"Enough! Enough!" he said.

Juana stood up, for she had knelt to comfort the boy. Philip looked at her coldly.

"You are not treating the boy as he should be treated."

Carlos's expression was cunning now. He said: "Juana loves him. Juana loves the little one."

"Your Highness," stammered Juana. "He is young yet . . ."

"I know it. He has told us. *El niño!* This pampering must be stopped. What of his lessons? I understand he cannot read his letters yet."

"Your Highness . . ." Juana's protective love for the child overcame her fear of her brother. "He is so young . . ."

Philip's mouth was tight. "Others read before they are his age. He must pay more attention to his books. He must learn to read at once. How otherwise can he learn anything?" Philip softened. "It is not fair to blame you, Juana. He must have tutors."

"He will not," muttered Carlos.

"Do not touch him!" commanded Philip. "Do not soothe him. There has been too much soothing."

Juana was pale. She was only a child herself. She had no mother; the boy had no mother; there was a bond between them. *El niño,* she had called him. Juana's *el niño;* and it was from her he had learned his first words. It was to her he came when he wished to be soothed or petted, and she loved him as though she were the mother who had died giving birth to him. She was afraid now, for she was beginning to be almost as much afraid of wild Carlos as of calm Philip.

"He needs discipline," said Philip.

"Little one won't have it."

"When you speak of yourself, please say 'I.' You are too old for childish talk."

Carlos clutched Juana's skirts and scowled at his father, and Philip felt suddenly that he must end this scene because he could bear no more. He had suffered too much tragedy. Was it not enough that he had seen Maria Manoela lying on her deathbed? Must he also have to look on this monstrous child with the heavy head, the low brow, the atavistic eyes?

"Tutors shall be appointed," he said, "and in the meantime, Juana, I command you, do not pander to his whims. Treat him sternly. If you do not, I shall have no choice but to forbid you to see him."

He strode past them. Juana sank to her knees.

As Philip left the apartment, he heard Carlos cry: "*Juana* loves him. Juana loves *el niño.*"

When Philip left his son's apartment it was to discover that the Duke of Alba had arrived at the palace. The Duke had just come to Spain from Flanders and brought dispatches from the Emperor.

The dispatches, said Alba, were of the utmost secrecy, and the Emperor had entrusted them in no other hands but his. Moreover, his instructions were to hand them to no one but Philip.

Philip took the packet and, dismissing the Duke, shut himself into his small privy chamber and prepared to examine the documents. He was glad of the work. He was glad of anything which would enable him to forget that nursery scene in which he feared he had played a somewhat ignoble part.

The Emperor had written with his usual fullness and frankness. He recalled the past in order to explain how he and Philip came to be in their present position.

"Your great-grandfather Ferdinand, as you know, my dear Philip, favored my younger brother Ferdinand. Doubtless because he had the same name as himself, for people do favor their namesakes. It is a human weakness. My brother Ferdinand was educated as a Spaniard while I went the way of the Hapsburgs. It was your great-grandfather's wish to make my brother Ferdinand King of Aragon, at one time, or even to create a kingdom for him in our dominions. He was to be Regent of Spain while I administered the Hapsburg inheritance in Germany and the Netherlands. But when old Ferdinand, your great-grandfather, died, I was the stronger. I was proclaimed King of Spain while I remained Emperor of my father's dominions. But I could not ignore my brother Ferdinand. I had troubles enough on hand and I did not want another enemy. I made him King of the Romans, and I let him believe that on my death or retirement he would become Emperor.

"Naturally, my son, I have always wanted you to succeed me; and I plan, in order that I may ensure this as far as possible, to transfer to you the Imperial Vicariate in Italy and to attach Flanders and Holland to the Spanish crown. This would mean, of course, that my brother, as future Emperor, would have nothing but the Austrian territory. Naturally, he does not much like this arrangement, but after many conferences I have won him to my side.

"To do this, I have had to agree to the immediate marriage of your sister Maria with his son Maximilian, and to agree that on Ferdinand's death, Maximilian—not you—shall succeed him as Emperor. Now, my son, you have traveled very little, and I should like to remedy that. Young Max has won the affection of the people whom he hopes one day to rule as Emperor. He is one of them. They follow him in the streets; they cheer him. They are a lusty people who will choose their own rulers.

"My dear Philip, it is time you visited your dominions. This is my proposal: Maximilian is on his way to Spain. When he arrives he shall be married to Maria. I have promised your Uncle Ferdinand that Maximilian and Maria shall have the regency while you are away. I believe this to be our safest move. Therefore, on receipt of this, make preparations for a journey, which will take you through Italy and Germany and Luxembourg to me here in Brussels. There is much that I wish to discuss with you in private . . ."

Philip stopped reading.

To leave Spain! To leave Carlos, who needed his discipline? To leave Doña Isabel and her two boys who gave him all the solace he needed when he escaped from his affairs of state, to face the *Cortes* and tell them that he was to follow his father abroad . . . he did not like it. And Spain would not like it either.

He guessed that one subject his father wished to discuss in private was another marriage for him. He had been a widower too long.

He did not want his life to be disturbed; yet if it was his duty to leave his country and to travel in foreign lands, to take a woman whom he did not want to be his wife, he would do that duty, as he always had.

Valladolid was preparing for *fiesta*. The marriage of the Emperor's daughter Maria to her cousin Maximilian was to be celebrated with even more pomp and splendor than was usual on such occasions; the populace must be appeased. The *Cortes* had protested against the departure of the heir to the crown; its members had even written to the Emperor begging him not to take Philip from Spain. Some of the statesmen had been outspoken: they had declared that the Emperor was ruining Spain with his campaigns abroad, and they wished to be ruled by a king, not an emperor.

Philip had faced them, calm and resigned. He had no wish to leave Spain; but if it was his father's desire that he should, then that must be fulfilled.

When he had left the *Cortes* he had gone to Isabel's house. She was waiting for him. The baby was a fine child, growing up like his brother, and it was a great pleasure to be with them. There was peace in Isabel's room; he could sit beside her, watching the children playing at their feet. If only he might enjoy domestic happiness! But even now, at this moment, he must break the news of his departure.

"My father has sent for me, Isabel, and I may be away from you for a long time."

She turned to him and, as that control which she had taught herself broke suddenly, she laid her face against his shoulder and began to cry quietly.

Philip was deeply moved, as he always was by a display of affection toward himself. "Isabel," he said. "Isabel . . . my love."

She spoke fiercely against the Emperor. "But why should you go? You are needed here. Are *you* going to be away from us forever . . . as the Emperor has always been? The people will not endure that. You must not go, Philip. Oh, you must not go."

He stroked her hair; he dared not speak for fear of showing her his distress.

Little Garcia came and stood before them, looking wonderingly at his mother. "What ails her, Father?" he asked.

Philip took the boy on to his knee. The baby stopped kicking as he lay on his cushions. When he saw their tears he let out a loud wail.

His mother went to him and picked him up; she sat with him on her knee, hiding her own grief in her effort to comfort the child.

"Father," insisted Garcia, "what is wrong, then?"

His mother answered for Philip. "It is nothing to be sad about. But . . . your father has to go away for a time."

"For a long time?"

"It will not be longer than I can help," said Philip.

"You will come back soon," said the boy.

They sat for a while in silence, the boy looking from the face of one parent to the other's. The baby put out a fat hand and grasped at a bright ornament on his father's doublet.

It seemed to Philip a scene of charming domesticity, saddened only by his impending departure. Oh, how happy he might have been had he not been born the Prince of Spain!

While the festivities which followed the wedding of Maximilian and Maria were still in progress, Philip left Valladolid on the first stage of his journey.

His departure took some of the merrymaking out of the revels, for even to the people in the streets he was the beloved Prince. The Emperor might be a foreigner, but Philip was one of themselves; they liked his quiet dignity, his Spanish haughtiness; they had never heard of any indiscretion on his part, and even his love affair with Isabel Osorio was conducted with decorum, and it was said—and all believed this—that Philip behaved like a respectably married man in his relationship with Doña Isabel, whereas his father's love affairs were mainly with foreign women.

Still, if they loved their Prince, they also loved merrymaking, and what good could they do by grieving?

On that October day, as Philip left Valladolid followed by a magnificent retinue to ride through Aragon and Catalonia, the people lined the streets and cried Godspeed and a quick return.

One woman watched him from her window. She held up her elder son that he might see his father, for she knew, though she did not tell the boy this, that it would be a year or two before they saw Philip again.

Was Philip aware of them as he rode past Isabel's house? She knew that he was, and she knew that he longed to turn and take one last look at the house in which he had known great happiness. But he did not turn his head to look. Not for one instant, however great the provocation, would he forget the decorum due to his rank.

Yet he had taken a public farewell of Carlos. He had lifted the sullen boy up that the crowds might see him, and he had solemnly kissed the unresponding lips. Carlos had enjoyed the ceremony, caring nothing for his father's departure.

Philip had said to him when they were alone: "I shall not see you for a long time, Carlos. I want you to promise me to be good and try to learn your lessons."

Carlos had said nothing; he merely gave his father that long, cunning stare.

"You must be good, my son, for, with your grandfather and your father away from Spain, you have a special duty to your people. You must show an example to all."

The boy continued to scowl; he did not like this talk of being good.

"You must make the people love you. You must, by your behavior, win the respect of your grandfather and father."

Then Carlos spoke. "Juana loves him. Juana loves the little one."

Philip rode through Catalonia to the Bay of Rosas, where Admiral Doria met him with fifty-five galleys and many sailing ships; and Doria fell on his knees before the Prince and, with tears streaming down his cheeks, cried: "Now, O Lord, let thy servant depart in peace, for his eyes have seen Thy salvation." Philip knew that the emotion of Doria was genuine; to him the Prince was like a god; and the Admiral reflected the mood of the entire Spanish nation.

This was gratifying indeed. His people—the Spanish—loved him; not as he craved to be loved, but as a ruler; his manners, which repelled in private, pleased in public. He had this devotion and he had the love of Isabel and their children to sustain him. Should he not be gratified?

But whatever he had, he would never forget that first he was a Prince, and, as he listened to the compliments that were showered upon him, as he heard the cheers of the people, he could not shut out of his mind the memory of that dark, lowering face; he could hear the peevishly triumphant whine: "Juana loves him. Juana loves the little one."

And although he had given Spain his life to make of it what his people wished, he had also given them Don Carlos.

He passed through Genoa to Milan and Mantua.

The Italians did not like him. They were courteous, paying him the respect which was his due; but he, as much as any, was aware of the impression he made.

"He is serious, this Philip," it was said. "Has he never learned to laugh and compliment the ladies?"

They talked of his father. There was a man! It was good to watch him at table and to mark his way with women. He was a man such as the Italians could understand.

Through the Tyrol and Germany to Luxembourg went the magnificent procession; and always it was the same story. "How solemn he is, this Prince!" They shook their heads gravely. They would not, if they could help it, further the chances of such a one. They wished to have a ruler who was a merrymaker. The Emperor Charles had a strength of his own, and that they applauded; young Maximilian, the Emperor's nephew and now his son-in-law, was like his uncle. But this quiet, calm Spaniard? No! They did not like him. Their cheers and homage were lukewarm.

It was April when he made his entry into Brussels.

A great ceremony had been prepared for him at the Emperor's instigation. Charles was perturbed; he had seen little of his son of late, but he was not unaware of the fact that Philip's personality would not appeal to those robust, pleasure-loving people, who cared little for ceremony. He knew the Flemings well, and he believed that they would not welcome a future ruler whose tastes and manners did not accord with their own.

Charles was waiting for Philip at the palace in the company of his

two widowed sisters—Mary of Hungary and Eleonore, who had been
the second wife of Francis the First. Mary was practical and capable;
Eleonore was warm and motherly. Both women were looking forward to
Philip's visit; Mary because she liked to have a say in family affairs and
she saw a big storm blowing up concerning the inheritance of Philip
and Maximilian; Eleonore because it was time Philip married and she
had a suitable wife for him in the person of her own daughter by
Manoel of Portugal, whom she, Eleonore, had married before she became the second wife of the King of France.

But neither of these ladies was more eager to see their nephew than
Charles was to see his son.

The Emperor stood at a window of the palace, watching the
crowds in the street, listening to the triumphant music. He saw the approach of the cavalcade; and at the head of all this pomp and magnificence rode Philip, the heir of Spain and as much of Europe as his father
could snatch from the eager hands of his brother and nephew.

But this was not the way in which a future ruler should ride into a
Flemish city! There, on his horse, he sat—a small man, too small for
these people who liked their men to be large and lusty; too pale for a
people who fancied the florid complexion; and worst of all, he did not
smile; he stared sternly straight ahead. Maximilian, Charles conjectured,
would have thrown kisses to the groups of pretty girls who were watching from the houses and that would have made them his slaves for the
rest of their lives; he would have doffed his hat, waved his hand, bowed,
smiled on everyone. But instead of that, Philip came on in stately dignity, a solemn Spaniard among the hearty men and women of Flanders.

The Emperor embraced his son with warmth, and he thought: You
and I will have much to say, my son. But before I lay my plans before
you, I shall have to implore you to discard this solemnity. When a
man—and that man hoping to become a ruler here—is in Flanders, he
must do as the Flemings do.

How Philip hated the life! How he longed for Spain!

He thought with particular sadness of the house of Doña Isabel
with its hangings that were neither rich nor luxurious, but seemed the

more beautiful to him because of their simplicity; he remembered her delight in the Flanders carpets he had given her; he longed to stride un-ceremoniously through the door which opened on to the *plazuela*, to walk into Isabel's apartments and pick up the baby, to speak to young Garcia.

He noticed that Charles had aged considerably since they had last met. His florid complexion had become almost sallow, and the rich purple-red color was replaced by a criss-cross of veins that showed up startlingly against the yellow pallor; he was less corpulent than he had been and the flesh of his face hung in folds; his hands were swollen with gout and he told Philip that his feet were affected in the same way. He was subject to a form of fever which attacked him now and then; his lips were cracked; his mouth was perpetually dry and there were times when he was so affected by the heat and dryness that he kept a green leaf in his mouth for the sake of its cool moisture.

"But enough of myself!" he cried. "It is of you we must talk, my son."

"I am at your service, Father," said Philip.

"The sight of you gives me pleasure. You are a son to be proud of. But you have come from Spain, and here things are different. These people will love you no less than the Spaniards do, but whereas the Spaniards wish you to be a demi-god among them, the Flemings wish you to go among them as a man. They would like to know you are lov-ing their women; they will wish to see you riding at the jousts, winning all the trophies. That is the sort of ruler they look for."

"Then I fear they will not find me to their taste."

"We'll make them. We'll show them at the joust tomorrow. I have ordered a special pavilion to be set up. It will be in your honor, and the great moment will be when you ride into the arena."

"Is that wise? I was never a good horseman. Even Zuñiga could not make me that."

"You'll do well, I know." He laughed, bringing his face close to Philip's so that it was possible to smell the mingling odors of garlic and green leaves. "Why, none will dare beat you at the tourneys! They know my orders."

"Perhaps all the people know of this," said Philip. "Therefore it may be a waste of time to joust."

"Ha! You have become a cynic. No! I want the people to see you triumph over all. You must do that, Philip. You know how my brother Ferdinand plagues me; and there is Maximilian to consider. There is one thing which you must understand: No matter what arrangements I am able to make for you, it is these people who will choose their ruler."

"Then I do not think they will choose me."

"They will. We'll make them. You were rather formal during your entry, but you will learn to smile and joke, eat, drink, and make love to the women. You should have a mistress without delay. That will be expected of you." Charles burst into hearty laughter so that some of the green juice ran down his beard. "You look not too pleased at the prospect."

"Such matters should surely come about naturally."

"Well, 'twill not be difficult, I am sure. The women are handsome here; and how long is it since you were a husband? Oh, I know of that very sober relationship with Isabel Osorio. Very creditable. But that is in Spain. Yes; you must have a mistress without delay."

More than ever Philip was longing for home as he watched his father's expression, which was one of affection mingling with approval and not a little exasperation.

"And there is one other problem of great moment which we must discuss," went on Charles. "You have been a widower too long. You must have a wife."

Philip's Aunt Eleonore craved audience with him.

He felt bruised and humiliated. In the tourney he had not shone. Charles had evidently not given his instructions clearly enough and Philip did not break even one lance. The people had been silent, and it was clear that they did not think very highly of their Prince.

He was homesick and weary. He hated their rough horseplay, their practical jokes, their loud laughter, their preoccupation with eating, drinking, and amorous adventure.

His father was undoubtedly one of them; he saw that now. And he, Philip, was a Prince of Spain, and would never be anything else.

Eleonore had perhaps come to commiserate, for she was a kindly woman. She had been good to the little sons of Francis the First when they had been prisoners in Spain, and they had grown to love her; but that was a long time ago now. The elder of those boys was now dead; he had died, it was said, through drinking from the cup brought to him by his Italian cupbearer who was in the service of the Italian woman, now Queen of France; the second of those boys was himself King of France, with that Catherine de Medici as his Queen who, many Frenchmen believed, had been responsible for the death of the King's elder brother.

Eleonore had been at today's tourney and she would have witnessed his humiliation. It was always to women that Philip turned for compassion—to Leonor, to Maria Manoela, to Isabel, and now ... perhaps to Eleonore.

She knelt before him.

"Have I your Highness's permission to speak frankly?"

"You have, dear Aunt."

He would have liked to embrace her, but he could not bring himself to do so. He could only sit straight in his chair, bid her rise, bid her be seated; and even while he longed for her compassion he could not behave otherwise than as the Prince of Spain.

"I wish to speak to you of my daughter."

"The Princess of Portugal," said Philip; and he felt excited, for Eleonore's daughter was the aunt of Maria Manoela.

"She is a charming girl," went on Eleonore, "and I am sure you would love her. She has already heard of you and talks of nothing else, so I hear. There would be a good dowry with her, and I doubt not that if you approved the match, the Emperor would also."

"Maria ..." He spoke the name so quietly that she scarcely heard. He was living it all again, seeing her ride into Spain with her Castilian cape about her shoulders, raising her frightened eyes to his—Maria Manoela who had gone and in her place had left him Carlos.

He rose and walked about the room, for he did not want his aunt to see his emotion. At length he stopped and looked at her.

"Have you spoken of the marriage to the Emperor?"

"No, your Highness; but I doubt not its possibilities have occurred to him."

"I will consider them," he said; and he bowed his head in a manner which told her the interview was at an end. She accepted dismissal and left him alone with his thoughts.

It seemed to Philip that life was ironical. He was required to have a wife; and he would, of course. When had he ever failed to do what was expected of him? It was almost as though he had reverted to his youth when his father had said to him: "Jeanne of Navarre is divorced from that fool of Clèves. What think you of taking her for a wife?"

He had thought of it. He remembered afresh his feelings for her. He recalled how she had gone to the Cathedral to present her protests to the bishops, how she had defied her mother and King Francis. At that time he had delighted in her bravery; now he saw her conduct in a different light. Such a flouter of authority was not a fit wife for him.

His Uncle Ferdinand was impressing on the Emperor that his, Ferdinand's, daughter would make a suitable Queen of Spain. Ferdinand would be ready to make concessions regarding this complicated matter of settling the inheritance if, now that his son had married the Emperor's daughter, the Emperor's son Philip married *his* daughter.

Philip wanted neither Ferdinand's daughter nor Jeanne of Navarre. Maria of Portugal roused memories, but he longed for the peace of Isabel's home and his own children playing at his feet.

His thoughts were uneasy. He knew that soon he must take a wife, and he wanted none of them—not Maria who might bring too poignant memories of Maria Manoela, not Jeanne of Navarre, that strong-willed young woman, nor Ferdinand's daughter, a union with whom would make the settlement so much easier. He wanted none of these women; he wanted only Isabel, whom he thought of as his wife.

He was melancholy, longing for home.

But, being Philip, he did his duty. He tilted in the tourneys; he accepted the prize as victor, although he disliked doing so, knowing that his victory had been arranged. The spectators knew it too; he was aware of their cynical glances.

He knew they whispered about him. "The solemn Spaniard was never able to break a lance in even combat. Lances have to be made soft when set against him, that he may wear the victor's crown."

The Emperor was uneasy, but he was too wise to arrange more jousts and tourneys with more faked victories for Philip.

In spite of his exasperation, he was full of affection for his son. Philip's grasp of statecraft was as sure as ever; he was never brilliant, but always intelligent. While he had a plan to follow he would plod steadily on, but if he had to make a decision, as surely every leader must, he would take so long to reach it that valuable opportunities were lost. No flashing genius this, but what admirable determination, what power of control, what steady, plodding virtue. When he contemplated Philip, Charles was reminded of François Premier merely by the wide gulf between the two. François had been witty and brilliant, but where had that led him? Once it had taken him to Pavia; and some said that his love of pleasure had driven him earlier to his grave than he might otherwise have gone. And Henri Deux, the son of François, who now ruled France, was another such as Philip—slow, steady, almost completely faithful to his mistress, Diane de Poitiers. Henri was not unlike Philip, and he was proving that he could successfully rule a kingdom. It might be that there was no need to worry about Philip; but Philip must please these foreigners; Philip might rule Spain as well as Henri ruled France, but Philip had an additional task; he must ingratiate himself with strangers if he was to succeed to the position held by Charles.

Every day father and son spent hours together. Every lesson of government and statecraft which the Emperor had learned at great cost and bitter experience, he passed on to Philip, and Philip absorbed this instruction with that thoroughness which was a part of his nature.

There were family gatherings, with Mary of Hungary giving her views. Eleonore was trying hard to bring about a match between her daughter and Philip. There were festivities and entertainments, and always Charles was trying to show the Flemings that his son was becoming more and more like them. He selected the most comely women for his son's approval, but while the Emperor was able to make his choice with the greatest ease, Philip hesitated.

There were titters in the court, and in the quietness of private apartments there was much bawdy chatter concerning the Prince of Spain.

This would not do, the Emperor decided. He knew that if he were to declare his son to be the future Emperor, the people of Brussels at least would rise against the judgment.

In desperation, Charles sent for a certain woman whom he knew well. She was by no means virtuous, but of what use to Philip at this stage was a virtuous woman! She was beautiful and there was about her a childishness combined with a motherliness which was very appealing. The Emperor looked at her with some regret as he gave her his instructions, for he would have liked her for himself.

To this lady he said: "The Prince is a strange man. Few understand him. He seems cold, and so he is; but there is passion somewhere within him. His religion has kindled it; so could a woman. He loved his wife but she died. Appeal to his chivalry. He has plenty to spare for ladies in distress, and I doubt not that before long you will be his mistress."

She turned her beautiful face to the Emperor and smiled. "Your Imperial Highness need have no fears. I will do this."

"Fears!" cried the Emperor. "I have no fears, dear lady. I have only regrets."

And so Philip had a Flemish mistress.

Strangely enough, he was in love, but this love was quite different from the emotion he had felt for Maria Manoela; nor was it in the least like the steady affection he had shared with Isabel. This was an intoxication, an introduction to the delights of the flesh such as he had never known existed. His new mistress was expert in the ways of love, and under her tuition Philip was slowly changing. There was, he discovered,

a voluptuous side to his nature. He saw no reason why he should not indulge it since his father approved. Charles had said: "My son, you are
becoming a man of the world, and that is a good thing to be."

But Philip was no lecherous philanderer; he was faithful to his mistress, and when she had his child he was as delighted as he had been at
the birth of Isabel's children.

Meanwhile eighteen months had passed, and the Emperor had
shown no inclination to part with him. There were continual negotiations, not only with regard to Philip's marriage, but also with the division of the family inheritance.

At length it was decided that Charles's brother Ferdinand should
succeed Charles as Emperor, but, on the death of Ferdinand, Philip
should be given the Imperial crown. Maximilian, Ferdinand's son, should
act as Regent in Austria while Philip governed Spain, although Philip
was to remain supreme over the Italian States.

"It is not what I would have wished for you," said Charles when he
and Philip were alone together, "but it is the best we can get; and now,
my son, it might be well if you returned to Spain, for you must not
overlong neglect your Spanish subjects. There is one matter which all
wish to see settled. Have you decided who your wife shall be?"

Charles looked up with some amusement at his son's face. Philip
could never make up his mind quickly.

At length he spoke: "I think . . . Maria of Portugal."

"Wisely chosen!" cried Charles. "There is a big dowry there. I should
dispatch Ruy Gomez da Silva into Portugal to discuss matters. Let us
hope her brother, King John, will be as liberal with his sister's dowry as
he was with that of his daughter, your little Maria Manoela, whose
dowry stood us in such good stead. Then after the Augsburg Diet is
concluded you can start your journey back to Spain. It will not do to let
Master Max rule too long in your stead."

"No, Father."

"I shall be very sorry to see you go. And I know at least one other
who will be heart-broken. It was a pleasant little friendship, was it not?
She has changed you. I envy your youth. Don't forget, my son, to take

your pleasures. You have responsibilities and anxieties before you. Leaven them with pleasure, as I have always done."

Charles sighed and looked sadly at his gouty feet. He spat out the leaf he had been holding in his mouth and took a fresh one.

He was thinking that he himself had been rejuvenated by this change in Philip.

And in that mood they went to Augsburg for the Diet.

The days passed quickly in Augsburg, for Charles as well as for Philip. There were state matters to attend to every day; there were the Fiefs of the Empire to be received. Charles had at last settled affairs with his brother, and although neither was entirely satisfied, they both realized that they had come as near to satisfaction as could be expected.

Reviewing the last years, Charles considered he had good cause for satisfaction. His son Philip was a young man of whom he could be proud. Very soon he would be able to leave the responsibility of government in the hands of that worthy young man. It was folly to have wished for a gayer son. Yet how pleased he would have been to have begotten a son who combined Philip's excellent qualities with charm, gaiety, and that bold manliness which the Flemings demanded of a leader.

Charles was in this meditative mood, sitting at his palace window, when he saw a beautiful girl below. Her fair thick hair was coiled about her head, and her costume proclaimed her to be a burgher's daughter.

He watched her, wistfully admiring her youth. He could see the shape of her strong, firm legs and thighs beneath her skirts; her profile was clear-cut, and she walked with a modest unawareness of her beauty.

He wondered about her, and he could not dismiss thoughts of her from his mind. He forgot to put a fresh green leaf into his mouth, and indeed the fever had abated considerably. He had not felt so well for years, and the sight of the blonde girl, and perhaps the thoughts of a perfect son, had made him feel almost a young man again.

He saw the girl again on another occasion and he, keeping watch for her, discovered that she walked past the palace every day. He played with the idea (so beloved of kings) of walking through the streets disguised, of making her acquaintance, and, temporarily setting aside his imperial dignity, wooing her as a nobleman.

But Charles was a realist. He was nearly fifty; the girl could not be any more than twenty. How could an aging man, with cracked lips, with gout and fever, disguise himself as a young lover?

No, he thought; I cannot cast off my imperial dignity, for what else have I to attract a beautiful young girl?

So, being unable to play the old game of masque and disguise, he sent for her.

She came, shy and trembling, and her beauty together with her youth delighted him. She was afraid, he had been told, that she or her father or some member of her family had committed an offense of some kind.

He waved away all his attendants and spoke to her very gently.

"Do not be afraid. You have committed no crime, nor has your father, unless it is a crime to be beautiful or to beget a beautiful daughter. I have watched you passing in the streets, and it gave me great pleasure to know that you were one of my subjects."

The girl was so frightened that she could not speak.

"Tell me your name," he said. "Here! Sit on this stool . . . close to me that I may see you better. Now . . . what do they call you?"

"Barbara," she whispered. "Barbara Blomberg."

"Then I shall call you Barbara, my Flemish maid."

She did not speak, and he went on: "I thought to come to woo you disguised as a nobleman. Then I realized that I was too old to play such games, so I sent for you as your Emperor, because I knew that there would be little in your sight to distinguish me from others apart from my Imperial crown, my palace, my servants."

He did not make love to her then. He felt unusually abashed, longing above all things that she should come to him willingly.

The burgher's young daughter had seen the mighty Emperor on other occasions; she had seen him surrounded by Imperial pomp. She had never in all her life imagined a humble Emperor.

And in a short while Charles—fifty, gouty, fever-racked—found that his wayward interest had grown to love, and he loved this girl with a passion he had never felt before, even in his youth. As for Barbara

Blomberg, she was at first moved by the imperial humility, and eventu-ally her feelings changed to love of him.

The Emperor, feeling young again, was eagerly devouring the fruit of passion's burgeoning. He was happy during those days in Augsburg when Barbara Blomberg became his mistress; and before Philip left for Spain it was beyond doubt that she was to have a child.

The Emperor was delighted. He believed that his child would be a son and that he would combine the staid virtues of Philip with the beauty of his mother.

Those were charmed days for the Emperor; and meanwhile Philip made his way back to Spain.

The Indian summer of the Emperor's life had changed abruptly to autumn, and he felt that winter was not far off. Gout and fever troubled him once more. He could no longer enjoy to the full his life with Barbara. A child was born; he was a bonny child and they called him Juan; he was of promising beauty and intelligence, but Charles realized that he would not live to see his hopes for the boy fulfilled.

The German Princes rose in sudden and unexpected revolt, joining with Henri of France against Charles. The cunning French King persuaded the Italians to turn against the Emperor and, being confronted with war on two fronts and finding he had not the means at his disposal to meet it, Charles saw nothing but disaster and defeat ahead.

He ceased to dally with his beloved mistress; he put himself at the head of his armies, but he was too late, too tired, too old. Defeat followed swiftly, and with it the peace which was dictated by Saxony. The French seized their opportunities and the Duke of Guise decimated Charles's armies at Metz.

He was beaten and he knew it. He did not see how he could ever regain what he had lost, so heavy was his defeat, so humiliating the peace terms to which he was forced to agree.

With great agony of mind, he knew that he had lost a great deal of what he had hoped Philip would inherit, and it seemed now that his son would be Philip of Spain in very truth.

Was it because he was old that all the fight was going out of him?

He tried to raise money, but the Spaniards were only too glad to see his dominions slipping away from him. They wanted their King to be King of Spain, to stay with his people, to develop Spain from within. Charles could see little security in what was left of his Empire; he could only see a future given over to continual wars.

Often he thought of days and nights spent in Augsburg, of the child who was to be all that he had longed for in a son, of the Flemish girl who had been all that he had hoped for in a mistress.

"But," he ruminated sadly, "Fortune is a strumpet who reserves her favors for the young."

And so tired was he, so filled with pains, that he longed not so much for Barbara Blomberg as for the quiet of some monastery where he might relinquish responsibility and repent his sins, thereby resigning his interest in this world in his contemplation of the next.

Back in Spain, Philip resumed his relationship with Isabel. He confessed his infidelity; not that he felt it incumbent upon himself to do so, but because it seemed to him that Isabel would rather hear of it from him than from others; and there would certainly be others to pass on news of the Prince's love affair in Brussels.

Although he was as kind and considerate as ever, Isabel noticed the change in him. His liaison with his Flemish mistress had broken down his previous reserve. The court began to whisper the name of Doña Catherine Lenez—a very beautiful woman of noble birth—in connection with Philip.

It was considered natural for a prince to have at least two mistresses. There was Isabel to provide the quiet, homey atmosphere which a wife of some years' standing might give, and there was Catherine to supply more erotic entertainment.

Throughout Spain there was rejoicing in Philip's return. Wherever he went people lined the streets to cheer him. News was bad from abroad. Let it be. The Prince was home.

And Philip continued to do what was expected of him. He summoned the Castilian *Cortes* in Madrid and asked for supplies which were so urgently required by his father. He pushed forward with negotiations which would bring him Maria of Portugal and her dowry. Philip was sorry to lose his beloved friend, Ruy Gomez da Silva, but he knew that Ruy with his suave diplomacy could lure more money from the coffers of King John of Portugal than anyone else could. So to Portugal went Ruy, and Philip prepared to receive his bride as soon as negotiations were brought to a conclusion.

But it seemed that King John was not prepared to be generous, and arrangements were delayed.

Philip was twenty-six; he had had a wife, and now he had two mistresses who completely satisfied him. For himself he did not need a wife. But he must not forget that although he had given his country an heir, that heir was Don Carlos.

Carlos was in the schoolroom; he was sprawling over the table, but he was not listening to his tutor. The tutor was afraid of him, as Carlos was beginning to realize most people were. They were not so much afraid that he would attack their persons—which he would do if the mood took him—but that he would attack their dignity. They did not know how to act when the Prince Don Carlos threw a boot at them. That made Carlos laugh so much that he would cry. To see them standing respectful, full of dignity, and then being forced suddenly to dodge in order to avoid a missile was, thought Carlos, the funniest thing imaginable.

They had taken his beloved Juana from him and married her to the Prince of Portugal. She had wept bitterly when she had gone, and she had told Carlos that she would continually think of him.

There had been only one matter which gave him pleasure at that time: his father was away from Spain. He had stayed for months which had grown to years, so that Carlos had forgotten what he looked like and remembered only that he hated him.

Maximilian and Maria hardly ever saw him; he was shut away from them because they were too busy to be bothered with him. Carlos alternated between bouts of anger and self-pity.

"Nobody loves the little one," he would say to himself, although he was not so little now. "Nobody loves *el niño.*"

He was afraid of his Governor, Don Garcia de Toledo, who was the brother of the mighty Duke of Alba. Don Garcia would stride into the apartment and everyone would bow low as though he were the Emperor himself. Carlos would watch him from under lowered brows, his lip jutting out, his eyes sullen. One of these days he would put Don Garcia to the test; he would throw something at *him*; he would arrange a trap, something over the door to fall upon him and spoil his magnificent doublet, splash his white kid breeches; or perhaps he would put something on the floor so that Don Garcia slipped and turned head over heels. Then Carlos would see what became of his dignity.

For all these mighty dons must remember that Carlos was a prince of Spain and that one day he would be their King; and when that day came he would have their throats cut if they displeased him—not deeply, but just lightly, so that he could watch them bleed to death as he did the rabbits he caught.

At the moment, though, he was not ready. He planned these tricks he would play on Don Garcia, but when the nobleman appeared he would seem so much bigger than the man Carlos had imagined, so much more powerful; and the young Prince had to content himself with plotting for the future.

In the meantime he was helpless. He must leave his bed at seven to attend Mass, and after eating he must go to the schoolroom until eleven, when it was time for dinner. After dinner he must go out of doors into the courtyards, and sons of noblemen were sent to fence with him or play games. He would have liked to fence without foils; he would have liked to run a sharp sword through his opponent's body. They were too quick for him. It seemed that all the boys with whom he played were stronger than he was, bigger than he was; they did not limp as he did; they could run fast and were never breathless.

He had cried to his tutors: "Let little boys be sent." Little boys, he thought, whose arms he could twist until they screamed; little boys who did not know the tricks which would enable them to escape his sword, who did not beat him at billiards and quoits.

Don Garcia had said gravely: "Only those worthy to share your Highness's leisure hours may be sent to you."

"Why? Why?" demanded Carlos.

"Because those are the orders of his royal Highness, your father."

His father was the source of all his misery. Well, there was one thing his father did not know. It was this: Whenever Carlos killed a rabbit or a dog, it was of his father that he thought. It was because of his father that he enjoyed taking a mole or a mouse in his hands and slowly squeezing it until it died, because then he imagined that it was his father's neck which his fingers were pressing, just as he imagined that the blood which flowed was his father's.

Hatred for his father was the greatest emotion in his life.

Everybody disliked Carlos; he was wise enough to know that. The only one who had loved him was Juana, and they had taken her away from him. She had cried so sadly when she went away. "Little one," she had said, "if only I could stay with you!" He had put his arms about her neck, had let his hands rest on her soft skin, and although that well-known thrill had crept over him and part of him had wanted to press and squeeze as it did when he touched soft things, the other part of him had only wanted to stroke and caress, for he loved Juana because she was the only one who loved him.

"Little one will kill those who take you away from him," he had snarled.

"It is no one's fault, Carlos."

"It is Prince Philip's fault."

"No . . . no."

"Everything is his fault."

He was sure of it; and everyone loved Philip, while only Juana loved Carlos. Carlos wanted so much to be loved. When he was King, he often told himself, he would have everyone killed who did not love him. But in the meantime he was merely a prince, a very young prince, who must perform all the irksome tasks which were set him.

Now that his father had returned to Spain there were more tasks. His father had found the bodies of rabbits in the schoolroom and had demanded to know who had put them there. The result of those inquiries was that Carlos was brought before his father.

"Why do you do such things?" asked Philip sadly.

"Little one does not know."

"Please speak of yourself as a grown-up person. You are no longer a baby."

Carlos was afraid because of the coldness of those pale eyes. Fiery anger he understood, but not cold anger.

He stammered: "I do not know."

"You must know. Why do you take defenseless creatures and kill them without reason?"

Carlos was silent.

"These bad habits must cease," went on Philip. "You are old enough now to come to some understanding of what your duties will one day be. Instead of occupying yourself with ill-treating defenseless animals, I wish you to develop a taste for reading. Nothing can improve your mind more than that. Understand that is what I expect of you, and if I hear further bad reports of your conduct I shall have to take measures which will not please you."

Philip dismissed Carlos then; and never, felt the boy, had he hated him so much. He fled to his own apartments, flung himself on to the cushions which were on the floor and, in a rage, began to bite them, tearing the velvet so that soon the down was escaping and floating about him like a snowstorm.

One day, he promised himself, Little One will kill his father.

His tutor came in and found him in a state of emotional exhaustion.

"You shall have a soothing drink, Highness, and after a rest you will feel better."

And while the tutor took the trembling body of his young master and helped him to his feet, he was wondering if he might ask to be excused the great honor of tutoring the heir. His duties were becoming more and more irksome, and he guessed that one day they would be more than irksome; they would be dangerous.

It was not long before Carlos was lashing himself to fresh fury and, as he did so, a cobbler arrived with a pair of shoes the Prince had ordered.

Carlos was glad to tear himself away from the fierce passion which beset him. "Send the cobbler in," he commanded. "He brings the new shoes and Little One wishes to try them on."

Carlos glowered at the cobbler because he was young and handsome.

The cobbler knelt and held out the shoes, which were beautifully wrought. He was obviously proud of his work.

"Your royal Highness will see that I have carried out your instructions in every detail. Might your royal Highness like to try them on to assure yourself that the fit is as perfect as I know it to be?"

Carlos sat imperiously in his chair, ordering one of his attendants to kneel and take off his shoes. This was done, and the shoes were put on his feet.

Carlos rose. The cobbler watched in delight. But Carlos was determined to be angry. He could not forget the recent scene with his father. Hatred filled his heart—hatred for his father. Yet he dared not show that hatred. He had enough sense to know that he could not pit his puny strength against that of the calm, solemn man who had the whole of Spain behind him. Yet Carlos would be revenged on someone. He looked at the smiling face of the cobbler.

"They are ill-made!" he shrieked. "They do not fit. You have made them badly on purpose to provoke Don Carlos, and Don Carlos will not be provoked. Scoundrel! How dare you stand there smiling, so pleased, when you have caused the shoes of his royal Highness Don Carlos to pinch him?"

"Your Highness, is it so? Doubtless we can remedy the slight fault. Mayhap the shoes which were copied were a little too small for your royal Highness. The fault shall be rectified."

"The fault shall indeed be rectified!" cried Carlos, his eyes flashing. "You . . . standing there . . . seize this man. Do you hear? Do you stand there refusing to obey Don Carlos!"

Two attendants came forward and took the bewildered cobbler uncertainly by the arms. "What . . . is your Highness's pleasure?"

"Your Highness will tell you. Take him. But first let him pick up his shoes . . . his odious shoes . . . which he has made too small in order to hurt his Prince."

"I assure your Highness . . ." began the cobbler.

"His Highness does not listen to you. His Highness thinks how he will punish you. You will soon wish that you had not dared to show your insolence to Don Carlos."

Carlos broke into loud laughter. He had thought of a wonderful plan, and it amused him; it made him happy; he would be revenged on the insolent cobbler, for how could he be revenged on the one whom he really hated? For the time being the cobbler could take Philip's place.

"March this man down to the kitchens. At once. Do not stand gaping there, or Don Carlos will have you whipped. He'll have you whipped until the blood runs." Carlos paused to contemplate that. Blood! He liked that. For a moment he forgot his amusing plans for the cobbler. Then he remembered and once more he shook with laughter.

"To the kitchens . . . your Highness?"

"You heard Don Carlos. At once. Now . . . march! You come too. And you . . . and you . . . and you. You will see how Don Carlos treats those who are insolent to him."

Perturbed, they marched down to the kitchens, hoping that some person of authority would see them and have the cause of such strange conduct investigated.

In the kitchens below the great hall of the palace the cooks were busy. Joints of meat were turning on spits and a great cauldron over a wood fire was sending off savory steam.

The cobbler was now sweating with fear; he had heard of the wild ways of the Prince, but he had not believed he could arouse wrath such as this by presenting him with a pair of beautiful shoes.

Carlos called to the cooks: "Here! Here! Come here, you cooks. Stand there before Don Carlos. What are you cooking in the cauldron? Take it off and put another on the fire filled with hot water. Now take these shoes. Cut them into pieces."

The cobbler gasped. In spite of his fear he protested: "Your Highness . . . such beautiful shoes!"

"Cut them! Cut them! Or do you want me to cut off your head instead? Here are sharp knives. They could cut heads as easily as shoes . . ." Carlos broke into mad laughter which terrified all those who heard it. "Here . . . you cook. Cut . . . Cut . . . Unless *you* want to be put in that cauldron and brought to the boil. What a dish that would make, eh! Ha . . . ha . . . ha . . ." His laughter seemed as if it would choke him, and there was not a person in the kitchens who did not hope that it would ... choke him to death so that they need never give a thought to the mad schemes of Don Carlos, which might involve any member of the household in pain and disaster.

"Cut the leather into pieces ..."

He watched the cook do this while he burst into peal after peal of laughter; and when the shoes were cut to pieces he ordered them to be put into the hot water. He peered into the cauldron of boiling water, while his mad laughter rang through the kitchens.

"This will show," he cried. "This will teach those who wish to play tricks on Don Carlos that they would be wiser to leave him alone. Now take the leather out of the water. Set Master Cobbler at the table. Give him a platter. Now ... set out his dish for him. Set out his shoes. By God and all the saints, Don Carlos swears he shall not leave these kitchens until he has eaten the shoes ... every scrap of them."

"Your Highness ..." cried the cobbler.

Carlos lunged at the man with his fists, but the cobbler was strong and the Prince was puny. Carlos wanted to cry with anger because his blows had no effect on the stalwart young man. He was acutely aware of his own weakness, the deformities of his body, the hump on his back which his loose doublet could not quite conceal, his pallid face, his rolling eyes and his loose jaw, of those legs which were not the same length.

He wanted to cry: "Love Don Carlos. Love this little one and he will not hurt you."

But there was disgust in the cobbler's eyes, and Don Carlos recognized this. He knew that all the people who watched him despised him, and that if he had not been a prince they would have turned against him; they would have driven him out of the kitchens, out of the palace, sent him into that world where nobody loved him.

So he would revenge himself on all those who were powerless to act against him.

"Eat ... Eat. You are commanded to eat."

The bewildered man put a piece of leather into his mouth. He swallowed and choked. He began to cough and vomit while the Prince roared with glee.

"More! More! Don Carlos will call in the whippers if you do not. They will make you eat."

And into his mouth the cobbler put another piece of leather. He choked, coughed, and was sick. His face was yellow now—yellower than that of Carlos. He looked ugly in his discomfort, uglier than Carlos. This was what the Prince liked; he was enjoying this. He must have more of such games.

There were still several pieces of leather on the platter, but it was clear that the cobbler would not be able to swallow them. He was writhing now in agony and Carlos was beside himself with mirth, commanding the onlookers to join with him in urging the cobbler to greater efforts.

There they stood, shocked into sullenness. Carlos would show them.

"Laugh! Laugh!" he screamed. "You there . . . You . . . cook! If you are sorry for this traitor, you may help him eat his tasty dish." Carlos laughed until the tears spurted from his eyes and moisture dribbled from his lips, spattering the black velvet of his doublet. Thus he did not immediately see the messenger from his father's suite who had entered the kitchen.

"Your Highness," said the messenger. "On the instruction of his most royal Highness, Prince Philip, I ask you to go at once to your apartments."

Carlos swung around, his face working with fury, the tears of laughter turning to tears of rage. He stammered: "You . . . you shall eat this. You . . . you . . . who dare to order Don Carlos."

"*I* do not order your Highness. I but obey orders, the orders of his most royal Highness, Prince Philip."

"They shall not be obeyed. Don Carlos is the Prince. Don Carlos shall not . . ."

The cobbler was lying unconscious on the floor; the cooks and kitchen workers stood very still, watching the conflict between the unbalanced Prince and the envoy from his father.

"Your Highness," said the clear, calm voice, "I beg of you, accompany me. Your father's guards await you. They will escort you to your apartments. So, I beg of you, let us go."

Carlos knew that he was powerless. Someone had carried the tale of his sport to his father, and his father had sent men to put him under what was tantamount to arrest.

Even as Carlos hesitated, Philip's physician came into the kitchens and went to attend to the unconscious man on the floor.

Carlos knew that he was beaten. He was a boy as yet and the whole of Spain was against him.

So, the men about him fell back, and while Philip's own physician attended to the cobbler, Don Carlos was obliged to walk, most shamefully, out of the kitchens with his father's messenger; and as he went along the corridors and up staircases to his own apartments, he could hear the steady footsteps of his father's guards tramping behind him.

Of all the people in the world, Don Carlos hates him most, thought Carlos. One day Don Carlos will kill Don Philip.

So Philip knew that he must marry again; without delay he must have another heir. That young monster called Don Carlos must not be his only offering to Spain. He was about to send dispatches to Ruy Gomez in Portugal, telling him to complete the marriage negotiations as quickly as possible, when news came from the Emperor.

Charles was evidently excited.

"My son," he wrote, "hold up the negotiations with Portugal. Something is happening in England which must command our close attention. We cannot afford to close our eyes to events in that island. Flanders is ours, but to keep it ours without the might of the Empire behind us will not be an easy matter. There are the French on one side, the Lutheran Princes on the other. The only way in which we can hold Flanders is to make England our ally. That is why we must earnestly consider what is happening there.

"For some years the young King Edward has been ailing. News has reached me that he is dying—some say of poison. By the time this reaches you Edward the Sixth of England will be no more. The Duke of Northumberland will try to put Lady Jane Grey on the throne. Our friends there inform me that this cannot succeed. The English will not have Lady Jane for their Queen; they are a determined people who will choose their own rulers. They are all behind our kinswoman, Mary Tudor, and I doubt not that in a short time the throne will be hers.

"You will readily see that if England and Spain were united in lasting union—and it must be lasting—we need no longer fear the French. With England beside her, the greatest power in the world today—in spite of all we have lost here in Europe—would be Spain.

"You see what I mean? Our kinswoman, Mary Tudor, is unmarried; and you, my beloved son, are unmarried. Philip and Mary could unite Spain and England. Not only would such a marriage restore the power of Spain; it could bring England back to Holy Church.

"Mary would make an excellent wife for you. She is only eleven years your senior; she is of the same stock, being a granddaughter of our own Queen Isabella the Catholic, your great-grandmother. She is a devout Catholic. My son, you are twenty-six years old; you are a man of sound judgment. I do not command you to this marriage, for I know full well that having considered it and seen it to be your duty to Spain, you will not hesitate."

Philip stopped reading.

Mary Tudor! A woman of thirty-seven, a niece of mad Queen Juana, who was still living her frenzied existence in the Alcázar of Tordesillas.

No; certainly he would not have chosen Mary Tudor.

He would have to go to England—to that dark and dreary island which he had never seen, but of which he had heard much; he would have to spend a long time among a barbarian people whose tongue he could not speak; he would have to marry an aging woman whom he was sure he could never love.

He resumed the reading of his father's dispatch. "I do not command . . . for I know full well that having considered it and seen it to be your duty to Spain, you will not hesitate . . ."

How well his father knew him!

He wanted to cry out against this suggested marriage; but there must be no question of his personal wishes.

He was the slave of his country.

TWO

*I*n the city of *Valladolid*, flags of rich velvet and brocade fluttered from the windows. In the streets the people stood about to admire the decorations and see what they could of the bullfights, the sports, and the tourneys. This was a great day for Spain, it was said, for now Spaniards would see an end to continual wars. When they were allied with England none would dare attack them; and they would soon be allied with England through the strongest tie it was possible to make—that of the marriage of their own Philip with Mary Tudor.

They would have to lose their Prince for a while, and that saddened them; but he, alas!, would feel the sadness more than they did. They had but to stay at home and await his return, while they reaped the benefit of the marriage; he had to marry the Queen of England. They had heard tales of her. She was a witch, it was said. She was ten . . . fifteen . . . twenty years older than Philip. She was eagerly awaiting him because she badly wanted a husband; she had been promised to so many and had never managed to get one. Their long-suffering Prince must make the sacrifice; he must make this marriage for the sake of Spain.

Philip himself, sitting in the palace of Valladolid, yet again reading dispatches from his father, thought sadly of his departure.

How glib the Emperor seemed: "Do this . . ." "Do that . . ." It was so easy to advise; to carry out the advice quite another matter.

Such thoughts were rare with Philip, and he dismissed them immediately. His father was right when he said this should end their troubles, and Philip was stupid to dream of a beautiful young wife whom he could love as he had loved Maria Manoela.

He continued the perusal of his father's documents.

"My son, let us look facts in the face. Your solemn manners did not please the Italians and the Flemings. Believe me, they will not please the English. They are a rough people, a hearty, lusty people. They eat and drink with more gusto than any other nation we know. You will have to learn to do the same and appear to enjoy it. As a rough, uncultured people, they will expect you to enjoy what they enjoy. Your clothes must not be too somber. These people love bright colors . . . scarlets . . . blues and gold. You must not ride among them simply clad. You must feign great pleasure to be among them. Do all you can to learn their language. Remember, you will be their King. We will try to bring about your coronation as soon as possible, but they are a difficult people. It would seem that since the death of Henry VIII they have been ruled more by their parliaments than by the monarch.

"I shall make you King of Naples. We cannot have you merely a Prince when you mate with a Queen. Your rank must be equal.

"My dear son, there is one matter which I know you will join with me in wishing to bring about more speedily than anything else: the saving of this island for Holy Church, bringing them back to the Catholic fold. Your bride will help you in this, for she is a fervent Catholic. But it will be necessary to act with the utmost wariness. I know from our ambassadors and spies—as you do—that we shall not be dealing with a docile people. Do not attempt to force the Inquisition upon them . . . at first. Wait until you are firmly settled, until your son is born; wait until you are indeed King of England. I doubt not you will soon have your way with this old virgin, who, I understand, is delighted at the prospect of the match. But remember . . . first of all tolerance, for these islanders are lovers of tolerance. They have never been as deeply religious as our people have. But we will make them so in time. But at first . . . tolerance, *bonhomie*, and popularity.

"So to England, my son, richly clad and in great splendor, carrying magnificent gifts, smiling on the people, quaffing their beer—it is loathsome, Renard tells me, but you will become accustomed to that—

dancing attendance on the ladies, being a bluff and hearty fellow rather like their old King Henry—one of the biggest rogues in Christendom, but well liked among his people, who forgave him his sins because of his hearty manners."

Philip let the dispatch drop from his hands. He went to the window and looked out on the shouting, laughing crowds in the streets.

He must go to England, marry an aging woman whom he disliked on hearsay, and get her with child; and he must be a jolly, hearty, bluff, splendor-loving man; he had to learn to become a person quite different from himself.

Ruy Gomez da Silva came into Philip's apartments. Philip had showered honors on this well-beloved friend. Ruy was now Prince of Eboli; moreover, Philip had arranged his marriage with Ana de Mendoza y la Cerda, one of the richest heiresses in Spain. The marriage had taken place, but had not yet been consummated on account of the youth of the bride.

Philip was glad that Ruy was to accompany him into the barbaric island, but he did not say so, being as chary of showing his feelings as ever.

"What news?" he asked.

"Not good news, Highness. The English are gathering in the streets of their cities, shouting insults against Spain. They smile on the Princess Elizabeth; and they wish the Queen to marry Courtenay."

"That we know," said Philip. "But the Queen is strong. She put down the Wyatt rebellion, and she is eager for our match."

"She is madly in love with your Highness."

"It is not her feelings for someone she has never seen which are important," said the Prince primly, for the thought of Mary's doting adoration disturbed him deeply. "It is the temper of the people with which we are concerned."

"Highness, doubtless they will try to keep this from you, but I think you should know it, for to be warned is to be armed: We go—and I thank the saints that I shall go with you—into a strange land; and there the people will hate us; they will mock us; they will watch us; they will misconstrue our actions."

"I have already been warned that I must change my very nature. I must be as one of them—gay, ribald, eating too much, drinking too much—a real English gentleman."

"Then you would assuredly win their hearts. But the English wish their Queen to marry an Englishman. They distrust us and are afraid of us; that means they hate us. I must tell you this: A fight took place in Moor Fields—which I understand is open land situated in or about the city of London. In the games the boys who played divided themselves into two parties, one representing Wyatt's men, the other the Queen's and your own troops. One urchin played Wyatt, another your Highness. And the one who was representing yourself was taken prisoner. The whole gang then joined to take vengeance upon him. They hanged that boy; and had they not been seen and the serious nature of the offense against yourself been noted, he would have lost his life."

"You imply that if they would hang my impersonator, what would they do to me if they could lay their hands upon me?"

"Highness, I imply that we must move with the utmost caution."

Philip smiled. He almost confided in Ruy then: It is not these barbarians whom I fear; it is not the rope they might put about my neck, the coarse food I must eat, the ale I must drink. No. It is the woman ... this aging spinster. I dread the moment when, the ceremonies over, I shall find myself with her in the marriage bed and with what I am led to believe will be her cloying affection, her long-delayed passion.

Philip got up and walked to the window. "How go the preparations?" he asked briskly.

"The Marquis de las Nevas has set out for England with the priceless jewels you are sending to the Queen. Egmont, Alba, Medina Celi, Feria, Pescara, and the rest are making their final preparations. I am ready. It will not be long now before your Highness rides out of Valladolid on your way to England."

"The sooner the thing is accomplished the better," murmured Philip.

"I rejoice to hear your Highness say so. Then you are reconciled?"

Philip turned away as he said almost haughtily: "How could it be otherwise? Is it for me to flinch from what I have to do for the good of our country?"

Ruy bowed his head. If Philip curbed his feelings, so did Ruy. There were times when Ruy wished to embrace his friend and to tell him of the love and admiration he had for him, which exceeded that expected of a servant for a royal master.

Tomorrow they would ride out from Valladolid in a glittering procession under a Castilian May sky. And Philip, as he lay beside his mistress, Catherine Lenez, felt as though he would be shedding the personality of one man and putting on that of another.

He was a very different man now from the lover of Maria Manoela. Too much had happened to him; it had changed him. He was hardened; he was sensual as he had never believed he could be. Alone with his mistress, he had ceased to be cold; he had plunged into deep seas of passion. Was this the real man? Was the cold solemnity a mask that he put on to guard himself from the world?

It was typical of this new Philip that his last night in Valladolid should be spent with Catherine and not with Isabel . . . with the woman whom he thought of as a mistress rather than the one he thought of as a wife. That would sadden Isabel. But he, Philip, was the one who must suffer most. Isabel must understand that. Could she not see that he must enjoy to the full the delights of carnal love before he walked into the marriage chamber of Mary Tudor?

Catherine was soothing as well as passionate; Isabel would have spent the night in weeping. Catherine understood, as the more conventional Isabel could not; she knew why he must plunge into these frenzies of passion; Catherine offered balm and sympathy, and she helped to banish thoughts of Mary Tudor from his mind.

In the streets that night the festivities had been robbed of their maddest gaiety. The people remembered that they were to lose their beloved Philip; moreover, news had come of the death of the Prince of Portugal, young Juana's husband, so that the royal house must be plunged into mourning.

Philip himself was not sorry that the Prince had died at this moment; it meant that Juana would be coming home to Spain to take up the Regency during his absence; it would mean making a detour in the journey to Corunna, because he must show the proper courtesy to his sister by meeting her at the borders of Spain and Portugal.

So, the following morning the cavalcade set out from Valladolid. All the nobles who accompanied Philip had received instructions from the Emperor, with the result that they and their followers were dressed in the gaudiest of costumes. Philip's guards—Spanish and Teuton— were magnificent in their uniforms; and, thought Philip, the livery of his servants, being red and yellow, would please the English.

Philip himself was soberly dressed; he was still in Spain, he had reminded himself, and although he intended to carry out to the best of his ability what was expected of him, there was no need to become an Englishman in appearance just yet.

Beside Philip rode Carlos. This was an added trial to Philip. He was unsure how the boy would behave; already the people's cheers for the young Prince seemed forced. No doubt they had heard rumors of his behavior.

Yet Carlos seemed a little brighter than usual as they rode out of Valladolid. There were two reasons for Carlos's pleasure; one was that his father was leaving Spain and it was possible that the English might hang him as they had tried to hang the boy who had impersonated him; the other was that his beloved Aunt Juana was coming home. It was nearly two years since she had gone away, and she had a little baby of her own now—Don Sebastian—but Carlos was sure that she would have retained her affection for her Little One.

Carlos looked quite attractive in his dazzling garments cunningly cut to hide his deformities. Seated on his mule with its rich trappings, it could not be seen that he was lame.

He was enjoying the journey and the rests at the various towns where great festivities had been prepared to welcome them. One of his greatest pleasures was to watch the bulls and the matadors. When the blood began to flow and the horns of a bull cruelly gored a victim he would cheer wildly. Then he wanted to stand on his seat and shout:

"More! More! Bring out more bulls!" But he was aware of his father's stern eyes upon him.

And at length, at the borders of Spain and Portugal, the two processions met. There was Juana looking rather unlike herself in her widow's clothes, tearful, weeping for her husband, kneeling solemnly before her brother. Yet when she took Carlos's hand and smiled at him, his heart beat faster with pleasure, and tears of joy filled his eyes.

"Juana! Juana!" He did not care for etiquette; he could not hold back the words. "You have come home to your Little One."

Philip conducted his sister back to Valladolid, instructing her every day during the journey on her duties as Regent. She would, among other tasks, have charge of the young Prince during his father's absence.

"Remember," said Philip. "There must be no pampering. Carlos gives me great anxiety. He must be curbed, and above all kept at his lessons. I have arranged a separate household for him under his guardian, Luis de Vives. But much will rest with you. I hope to see an improvement in Carlos when I return."

"Your Highness shall."

Philip, looking at his sister, saw that she was weeping softly. Had she loved her husband so much? Was she the best person to look after Carlos? She lacked his own calmness and the common sense of his sister Maria, who was now in Austria with her husband, Maximilian. It was too late now to alter arrangements. Besides, it would be a breach of etiquette to leave any other than Juana in charge of the boy.

He reminded himself that he would beget more children; and that thought led him to another; he was getting nearer and nearer to the marriage bed of Mary Tudor.

"My son," said Philip as they left Valladolid on the way to Corunna, where Philip would embark for England while Carlos returned to Valladolid, "we shall pass through Tordesillas on our way and visit your great-grandmother."

"Yes, Father." The boy's eyes were alight with excitement. Each day brought nearer the farewell between himself and his father; then he would return to Valladolid and Juana. In the meantime, here was an-other treat; he was going to see his great-grandmother of whom he had heard so much. There were many rumors about her, and Carlos had bullied one of the younger boys into telling all he knew. He had kept the boy in his apartment, and even tickled his throat with a knife while the boy, with bulging eyes and twitching lips, had told all he knew.

"She is mad . . . mad," he had said. " 'Mad Juana' they call her. She lives in the Alcázar at Tordesillas, and she has jailors who are called her servants. She speaks against Holy Church and once she was tortured by the Holy Office."

Carlos's eyes had glistened. Tortured! Carlos must know more. He must have details of torture by the pulley, when men or women were drawn up by means of ropes, and left hanging by their hands with weights attached to their feet, until every joint was dislocated; he must know of the burning of the soles of the feet, of the red-hot pincers, of all the wondrous arts of the Holy Inquisition.

And the fanatical monks had dared to torture his great-grandmother, who was a Queen!

"They would have burned her at the stake," his informant had said, "but for the fact that she was a Queen."

And now he was going with his father to see this mad great-grandmother. It seemed that life was smiling for him at last.

As they rode the few miles between Valladolid and Tordesillas, Philip was wondering what effect Juana would have on Carlos. He would have preferred not to have his son accompany him, But how could it be arranged otherwise? Juana was a Queen, if living in retire-ment, and Carlos was her great-grandson.

Philip said as they came near to Tordesillas: "You will find your great-grandmother unlike other people whom you have known. You must be quiet in her presence and speak only when spoken to. Do not be alarmed by what may seem strange to you. I shall speak with your great-grandmother, and you will stand very still. You will receive her blessing."

"Yes, Father."

Was it imagination, thought Philip, or had the boy improved?

"You may hear me speak to your great-grandmother on religious matters," went on Philip. "She is a little strange and needs guidance."

"Father, is it true that she has offended the Holy Office?"

"You should not have heard such things. None has any right to say such things of a Queen."

"But even Kings and Queens should not offend the Inquisition, should they, Father?"

"My son, one day, I hope, you will support the Inquisition with all your might . . . as I intend to do."

Carlos seemed almost reverent. He was thinking of the torture chambers below the prisons of the Inquisition, where the walls were lined with heavy, quilted material so that the cries of the sufferers might be deadened. Carlos thought of blood and pain, but with less excitement than usual.

Carlos walked beside Philip into the apartment of Queen Juana.

A few candles were burning, but they gave little light to such a vast room and the effect was one of gloom. On the floor food lay about in dishes on which flies had settled. The air seemed to hold the smell of decay.

Carlos thought it was a very strange room, and as his eyes grew accustomed to the dim light he became aware of the woman in the chair, and she was stranger than anything else in that room. She sat on a chair with ornate arms; she looked like a witch. Her mouth was toothless; her gown was tattered and splashed with food; her hair hung loose about her shoulders; her long thin hands lay on her lap, showing uncared-for nails, black and overgrown.

So this was Juana, the Queen, who might now be Queen of Spain had it not been decided that she was mad, and that it was best for her to live out her crazy life in solitude.

Carlos was filled with horror that held something of fascination.

Members of Philip's entourage had followed him and Carlos into the apartment; they stopped at a respectful distance.

Carlos felt his father's hand on his shoulder, forcing him to his knees. Obediently he knelt before the Queen in the chair.

Philip, conquering his repulsion, took Juana's hand and kissed it.

"Your Highness," he said, "I have brought your great-grandson to pay you homage and receive your blessing."

"Who is that?" asked Juana, her eyes growing suddenly wilder yet alert. "Carlos! Where is Carlos?"

"Here, at your Highness's feet." Philip took one of the dirty hands and laid it on Carlos's head.

"Carlos," she muttered, leaning forward. Her hair fell over her face and she peered through it as though it were a curtain. "Carlos. Carlos. That's not my Carlos. That's not Caesar . . . ruling the world."

"Not your son," said Philip. "But my son. Your grandson's son. You are thinking of my father, the Emperor."

"Ah!" The eyes were cunning. "You are trying to deceive me. You bring him here . . . as Esau was brought to Isaac. I know. I know."

"Give him your blessing, I beg of you, Grandmother."

Carlos then lifted wondering eyes to her face. She laughed, and Philip was reminded of the laughter of Carlos. There was the same wild abandonment which he had heard his son display.

But the old woman was looking at Carlos, and she seemed to sense some bond between herself and the boy. "Bless you," she said quietly. "May God and the saints preserve you . . . give you long life, little Carlos, great happiness and many to love you."

"To your feet, my son," commanded Philip. "Kiss your great-grandmother's hand and thank her for her blessing."

Carlos, still as though under a spell, obeyed. The woman and the boy kept their eyes fixed on each other; then slowly tears began to flow down Juana's cheeks, making furrows through the dirt on her skin. This was comforting to Carlos, but to Philip quite horrible. He signed to one of his attendants.

"Escort Don Carlos to his apartments," he said. "And leave me alone with the Queen and Father Borgia."

Carlos was led out of the room, and Philip was alone with the priest and his grandmother.

"Grandmother," said Philip, "I have heard sad stories of your state.

I understand that you have once more spoken against Holy Church. Grandmother, cannot you see the folly of this?"

She shook her head, mumbling to herself: "We should not be forced to perform religious rites . . . We should worship as we please. I do not like these ceremonies . . . and if I do not like them I will not perform them . . . nor have them performed in my presence."

"Grandmother, such words are in direct defiance of the Holy Inquisition itself."

"So you have come to torture me . . . as I was tortured once before! I was tortured when I spoke against the Catholic Church and the Inquisition. They take people to their dungeons, they tear and burn the flesh . . . all in the name of God. Is He happy, think you? Does He say: 'Look at all the blood they have shed in Spain! It is all for Me. It is all in My Name . . .'? Ha . . . ha . . ."

"Grandmother, I beg of you, be calm. Father Borgia tells me that you have been a little more reasonable of late, but that your conduct leaves much to be desired."

"And who is this come to torment me, eh?"

"I am Philip, your grandson . . . Regent of Spain in the absence of the Emperor, but I have not come to torment you."

"Philip . . . oh, speak not that name to me. You come to torture me with memories . . . and memories torture even as do the red-hot pincers . . . even as does the rack . . . Philip . . . oh, my beautiful Philip, I hate you. Yes. I do. I hate you . . . because you are so beautiful . . . and I love you . . ."

Philip looked helplessly at Father Borgia.

"She swept everything off the altar we set up for her, your Highness," said the priest, "screaming out that she would not have it thus. But I beg your Highness not to despair of her soul. She grows more reasonable as her health fails."

"What are you mumbling about, eh, priest? What are you mumbling about there in the shadows? You are a woman in disguise, I believe. I won't have women about me. He's not to be trusted with women, that Philip!"

"There seems nothing I can say," said Philip.

"We might apply . . . a little force, your Highness."

Philip looked at the sad figure in the chair, the filthy hair, the tattered garments, the legs swollen with dropsy. Philip hated cruelty for its own sake. He hated war because that meant much bloodshed; in his opinion, the tortures of the Inquisition were only inflicted for the purpose of guiding heretics to the truth and saving their souls, or preparing them for eternal torment. That seemed to him reasonable. But to inflict suffering when no good could come of it disgusted him. And how could they, by torturing this woman, make her see the truth? She might see it for a day, but after that she would lapse into the old ways. She was mad; they must remember that.

He would not have her hurt. They must accept her madness as an additional burden on the royal house. They must try to lead her gently to salvation.

"Nay," he said. "Persuade her with words only. I forbid aught else."

"Your Highness has spoken. And it is a fact that she did not resist this day when I conducted the usual rites. Though I must report to your Highness that she always closes her eyes at the elevation of the Host."

Philip sighed. "Continue to reason with her."

"I will, your Highness. And I think you should know that there was an occasion when she stated that the blessed tapers stank."

"You must have done well, Father Borgia, since she is quieter now. Continue with your work. I doubt not that we shall save her soul before she leaves this Earth."

"That is what we will strive for," promised the priest.

They looked at Juana; she had suddenly fallen asleep, her head lolling sideways, the mouth open as she emitted loud snores.

Philip said: "There is nothing more to be done at this stage. Let us leave her now."

He went slowly to his apartments; he would be almost glad when next day they continued the journey to Corunna and England.

Carlos could not sleep. He could not forget the old lady in the strange room. He wanted to know such a lot about her, because vaguely he believed she could tell him something which others would not.

He sat up in bed. It was very quiet and must be past midnight. His heart was beating very fast, but he was not afraid.

She would be in that room still, he knew, for he had heard that she rarely went to bed. She sat in her chair and slept at any time of the day or the night; and sometimes she lay on the floor.

If he tiptoed out of his apartment and went along the corridors he would come to that room. He knew the way, because he had noted it carefully.

Cautiously he got out of bed and tiptoed to the door. He could hear the rhythmic breathing of his attendants. They were all fast asleep.

He was in the corridor, clutching about him the cloak he had picked up as he had got out of bed. Along the corridors he went, creeping cautiously past the sleeping guards. Outside the door of his great-grandmother's room were two men-at-arms. They were slumped on stools and both were fast asleep. Quickly Carlos slipped past them and into the room.

The candles were still burning and she was in her chair, sitting there just as he had seen her when he had entered this room with his father. He shut the door very quietly.

She moved in her chair. "Who is there?" she croaked.

"Carlos," he whispered. "The little one."

He limped across the room.

"You limp, little one," she said. "Philip limped at times. It was one of the joints in his knees." She spoke in whispers, as though she realized the need for quietness. "That did not stop his running after the women, though."

"Did it not?" said Carlos.

"Sit at my feet."

He sat, and she let her fingers run through his hair.

"He had thick hair," she said. "Ripples and curls. He was the loveliest man in the world. Who are you? You're not Philip."

"He is Carlos, this little one. Philip is his father."

"Carlos . . . Not that Carlos! Not my son. Not Caesar."

"No . . . no. I am your great-grandson. The son of Philip."

"My Carlos took him from me . . . He took my Philip. He said: 'My Mother, you cannot keep a dead body with you forever. I must take him away for decent burial.' But my Philip was not dead. I would sit by the coffin and I would have it open . . . and I would kiss his lips . . . He could not escape me then. He could not run to other women then."

"The Emperor who took your Philip away is this little one's grandfather. There is another Philip now. He is this little one's father. Carlos hates that Philip. He hopes he will soon die."

"Your Philip, Carlos? Your Philip. He is not my Philip. They said I must marry my Philip and I wept and I stormed. I could weep and storm, little Carlos. Oh . . . I could. And my father . . . Great Ferdinand . . . the King of Aragon . . . he said I was mad when it was good for me to be mad . . . Good for me . . . Who cared for me? It was good for him that I should be mad . . . and sometimes it was good that I should be sane . . . Mad . . . sane . . . mad . . . sane . . ."

"They look at Carlos as though he is mad."

"Mad . . . sane . . . mad . . . sane," she murmured.

"You hated your Philip, did you not?" asked Carlos.

"Hated because I loved . . . loved because I hated. I sat by the coffin. I'd take off the lid and kiss him . . . fondle him . . . I said: 'You cannot leave me now, Philip. Where are your women now?' Ha . . . ha . . ."

Carlos joined in her laughter, then held up his fingers to his lips to remind her of the need for quiet.

"I would let no woman come near the coffin," she murmured.

"Why not?"

"I could not trust him. He was full of cunning. I thought he might slip out . . . I could not keep him from women. Could death?"

"Could death?" asked Carlos.

"They have taken him from me . . . Carlos . . ."

"Not this Carlos. The other one . . . the father of my father. Not this Carlos. He loves you. This little one is your friend."

"This is my friend, this little one."

"He wants to bring his Aunt Juana here and live with you forever."

"Carlos . . . you will live with me here, then?"

"Yes . . . yes . . . When Philip goes to England, Carlos will run away . . . he will come to you . . ."

"They wished to send me to England."

"No, no . . . It is Philip who goes to England."

"They said the King of England cannot marry a mad woman. I was mad then, you see, little one. Mad . . . sane . . . mad . . . sane . . . *Mad!* They said the King of England did not mind insanity. Insanity did not stop the bearing of children . . . So said the English . . ."

"The father of Carlos is going to England. He is to marry the Queen."

"Henry Tudor wished to marry me. King Henry the Seventh of England. They said he was such a good man that he would make me sane again . . . mad . . . sane . . . mad . . . *Sane!*"

"Great-grandmother, you must not laugh so. They will hear, and send Carlos away from you."

"They poisoned him, you know."

"Whom did they poison, Great-grandmother?"

"My Philip. My father sent his agents to poison my Philip."

"Then you hate your father. Carlos hates *his* father too."

"It was after a banquet that he died. They said it was a fever . . . but I know what it was."

"Poison!" cried Carlos.

"I stayed by his side and none could move me from him. And when they said he was dead, I had him set upon a catafalque covered in cloth of gold, the color of his hair. I wrapped him in brocade and ermine. I sat beside him . . . through the days and nights. They could not tear me from him. Do you know who did it?"

"Your father? And you hate him?"

"My father's friend and counselor. What was his name? I forget it. He was an Aragonese gentleman. I know! It was Mosen Ferer. He was a wicked man. They set him in charge of me . . . He said I was a heretic and he tortured me."

"Tortured you! Tell Carlos."

"Oh . . . torture . . . torture . . ." Her mouth twitched and she began to cry. "They told me they must save my soul." She was silent for a while; then she began to mutter under her breath: "Mad ... sane ... sane ... mad. Carlos ... Carlos ... are you there, little one?"

"Carlos is here," whispered Carlos.

"Never ... never let people make you do what they want, little one."

"No!" breathed Carlos. "No."

"Love that is hate ... and hate that is love ... mad that is sane and sane that is mad ... My Philip was the handsomest man in the world. I would have a throne made for him and I would set him on it. I would sit at his feet and he would be my prisoner. I would never have women near him. I never will, Carlos ... never ... never ... None save my washer-woman. She is ugly. He would not care for her. Carlos ... come near to me and I will tell you something."

"Yes ... yes? Carlos is near you."

"The whole world is mad, Carlos, and only you and I are sane ..."

He looked wonderingly into her face, but she had closed her eyes suddenly; he watched the tears running down her cheeks; he thought that they were like rivets pushing their way through the soil.

There was silence in the room. One of the candles had gone out. He put his head against her ill-smelling gown, but he did not mind the smell. He was excited because he and she were the only sane people in a mad world.

"Great-grandmother," he whispered; but she did not answer; the effort of talking so much had tired her and she had fallen asleep.

He sat there for a long time. He did not want to leave her. He and she had much to say to each other; but after a while he, too, fell asleep; and he lay against her, keeping his hand in hers.

The guards looked in, as they did periodically, to see that all was well.

She awoke and immediately was aware of the boy on the stool at her feet. There was queenly dignity in her voice as she said: "Don Carlos visited me. We talked and he grew tired. Carry him back to his apartments and carry him gently. Do not wake him. He is but a child."

And the guards, who were never surprised at what she might do or say, bowed low, and one of them picked up the sleeping boy and with him went quietly out of the room.

The next day the brilliant cavalcade set out on its journey to the coast.

Carlos, riding beside his father, hated him more than ever. Carlos did not want to ride with his father; he wished to stay with his great-grandmother in Tordesillas. But he was quieter than usual and he did not make his wishes known. He believed that his father was going among savages who—if he managed to survive the terrible sea journey—would make short work of him.

At Santiago de Compostella, the procession halted. There they must stay for several days that Philip might pay his respectful devotion at the shrine of St. James, the tutelar saint of Spain. There were always many pilgrims gathered in this city, but on this occasion their numbers were increased on account of the royal visit.

The sojourn in this town was devoted to religious ceremonies, which were a change after the tourneys and bullfights which they had had to witness at Astorga and Benavente.

Here they met the envoys from England.

When Philip received them, his friends and followers were astonished by the change in him. It was as though he had found a lifelike mask which he had put over his severe features. He smiled at these Englishmen; he greeted them with warmth; and those of his friends who were not amazed were jealous.

"See," they said to one another, "what smiles he has for these English! When has he ever given us such smiles?"

Only Ruy seemed to understand and, when they were alone, congratulated him on a masterly performance.

When Philip had given every Englishman in the Duke of Bedford's embassy a costly present, the party began the thirty miles' journey to Corunna.

A wonderful sight greeted them in the harbor there. A great armada had assembled to escort Philip to England, and protect him if need be from the French King's fleet; for that monarch would doubtless do his best to prevent Philip's arrival in England, as he was hoping to secure the English throne for his daughter-in-law, Mary Queen of Scots.

None watched that array with more delight than Carlos. As he looked at the banners of red silk and the brilliantly colored pennons, as he admired the crimson damask and the great standard decorated with the Imperial arms, he was thinking: "Philip is going, and may it please God and the saints that he never comes back."

Then Carlos bade a public farewell to his father, and the fleet of a hundred ships set sail for England.

Ahead lay Southampton.

Philip stood on deck and looked at the land he had come to conquer, not by war, but by marriage with its Queen, by the son he would have, and by the new man he must become for the sake of the English.

On the deck with him stood the important men who had accompanied him on this great mission. Ruy was there, ever a comfort, shrewd and calm, always to be relied upon; there was noble Alba of great experience, the handsome Count of Feria, Egmont, and the rest.

A boat was being rowed out to their vessel. In it were Lord Howard, the Queen's Admiral, Lords Shrewsbury, Arundel, and Derby with Sir John Williams.

Philip was dressed in black velvet and cloth of silver, and his doublet was hung with chains of gold. His garments were decorated with dazzling jewels of many colors; he was a glittering and magnificent sight; and in such garments he, who had always insisted on wearing the simplest clothes except for state occasions, seemed almost a stranger to his friends.

He spoke to the English in Latin, and apologized for his ignorance of their tongue. His manner was gracious and charming; it was clear—for the English made no secret of their feelings—that these men who had come to welcome him in the name of the Queen were agreeably surprised.

Now a barge, lined with cloth of gold and manned by men in the white and green of the Tudor livery, approached the vessel. This was the royal barge which had been sent to carry Philip to English soil; and when he reached the land, the Earl of Arundel begged his leave to perform a little ceremony which, he said, he would do at the express command of the Queen. Philip was then presented with the Order of the Garter.

The company rode to lodgings which had been prepared for them, and there, to the further astonishment of the *hidalgos*, Philip expressed his desire to pledge his friendship to England in a draught of English beer.

This he drank as though it were Spanish wine, smacking his lips, declaring that he could wish to be drowned in such nectar.

The Englishmen were deceived. Who had said a moody, morose man was coming to wed the Queen? Someone had lied to them. This Philip of Spain was a hearty fellow—for all that he was of such low stature.

Only when he was alone with Ruy in that alien house in that alien land did Philip's features relax into their familiar expression.

"Highness," said Ruy, "your father would be proud of you. This night you have shown these barbarians a man they will love. You might have been one of them, Highness. It was as though you played a part with mummers."

Philip was reflective. "There are times, Ruy," he said, "when I wonder what manner of man I am. I am sober, am I not? And yet perhaps there is in me something of the barbarian I showed these people tonight. But the test lies before me. Oh, fortunate Ruy! You who are soon to delight in the beautiful Ana!"

Ruy lifted his shoulders and smiled. "Perhaps she has lost her beauty before I shall enjoy it. She has been fencing with a page and lost an eye."

"She is a wild girl, Ruy, but the loveliest in Spain. The most haughty too, I'll swear. I doubt even the loss of an eye could entirely alter that. Well, your trials will come, Ruy, with Ana. In the meantime . . . think of me . . . with Mary. Think of me and pray that I shall not flinch from my duty."

"Your Highness flinch from his duty! As well imagine that the sun will not rise."

"Yet pray for me, Ruy, for in this alien land I need your prayers."

So Philip set out from Southampton.

The coldness—although it was July—seemed to penetrate every

garment to his bones. His surcoat was of black velvet, twinkling with a hundred diamonds; his trunks and doublet were of shining white satin with a pattern of gold. It was fine at first, yet it seemed drear to the Spaniards, because there was a mist in the air; and they had scarcely begun the journey when the rain began to fall.

It was necessary then for Philip to put on the thick cloak of red felt, but the rain seemed to penetrate even that thickness. People had gathered at the roadside to watch them; they were an ill-mannered crowd. Some of them shrieked with laughter, which could not be misunderstood; they were shouting their derision of the foreigners who were afraid of a drop of rain.

At Winchester it was necessary to stop and change their garments; and here at the Cathedral the bishops paid their homage to Philip. Here the Prince met that Bishop Gardiner—the Queen's favorite—who rejoiced in his coming and believed that here was a Moses come to lead England back to the promised land.

Philip and his followers were then taken to the Dean's house.

"Our Queen, being a maiden lady of great delicacy," explained the Dean, "does not think you should spend a night under her roof until after the ceremony."

Philip smiled approval of the Queen's delicacy, and declared that he would be delighted to accept the hospitality of the Dean.

"Her Majesty is lodged in Bishop Gardiner's Palace, which adjoins the Deanery."

"Then I see in that a delightful arrangement," said the new and charming Philip.

In the Deanery a banquet was prepared for Philip and his men.

Once more they removed their wet clothes, but they found the rooms draughty, and in spite of the time of year they were shivering with the cold. The Spaniards were disgruntled; they sensed the contempt of the English; and the new character which Philip had assumed, while delighting the English, was distasteful to them. Never, they declared, had Spaniards been treated with such lack of courtesy. These English had no manners; they were too bluff, too hearty. During the sojourn in Southampton, when his Spanish followers had gone to church

with Philip, they had at the end of the service been ordered out by offi-
cious Englishmen, they were told that the people would like to see
Philip leave the church surrounded by Englishmen. Nor had Philip
protested; in his new role he seemed prepared to do everything these
people wished. And as they left the church the rain had teemed down,
and Philip borrowed a cloak and hat from one of the English and
walked forth in the rain in these most undignified garments.

Now at the banquet in the Deanery they were expected to eat the food
prepared for them—and not eat delicately either. They must partake of
every dish upon the table, and while the English were prepared to tackle
the great mounds of beef, venison, peacocks, and pastry, and to wash these
down with quantities of beer, the Spaniards must follow their master's
lead and feign to enjoy barbarians' food with barbarians.

When they had retired to their rooms for the night, Philip said to
Ruy: "We have been but a few days in this country, but it seems like
years."

"Your Highness will grow accustomed to it before long."

"I rejoice that one more day is over."

But that day was not over, for there was at that moment a knock on
the door. Ruy, grasping his sword—for there was not one member of
the party who trusted the English—went to the door.

A woman stood there. She said in halting Spanish: "My lord, I am
Mistress of the Queen's Robes, and I come to tell His Majesty that Her
Majesty the Queen wishes him to visit her in her closet tonight. It is her
wish that he should bring with him but few of his followers."

"I fear His Highness has retired for the night," began Ruy.

But Philip was immediately beside him, forcing a smile. The woman,
seeing him, dropped a deep curtsy.

"The Queen wishes to see me!" cried Philip. "Then I am delighted,
and eagerly will I go to her. But I must have a few moments in which to
make myself presentable."

The woman rose and looked at Philip with admiration. He could
see by her expression that she was wondering who had circulated those
ridiculous stories about Philip of Spain. Solemn! Full of ceremony!
Nothing of the sort! She would go back to her mistress and report that

she had seen him and that he appeared to be not only handsome, but the kindest of men.

"Then may I send the Queen's envoy in ten minutes to conduct your Highness to her?"

"I am all impatience," said Philip.

The door shut on her and the two men looked wearily at each other.

"There is no help for it," said Philip. "Now . . . for another change of costume."

Ruy helped him put on the French surcoat with gold and silver embossments; the doublet and trunks were made of white kid, decorated with gold embroidery.

"We must not go alone," said Ruy. "How do we know what these people plan? I'll summon Feria and Alba . . . and I think Medina Celi, Egmont, and Horn . . . with perhaps a few more."

Philip did not answer. He was thinking: Now the moment has come. Now I shall be brought face to face with my bride.

In ten minutes he was ready, surrounded by those grandees who Ruy had considered should accompany them.

The messenger from the Queen led them out of the Deanery and across a small garden to the Palace of the Bishop of Winchester. They mounted a staircase, and the messenger threw open a door and announced: "His Highness King Philip."

Philip went forward. He was in a long gallery, the walls of which were hung with tapestry. Pacing up and down in a state of acute nervousness was a little woman. With her was Gardiner, Bishop of Winchester; some other gentlemen and ladies, obviously of high rank, were also in the gallery.

She stood still as Philip entered.

For a moment he thought her a charming sight. She was magnificently dressed in black velvet, cut away at the waist to show a petticoat of silver; the coif which adorned her sandy hair was of black velvet and cloth of gold; about her waist was a girdle made of flashing stones of many colors.

Philip approached and with a qualm kissed her on the mouth in accordance with the English custom. He saw the warm color flood her transparent skin; he saw too that, although she was far from being as ugly as she had been represented, she was a woman completely lacking in physical attractiveness. On her face were lines put there by ill-health and bitterness; clearly she showed herself to be a woman who had so far gone unloved through life.

What had she heard of him? he wondered. That he was cold, moody, and hardly ever smiled? Now he was all smiles, all eagerness.

"It was good of your Highness to come," she said in Latin, for although she understood Spanish well enough to read it, she did not speak it.

He answered in Latin: "The Queen commanded. She must be obeyed. Nor was it any hardship when she commanded me to do that for which I have been longing these many weeks."

What is happening to me? he asked himself. How can I talk thus? Have I really become this hypocrite, this sly schemer?

But it was not only expediency which made him wish to please; she moved him—not with love nor physical desire, but with a deep pity.

She looked a little younger now, flushed, excited, clearly liking the looks and manners of the man who was to be her husband. She led him to a canopy, at one end of the gallery, beneath which had been placed two royal chairs. They sat, and one by one the Spaniards came forward to kiss the Queen's hand.

When this was done, the party went into the next room that Philip might greet the Queen's ladies; and this he did by kissing them all on the mouth. As the Queen watched him, it was clear to many of the Spaniards that she did not care to see Philip salute her ladies thus. They considered that significant. Was she already half in love with her Spanish bridegroom? That augured well. Soon England would be completely under the domination of Spain.

After he had saluted the ladies, the Queen led Philip back to the gallery.

"Your Majesty will have a busy time before her," said Philip solicitously. "I will not stay to tire you."

"Nay!" cried Mary. "I am not tired. It is so pleasant to see you. Let us stay here and talk for a while."

There was nothing to be done but sit under the canopy. The Queen signified that ceremony was to be set aside. The Spaniards might talk as well as they could with those of her ladies and gentlemen who were in the gallery, and leave Philip to the Queen.

She looked at him almost shyly. "You are different from what I have been led to expect," she said.

"I trust I do not disappoint you?"

"Far from it. Far . . . *far* from it. You . . . you please me."

"Then I have my heart's desire."

"I was afraid . . . being so unversed in the ways of love and marriage. I thought you might be a lusty gentleman given only to carnal pleasures and . . ."

"Nay," he said with a smile. "I shall be a sober husband."

"And not too sober," she answered. "I was told that you never smiled. I have seen you smile this night."

"That is due to being in your Majesty's presence."

"Ah!" sighed the Queen. "You are gallant . . . you Spaniards."

"Your Majesty is half Spanish."

"That is true. My mother would often talk to me of Spain." Her mouth squared, as it always did when she spoke of her mother. "I longed to visit that country and know more of my mother's people."

"And now one of them comes forth to wed you."

"There was talk, at one time, that I should marry your father."

"That was when you were a baby and he a young man."

"He wrote to me recently and said he remembered that he was once affianced to me. He said it was ever a matter of regret with him that nothing came of it. He said he was sending me his son, who was young, handsome, and strong, while he had grown ugly, old, and tired. Why, had I married him you might be my son!"

"Impossible! Impossible! We are of an age."

She was pleased. Did she really think that he did not know she was eleven years older than he was? That was impossible, for time had not been very gracious to her. It had engraved its marks on her face— lines of suffering, lines of bitterness, anxiety, and sickness. Poor Mary!

He said: "What must you think of me—unable to speak your language?"

"I will teach it to you . . . Philip."

"I trust, Mary, that I shall be an apt pupil in all that you teach me."

"Nay, you must be the one to teach, I the one to learn."

Yes, he thought; that must be. I must make you see that I will govern this kingdom in accordance with the Emperor's wishes.

He longed to leave her, but now she was growing bolder. She let her hand rest on his sleeve. He looked at it, and with an effort he took those heavily ringed fingers in his. She was smiling and he could feel her trembling as he raised her hand to his lips.

He knew that he was watched, that the English were saying: "He is winning the Queen's heart with his chivalrous Spanish manners." And the Spaniards were saying: "We did not know Philip. What a man he is! He can act any part for the glory of Spain, for he surely cannot be as enamored of the old lady as he pretends to be—particularly when some of the other ladies are so charming."

At length Philip said: "I will not keep you from your sleep any longer, gracious lady. Now you shall teach me to say 'Goodnight' in English, and I shall say it to the ladies here and in the next room. Then I shall leave you until the morning."

She enjoyed teaching him the words for he found them so difficult to say. "*Good*night. Good*night* . . ." The Queen burst into merry laughter and brought her face close to Philip's. "No . . . this way. Goodnight. You see? Goodnight."

Then Philip kissed her hand and went to the door of that room in which the ladies were, and there he cried out in Latin: "But I have forgotten. What is it? Gooda . . . What is it?"

Then, while the Queen smiled in almost childish pleasure, he went back to her and learned the words again; then he went to the ladies and said it in such a manner as to set them all laughing and repeating "Goodnight" with that Spanish accent which they said was so charming.

"Your Highness," said Ruy, when they were alone, "goes from strength to strength. Why, the lady dotes on you already."

But his words did not please Philip. He had discarded the gay mask of the wooer and become the sober young man whom his friends knew so well.

In the Queen's bedchamber her ladies were helping her to disrobe.

Mistress Clarencius, her old nurse, whom Mary regarded as one of her true friends, was obviously in a state of high delight.

"He is a lovely little King," she declared. "I thank God for the day he landed here to make your Majesty the good husband I know he will."

Tall Magdalen Dacre said: "How magnificent he looked, your Majesty! And he had eyes for none but yourself!"

Mary said sadly: "But he is so much younger than I."

"None would guess it, your Majesty."

But Mary knew that they did not speak the truth.

Jane Dormer had said nothing, and, turning to her, the Queen inquired: "And what think you, Jane? What thought you of our visitors?"

"The Spanish gentlemen are very handsome, your Majesty. And it is a great joy to us to know that your Grace is to marry a strong adherent of the Holy Catholic Church."

Janet was thinking of the handsome Count of Feria, whom she had found at her side in the gallery. They had talked together, for he spoke English with remarkable fluency. Jane was as excited as her mistress; if she was struck with the handsomeness of the Spanish gentlemen, Feria had been equally impressed with the beauty of at least one English girl.

Mary looked at Jane and smiled, for she had noticed her with Feria during the evening; she had felt envious of the girl's youth and beauty. How wonderful it must be to attract by those qualities, she thought, and not because one was the daughter of a king.

They put her to bed and drew the curtains. "Your Majesty must sleep well," they told her.

But how could she sleep? She had seen him, and he was kind and gentle; he would be loving and tender, she was sure.

But was she as foolish as a young girl to imagine he had really meant those handsome compliments which he had paid her? Did she not know the truth? Strip her of her silks and velvets, take away her jewels, and what was left but a plain, aging woman who had lost almost everything in life but her throne?

Courtenay had deceived her; he had pretended to love her, and all the time he was plotting to marry her younger and more attractive sister Elizabeth, and take the throne from her. Courtenay and Elizabeth had both deceived her; they treated her with great respect because she wore the crown, but they were awaiting their opportunities to destroy her.

Gardiner and Renard, the Spanish Ambassador, had tried to persuade her to have Elizabeth executed. Why did she not? Would it have been so difficult to prove her guilty of treachery? Had not her name been mentioned in connection with the Wyatt rebellion? But she could not forget Elizabeth . . . Elizabeth as a little girl of three, so desolate, so alone, when her mother fell from favor. Although their mothers had been so different, they had the same father—there was no doubt of that. They were sisters.

What a bitter childhood Mary's had been! The grand marriages which had been prepared for her had all come to nothing, for the King had sworn that her mother was no true wife to him, and Mary who had been the beloved daughter, became a bastard. How many times had her life been in danger, not only from sickness, but from the axe?

And now she was thirty-eight—old for any woman, but for one who had passed through such desperate hazards desperately old; and now a young man had come from across the seas to marry her.

She smiled, thinking of him. He was beautiful with his trim figure, his golden hair and beard, his pale skin. When she had touched him she had thrilled with pleasure . . . more than pleasure—excitement. She was a virgin; she had never dared think of carnal love before this; if in her youth the sight of a handsome man had aroused such thoughts, they had been instantly suppressed; she had stifled her feelings then by kneeling before her altar, until she was cramped with pain, and must think of that rather than the strong arms of a lover.

But carnal love had become legitimate love. Love between herself and Philip must be more than pleasure; it must be duty. Without it, how could they produce the heir for which England and Spain were waiting?

So now . . . there need be no suppression. Now thoughts could run riot like mischievous children in hitherto forbidden gardens.

"Philip," she murmured; and all through the night she dreamed of him.

They were married in the beautiful Cathedral of Winchester. Gardiner, with the help of three bishops, performed the ceremony; and not since the days of the Queen's great father had such pomp been seen.

The greatest nobles of Spain and England were assembled in the Cathedral. Many of the English—chief of whom was Bishop Gardiner—were in a state of exultation, for they saw in the marriage that for which they had long prayed since King Henry broke with the Pope: the return of England to Rome.

After the ceremony had been performed, Philip and Mary, surrounded by the noblemen of both countries, went to the Bishop's Palace, where a great feast was awaiting them.

Here dishes were served with the utmost ceremony, as though the food itself were royal. The minstrels played gay music while the guests ate; but all the Spanish guests were furious because Philip ate from a silver plate while Mary had a gold one. They realized that these people meant to show them that Mary was Queen of England, Philip but the Consort; and that England would be ruled by the English.

It was a matter over which hot-headed Spaniards would have drawn the sword had they not been warned against this by Philip himself. They must content themselves with smiling at the Queen's loving expression when her eyes fell on Philip. Soon she would be his slave; then her parliament and her courtiers would follow.

Nor were the Spaniards allowed to serve Philip at table.

"Nay," said the hearty English: "he is our guest. He has married our Queen and we demand the privilege of serving him."

And what could be done? Nothing. The Spaniards could only marvel at these people, at their crudeness, their huge appetites, and their ability to sweep aside etiquette and make the rules which best suited themselves. Spanish discipline was needed here, thought the guests. Let

them wait until Philip's son was born! Let them wait until the Holy Inquisition was set up in this land!

The Queen gave the toast of her guests, and this she drank from a
golden cup. Then she drank the health of her husband, whose titles
were proclaimed by a handsome herald. "King of England, Naples, and
Jerusalem, Prince of Spain, and Count of Flanders."

And every eye of every Spaniard gleamed with loving devotion.

To Philip it seemed that the celebrations would never end, yet he
dreaded their climax. Mary was growing fonder of him with every passing moment. What tenderness had she known in her life? Very little.
And when this young man—one day to be the greatest monarch in the
world—showed her kindness, it was almost more than she could bear.
All her feelings, so carefully suppressed, were about to burst forth like a
river in flood; she was longing for the consummation of her marriage.
This Philip had everything to offer her; youth, quiet dignity—which
penetrated his new aspect of *bonhomie*—tenderness, kindliness, and understanding. Mary was happier at her wedding feast than she had ever
before been in the whole of her life. There was one thing she regretted
besides her lost youth—that her mother could not see her now. How
happy Katharine of Aragon would have been to see her daughter,
Queen of England, married to her kinsman, that together they might
rule the world while they led it to the only true faith.

After the banquets the great ball began. To the Spaniards and the
English this was a further cause for dissension. For could Spaniards
dance the crude English dances? It seemed to them that the English had
no notion of grace; they pranced, leaped, and laughed as they danced,
as though a dance were an expression of joy rather than of grace. They
laughingly declared—in their barbaric tongue, which only a few of their
guests could understand—that if the Spanish dances were danced they
would all die of laughing, for such laughter as they would be unable to
suppress would result in death after such a surfeit of beef, mutton, and
roast peacock. As for the grandees, the *hidalgos*, and the stately dons, how
could they so fling their arms about? How could they leap into the air,
guffawing as they did so?

Only the King and the Queen seemed to find the contrast between Spanish and English customs amusing. Philip, charming and courtly, discovered that the English knew the German style of dancing, which was not quite so crude as the English and was known to the Spaniards. So, in German fashion, they danced, led by the short, trim Philip in his dazzling wedding garments, hand-in-hand with the Queen, who was made almost handsome by the glitter of jewels and the shine of happiness.

Had that been all that was demanded of him, Philip would have felt great relief. But now the night was upon them. He and his Queen had been disrobed; their attendants had retired, and all but a few candles doused.

She was waiting for him—her eyes ardent, her thin arms eager. She was frightened yet desirous, seeing in him the embodiment of a dream. He was the belated lover; he was the savior who would help her to lead her country back to Holy Church.

And he? He was smiling; she did not notice that the smile was fixed on his lips to make of him an eager lover, as a crown, set on Mary's head, had made her a Queen. He was seeking to sharpen his pity for her into some semblance of desire.

She, so thin, so tense, so trembling, shocked him. How could he make love to her? He thought of Maria Manoela, the bride of his youth; he thought of Isabel, Catherine, and his Flemish mistress. He longed for them—any of them—anyone but Mary Tudor.

Fervently he beseeched the saints, and the saints, it seemed to him, came to his aid. He thought of his father's words; of the cheers of the people which had never failed to greet him; momentarily he thought of the misshapen body of Don Carlos. With his life Philip wished to serve Spain and the Holy Inquisition. He felt single-minded in his devotion to them. He was ready to serve Spain and the Holy Inquisition in the arms of Mary Tudor.

THREE

A slight mist hung over the great chamber in the Palace of Whitehall. It was the month of November, the most significant day, said all Spaniards and some Englishmen, in England's history. That morning, Philip, making his way to hear Mass in Westminster Abbey, had been accompanied by English, Spanish, and German guards, all clad in dazzling uniforms. The people in the streets had gathered to watch them—some with approval, some with lowering glances.

"This is the return to God," said some.

Others muttered: "Now we shall see terrible sights. Now we shall have the Inquisition in our land. That is why they made the Spanish marriage; this is the darkest day in English history."

Thus the people were divided.

During the last four months there had been numerous affrays between Englishmen and Spaniards; many a Spaniard making his way through a lonely place was set upon and robbed. He might call for help, but no Englishman would succor him.

"Get back to your own country!" children shouted after the foreigners.

"These are the worst people in the world!" wailed the Spaniards. "This is the least Christian nation. The English make no attempt to understand our language. They are barbarians."

Barbarians they might be, but the Spaniards knew them to be no fools. They managed to get their own way and they would not crown

Philip King. They insisted on treating him as Consort only, and, although the Queen loved him to such an extent that she would grow hysterical when he was absent, it was still the English who were ruling England.

Once the Queen is with child, the Spaniards promised themselves, we shall return home.

Those were Philip's thoughts, as he sat with Mary in the Palace of Whitehall on that misty day. Today he would see the first of his missions accomplished; it but remained to get a son. This was the great day of England's return to Rome.

Cardinal Pole, who had long been exiled, had come back to England, where he was being treated with honor by Philip and Mary. Pole came as envoy from the Pope. He was a sick old man now, but his face was lit by great enthusiasm. Here was the fulfillment of a dream; and he was the one chosen to bring it about.

Now he sat in his chair in the great hall, looking frail in his Cardinal's robes, while Philip and Mary, hand-in-hand, came to him and asked with great humility if he was prepared, as the Pope's ambassador, to receive the submission of England.

Philip and Mary then went back to their chairs while the Cardinal read messages from the Pope in which His Holiness proclaimed that he rejoiced to welcome back this great country which had strayed from the fold.

Philip and Mary knelt, pressing the palms of their hands together, their heads bent in attitudes of devotion, while the Cardinal pronounced the Pope's blessing and gave the Absolution.

There was a deep silence when he had finished speaking. The silence spread through the Palace and into the streets, where people stood about in groups, some exulting, some fearful.

England had become a Catholic country.

The royal procession passed in state through the City of London to St Paul's.

Cardinal Pole, in his own procession, with its banners, censers, crosses, and churchmen, took a different route to the Cathedral.

Great crowds were in the streets to see the splendors; but what caused most excitement—and anxiety—among the crowd was the sermon Bishop Gardiner preached that day.

He quoted St. Paul: "Brethren, know ye that it is time we rose from slumber..." They must start afresh, he said: they must forget the fearful days through which they had lived. The blackest day in England's history was when she broke from the Church of Rome. Now she was back in the fold. Let all men hear that and rejoice.

Then came the significant part of Gardiner's sermon.

He cried in a voice of thunder: "Brethren, we have been lax in these matters. We have stood aside and looked on indulgently at abominable heresies, tumults, and insurrections. These we could have averted, my friends, and England might have been saved much shame, had we *taken* these offenders and *purged* them of their wickedness..."

The news spread through the city and gradually to the provinces.

"It is here. Persecution is here." Every man looked at his neighbor and wondered whether it was remembered that this year...last year... he had spoken against the Pope.

The fires of fanaticism had burned in Gardiner's eyes. That fire would light other fires.

On that day it seemed to the people of London that they could already smell the smoke over Smithfield.

𝒯𝑜 𝒫𝒽𝒾𝓁𝒾𝓅 𝓉𝒽𝑜𝓈𝑒 were not unhappy days. He felt that his journey had not been in vain. He knew that throughout Spain there would be rejoicing. God and the Emperor would be pleased. But there was one thing the Emperor wished to hear more than anything. It was four months since Philip had left Spain, and still there was no news of a child. Charles had written several impatient dispatches. Philip could only reply that no one longed for the child's conception more than he did.

But...these were the happy days, for during one of them an excited Mary came to him as he sat in his privy chamber at Hampton Court turning over the dispatches from his father. He wondered at her interruption, for she, knowing that he wished to be alone when working, had given strict instructions that no one was to approach him at such times. And she herself came in.

"Philip," she said, and she looked almost like a young girl as she spoke, "I could wait no longer. I had to see you. I have wonderful news."

He took her hand and kissed it.

"It has happened," she went on. "I bring you the tidings we most want to hear. I am with child." She threw back her head and laughed. He kissed her cheek.

"I am so happy," he said.

"Happy!" She had turned away. Her joy was almost uncontrollable. She, who had led such a miserable life, was now the happiest woman on earth. She began to walk up and down the room, making no effort to hold back her tears. This was the happiest moment in her life . . . so far, because when the child was in her arms and she knew him for a boy, that would be the supreme moment.

She loved Philip, but that love was a torment. How could she help knowing that she was old, plain, and worn out with illness? How could she believe in his protestations of affection? She was aware that she must be grateful for his kindness rather than his love.

She faced him suddenly and said: "This I have desired all my life. A child of my own! In a few months I shall be brought to bed, and soon I shall hold him in my arms. I thank God for letting me live until this moment."

Philip was moved; he went to her and laid an arm about her shoulder. "I share your joy, Mary," he said.

"Nay, Philip. You have not lived as I have. But everything I have ever suffered is of no account now. 'My soul doth magnify the Lord and my spirit doth rejoice in God my Savior, for He that is mighty hath magnified me . . .'" Magnified me, Philip; and made me the happiest Queen . . . the happiest woman who ever lived."

He watched her. Surely he was almost as happy. I have done my duty, he told himself. Now I shall be free. I may escape. I may leave her and return to all I love.

The news quickly spread, and in the streets the people talked of the Queen's condition. The bells rang out. In a few months' time it was expected that the heir of Spain and England would be born.

It was now not so difficult to make a show of gaiety. He would say to Mary at night: "My dearest wife, you must rest. Remember the child you carry."

She would smile, for her thoughts of the child absorbed her; she would collect her women about her and they would discuss children for hours; and all the time she would sit among them, that rapt expression on her face, while now and then she would smooth the folds of her dress over her swelling figure.

As for Philip, he could not understand himself. Perhaps a man had to rebel. What happened when a man deliberately assumed a character he did not possess? Did he become something of the character he aped? Was he become cruder, more lusty?

He had watched Magdalen Dacre for some weeks, and each time he saw her she seemed to be more beautiful. She reminded him a little of Isabel, a little of Catherine.

During the dance he would seek to partner her; she would accept the honor graciously. Why did she appeal to him? Because she was tall and well formed, and Mary was small and thin? Because she was vital and young, and Mary was old and tired?

There were times when he was conscious of a strong desire for Magdalen Dacre; yet frequently other matters obsessed him. There was a Princess whom he had not yet seen because she was exiled from the court and living in seclusion at Woodstock.

He had heard a good deal of this Princess, for many scandals were attached to her name. Many said she had born the Admiral Thomas Seymour a child; and he knew that she had come near to losing her head at the time of Seymour's execution because she was suspected of complicity in his schemes. That was not the only time she had been in trouble. Whenever there was a rising, Elizabeth was suspect.

She was a gay jilt, he had heard; she was coquettish, wanton, but so like her father and so full of vitality, so very much one of these barbarians, that the people loved her and shouted for her every time she was seen. That was one of the reasons why Mary liked to keep her hidden away either at Hatfield or Woodstock.

Moreover, said some who were less kind, Mary was jealous. Here was a young girl of twenty-two, with startlingly red hair and bright blue eyes—not exactly a beauty, but fair enough, and with youth on her side.

Philip was eager to meet this Princess.

He broached the subject while Mary was pretending to take an interest in the arrangements for the Christmas revels. She was, of course, not interested. Mary had no interest beyond the infant she hoped soon to bear.

"Your sister should be welcomed back to court," he said.

Mary looked at him. Now he became aware of that obstinacy of his wife's; he could see in her face the ugly temper which she had never before shown him, though he had heard of it.

"You do not know what she has done," said Mary.

"Has aught been proved against her?"

"Plenty could have been proved."

"But has not?"

Mary's eyes, beneath the sandy brows which were so pale that they were scarcely visible, blazed suddenly. "Do you forget that it was due to her mother that my mother suffered as she did? When Elizabeth was born, my father declared me a bastard."

"Her mother suffered in her turn," said Philip. "Elizabeth was called bastard, and still is."

Tears gathered in Mary's eyes; they came easily during these days. "It is such a short time since Wyatt rebelled. Some of my ministers declared at that time that it was folly not to send Elizabeth to the block."

"You should forgive her now and bring her to court."

"Forgive her for trying to take the crown! Forgive her for winning over the people against me!"

"It is for the sake of the people that you should bring her to court. In governing a country, it is always unwise to ignore the people. They are not pleased that she should be banished from the court. Bring her here. Forgive her. Make friends with her, and you will please the people."

"Forgive her! I cannot do that."

"My cousin, Emmanuel Philibert of Savoy, will pay us a visit soon. He would be a good match for your sister."

"You think he would consent to marry a bastard?"

Philip was silent. He would go to work slowly. He would not suggest to Mary just yet that she might as well make Elizabeth legitimate, because that was how the people regarded her, and if some still declared Elizabeth illegitimate, there were also those who had doubts of Mary's legitimacy. Legitimacy was a ticklish subject where such a man as Henry VIII was concerned.

He said cautiously: "We could try to make the match, which would be advantageous from the points of view of both our countries, for, my dear wife, it would be a good thing for us if the Princess were out of the country."

"Yet you ask me to have her at court for Christmas!"

"As a preliminary step toward getting her out of the country, my dear wife."

When the Princess Elizabeth heard that she was summoned to court, she was torn between delight and apprehension. To one of her nature exile was purgatory; she loved gaiety and fine clothes; she hated obscurity and poverty. With her governess, Katharine Ashley, to whom she was alternately confiding friend and haughty mistress, she talked throughout the night after she had received the summons.

Katharine Ashley, who herself had spent many uneasy nights as a prisoner in the Tower, was terrified. She had been terrified of what would happen to her charge ever since she could remember. For haughty, wilful, arrogant as the Princess was, she was also warm-hearted, loyal, and brave—only Katharine knew how brave; and Katharine loved her better than anything in her life. It was Katharine's dream—as it was Elizabeth's—that one day the Princess would be Queen.

. They had been breathless with eagerness when little Edward had died and they had seen first Jane Grey and then Mary take the crown.

"She is old, Kat," Elizabeth often whispered in the quietness of her apartments at Hatfield or Woodstock. "She cannot live very long, for not only is she old, but she is sickly."

"Hush!" Kat would mutter, her eyes gleaming with an excitement which never failed to urge Elizabeth to great indiscretion. "That's treason!"

"Very well, Madam Ashley, report it."

"What . . . report the future Queen of England!"

Then they would pretend to laugh together at their presumptuousness, knowing that neither of them thought the idea in the least presumptuous.

But Philip of Spain had married Mary and now Mary was to have a child; that child would stand between Elizabeth's hopes of the crown forever. But Elizabeth was optimistic. She did not believe that Mary's child would live even if Mary came safely through her pregnancy. And then? . . . Well, that was just what she and Kat liked to brood upon.

And now this summons to court had arrived.

"It is my brother-in-law who has asked to see me," said Elizabeth. "You may depend upon that."

"And why should he?"

There were several reasons, Elizabeth said. Would not a husband wish to meet his bride's family? Might he not feel it was safer to have at court such an important personage as the Princess Elizabeth?

"You think the real reason is that he has seen your picture and fallen in love with you!" declared Kat.

"You have said it!" retorted Elizabeth. "Not I!"

They laughed frivolously together, as they did so often to enliven the monotony of their days of captivity.

They loved each other the more because they recognized each other's weaknesses. Kat knew that her mistress was the vainest creature in England, that she really did believe that every man who smiled at her was in love with her; she was haughty; she could be mean; she could fly into sudden rages; but how Kat loved her! And Elizabeth loved Kat, for a host of reasons. She was her mother's kinswoman for one; for another, she had taken the place of that mother whom Elizabeth had lost when she was three years old; and although at the time of Seymour's execution it had been Kat and

Elizabeth's cofferer Parry who had been so indiscreet before the Council regarding Elizabeth's and Seymour's flirtatious conduct, Elizabeth knew that Kat had talked because she could not help talking—it did not mean that she loved her mistress any the less.

"In love with you?" cried Kat. "This gentleman from Spain? Why, he has all the beauties of the world at his disposal."

"They say he is moderate and entertains only one at a time; and that one, for so long, has been my sister."

"Now don't you try your tricks with him, your little Majesty."

Elizabeth laughed and then was serious as she tried to look into the future. She was frightened. How could she, who had known the loneliness of a prison in the Tower and the fear of what footsteps outside her cell might mean, receive with equanimity a summons to appear before that sister who she knew had little cause to love her? There was only one way to meet such an ordeal bravely; and that was not to think of an angry sister, but an amorous brother-in-law who, having seen her pictures, surely must find her more attractive than his wife.

"My darling," said Kat, "have a care."

"Silly Kat! What is there to fear? Go now and read what I wrote with my diamond on the window of this very room. Go, Kat, and read it aloud to me now."

Kat made a mock curtsy and went to the window. She read slowly:

> *"Much suspected—of me,*
> *Nothing proved can be,*
> *Quoth Elizabeth, the prisoner."*

" 'Tis true, Kat. 'Tis true now as it was when I wrote it."

"Well, sweetheart, if you go tossing your head and frivoling with your sister's husband as you once did with your stepmother's, *I* shall be trembling in my shoes."

"Nay," said Elizabeth, smiling a little sadly, for memories of the gay and dashing Admiral Seymour always made her sad. Then she turned suddenly to Kat and cried: "I was a child then, Kat, and do you not remember him? There was none like him . . . nor will ever be. And they say this Philip is quiet and sober . . . everything that Tom Seymour was not."

"None the less dangerous for all that."

"Say you so? Well, Thomas nearly brought me to the executioner's axe; and this Philip, for all he is a King, could not take me further than that, now could he, Kat? For, stupid one, I have only one neck, you know; and it has been in danger so many times that once more . . . well, what is that?"

Then she laughed and Kat laughed with her. In their hearts they both believed that she was clever enough to come through danger and that she would rise to that high eminence which must one day be hers.

The next day she set out from Woodstock. She was cheered as she passed along the way, for many had come out to see her; the more unpopular the Spanish marriage became, the more they looked to Elizabeth. There were many ugly whispers throughout the country as to what would follow this return to the Catholic fold.

"Long live the Princess Elizabeth!" cried the people, at which Elizabeth would become demure, curbing her smiles, remembering that if there was one thing which angered Mary more than another it was to hear how spontaneously the people had cheered her sister.

After several days' journey, Elizabeth arrived at Hampton Court, where she was taken to the "Prince's Lodgings"; but no sooner had she entered with a few of her trusted attendants than the doors were locked behind her, and she knew that she was again a prisoner.

Before she had been in her lodgings an hour, messengers came to tell her that Bishop Gardiner, with some members of the Cabinet, was on his way to see her.

Kat was trembling as she helped to adjust her mistress's robes. "Gardiner . . . that man?" she cried. "If he could have his way . . ."

"Yes, Kat. If he could have had his way my head and body would have parted company."

"How I hate him!" cried Kat.

"Such indiscretion!" mocked Elizabeth.

"I never forget the way in which he persecuted your father's sixth wife."

"But she outwitted him. Remember that also. My quiet stepmother outwitted the mighty Gardiner. Do you imagine that what Katharine Parr could do, the Princess Elizabeth could not? Then you are guilty of double treason!"

"Hush, hush, my darling. Now are you ready? I beg of you, I pray you, my precious love, be careful."

They kissed fondly. "I give you my special permission, Kat, to listen at the keyhole. Though you do not need such permission. Get along with you at once."

"God bless . . . your Majesty."

"Hush! At such a time! You'll make me give myself too many airs. I must be modest . . . at least outwardly."

The Bishop was at the door, so Kat hurried away to take up her position at the keyhole and to experience great fear mingled with pride and love.

The Bishop came forward and Elizabeth gave him her hand to kiss. He bowed over it. Greatly, she thought, would I like to see your head on London Bridge, Sir Bishop; for if I could witness that cheering sight, mine would feel much happier where it rests still, in spite of your efforts to dislodge it.

She did not wait for him to speak. She said: "My Lord, how glad I am to see you! I have been kept a great while from you, desolately alone. I would entreat you to be a means to the King's and Queen's Majesties that I may be released from my imprisonment."

Gardiner replied: "Your Grace speaks truth. Her Majesty has, alas!, found it often necessary to keep you under restraint. And if you would remedy this permission, my advice to you would be to confess your fault and put yourself at the Queen's mercy."

It would indeed, Sir Bishop! she thought. Confess my fault! Admit my treason so that she could with free conscience lop off my head? Naturally, that is your advice, my Lord, for are you not at the head of those whose greatest wish is to see me headless?

Her eyes were clear and innocent as she lifted them to the Bishop's face. "Confess, my Lord? How could I, when I know not what my fault might be? Should I lie to the Queen? Should I invent a fault that she might forgive me for that which I have not committed? Rather than be so false I would lie in prison all my life. I have never offended against the Queen; therefore I can crave no mercy at her Majesty's hands."

The Bishop hid his exasperation. He said: "I marvel at your Grace's boldness. Say you then that the Queen has wrongfully imprisoned you?"

"Nay, my Lord. How could that be? I am the Queen's subject, and it is her privilege to punish me if she thinks fit so to do."

"Her Majesty would have you know that you must tell another tale if you would be set at liberty."

"Then, my Lord, if I must say what is not true, if I must plead for forgiveness when I have done naught to need it, I would rather lie in prison than say aught against my conscience."

Gardiner changed his method. He insinuated that the Queen was not pleased with Elizabeth's religious views. The Princess's eyes were wide with astonishment. Had she not heard divine service after the manner of Rome? Had she not frequently been confessed?

"These things you have done, some say, for expediency only. I should like to hear from your own lips what is your opinion as to the real presence of Christ in the sacrament."

Elizabeth was prepared for this. It was a question asked of all those who were suspected of being heretics. She spoke earnestly the lines which she herself had composed:

> *"Christ was the word that spake it,*
> *He took the bread and brake it,*
> *And what His word did make it,*
> *That I believe, and take it."*

What could be done with such a woman? wondered Gardiner. He rejoiced that the Queen was with child, for he could imagine what would happen to such as himself if ever this wily termagant came to the throne. It seemed little use trying to entrap her; she would have one of her cunning answers ready for every emergency.

"I advise your Grace to ponder well your position," he said severely; and then he left her.

Kat came in as soon as he had gone; she embraced the Princess, and Elizabeth tore herself away to give an impression of the dignified Bishop. Louder and louder grew their laughter, more boisterous their play-acting, until Kat cried: "Be silent. The danger is grave."

She fancied she had caught an echo, in Elizabeth's laughter, of that which beset people when they played with death. Thus her mother was said to have laughed in her gloomy lodging of the Tower.

Mary was nervous. As she paced the apartment, Philip walked beside her.

"You do not know what you ask," said Mary. "She is deceitful. She works with my enemies. She seeks to depose me and take the throne."

"How could she do that, my dear Mary, when you are the rightful Queen, and now are to have a child?"

The mention of the child never failed to soften her. "Ah, yes . . . But what if a rising against me were successful? I have to be doubly careful now . . . because of the child."

"Forgive her and please the people. Be calm when she comes . . . and she will be here at any moment. I shall hide myself behind these curtains that I may observe her without her being aware of my presence. I will draw my conclusions of her character; and when we have married her to Philibert, she will give us no more anxiety."

"Could you ask him to marry a bastard?"

"He is a vassal of my father's, and doubtless it would not be difficult to persuade him." He paused listening. "I hear them coming."

There was a knock on the door, and Mary cried: "Enter."

The door was opened, and a herald announced: "The Princess Elizabeth."

Philip had hastily hidden himself behind the curtains. His heart had begun to beat faster. He had heard so many tales of his young sister-in-law. Was it, he wondered, that nowadays every woman except his wife must excite him?

Mary was sitting in her state chair when Mistress Clarencius and Sir Henry Bedingfield brought in the Princess. Mary dismissed Mistress Clarencius and Bedingfeld as Elizabeth fell to her knees.

Through a small gap in the hangings, Philip watched the girl. He saw an elegant young woman with reddish hair and blue eyes; she was rather pale, no doubt because she had suffered many an illness in recent years, generally supposed to be due to her imprisonment and her perpetual fear of death. She lived midway between the executioner's axe and the throne, and would never be sure which way her steps must take her.

He noticed how cleverly she had dressed herself to enhance what beauty she had; he saw the rings which glittered on her beautiful white hands, and he was aware of how she deliberately displayed them even at a time such as this.

She said: "Your Majesty sent for me?"

"How else could you be here?" asked Mary coldly.

The long, sandy lashes were immediately lowered over the blue eyes. Philip sensed how vital she was. She looked demure, but she did not deceive him for a moment. She was all fire; within her ambition mingled with her womanliness. She might wish, as he had heard, to be a much-desired woman; but her burning desire was to be a Queen.

He must watch her very carefully. She must indeed be made to marry his cousin of Savoy and banished from her country, for one thing was certain: where she was, there trouble would be also.

Elizabeth kissed the Queen's hand, but Mary withdrew it immediately.

Elizabeth cried with passion: "Your Majesty must believe in my loyalty. Much slander has been spoken against me."

"Why is it that you always attract such slander?"

"Because it is the desire of mean-spirited people to misrepresent me, to undermine your Majesty's faith in me. I have never sought to rival your Majesty."

"What of your relationship with Courtenay?"

Elizabeth fluttered her eyelashes and allowed herself to look even more demure. "That, your Majesty, was no fault of mine."

She implied, as she said this, that she could not help it if men such as Courtenay found her so attractive that they risked their heads for her sake, even though she knew them to be acting foolishly and had no wish to accept what they offered her.

Elizabeth's vanity always annoyed Mary; yet, knowing this, and being wise and quick-witted in all other matters, Elizabeth could not eschew it, such was the pleasure of flaunting herself as the irresistible woman.

"I think otherwise," said the Queen. "I doubt your innocence. There are too many stories."

"Your Majesty, it is true that men when racked have spoken against me, but can confession made under torture be relied upon?"

Mary said: "Do you swear that you have never been involved in any rebellion against me?"

"I swear it, your Majesty."

"Would I could believe it!"

"Your Majesty must believe what is true."

"If you would confess your offense, sister . . ."

"Your Majesty, gladly would I do so if I had aught to confess."

"You stand stoutly in your truth, then?"

"I do, your Majesty."

"I pray God that it will so fall out that you speak the truth, for if you do not and we discover it, then your punishment would be the greater for your deceit."

"If your Majesty discovered aught against me to be true, then should I deserve all that befell me, and I should never sue your queenly mercy."

"That we shall see," said Mary. "Now I am tired. You may go back to your apartment. I have decided to forgive you this time, and unless I find aught against you, you may join our Christmas revels."

The Princess took the Queen's hand and insisted on kissing it. "Beloved sister," she said, "never shall I forget your clemency."

What was going on behind those blue eyes, Philip wondered. Was she already deciding what dresses, what jewels, she would wear to charm the courtiers? Was she praying that the child in Mary's womb might sicken and die before it saw the light of day? Was she waiting for the moment when none stood between her and the crown? It might be any of these things; and Philip realized that it could be all of them.

When she had gone he stepped from behind the curtains.

"What did you think of my sister?" asked Mary.

"Comely enough. Shrewd too, I should say."

Mary looked at him, noting the flush on his pale cheeks. Had he been slightly attracted by Elizabeth? Elizabeth herself so believed that every man must fall in love with her, that others found themselves believing it also. But Philip was no philanderer.

His next words disarmed her suspicions. "It would be well to marry her to Philibert. She is ripe for marriage."

But on looking at him more closely, Mary began again to wonder.

That was a merry Christmas. What tournaments, what jousts there were, with all the nobility of Spain to tilt against the lords and dukes of England!

There were the usual rivalries; there was sly English laughter at Spanish dignity, Spanish disdain of English crudity.

Philip was happy thinking: Before the summer is here, I shall have left England. Once the child is born, I shall be away—and if he is healthy, my duty is done.

He was watching Magdalen Dacre, that strange girl who seemed remote yet conscious of the honor he conferred on her when he singled her out. It was not always true that English and Spaniards did not get on well together. There were the Count of Feria and Jane Dormer to prove that. Feria had told Philip that he had fallen in love with the English girl and wished to break off the engagement he had made with a Spanish lady of noble birth. What could Philip say to that but wish him luck? If Feria could satisfy the family of his first love, there was no reason why he should not marry Jane Dormer. What a useful spy that lady should make for Spain!

The red-headed Princess, who, delighted to be back at court, was throwing herself wholeheartedly into the revels, gave him cause for anxiety. He suspected her of...he knew not what. Every action which seemed so spontaneous could have its motive. Courtiers said: "How gay it seems now that Elizabeth is back at court!" and he knew they meant to convey: What gaiety there could be, what merrymaking, if she were Queen! That was what she intended; while she was demure she was bold; she seemed full of humility, but what arrogance shone from those blue eyes!

He could not forget her; she turned his thoughts from Magdalen Dacre. When they had met she had made a charming speech of welcome as his sister-in-law. Yet what had she really thought of him? He could not understand her; she was all that he was not, and he felt that that gave her an advantage; he could not look at her without being reminded of the immensity of her importance. He was determined to get her married to Emmanuel Philibert of Savoy.

Philibert sat beside him now. What more handsome man could she hope to marry? He was the hero of many a battle. Alas! he had little fortune to offer; but what had Elizabeth apart from her questionable birth and her high hopes?

He watched her in the dance, flushed, excited, lifting her eyes to her partners—flirtatious and yet so regal. He whispered to Mary: "I would speak with the Princess. Summon her here. Philibert must have his answer."

Mary was nothing loth. She would like to see Elizabeth banished from the country, but there was one thing she would not do, even for Philip, and that was acknowledge her sister's legitimacy. To do so would cast a slur on her own birth, for how could Elizabeth's mother, Anne Boleyn, have been the true wife of Henry VIII, while he had another wife living, and that wife Mary's own mother, Katharine of Aragon? No; at all costs she must stand out against Elizabeth's legitimacy.

Elizabeth came and took the seat indicated by Philip. She glanced at him in a manner which made him uncomfortable. Was she suggesting that he found her so fascinating that he must have her beside him?

He said coldly: "I trust your Grace has considered the proposals of Emmanuel Philibert?"

Her eyes clouded. "Alas! Sire, it is so difficult for a young girl to know her mind."

"Oh, come. You have had plenty of time."

"But marriage is such an important matter, your Highness."

"His Grace of Savoy has paid a visit to England for the express purpose of wooing you."

"And of beseeching your Majesty to restore to him his estates," she said quickly.

She knew too much. How did she learn these things? At one moment she was a frivolous girl; at the next a statesman.

"He has forgotten the latter in his desire to achieve the former," said Philip.

"Does your Majesty think so, then?" She laughed—the frivolous girl again. "Would it be improper of me to ask how your Highness could have imagined it could be so?"

"You are so young and . . . fair." He was playing the game she wished him to play. She threw him a glance from under those fluttering sandy lashes.

"Your Highness honors me. I shall always remember that the King said I was young and fair."

He felt vexed. He said coldly: "It would please us if you gave him your answer before he leaves."

She pouted slightly. "And I thought your Majesty liked to see me at court!"

"I do indeed . . ."

"Then I am twice honored. I am a fair young lady whom your Highness likes to see at his court."

"I would like to see you married."

Her eyes were reproachful. Then she smiled brightly. It was as though she were telling him she understood his meaning; he wished her to marry because her presence at court disturbed such a respectable married man as himself. What a pity, her eyes went on to suggest, that the younger prettier sister had not been the Queen whom it was expedient for him to marry. Then there would have been a different tale to tell!

How could she say so much with her eyes? The answer was: Because besides being the vainest woman in the world she was one of the cleverest. She angered, exasperated, and attracted him.

"The match is a good one," he said swiftly.

"An excellent one for a bastard Princess," she said, and her looks belied her humble words. "Ah, your Majesty," she went on, "*you* know what it means to leave your native land. I think if I left mine I should die."

"I should have thought you would have been glad to leave these rains . . . these fogs . . ."

"Your Majesty has not been here when the first primroses are seen in the hedgerows and the blossom bursts on the trees."

"Well," he answered, "I doubt not that Savoy could offer you primroses and blossoms."

"Not English primroses," she said passionately. "Not English blossoms."

Now she was speaking loudly that those about them could hear her. She is one of us, they would say. She loves us and our land; and she is the one for us!

Philip looked at her sternly and wondered whether she should be forced to the match. He sensed that she was the most dangerous person in the country. Now she was trying to lure him to what? . . . To flirtation! To some indiscretion?

As he would have turned again she laid her hand on his arm with a gesture of charming timidity.

"It is so comforting to a young lady to know," she said with the utmost simplicity, "that the King has her welfare at heart."

He could not stay with Mary that night. He was disturbed. He showed the utmost solicitude toward his wife. "These festivities have been too much for you. You must sleep now. Remember the child."

She was not sorry to be cosseted, to be left alone with her dream of the child.

As he made his way to his apartments, he felt dissatisfied. What did he want? To play that old game of kings? To disguise himself, to stroll out into the streets and join merry bands, to find strange women and make love to them; in any case he wished to escape from the restraint he had put upon himself.

Passing along a corridor, he saw, from where he was, a lighted window. He looked at it idly, and as he did so he saw a woman on the other side of it. She had taken off her coif and was shaking out her beautiful long hair. He recognized her as the beautiful Magdalen Dacre. It was not often that he acted on impulse, but this was one of the occasions when he did.

His heart beating fast, his need for excitement urging him on, he went to the door of Magdalen's room and silently opened it.

Magdalen had taken off her gown. She stood in her petticoats, her long hair, cloak-like, covering her bare shoulders. She paled when she saw him, and strode to the door where he stood hesitating. She did not speak, but as she laid her hand on the door, he saw the vivid flush in her face. Her excitement was as great as his.

She tried to close the door, but his foot was inside.

"Magdalen . . ." he began; and he put out a hand to touch her.

But he did not touch her. To his profound astonishment, before he could do so, Magdalen lifted her hand and administered a stinging blow on his cheek. He could only drop his hands and stare. There was no time to do more. This English amazon had, with a second gesture, pushed him backward and shut the door in his face.

As he stood there, bewildered and horrified, he heard her turn the key in the lock.

The new year had come.

Emmanuel Philibert had left England, and Elizabeth had gone back to Woodstock, not exactly a prisoner, but under some restraint. She had declared in the presence of several people that her heart would be broken if she were forced to leave England. Philip realized that between them the royal sisters had defeated him. Both were obstinate: Elizabeth in her determination to remain in England, Mary in hers to insist on Elizabeth's illegitimacy.

Their behavior was typical of them. Elizabeth, fervently believing in her destiny, though her sister was securely on the throne and about to have a child, was refusing to leave England because she felt that when her great opportunity came she must be in the right spot to exploit it. Yet Mary, secure, with the child in her womb and the might of the

Anglo-Spanish alliance behind her, was so afraid of that young girl that she denied her the benefit of legitimacy.

Certainly these had been uneasy weeks for Philip. He could not forget his humiliating encounter with Magdalen Dacre. He did not blame her; he blamed himself. When they met about the court there was no change in her manner to him, nor in his to her; he was as gracious as he had ever been, she as humble and courteous. Neither gave a sign of having remembered the incident. He did not believe she would be so foolish as to report the matter to Mary. Magdalen was clever enough to know that, however angry Mary might be with Philip, she would be doubly so with Magdalen.

Magdalen herself had spent a sleepless night after the incident. She believed that Philip would not allow her behavior to go unpunished. She saw herself disgraced and exiled on some trumped-up charge. She had heard of Spanish vengeance, and she had seen how some of the *hidalgos* were ready to fight to the death in order to avenge an imaginary insult.

Daily she waited for the storm, but nothing happened. Once she fancied she saw a mute apology in his eyes. Could he really be so reasonable, so just? If so, she must admire his character, for it was not in the nature of powerful kings to see their own faults.

Magdalen eventually became grateful and sought to defend Philip when he was maligned. She mentioned the incident to one of her friends, in strictest confidence, to whom she pointed out that while he might be human in his desires, he was at least man enough to know himself in the wrong and not to seek to avenge a loss of dignity. That, said Magdalen, was admirable, in a King . . . and a Spaniard.

But how could such a secret be kept? Others must savor it. They *must* laugh in secret because Philip of Spain had had his face slapped by an English maid of honor.

As the weeks passed the fires of Smithfield had begun to blaze. Gardiner and Bonner had put their heads together; this should have started long ago, they declared. Now that England had returned to the Catholic fold, heretics should learn the folly of their ways, and those who wavered toward heresy should watch the writhing bodies in Smithfield Square and turn from their wickedness.

The people of London looked on sullenly. It seemed to them that a pall of smoke continually hung over the square. They could not get the smell of burning flesh out of their nostrils.

It was the Spanish marriage, the citizens declared. "All was well in this land until we had foreigners among us . . ."

Spaniards were set upon in the streets from time to time, and soon none of them dared venture out after dark. In the taverns threats were whispered, and the question asked: "Why has this happened to us?" The answer was: "Because of the Spaniards."

The Smithfield ceremonies were no *autos-da-fé*. There was not, said the Spaniards, the same reverence in England as in Spain. The English liked a merry spectacle, eating till they could eat no more, drinking until they were boisterous . . . mumming, dancing. They could find little satisfaction in a religious ceremony that was a solemn dedication. Some came to watch the burnings, but they were a sullen crowd. There was none of the ecstasy which was such an essential part of an *auto-da-fé* in Spain.

No; the people were sullen, and when these people were angry they showed their anger in ridicule. So now they jeered; and this time they did not spare Philip. The story of Magdalen Dacre and the Prince of Spain had spread to the streets, but it had changed considerably in transit. It was not only a lady-in-waiting whom he pursued; it was every woman he set eyes on. And since the ladies of the English court would have none of him he began to look elsewhere; he prowled the streets at night, said the people, seizing any young girl who happened to be abroad.

In the taverns they sang of Philip's amours.

> *"The baker's daughter in her russet gown*
> *Is better than Mary, without her crown."*

Philip was alarmed by the ferocity with which Gardiner was conducting the burning of the heretics. He approached Mary on the matter.

Mary, thinking perpetually of the child, was lethargic; she was worried because she did not increase her girth sufficiently to please herself; nothing interested her so much as the stories other women had to tell her of their experiences of pregnancy. Sometimes she would cling to Philip with fear in her eyes. She was terrified that the child might not be living within her. He would soothe her, believing that she was pleading for a renewal of that relationship which was so repugnant to him.

He now felt it necessary to speak to her about the fires of Smithfield.

"Gardiner has no restraint," he said. "No sooner is England returned to Rome, than he begins the burnings."

"Is this not as it should be?"

"Yes, yes; but it is always necessary to consider the people."

"Is that not what we are doing?" Mary was fond of Gardiner. If he was the cruellest and most vindictive of men where heretics were concerned, he was a great statesman and a loyal supporter of the Catholic Queen.

"No!" said Philip. "The people are unready as yet."

"But what are these ceremonies compared with the great work the Inquisition is doing in Spain?" demanded Mary.

"The Spanish people support the Inquisition."

"And do my people then support the heretics?"

He was irritated when she said *my* people in that way, and he retorted: "No. I agree *our* people do not."

She gave him her tremulous smile then. "Oh, Philip, *our* people, of course. That is how I would have it. You and I . . . together always . . ." She held out her hand, but he pretended not to see it.

This was so difficult to endure, this wavering between the arrogant Queen who was Queen in her own right, reminding him that the English people would allow him to be nothing more than Consort, and the hysterical woman come late to passion and therefore determined to drain the loving cup to the dregs.

"But the people are not ready," he said firmly. "Later we will install the Inquisition here. We will have an *auto-da-fé* in Smithfield Square. But that time is not yet. *Your* people are irreligious by nature. They prefer laughter to prayers, to forget the sins of their neighbors if they may laugh with them. But we will remedy that in time. Now they are sullen. They like not the fires. They blame my countrymen. They blame *me*. Their insults are more mephitic than ever."

"We'll stop it!" cried Mary shrilly. "Any who insults your country-men shall himself be burned at the stake."

"Nay; that is not the way to deal with subjects. I have tried to speak to Gardiner on this matter, but it seems he fancies himself the ruler of this realm. He is thirsty for blood. He has longed for this day and is like an excited child!"

"He is a true servant of God!" said Mary vehemently.

"Yes; but do not upset yourself, my dear. I shall command my friar, Alphonso di Castro, to preach a sermon urging leniency toward heretics, suggesting that they should be given time in which to repent."

"I see you are angry with me," said Mary. "You are cold. When I give you my hand, you look the other way."

"I am deeply concerned for you. You must remember the precious burden you carry. You must be calm . . . live quietly."

"What would you have me do, Philip, my love? There is nothing I would not do for you. Command me, I beg of you. Shall I send for Gardiner?"

"There is no need. I would have you rest. It is better that the sermon should be preached by my friar. The people will then see that I am not the monster they believe me to be, for they will know that a servant of mine would not dare preach such a sermon without my consent."

"The people do not know you, Philip," she said passionately. "They say ugly things of you which are . . . untrue . . . so untrue."

He looked at her anxiously. How many rumors had she heard? He had endured her cloying devotion; must he yet suffer from her bitter jealousy?

In the Palace at Valladolid Juana told Carlos of the news from England.

"You are to have a brother, Carlos. He will be half English."

Carlos did not care whether or not he had a brother; he was angry with the English because they had not killed his father, as people had believed they might.

"He will come home," said Juana. "As soon as the baby is born he will come back to Spain."

"That will be a long time yet," said Carlos.

He enjoyed those days. He was a little less wild, although he gave way to bouts of frenzy when any suggested he should learn his lessons. Always he would fly to Juana for protection, calling on her to save him from the monsters.

He continued to call himself Little One; nor would he allow even Juana to try weaning him from the habit.

His tutor, Luis de Vives, felt that, as it was almost impossible to teach Carlos anything, there was no point in forcing matters. To force the boy meant kicking, unpleasant scenes, and injuries to his health, which in their turn meant no lessons. There was hardly anyone who could be persuaded to whip the boy, for none could forget that he was destined to be the King of Spain, and they were sure Carlos was one to remember past injuries.

Only his father and grandfather would dare punish him, and they were both absent.

Often Carlos talked to Juana of her namesake; he remembered vividly that night when he had crept into Mad Juana's room and talked to her. He told his aunt that she had said that he and she were the only sane ones in a mad world. "But she did not know you, dear Aunt. You are sane too," he told Juana.

One day during that spring there came news from the Alcázar at Tordesillas. A messenger arrived at the Palace of Valladolid and asked audience of the Queen Regent.

Juana put on her cloak and hood to receive him, fastening the hood about her head so that she was just able to peep out of it. It had been a habit of hers to hide her face as much as possible since she had become a widow. It was remembered that that other Juana had adopted the habit after the death of Philip the Handsome when she had kept with her the coffin containing his body.

"Bad news, Highness," said the messenger. "Queen Juana is ill and we fear for her life. Her illness started three weeks ago. She demanded to take a hot bath. She was wandering in her mind and she said that the King, her husband, would visit her that night and, as it was years since she had taken a bath, he would find her dirty. The water was brought, and she would have it almost boiling, your Highness."

"And this bath . . . it was too much for her?"

"Her legs have been swollen to more than twice their usual size, your Highness. The water was so hot that the skin burst and it has not yet healed. The Queen was carried to a bed, and there she has been since. She will allow no one to touch her. She lies . . . without attention . . . and it has been thus for three weeks."

"Have you not had doctors brought to her?"

"She will have no one, your Highness. She screams if any approach. Her legs, your Highness, are in such a state of corruption that she screams in agony the whole day and night."

"Something must be done," said Juana. "I will visit her myself and take my brother's physicians with me."

So Juana set out immediately for Tordesillas, taking with her Philip's physicians, but when they arrived at the Alcázar the old Queen refused to see anyone but Juana.

Young Juana caught her breath in disgust at the condition of the bedchamber. The legs were exposed in all their horror, for the old Queen screamed in agony when they were touched by even the lightest covering.

The Queen called out: "Who are you then . . . come to torment me? You are Mosen Ferrer, are you . . . you torturer? See what you have done to me with your tortures!"

Juana fell to her knees and put her hands over her face to shut out the hideous sight. She began to sob hysterically.

"What ails you?" asked the Queen.

"It grieves me to see you thus . . . and you . . . a Queen."

"To see me thus . . . old, crippled, covered in sores . . . dying . . . ah, dying! But why be surprised? This is a fitting end for me."

"Oh, Grandmother, no . . . no! The doctors can help you."

"No one can, but I do not care. Soon I shall be past my pains. I shall be with him."

"Grandmother, your soul is in God's keeping?"

"I shall be with my Philip. What happens up there, eh? What happens in Heaven? Shall I find him there with his women about him?"

"Grandmother, hush . . . hush. I must call Father Borgia. You will see the doctors? You must see them."

"Father Borgia! He is Mosen Ferrer in disguise, I believe."

"No . . . no."

"He poisoned Philip. Comes he now to poison me? Then let him. For soon I shall be with my Philip. Oh, to be with him again! We shall fight . . . It matters not. Better to fight with him than to live, weary and lonely, without him."

"Here is Father Borgia, Grandmother. I sent for him. I implore you, listen to him before it is too late."

"I'll not see him."

"You must, Grandmother. I beg of you, do not depart this life with all your sins upon you."

She began to whimper: "I am tired. Let me go in peace."

Young Juana beckoned to Father Borgia, who had come close to the bed. "Pray for her," she whispered.

So he prayed. "Repent," he urged. "Ask for forgiveness of your sins."

She nodded—whether or not in answer to him, none of those who had come to the apartment could be sure.

A messenger came to say that learned priests, having heard of the Queen's condition, had come from Salamanca to do for her what must surely need to be done.

They crowded about the bed, and one held a crucifix before the dying Queen.

"Your soul is in jeopardy," he cried. "Speak and ask forgiveness. Say after me, 'Christ crucified, aid me.'"

She lifted her eyes to his and the death rattle was in her throat. She murmured: "I feel no pain now."

"Beg for mercy. Say after me, 'Christ crucified, aid me.'"

Her lips moved. "Christ . . . crucified . . . aid me."

The priest held the crucifix close to her face. Her breathing was very faint and suddenly she smiled.

Juana, watching her, saw her lips form the name: "Philip!" as she slipped away from the world.

It was April. A fitting time for the heir of England to be born. All the trees were in bud; the birds seemed riotously gay as though to welcome the baby Prince. Even the Spaniards seemed reconciled to England in the spring, perhaps because they knew they would soon be leaving it.

In Hampton Court there was a bustling and a hurrying to and fro and many an excited whisper. Any moment now, it was said; and all England and Spain were on tiptoe for the news. The French were hoping for a hitch, for the birth of a Prince would be the death-knell to the hopes of Henri II of securing England's crown for his son through Mary Queen of Scots.

A peal of bells was rung at St. Stephen's in Walbrook, and in less than ten minutes bells were ringing all over the city of London. This was taken as the signal.

"The child is born!" cried the populace.

"And is it a boy?"

"Of course it's a boy!"

Nothing less than a boy would please the people. The bonfires were lighted. There was singing and cheering in the streets.

And on her bed at Hampton Court the Queen was tossing and turning.

Here was all the ceremony that must attend a royal birth. There must be no doubt that the infant was the one born of Mary; therefore there must be important witnesses at hand.

Some of the experienced midwives were looking furtively at one another. They dared not speak their thoughts for fear of being charged with treason.

The Queen screamed aloud in agony and the women closed about her.

One of the women, more bold than the rest, said: "The Queen's time has not yet come."

The other midwives nodded in agreement. Mistress Clarencius, her eyes filled with anxiety, whispered to the Queen: "Your Majesty, will you try to rest? The time is not yet here. You should try to rest, they say."

"Not yet come!" screamed the Queen. "But I swear my time has come. I feel it. I know it. What mean they?"

"They are craving your Majesty to be patient."

"The child . . . the child is safe . . . ?"

"Safe, your Majesty," said Mistress Clarencius, "but not yet ready."

"Ah! I have come to my bed too soon."

"Your Majesty should rest. Here is a soothing draught."

She sipped it and lay back on her pillows. She looked very old without her jeweled coif; her light sandy hair was disordered on the pillows, her sallow face piteously lined. The women looked at her with a terrible fear in their hearts, but they saw that all the Queen's hopes were with her still.

"I hear bells . . . shouts . . ." said Mary.

"It is the people, your Majesty. They rejoice in the blessing which is about to be yours."

A tired smile was on her lips. "My husband . . ." she began.

Philip came forward. He could be relied upon to do what was expected of him. He looked at Mary and tried to hide the repulsion she aroused in him. He was not unaware of the tension in the apartment, and he knew that all was not well with the Queen.

Unless this child was born, the discomfort and the humiliation of the last months would have been in vain. If the child died and Mary died, he would have no hold on England. The red-headed Elizabeth would mount the throne; and he doubted that not very soon after such an event she would be snapping her fingers at the Pope himself. And something was wrong . . . very wrong.

He took Mary's clammy hand and kissed it.

"It is so long," she said piteously.

"You were too anxious, my love. There has been a slight miscalculation. You have been brought to bed too soon."

She nodded. "It seems as though it will never be."

The draught they had given her was beginning to have its effect. He said: "Sleep, my love. That is what you need. And when you wake . . . who knows, your time may have come."

She would not release his hand. Those cold fingers twined about his, pressing, squeezing, like snakes, he thought. As soon as he was sure she was asleep, he gently withdrew his hand.

"What is it?" he asked the midwives.

They lowered their eyes.

"Let us leave the apartment," he said. "The doctors also. If aught is as it should not be, I would know of it."

In the antechamber to which he had led them, one of the doctors said: "Your Majesty, I never saw such a strange pregnancy. There seems to be no child . . . no movement."

"You think the child is dead?" His voice was cold and precise.

"It is not that, Sire. It is as though there is no child."

He looked at the doctors. "Well, you are learned men!"

"It is true, your Majesty, that there is all the outward appearance of pregnancy, but . . . a softness, you understand? It would seem that there is . . . no child."

"But how could this be?"

"Sire, there have been similar cases. There have been ladies of the Queen's age whose desire for children was intense. There followed all the outward signs of pregnancies . . . but *mock* pregnancies, your Majesty. The would-be mothers were completely deceived."

"But this is . . . impossible!"

"We crave your Majesty's pardon, but it has happened thus in other cases. Ladies long for children, their longings become hysterical, and they may not be in the best of health. We fear that the Queen's age may not allow her to bear children, and that in the greatness of her desire she has created a mock pregnancy."

"I cannot believe this. It is fantastic."

One of the women curtsied low. "Your Majesty, the Queen expected to be brought to bed last month. She was waiting for her pains. Many times she thought they had started, but they had not. And so it was on this occasion. She waits for her pains in vain."

Philip said: "Leave me now. Not a word of this to the Queen. It would kill her. We must wait and hope. There *must* be a child."

There must be a child. The bells were ringing throughout London. Soon the news of the supposed birth would be all over the country.

And if there is no child, pondered Philip, what hopes are there for Spain? How Henry of France would be laughing up his sleeve! The whole of France and England would be laughing at poor, plain Mary and solemn Philip, who could not get a child.

There must be a child. News of it had been sent to the Emperor, who had written back gleefully to Philip to say that he had heard that the Queen was "hopeful and that her garments waxed very strait."

Could the hopes of the last months have grown from nothing more secure than a hysterical woman's delusions?

All through the palace the rumors were circulating. Philip was filled with pity for Mary, that sad, frustrated woman who had already suffered more in one lifetime than anyone should. What would her reactions be if she knew the truth? He must order the cessation of the bell-ringing. Yet how could he tell the people that there was to be no child because it had never existed outside the Queen's imagination?

Mary was wild-eyed. They had tried to break the news to her. She screamed: "It's a lie. It's a conspiracy. My sister has set these rumors abroad. Look at me. Am I not large enough?"

Her women were weeping about her; but she paced up and down her apartment, her hair wild, her eyes blazing. Let others doubt the existence of the child; she would not.

"Send the doctors to me. Send to me the men who have set these rumors working. I'll have them racked. I'll get the truth of this matter."

Philip alone could soothe her. "Wait," he begged. "I doubt not that shortly you will prove these rumors false."

She took his hands; she covered them with burning kisses. "My love, you are with me. Oh, Philip, how happy you make me! How we shall laugh at these people when I hold my son in my arms!"

"You shall," he said. "But calm yourself now. Rest. You must be strong for the ordeal when it comes."

"How you comfort me! You are always right, and I thank God for bringing you to me."

He felt the smile freeze on his face at these protestations of affection. Did she notice that? She was watching him suspiciously. "What do you do while I am resting?" she asked. "What do you do at night?" Her voice grew shrill. "Is it true what they say of you? That you are with . . . women?"

"No, no," he soothed. "You are distraught."

"They plot against me," she cried. "They tell me that I am to have no child. I feel it within me. I know my child is here. And you? How can you love me? Do I not know that I am old and tired and worn out with my miseries? You wish me dead that you may marry Elizabeth, because she is young and healthy and more pleasant to look at than I."

He shrank from her. He could not bear these noisy scenes; her jealousy shocked and humiliated his reserved nature almost more than did her cloying affection.

"You are not yourself," he said gently. "I beg of you, for the child's sake, and the sake of our marriage, be calm. Lie down, Mary. Rest, I say. Rest is what you need."

"And you?"

He was resigned. "I will sit beside your bed."

"You will stay with me?" she asked piteously.

"I will stay as long as you wish me to."

"Oh, Philip . . . Philip!" She flung herself at him, clinging to him, pressing her face against his. He steeled himself to return her caresses. Then he spoke firmly: "Come. You *shall* rest. This is so bad for you, and the child."

Then he made her lie down, and tenderly he covered her; and he sat by the bed, her hand in his.

"There is comfort in this," she said; "my child within me and you beside me—the two I love. I cannot help the fierceness of my love; I went so long without love."

He sat silently beside her bed, wondering what would happen when she was forced to accept the truth that there would be no child.

Another month had passed. Mary went about with the light of determination in her eyes. She would see none of her ministers. She declared that the child would be born at any minute.

One day a woman came to the palace and asked to see the Queen. She said her mission was concerned with the Queen's condition, so that none would turn her away, and eventually she reached Mary's presence.

"Your Majesty," she said, "I was forty when my first child was born."

Then the Queen made her sit in a chair of honor while she told her story.

"Doctors are not always right in their reckoning. My child was three months overdue, your Majesty, and everyone declared it was a mistake. I was forty at the time, and a fine, healthy boy is my son today!"

Mary was delighted. She gave the woman a jewel and thanked her for her visit.

In the streets the townsfolk made sly jokes. "Now we know these Spaniards! They beget children who are too shy to put in an appearance!" The jokes became more and more ribald. And more and more women came to call on the Queen. Toothless old women presented themselves with their granddaughters' latest. "See!" they wheezed. "Old women can have children!" It was well worth a journey to see the Queen and pocket the royal reward.

Every day the midwives and doctors waited on Mary. Continually she was declaring that her pains had started.

But May was almost out and the child was as elusive as ever.

The Emperor wrote impatiently to Philip, demanding to know the truth of this strange story. He feared that Mary was too old to bear children. "Ingratiate yourself with Madam Elizabeth," he wrote. "I know she is suspected of heresy and that if she takes the throne all our work of bringing England back to Rome may be undone. But remember! Better a heretic England which is a friend to Spain than a Catholic England dominated by France. We must at all costs have the English with us, but I doubt you can do much good by staying in England now. Proclaim yourself Elizabeth's friend and come to me in Brussels. I grow so feeble I can no longer rule. I wish you to take over my crown; and you must do that here in Brussels that all my vassals may, in my presence, swear fealty to you."

To leave England! There was nothing Philip wished to do more. But how broach the matter to the love-sick woman who insisted on imagining that she carried a child in her womb in spite of all evidence to the contrary?

The Queen shut herself in her chamber and would see no one. She did not weep. She stared before her in such utter misery as she had never before known in the whole of her life.

She thought of her mother, longing, always longing for the son who would have made her life such a different one. She remembered Anne Boleyn could not bear a son. It seemed as though the very walls of this great palace echoed with the cries of defeated motherhood. "A son . . . a son!" wailed the wind driving through the trees in the gardens.

She was barren. Her swelling was due to some ailment, they told her now. The new physician had given her potions and had considerably reduced it.

She had said to Philip: "Perhaps there is yet time for us to have a son."

How could she be blind to the look of horror which had passed over his face? Even his accustomed control could not hide it. What did it mean? That he believed her to be too old to bear children? That he found her repulsive? He was evasive, as he ever was. He spoke with quiet, yet firm tenderness: "In view of the ordeal through which you have passed, it would be advisable for you to have a long rest . . ."

Rest! All he could say was: "Rest!"

She must still delude herself, for a woman could not face, all at once, too much that was so tragic.

Mistress Clarencius, that privileged person, came to her. She shook her head sadly, for when they were alone there was little ceremony between them.

"Your Majesty gives way too quickly. Your hopes have been disappointed, but you are still a bride."

Mary put her arms about her old nurse and wept quietly.

"It was a bitter disappointment," soothed Mistress Clarencius. "But there will be another time, dearest lady."

"My dear, dear Clarencius, will there be? Can there be?"

"Of course there can be. And the King is coming to see you. You must look beautiful, because that is how he will want you to look, is it not, dearest Majesty?"

It was good to be petted, to let oneself believe that one could be made beautiful, to sit while one's hair was dressed and a glittering coif set upon it, to have one's black velvet gown with its dazzling ornaments arranged to perfection, and to await the coming of Philip.

He came unattended, and as soon as he arrived Mary dismissed Mistress Clarencius. Philip kissed Mary's hand.

"I rejoice to see you so improved in health." He hurried on: "Oh, there is need for great care yet. You must rest and not excite yourself. We must take great care of you."

"It was good of you to come and see me, Philip," she said meekly.

"I have had an urgent letter from my father."

Before he spoke she knew what he would say, and she sent up a silent prayer to the saints for fortitude to help her bear it.

"He says it is imperative for him to see me."

"Where is he now?"

"Only in Brussels."

"And you will go?"

"I fear I must."

She wanted to shout at him: You *fear*! You are filled with pleasure at the thought of going. You long to leave me because I am old and unattractive and the strain of pretense is too much for even you to bear.

"There is no help for it," he went on with an apologetic half-smile. "He is going to renounce his crown, and I must be there to take it."

She looked at him with pride and longing. He was so slight, frail almost, and she thought how beautiful he was with his fair skin and hair that seemed almost silver in the sunlight. He was her beloved husband who would soon be the most powerful monarch in the world.

"You will not stay long?" she implored.

"Nay. A month perhaps."

Four weeks! To her they would seem as long as years; to him they would be so short. But they both knew that once he escaped he would not be back in a month.

"Oh, Philip . . . must you go?" He recognized the hysteria in her voice. He was poised for flight; he was ready to call her attendants so that he might not be alone with her and suffer her protestations of affection, her cloying embraces.

"I fear so," he said briskly. "But the sooner I leave the sooner it is over. Now . . . I have my dispatches to answer."

"Philip . . ."

"I will send your women to you."

"Nay, Philip. Just a moment. I will send for them when I need them."

"I see I must take charge of you. You do not take enough care. We cannot have you running risks." He was edging away from her. He was now at the door. He opened it and the men-at-arms saluted. "Send for the Queen's ladies at once!" he commanded.

And they came in great haste, thinking she had been taken ill again. But they found her with her husband, yearning and wretched, knowing that his solicitous care for her was really a means of escape.

It was August when the royal party left Hampton Court and came by water to Westminster, where they disembarked and went by road to Greenwich, riding through the lines of sight-seers. Mary was too weak to ride on horseback and was carried in a litter.

Her subjects cheered her, for, they said, she looked like a corpse dug up from the grave. There were no jokes about the imaginary baby on that day.

All about Philip was an armed guard, for he rode at the head of the procession with Cardinal Pole beside him, and his friends would not allow him to go undefended through the city of London.

Philip was smiling in a manner which would have pleased his father. In three days' time, if there was a good wind, he would step aboard and sail away from England and Mary. It was little more than a year that he had spent in England—yet, to him, it seemed a lifetime.

Three days had to be lived through, and in Greenwich Palace it was necessary to spend most of the time with Mary; but at length came that day, so happy for Philip, so wretched for Mary.

She could not contain her grief, and wept bitterly when the farewells were said. Philip returned her fervent embrace. He hoped it was the last he would have to suffer for a long time.

"Good-bye, my dearest husband."

"Good-bye, dear wife."

"You will be back in a month?" she begged.

"In a month," he promised, "unless . . . something happens to prevent my coming."

"You *will* come back? You must. I shall be counting the days. It will be the longest month in my life."

"I also shall count the days."

He was looking at the barge and thanking God for it. He could wait no longer. One last embrace; one last farewell, and the barge was slipping away from the shore while, with his attendants about him, he waved to the desolate Queen who stood watching until he was out of sight.

What had happened to this son of his? wondered Charles. What had the English done to him? Was the change for the worse or the better? There were two Philips now—warring one with the other. Tales had reached the Emperor of the Prince's conduct. At last, it seemed, Philip was indulging in those adventures which others before him had enjoyed in the days of their youth. He had run wild since he left England; he had had many light love affairs. He had roamed the streets in the disguise of a nobleman, accompanied by the merriest of his followers.

Lines appeared about the pale eyes; there was a hint of sensuality which had not been apparent before. Yet the well-known Philip was never far away; he was always ready to emerge unexpectedly—calm, aloof, and controlled.

The Emperor was amused to think that he should ever contemplate remonstrating with Philip concerning his wildness. To think that he might warn *Philip* to take heed, to choose his companions with more care, to lead a less dissolute life! Charles could not help breaking into loud laughter at the very thought.

But he decided that it was not for him to change his son. Let this madness work out of him. It was the result of several months' matrimony with Mary Tudor—nothing more; and Philip would come to reason of his own accord. Charles reminded himself that he was about to transfer his imperial dignity to Philip, who was no longer a boy to be admonished. If he wished to wander the streets in disguise, if he wished to share the beds of loose women, that was for him to decide; and there was no one who could say it was not a kingly habit!

Charles was feeling his years sorely. His hands shook with palsy and his gout was painful. His fever had increased, and he told Philip that he longed to pass on his responsibilities at the earliest possible moment.

"Was it very unpleasant in England?" he asked.

Philip's face hardened as he answered: "I drained the cup of my sacrifice to the very dregs."

"My son, I know you suffered. Well, it is over; and you wrote of her as though you pitied her."

"Aye," said Philip. "I pitied her, for she is pitiable."

"And pity is said to be a sister of love, eh?"

Philip laughed with bitterness. "A poor sister . . . a poor relation. And do we not always feel uncomfortable in the presence of our poor relations?"

Charles laid his hand on his son's shoulder. "You suffered the lot of princes," he said. "But it is clear the Queen of England is past childbearing. I would they had crowned you King of England, but you will have kingdoms enough when you have taken them over from me. I rejoice in you and all that you are; and there are not many fathers who can say that."

Philip took the palsied hand and kissed it.

"We shall have much to talk of during the next weeks," went on the Emperor. "But there is one matter, a little outside statecraft, which has been giving me some thought lately. It concerns your brother. Ah! You wonder to whom I refer. When we were in Augsburg I had a son by a burgher's daughter. She was a good girl, and this child of hers is a good child. He is strong and healthy; and I am having him brought up far from any of my courts. He lives simply and has no idea who his father is. When he is older I wish you to send for him. He will make a good general for your armies. His name is Juan. I think of him as Don Juan of Austria. How sounds that? He will serve you well, and be more use to you than young Carlos ever will. Look after him, Philip. Give him opportunities. Remember he is your brother, though illegitimate. You'll thank God for him one day, as I doubt not you will for Isabel Osorio's boys. It is good to have the members of your family about you . . . even though some of them were not born in wedlock."

"I will remember. Where shall I look for this Don Juan?"

"In the household of my steward, Luis Quixada. For some years I let him run wild, barefoot, playing with boys in the village and being taught scraps of learning by a priest. Luis's wife continually bemoaned the fact that she had no children, so I said: 'Take this boy and bring him up as though he is your own.' Poor woman, she seized that offer with delight, and now he is to her as her own son."

"And where are they now?"

The Emperor gave a half-embarrassed smile. "I must have my steward in my household; I must have him with me at the monastery—for which I shall leave when the ceremonies are over. And could I separate a husband from his wife? Nay, I could not. So Doña Magdalena Quixada will remove to a small village close to the monastery of Yuste that she may be near her husband."

"You will see this boy, then?"

"Oh, I shall seclude myself. That is my wish. I shall not see many people."

But of course he would see the boy. Philip realized that he doted on him.

"I will do as you wish," said Philip.

"My blessing on you. It is a good thing for a man to have bred a son like you."

Philip knew that the Emperor was pleased with his two sons—the legitimate one who would shoulder his responsibilities, and the illegitimate one whose charm and intelligence would lighten the days of his seclusion.

The ceremony which surprised the world took place on an October day in the great hall of the Palace of Brussels.

Here were assembled the vassals of the Emperor. Coats of arms decorated the walls; there were banners displaying the heraldic devices of all the countries and provinces under the Imperial sway.

The hall was crowded with members of the nobility—statesmen and heads of states, magnificent in their rich uniforms.

A dais, hung with rich arras and decorated with griffins, eagles, and unicorns in all the colors of the various provinces, had been set up at one end of the hall; and with a flourish of trumpets the Emperor came forward, leaning heavily on the arm of William of Orange. Behind these two came Philip with his cousin Maximilian and his aunt, Mary of Hungary, whom Charles had made Governess of the Netherlands.

The Emperor looked very ill. He could scarcely hobble to the dais, and William of Orange had to help him mount it and take his seat on the royal chair.

Philip took the chair on the Emperor's right hand. He could not help resenting the intimacy which seemed to exist between his father and Orange. He had heard rumors of this clever young William of Orange, the Count of Nassau; he was reputed to be a secret supporter of the heretics. Was the Emperor in his dotage that he must favor a man because he was young and handsome?

Orange seemed a little arrogant as he caught Philip's eyes upon him. Doubtless he bore in mind that he had all the Flemings behind him. But neither Orange nor Flanders must forget that they were vassals of Spain; and Orange was a fool to show arrogance to one who was about to step so publicly into his father's shoes.

The church bells all over Brussels began to chime, and the President of the Council rose and announced to the gathering that their great Emperor Charles the Fifth had decided, because of his age and infirmity, to pass over to his son his possessions in the Netherlands.

There was a deep silence while the Emperor rose slowly to his feet. He explained to them that he was a tired old man. They would love his son even as they had loved him, for they would find Philip the best of rulers.

Charles was overcome with emotion; tears came to his eyes. They would be loyal to his son, he knew. They would show him that devotion, that friendship which they had always given to himself.

Philip, from the dais, looked down on these foreigners, these Flemings; he stood on one side of his father, and it seemed a pity that William of Nassau, the Prince of Orange, should be standing on the other. The people were accepting Philip now; but their eyes were turned—was it with hope?—toward William of Orange.

Philip felt the full weight of his responsibilities. He was King of Spain—Castile, Aragon, and Granada; he was King of Naples and Sicily; he was the Duke of Milan; he was Lord of the French Compté and of the Low Countries. He was the titular King of England. Unfortunately, the crude islanders had made this seem but an empty title so far. The Cape Verde Islands of Africa and the Canaries belonged to him. Tunis and Oran were his, as were the Philippines and the Spice Islands of Asia. He had possessions in the West Indies; Mexico and Peru were part of his Empire. He was the most important and powerful monarch in the world—a young man under thirty, morose by nature, although he had recently shown that he could enjoy isolated adventures in sensuality; he was conscientious, determined to do his duty, eager to serve God first, then his immense Imperial responsibilities. His great wish was to bring the whole world together under Spanish domination and to set up the Inquisition in every country. All this he would do, not for the glory of Philip, but for the glory of God.

In the meantime he wished to keep away from his wife for as long as possible. He could do this now with an easy conscience because he was certain that she could never bear a child.

So Charles made his slow journey to the monastery of Yuste, and Philip became titular ruler of half the world.

He had excuses to spare for not returning to Mary, since war had broken out. This was war against the Pope himself. Spain was devoutly Catholic, but Spaniards believed that the heart of Catholicism was in Spain, not in Rome; and Charles had, over the years, gradually taken many of the rights so dearly cherished by pontiffs of the past and kept them to himself. This meant that Charles had been using some of the Church revenue to serve his political ends. Spaniards had encroached on Italian territory, which disturbing fact many of the Popes had accepted with as good a grace as possible; but the present Pope was a fiery Neapolitan, and the French King had persuaded him to join France against Spain.

So, on his accession to power, Philip, who hated war, found himself in the midst of it.

Though it might be difficult to get English troops to fight the Pope, they would not be reluctant to attack the French, who were their perennial enemies; therefore, it was decided that the English must be persuaded to take up arms against the French; and who could better persuade the Queen to this than her beloved husband?

The unpleasant duty faced Philip again. He must return to England; he must once more endure the devotion of his wife, for Spain must have the help of England.

Mary could neither sleep nor eat. He was coming again. Many times during the last year he had promised to return, but he had not kept his promises. He had said he would be away for a month. It was August of the year 1555 when he had gone away; it was now March 1557. And he had said one month!

But no matter; the waiting was unimportant now since he was to come at last. She had aged during his absence. She had spent many nights in weeping. That did not improve a woman's appearance. She had a return of her ailments and her skin was more sallow than ever; she was very thin, apart from her dropsical swellings.

Last autumn had brought much rain and the Thames had overflowed.

Westminster Hall had been flooded, so that wherries had been able to pass through it. The resultant damp had brought epidemics with it. Mary herself had developed a fever at that time and there seemed to be nothing to cure it.

So lonely, so dreary her life had become. Gardiner had died, and on him she had relied more than on any, with the exception of Philip and Cardinal Pole.

Her sister Elizabeth, she believed, was plotting against her once more. She had entertained soothsayers at Woodstock and it was said that she had wished to be told how much longer the Queen would live. Some gentlemen of her household had plotted to put her on the throne, and they confessed on the rack to her complicity in their schemes. Why should Elizabeth be allowed to live? When she went into the streets the people applauded her more loudly than they had ever done. She was young and pleasing to look at. She did not suffer from complaints which made her a grotesque object of pity.

Philip had written urgently from Europe that she must be lenient with Elizabeth. He said he was convinced of her innocence. He pointed out that if Mary harmed the Princess the whole of England would be against her.

Why was he so concerned for Elizabeth? Sometimes Mary would be amazed at her own passion. She would stand before his picture and demand to know of that concern.

"Do you hope that I shall die and you may begin to woo another Queen of England?"

If he had been there to answer, he would have reminded her coldly: "I wish to preserve her that the throne of England may not go to Mary Queen of Scots."

That might be true, but did it not mean that he had her death in mind?

"I have never really lived," she murmured. "That's the pity of it."

But now he was coming to her again. As she stitched at the tapestry which her mother had started and which when finished would hang in the state apartments of the Tower, she thought that waiting for him was like waiting for the child. The child had not come. Would he?

Then her hopes would rise again. Was she so old that she could not have a child? She did not believe she was.

And at length on a sparkling March day when the sun was shining on the river and the marsh marigolds made a golden pattern on the banks, Philip came.

He took horse at Gravesend, and she was almost fainting with joy when he arrived at Greenwich. She could not tolerate ceremony at such a time. Surely now and then in the lifetime of a Queen she could dispense with it?

"Philip!" she cried, as she threw herself at him. He was smiling as all would expect a husband to smile who was returning to his wife after so long an absence.

He returned her embrace. She noticed that in appearance he had changed little; she was sadly aware that she was a little more lined, a little less attractive than when he went away. But she would not face the truth. Her loved one was back, and she must believe that he had come back for love of her, and not to win her assistance in his war with France.

How she schemed to keep him at her side! As for Philip, he had returned to the old relationship and he was once more sacrificing himself on the altar of Spain's needs. He schooled himself to be the pleasant and charming husband, and that in itself seemed a folly because the better he played the part, the more enamoured she became.

From Mary came occasional outbursts of jealousy, and these often concerned the Princess Elizabeth. Philip was once more urging the marriage of the Princess with Emmanuel Philibert of Savoy.

Mary turned to him crying in a passion of jealousy: "Why should you wish for this marriage? Do not answer me with soft words. Do you not think I know? You would have her the wife of a vassal that she may be near you. Is that the answer? Tell me. I demand to know."

"I think," said Philip, "that you have lost your senses."

She laughed shrilly and hysterically. He thought how ugly she was at such times, even uglier than in those pitiable moods when she would cajole him to indulge her passion.

"She would be near you, would she not? She would be in Flanders, and you would find it necessary to visit her household often. Do you think I do not know why you continually press for this marriage?"

"It would seem that you need to be alone for a while, to calm yourself, to bring yourself back to reason."

"You suggest that so that you may escape from me."

"Why should I wish to escape?"

"You ask me that: Do you not always wish to escape? Are you not thinking all the time, 'How can I get away from this old woman who, by great bad fortune, is my wife?' Why were you so long in coming to see me? Were you really so involved in matters of state? Do you think I am blind?"

She fell into a passion of weeping, and once again his pity chained him to her side. "Mary," he lied, "it is not true. You distress yourself without reason."

So sad she was and eager to be reassured. "Is it truly so, Philip, my dearest, my beloved?"

He forced himself to kiss her.

"I am so jealous, Philip; and jealousy such as mine is worse than death."

These scenes became more frequent, and after four months of such strain he could bear no more. He must escape. He had succeeded in making her declare war on France, so there was no longer need for him to remain.

She was again obsessed with the idea that she was to have a child. No one but herself believed this possible; but she clung to hope.

All over England men and women were perishing in the flames. Cranmer, Ridley, Latimer, and Hooper, with other such great men, suffered the dreadful death. Mary was conscious of her people's dislike, even as she was of Philip's. She must therefore cling to the hope of a child, even if that hope was delusive.

In her litter she accompanied Philip once more to Gravesend. Again she suffered that poignant parting; she stood watching him until she could see him no more; then she returned, sorrowing, to her loneliness.

Philip was to receive one of the greatest of all military defeats at St. Quentin, although the great Montmorency and Coligny fell prisoners to his soldiers and the road to Paris was open.

Never had the Emperor had such an opportunity of subduing the French for ever. Never did a soldier fail at the peak of success as Philip failed then. And yet, being Philip, what else could he have done?

St. Quentin would haunt him for the rest of his life, not because that great victory was turned to defeat through his personal indecision, but because Philip would never forget the sights which greeted him when he made his triumphant entry into the captured city.

Philip hated war. He was no soldier and he knew it. The prospect of war never failed to fill him with dread. He had given orders, when the besieged city was surrounded, that there were to be no reprisals. But he did not understand the nature of the men serving under his banners. The English and the Spanish in his armies had worked themselves into a fury against each other; the German mercenaries looked upon the spoils of a defeated town as the natural rewards of conquest.

Philip's orders were ignored, and when he saw the terrible carnage in St. Quentin—murdered citizens lying about the streets horribly mutilated, burning houses, the nauseating treatment which had been meted out, not only to women and children, but to monks and nuns—he was horrified. To him it seemed a disaster as shameful as the Sack of Rome.

He came to the Church of St. Laurence; he saw the blood of human beings befouling the altar, the burning pews, the slaughtered bodies of monks on the floor of the church, and in horror he swore that he would never forget this foul crime as long as he lived, nor that it had been done in his name. He fell to his knees and vowed that he would dedicate his life to building a monastery in Spain to the glory of St. Laurence.

His young cousin, Emmanuel Philibert, warned him that they must take the advantage such a victory had given them. The road to Paris was now open and it would be possible to defeat the French for all time; but

Philip, having looked on those terrible sights, wanted to put an end to the war. In vain did Emmanuel Philibert plead. Philip was adamant.

"The risk is too great," he equivocated. "Our men are weary. I am weary . . . weary of death and destruction. Here Catholic fights Catholic; Catholic churches are destroyed. There is only one war I wish to fight: God's holy war; the war against the heretic."

So at St. Quentin he stayed, and his men were idle and disgruntled, so that they did as mercenaries were accustomed to do at such times; they deserted. Meanwhile, the Duke of Guise, who had been fighting in Italy, made a hasty peace on that front and came with all speed to the defense of his country.

Paris was soon bristling with defenses. The great moment was lost; and Guise, with that intuition which had made him the greatest soldier of his day, made a surprise attack on Calais and took it.

He knew that there could be nothing more likely to cause strife between Spain and her English allies than the loss of that town which the latter looked upon as a foothold which would one day lead to the conquest of France.

In the monastery of Yuste, which was not far from the town of Placentia and was surrounded by thick woods and mountains which kept off the cold north winds, the Emperor was enjoying his days of retirement.

The climate was good for his gout and he had employed architects to make a lodging worthy of him; he had installed great fireplaces in every room; he had brought some of his treasured pictures with him. His favorite, *Gloria*, painted by the great Venetian, Titian, and which depicted himself and his late wife surrounded by angels, he had had set up in his bedroom. Beautiful gardens had been laid out for him, and in these orange and citron trees grew; he himself attended to the weeding and pruning when the gout permitted. He had also brought numbers of clocks and watches with him, and one of his great pleasures was to take these to pieces and examine their works; the winding of the clocks was a ceremony which, whenever possible, he supervised in person.

He attended religious services regularly, and the window of his bedchamber looked onto the chapel, so that if he were not well enough to get up he could hear Mass in bed, and from where he lay see the elevation of the Host. His rich baritone voice often mingled with the chanting of the monks in the chapel.

He felt content with the monastic life and would stand at his windows looking out across the jagged sierra at the stunted orange trees and the rushing torrents that tumbled down the mountainsides. But his great delight was still in his food. In vain did his physicians implore moderation. Abstinence might be a virtue, but not even for the sake of his soul could Charles deny his stomach.

He would sit at a meal with his favorite servants about him. There were his major-domo, Quixada, and the Fleming, Van Mole, his gentleman of the chamber, to beguile him with their conversation. There was another whom he greatly favored—a boy of handsome looks and bright intelligence, young Juan, who did not know that besides being the Emperor's page he was the Emperor's son.

When Charles was melancholy, Juan was sent to charm him; and this he never failed to do. Charles treated him as though he were much older than his age; he would show him charts and maps and discuss with him the progress of the war which Spain was now fighting against the French.

Juan was with Charles when the news was brought of Philip's action at St. Quentin and his subsequent hesitation.

The Emperor's face grew purple and the veins showed in angry knots at his temple.

"Holy Mother of God!" he exploded. "Why . . . why . . . in the name of Christ, why? The greatest opportunity a general ever had . . . and lost . . . lost! Philip is useless. Is he as mad as his grandmother? Had I but been there . . ."

He paced the apartment and all feared that he would injure himself. But suddenly he stopped and looked at the boy.

"One day," he said, "you may be a general leading your armies. Then . . . you will remember this day. But, Juan, you will learn . . . you will profit from the mistakes of others . . ."

And, contemplating the boy beside him, he grew calmer. He shrugged his shoulders. He was an old man in retreat from the world. He had but to brood on his sins and win absolution. The conduct of wars was no longer any concern of his.

He fell to wondering what he would have for dinner—a rich capon, chickens, a fat goose, peacocks roasted by the best cooks in Spain, who now resided at the monastery of Yuste?

Mary Tudor shut herself away; she lived almost completely in retirement now. She had failed. She had lost Calais, and her people were saying that in the five years of her reign she had brought disaster on England. She had burned men's bodies—respected men such as Archbishop Cranmer; she had put England under a foreign influence. There was disaster everywhere.

And she was old and ill. She could only write passionate letters to Philip, some of which she did not send. She even offered him coronation if he would return to her. For as long as she could, she had believed in the coming of the child; but the months were passing, and it was nearly a year since Philip had gone.

Philip was still urging the marriage of Elizabeth with Emmanuel Philibert. He had made peace with the French, and his son Don Carlos was to marry the eldest daughter of the French King; but Calais was still in the hands of the French.

Jealousy tormented her. Great attention was being paid to her sister Elizabeth, and many of those whom she had believed to be her friends were slipping away to Hatfield and begging to be of service there. Cardinal Pole, that dear friend and staunch supporter, was as sick as she was herself. And Philip did not come back.

He sent his cousin, Christina of Denmark, to try to persuade her to permit the marriage of Elizabeth with Savoy. How she had hated that visit and the visitor!

Christina was noted throughout Europe for her charm and beauty, and there were rumors that Philip had been deeply enamored of her and would have liked to marry her.

Mary's jealousy would not allow her to treat Christina with the honor due to her rank. She was coldly received in England, and went back, her mission unaccomplished.

And on the day she left, Mary stood before Philip's latest portrait, which represented him in armor, and in which he looked very handsome, in spite of the fact that he wore no helmet. She recalled the message he had sent with the picture: It was not in accordance with etiquette that he should stand, his head covered, in the presence of the Queen.

She had been delighted with picture and message. Now she thought with great bitterness how very devoted he could be when he was absent!

And as she gazed at the picture, she cried: "You are cold! You will never come back to me. You are not faithful to me. You stay away, not because of state affairs, but because you hate to be with me. You could be at my side if you wished. But you hate me . . . hate . . . hate me . . ."

She took up a knife and slashed the canvas to ribbons.

Then, in frustration, she fell sobbing to the floor.

Jane Dormer found her thus; she called to Mistress Clarencius and tenderly they carried her to her bed.

The Emperor knew that his end was near. It was September at Yuste and he felt at peace. His confessor, Juan de Regla, sat on a stool at his bedside. The Emperor was ready to leave this world.

He prayed for Philip, who had so many good qualities. He feared for Philip. What would happen in the great dominions? wondered Charles. Philip was surrounded by enemies. He had shown himself to be a man who could not make the quick decisions which could shape his destiny. He consoled himself; there was much to be said for caution, patience, and steady virtue.

He thought of Orange and hoped that young man would not give Philip any trouble. Orange was a man born to greatness. And Philip was not one who could combine religion and statecraft. Philip had been taught that he must serve God first, his country second; and he believed it. Philip took these precepts too literally. Charles had been Emperor first, Catholic second. That was a sobering thought now that he was nearing his end, but he was too much the realist to deny it.

"God help him . . ." murmured the Emperor. "God help Philip in the tasks that lie ahead . . ."

But now Charles was smiling, thinking of little Juan. There was a son to warm the heart of a dying man.

Philip would look after little Juan. Thank God and all the saints that Philip could be trusted. Philip would do his duty. What more could a man ask of his son?

He had been blessed in his sons.

But he must think of his own passing. The time was short. Philip would do his duty. Juan would be a great soldier—he was sure of it— handsome and strong so that the people would love him; it might be that in the future they would speak of Don Juan as they now spoke of the Cid.

He had had a long life and it had been a satisfactory life since it had given him two such as Philip and Juan.

To his eyes, the light in the room seemed dim. His priest was at hand. They were giving him extreme unction. So the end was as near as that. All the sins of a long harsh lifetime were forgiven . . .

"Christ . . . crucified . . . aid me."

He was fast sinking; his lips moved. "Christ crucified . . ."

But his hazy thoughts were reaching into the future . . . that future which was Philip's and little Juan's.

𝒟eath did not come singly. Hard on the news of the Emperor's death came the messenger from England with news of Mary's sickness.

Philip would not believe that she was dying.

"How can I go to England now?" he demanded. "My father is dead. My duties increase. Moreover, the Queen has been ill before."

She had had a false pregnancy, he was remembering. Might not this also be a false alarm?

He decided to send Feria with a message and a ring.

"If the Queen is dying," he said, "we must at all costs secure the accession of Elizabeth. She is suspected of heresy, and that is deplorable; but if she does not succeed to the throne, the King of France will have the crown for Mary of Scotland. That we must prevent. If France succeeds, all our work will have failed. We shall lose our footing in England; and before long we shall have the English and French banded together against us."

"There is the match between Elisabeth of Valois and Don Carlos," said Feria.

"These matches! They sometimes come to naught. We will not rely upon it. The English law says that the reigning monarch must name his successor. Mary must name Elizabeth."

"I will make known your Majesty's wishes to her."

"And, Feria, give her loving greetings from me. Explain that I cannot come. Speak of my duties here . . . my father's death . . . Surely there are excuses enough; and even she must see that I must be here."

"I will endeavor to make her see reason, your Highness."

When Feria had gone, Philip stared ahead, seeing that bed-chamber which he felt would be engraved upon his mind for ever. Could it be true that his wife was dying? If so, it would mean the loss of Spanish power in England, but oh, what glorious freedom for the King of Spain!

𝓜ary was tossing on her bed. There were few ladies to attend to her wants, and she knew why. They had deserted her—so many of them—and were on their way to Hatfield.

There, her red-haired sister would have put on new dignity. That haughtiness which ever lurked behind her blue eyes, would emerge. Elizabeth . . . Queen of England.

She, so young, would be so powerful. She would choose her own husband. Perhaps Philip would sue for her hand. No, not that! She must not imagine such things. She must try to be calm.

The fever was with her again. It had been decided that the Palace of Richmond was too damp and had aggravated her fever. Her dear friend Reginald Pole suffered from the same fever. He was not expected to outlive her.

Will Philip come? she wondered. Surely none could refuse the request of a dying woman?

This time she wished him just to touch her hand and to smile, to pretend to the last that he loved her. Was that asking too much of him?

Ah, but he had hated her. Her people hated her. They would say after she was dead: She brought strangers into the land; she restarted the fires of Smithfield; she lost Calais.

How bright had seemed her future on that day five years ago when she had ridden into London to the Tower to be crowned. Queen of England! And all England was with her then, all shouting: "Death to the false Jane Grey!"

But now it was a different tale. Now they would shout: "Death to Mary. Long live Elizabeth!"

One of her ladies came to tell her that the Count of Feria was without and craving audience.

The Count of Feria! But it should have been Philip.

Yet why should Philip come? There was nothing he wanted of her now.

She greeted the Count with her melancholy smile. There was one who would be more glad to see Feria than Philip. Might he prove a good husband to Jane Dormer, better than the husband the Queen had had!

But she would entertain no evil thoughts against Philip. He was good and noble. Was it his fault that he could not love her? He had tried. How he had tried!

The Count knelt by her bed and, kissing her burning hand, gave her the loving message and the ring; then he told her the real reason for his coming. "His Highness declares it is imperative that you name the Lady Elizabeth as your successor."

She smiled wanly. Ah, yes, of course. She must ensure English friendship with Spain. She must remember Spain's enemies, the French. She nodded feebly.

"If Elizabeth will pay my debts and swear to keep our religion as she found it, then I agree."

When Feria had left her, she lay half-conscious, thinking that Philip was beside her. Then she became disturbed. She cried out that she could hear the screams of men and women in agony. Were they burning now outside the Palace? Did they not know that Smithfield Square was the appropriate place?

Mistress Clarencius soothed her. "Nay, your Majesty. All is well."

"But I smell the fires."

"It is the one here in your chamber, your Majesty."

"I hear the crackle of wood. What of Cranmer?"

"It is not for your Majesty to concern yourself with heretics at this time. Rest is what you need."

She said: "He held out his right hand that it might burn first. My father was fond of Cranmer. He gave him much honor. Oh, Clarencius, less than three hundred were burned under my rule; and in my husband's land there have been three hundred at one *auto-da-fé*."

"Do not speak of it, dearest Majesty."

"In the streets they speak of it. They call me Bloody Mary. I know it. There are things which cannot be kept from me. They are all going to Hatfield now. They will shout for her. She is young and fair enough... though not so fair as she thinks she is. She will have many suitors for her hand, and Philip... Philip..."

"Rest, your Majesty, rest."

She closed her eyes and the tears rolled slowly down her cheeks. She smiled suddenly and said: "What matters it, my friends? This is the end."

She asked for extreme unction and that afterward Mass should be celebrated in her chamber; and at the elevation of the Host she lifted her eyes and she bowed her head at the benediction.

Then she seemed contented and at peace. She seemed to have forgotten the martyrs who had perished in her reign, that the people had called her Bloody Mary, and that she had lost Calais.

Her smile almost beautified her face in those last moments, and those about her bed thought that she could only have smiled thus if she had believed that Philip was with her.

ELISABETH DE VALOIS

arlos had changed. He had grown quieter; he had assumed more dignity; he no longer referred to himself as little one. He was Don Carlos, heir to the throne, and he did not forget it.

The reason was that he was to have a bride.

He had seen her picture and as soon as he had seen it this change had come upon him, for never had he seen anything so beautiful as the face in the locket which he carried about with him. She had a small, oval face, great dark eyes, and masses of black hair; she was half French, half Italian, and she was the daughter of Henri, King of France, and the Italian Catherine de Medici.

He had heard some time ago that he was to have this bride, but he had taken little heed at the time because, as Prince of Spain, many brides had been suggested for him. It was not long after his father had left for England on the first occasion that his father and the French King had decided Carlos should marry the young Princess when the Peace of Vaucelles had been signed. That seemed to have been forgotten, as so many plans were; but now there was a new treaty with France, the portrait had arrived, and, having seen it, Carlos could think of little else but the Princess of France.

At first he had thought it would be amusing to have a bride, to be the master, to force her to do all that he desired; but when he looked at the picture, those feelings left him. There was nothing within him now but a tenderness and an apprehension, for what would she, this beautiful

Princess, think of him—stunted, crippled, and so ugly when the fits of anger came upon him?

Once he had loved his Aunt Juana, but she was strange now. She prayed constantly, and she thought of nothing beyond saving her soul for the future life; and she went about with her face half covered, withdrawn, remote from the world. People said she was strange; but it was not the strangeness of himself and his great-grandmother; there was no wild laughter, no impulse to do extraordinary things. Juana's strangeness was a religious fervency which resulted in deep melancholy. She was, Carlos reflected, very certain of her place in Heaven, but that did not make her such a good companion here on Earth.

But to whom else could he talk? There was so much he wanted to know. He wished that he had not neglected his studies. He did not understand French; nor did he know Latin. He knew very little of the history of his own country, let alone others. If only he had worked harder! But how could he have known that they were going to give him a beautiful and learned Princess like this one for his wife? And how could he have known he would want to shine so much in her eyes?

"Juana," he asked, "Aunt Juana, what is it like at the court of France?"

She drew her hood closer over her face, and he saw her lips tighten. "The French are godless," she said. "Although they have improved under the present King's reign. In the time of his father, theirs was the most immoral court in the world, and still is, I doubt not, for the French are wicked by nature."

"That was *her* grandfather—this wicked King," said Carlos with satisfaction. His brain was more alert; he was determined it should be. He was not going to be ignorant any more. He was going to learn and be clever for the sake of Elisabeth de Valois. "What did they do at her grandfather's court?" he asked.

"There were masques and balls all the time. They read books. They fêted those who wrote them. They were not good books. King François was your grandfather's greatest enemy . . . the most lecherous man in the world . . . the most pleasure-loving and the most wicked."

"You speak of him as though he were a heretic."

"Nay. He was not as wicked as that."

"My grandfather took him prisoner," said Carlos, eager to show that he remembered that bit of history. "Her father was my grandfather's prisoner too when he was a little boy. And now she is coming here. We shall have much to speak of, Juana. When do you think my father will let her come?"

"We do not know. Everything depends on her father and your father. They are at peace now, but if there should be another war..." Juana lifted her shoulders.

"Do you mean that they might have a war?" His face puckered; his lips began to twitch. "If my father goes to war with the French King now, I...I...will...kill him."

"Hush, Carlos! The bad mood is coming on you again. You know what I told you to do when that happens. Get down on your knees and pray."

"I don't want to pray. I don't want to. I want to kill...kill..."

"Carlos, you promised to be better. What will she think of you if she sees these bad moods?"

His face puckered again. "But there will be a war... They will keep her from me."

"There is no war, and as arrangements stand she will come to you in good time."

"My father will never let her. He hates me. He hates me to be happy. It has always been so."

"It is the bad mood that makes you think that. Your father will be glad of the link with France. Your father tries to make peace. That is why he arranged this marriage. Look at her picture again. There! You are right, Carlos. She is beautiful. And your own age too. That is charming."

He was sobbing as he took the locket in his hands, and his tears fell on to it; but the sight of it calmed him, as it always did.

"I fear my father will not let me have this happiness."

"Of a surety he will. He wants to see you happy, Carlos. He is pleased because we can truthfully tell him how much you try to be worthy of your bride."

"I am learning now. I am trying to be clever."

"And you are praying, Carlos?"

"Each day, each night. I pray that her coming will not be long delayed. Do you think the saints will intercede for me?"

"If it is good for you, they will."

He stamped his foot. "Will they? Will they? It *is* good. I know it is good. She makes me good . . . because I learn my lessons. I am calm because I want her to love me."

"Only *they* know if it is good for you, Carlos."

"*I* know. *I* know!" cried Carlos.

"You must learn, dearest nephew. Something which is bad may happen, but that may be for our good. Those on high know best what is good for us."

"If they do not let her come, I . . . I . . ." She flashed a glance of horror at him, for blasphemy terrified her. But he went on: "I shall hate all who keep her from me. Hate . . . hate . . ."

She had crossed herself and fallen to her knees, lifting her hands toward the ceiling. Her hood fell open, showing a face so strange that for a moment Carlos was silent.

He watched her moving lips; he listened to her words. She was praying for him; and something in the expression of her face filled him with sudden fear. He looked over his shoulder furtively. There were times when his Aunt Juana made him feel that, although the room was empty, they were not alone.

He began to whimper: "I pray every night, Juana. I only want to have her here . . . to love her . . ."

Juana rose from her knees. "If God wishes it, it will come to pass," she said.

With trembling hands, he took the locket and looked at the picture. "Elisabeth," he said. "I love your name, but it is hard to say it. It is French, is it not? Here we say Isabella. I shall call you Isabella. Isabella . . . little Isabella . . . are you praying that you will soon come to Spain?"

In the Old Palace of Brussels, the royal widower sat alone in deep concentration.

He had felt nothing but relief during the last few weeks. He knew that he could not continue in that state, for there was great work to be done, and his position as monarch was not made easier by the death of his wife; it was only the husband who had escaped from a particularly irksome situation.

On the table before him documents were neatly arranged; he could not endure untidiness, as all his secretaries knew. He was dressed this day in the plainest of black velvet garments; he might have been mistaken for one of his own secretaries but for his quiet dignity and that excessive cleanliness—so rare, even among Spaniards—which was accentuated by the pallor of his skin.

He had furnished this room in accordance with his own tastes, and they did not please the people of Brussels; he knew this, but he did not care. These people were going to need a firm hand. Already they were turning against him. He was appalled by the increasing number of heretics, and was planning harsh action against them; as soon as possible he would consult Alba, that fiery Catholic, and doubtless he would set him up as Governor of this land, with the Holy Inquisition to work with him.

Philip looked at the silver crucifix on the wall. There had been too little devotion to God in his father's day. Charles's *bonbomie* and his love of fleshy delights had pleased the people. But Philip believed that a ruler's first duty was toward God, and if he jeopardized a hundred crowns in God's service then must he count himself blessed to lose them all, if that was God's will.

Philip remembered with shame that outburst of sensuality which had followed his departure from England. He remembered also the terrible sight of St. Quentin.

He had already found the site for his monastery. It was to be built on the unfertile Guadarrama steppes; there he would build his Palace of the Escorial, a home for a hermit king, a monastery where he could live a life of prayer and devotion while he ruled the world and brought it, through the blood and fire of the Inquisition, to the truth.

His cold eyes were suddenly like hot blue flames when he thought of the future; and as he sat there at the table, immersed in the relief of his escape from Mary Tudor, he vowed that he would wipe heresy from the world, that he would rule it in his own way, not that of his father, and he would dedicate himself in the future, not to ambition, not to love of power, but to the service of God. He saw himself as God's vicar on Earth, the junior commander in the battle against the Devil.

Meanwhile, he must turn his attention to affairs of the world, and with the death of Mary and the accession of Elizabeth, England gave him much to think of.

He took up the dispatch Feria had sent from the English court. Feria was the most suitable ambassador at this time, for Feria was one of the handsomest of men, and the new Queen was very fond of handsome men; Feria was well versed in the art of flattery, and the new Queen was the vainest woman on Earth; moreover, Feria spoke fluent English and was affianced to Jane Dormer, so that he possessed many qualities which would enable him to fill the post satisfactorily.

But Feria was made uneasy by the new Queen.

Although she still heard Mass, and the religion of the country appeared to be the same as in her sister's day, there had been an immediate cessation of the persecutions. The woman was at times a ridiculous coquette, and then suddenly it would be as though a shrewd statesman looked out from behind her fan. It was impossible to get a straight answer from her on any subject of importance; she would prevaricate, giving neither "Yes" nor "No," holding out promises one day, repudiating them the next.

Her response to her sister's stipulations had been typical of her. Mary, in bestowing upon her the succession, had said she did so on these conditions: That she would not change her privy council; that she would make no alteration in religion; and that she would discharge Mary's debts. Elizabeth's reply was that the debts should certainly be paid; but as regards the council it was Elizabeth's opinion that one Queen had as much right to choose her councillors as another. "As for religion," she said, "I promise this much: I will not change it, provided only that it can be proved by the word of God, which shall be the only foundation and rule of my religion."

"You see, your Highness," wrote Feria, "the kind of woman with which we have to deal. There is a sharpness beneath the soft answer. She says 'Yes' in such a way as to mean 'No.' She said: 'There is no reason why I should thank Mary for bequeathing the crown to me, for she has not the power of bestowing it upon me. Nor can I lawfully be deprived of it, since it is my hereditary right.' Your Highness will see that this is a direct rebuff to yourself, as the new Queen has been assured of your efforts with Mary on her behalf.

"There is one other matter which gives me concern. I sought to extract from her a statement concerning her religious policy, and I tackled her while she was in the midst of her courtiers and statesmen, as I felt that if she publicly stated her intention to uphold the true religion, she would perforce be obliged to carry out that intention. I said that your Majesty had ordered me to beg her to be very careful about religious matters as they were what first and principally concerned you, implying that if she did not continue in the established religion your Majesty would become her enemy. Her answer came in a tone of mild reproach: 'It would indeed be bad of me to forget God, who has been so good to me.' Your Majesty will see how, with such an answer, she can say nothing or everything.

"There are, of course, many suitors for her hand ... and crown. This makes her very coquettish indeed; she plays the part of desirable woman with such verve that in her presence it is difficult to believe that it is her crown and not her person which is so attractive. There is Prince Eric of Sweden, who, at time, she feigns to favor. There are your Majesty's own cousins, the two sons of the Emperor Ferdinand. And, of course, Savoy.

"There is another who is considered a possible suitor. This is an Englishman, Lord Robert Dudley. This young man is very handsome and the Queen favors him, keeping him beside her and at times treating him as though he is her acknowledged lover. His wife has recently died in mysterious circumstances and there are unsavory rumors about this matter among the people; but the Queen is so set on the young man, and she being as she is, it is thought that she may make up her mind to marriage with him.

"I feel this matter of the Queen's marriage is of the utmost importance to our country, and that while she is playing with the idea of making her subject Dudley her husband, she is obsessed by her vanity; and the way in which we could appeal to that would be to suggest to her the greatest match the world can offer."

Philip laid down the documents and considered this. Himself once more the husband of a Queen of that bleak land! He shrank from the idea.

He thought of her—sly, yet demure—dropping to her knees before him, yet raising her eyes as though to say: I salute you because the world recognizes you as its greatest monarch; but to me you are just a man, and one day there will be a greater monarch—and that a woman. One day there will be a greater country than Spain, and that will be England; for I shall be Queen of England, and I will have none but the best.

She was arrogant and insolent, yet so clever that it was impossible to protest against that insolent arrogance.

He thought of her pleading with her sister, when he had seen her from behind the curtains. Then she had been afraid, and yet what pride there was in her, and how different she had seemed from poor, sickly Mary, doomed to defeat, frustration, and failure!

And to marry her! That was what Feria was suggesting. Marry that coquette, that virago, that conceited, foolish, shrewd woman!

She was not repulsive to him, but why should he concern himself with her physical attractions? It was not for him to marry for such reasons. He must think only of his religion and his country.

He looked again at the crucifix on the wall. To bring England back to Rome was worth any price that might be asked of him. And now this Queen was about to break away from Rome; he was fully aware of that. If she did so, Henri of France would have little difficulty in getting the Pope to excommunicate her; then the Pope would be ready to support the claim of Mary Queen of Scots to the English throne.

There *must* not be an English-French alliance.

He rose from his table and fell to his knees before the crucifix. There had come to him suddenly a vision of married life with the

Queen of England. It would be an exciting life, he doubted not; quite different from that which he had shared with her half-sister. He thought of her red hair and blue eyes which veiled her secret thoughts. Desire? A little perhaps. She appealed to something in him. But he knew he could never subdue her. He knew that life with her would be one long battle. He was not a warrior; he was a man who hated war. Moreover, he felt that she, with her wiles and sly cunning, would get the better of him.

Marry Elizabeth? "No!" he murmured.

Yet such a marriage would be good for his country; it would baffle the French. He must pray; he must ask for guidance. Was it God's will that he should marry Elizabeth of England?

Quite suddenly he knew that it was so. She was wavering toward heresy, and only marriage with the Most Catholic King might save her. He could make her abandonment of heresy a condition of the marriage; in fact he must do this.

Then the Inquisition should be set up in England. Was it not Philip's task in life to save the world for Catholicism?

He wrote to Feria:

"I highly approve the course you have adopted in persuading the Queen not to marry a subject. As regards myself, if she were to broach the matter to you, you should treat it in such a way as neither to accept nor reject the suggestion entirely. Many obstacles present themselves. I could not be much in England, as my other dominions claim my attention. The Queen is rumored to be unsound in religion and it would not look well for me to marry her if she were not a Catholic. Such a marriage would, in view of the claims of Mary of Scotland, mean perpetual trouble with France. So there is much against the marriage; but I cannot lose sight of the fact that such a match would be of great moment to Christendom, and it is my great wish that England should not lapse into former errors.

"I have decided, therefore, to put aside all other considerations and render this service to God by offering to marry the Queen of England.

There must be conditions, and the first is that the Queen must profess to be a staunch Catholic. Dispensation from the Pope will be necessary, but if she is a good Catholic that will present no great difficulty."

When he had finished he read through the letter. To bring her and her country back to the true faith would be a great achievement and give him much credit in the eyes of God.

But was that the real reason why he wished to marry Elizabeth?

There were two others. She interested him. Her perpetual assurance of her own desirability had apparently made him feel that there must be some truth in it. Her past appeared to be far from unsullied; there had been adventures. She was young; she was all that Mary had not been.

And the last reason? As King of Spain, he must not lose the friendship of the English. Henri of France was awaiting his opportunities. If Mary Stuart ever reached the throne of England, then France, with England her close ally, would threaten to become the greatest world power.

There were so many reasons. Which was the most important of them all? Philip was not sure.

But the Queen of England was not overcome with joy by the proposal of the King of Spain. She flirted with Dudley and her Spanish suitor's ambassador; she was absurdly coquettish, declaring that since Feria was her suitor by proxy he must not have lodgings under the same roof, for that would be most improper (yet this, Feria wrote, was she who, rumor had it, had borne Seymour a child!). First she favored one, then another; she accepted the rich present of jewels which Philip had instructed Feria to give her—jewels which he had previously given to Mary—but she had accepted them with a speculative light in her eyes which had meant: What does he want for this? Philip would never give something for nothing!

At times she snubbed Feria; at others she petted him. She could not see him; she was too busy; she was not well. Then he must sit beside her; he was her very dear friend and she would have him know that he was always welcome.

Feria wrote to his master in exasperation: "She is the daughter of the Devil, surrounded by ministers who are heretics and scoundrels."

The "courtship" dragged on. Elizabeth was favoring one suitor after another, behaving as though the humblest of them was as interesting to her as the most powerful.

Such a state of affairs could not continue. Spain could not be slighted forever.

Philip suddenly decided on a change of policy. He was no longer going to ask for Elizabeth's hand; and it seemed to him that God was guiding him, for just at that moment when the conduct of the English Queen was exasperating him beyond endurance, the French Ambassador brought dispatches from the King of France in which Henri declared that he was becoming alarmed by the growth of heresy in his country; and he felt it behooved the great Catholic powers to stand together against it throughout the world. It was irreligious for Catholic to fight Catholic while the enemy of their faith was growing to alarming power. Should not the Kings of France and Spain stand together, forget their differences, and isolate England, which, in spite of the prevarication of its Queen—or perhaps because of this—was daily growing more heretic?

Let the marriage between Carlos and Henri's daughter Elisabeth take place at once, and so show the world that the two Catholic Kings were united against the heretic.

Surely this was the answer, thought Philip. It should be done.

Carlos was quietly happy.

At last she was coming to him, this beautiful girl. He had worked hard with the French language; he could speak many words now. He could say: "I shall call you Isabella, because that is a beautiful name in this country. It is Spanish, and Elisabeth is French. You are Spanish now, dear Isabella."

He talked to her when he was alone; and he fancied the picture in the locket smiled at him.

He would show her the countryside; he would tell her about his ambitions, how he had always longed to be a great soldier, and that perhaps now that he was so much better, he could be.

"Isabella . . . Isabella . . ." he whispered. "I am so glad you are here.

There is no one who loves me. Now there will be. There will be you, Isabella."

Sometimes he pictured darker scenes when he was angry—not with Isabella though; he would never be angry with her. But he fancied that one of his black moods came upon him and he struck his servant until Isabella came to him and begged him to show mercy to the man. And for Isabella's sake he would pardon the servant. She would be delighted. "Thank you, Carlos," she would say. "How happy you make me!"

Isabella was gentle. He could see that by her picture. She would be sorry for helpless little animals. She would beg him not to roast hares alive as he liked to do; she would beg him not to cut their throats and let them bleed slowly to death.

"I know I am silly, Carlos," she would say, "but it frightens me."

Then Carlos would answer: "I will not do it, Isabella, because I wish to do what you want always . . . always . . ."

Then they would laugh together and he would tell her of the black moods. She would kiss him and say: "I will charm them away, dear Carlos."

"Oh, Isabella . . . Isabella . . . at last you are coming! Even my father cannot keep you from me now."

In the Brussels Palace Philip thought continually of this marriage, and how could he possibly think of the marriage without sorrowfully pondering over the prospective bridegroom?

He shuddered, remembering Carlos in a hundred ugly moods.

"Holy Mother," he groaned, "why was I burdened with such a son?"

What could Carlos do for his father? What could he do for Spain? The reports from his tutors were alarming; there was not one of them who, having been given a high post in the household of the Prince of the Asturias, did not hint that he would be delighted to dispense with it.

Philip must face the truth. Carlos might not yet be as mad as his great-grandmother Juana, but he was not entirely sane. What trouble Juana had caused! Philip recalled the stinking apartment and the wild-eyed woman. He remembered how she had kept her daughter Katharine in seclusion in the Alcázar of Tordesillas. He remembered how she had screamed from her window, ordering the guards to kill one another.

Carlos was unfit for marriage.

Philip himself must have another son; if he did so, this marriage of Carlos with Elisabeth of Valois would be unnecessary. The important matter at issue was alliance with France, and Philip was the one who needed a wife. Why not continue with the French marriage, but with a different bridegroom!

He reached for the marriage contract. It was so simple. All he need do was substitute the name of Don Philip, King of Spain, for that of Don Carlos, Prince of the Asturias.

And what would the King and Queen of France say to such an exchange of bridegrooms? He could rely on their attitude. Instead of marrying their daughter to a weakling boy who had no power they would be offered alliance with the most powerful monarch in the world. What would any ambitious father and mother say to such a project?

And what would Elisabeth herself say to such a dazzling prospect?

But did it matter what such a child would say? She would of course obey first her parents and then her husband.

The more Philip thought of the project, the more he liked it.

It was left to Juana to tell Carlos.

She came to him, her face, as usual, half-hidden; and there was a terrible fear in her heart. She knew why he had improved so much during the last months; she knew of the picture in the locket, which was his perpetual solace.

She dreaded telling him, yet she knew he must not hear the bad news from any other. Who knew what wildness would take possession of him? He would be capable of a murderous assault on anyone who told him what had been decided.

She came to him while he was studying a book written in French.

"Carlos!" she cried. "Little One!"

He looked at her haughtily. He was not Little One now. He was grown up. He was about to be a husband.

"Carlos, there is sad news, dear one. It is hard to tell."

"My father is coming home," he said scowling.

"Yes, yes. I doubt not that he will be home. Carlos, he is to marry."

"Ha! Then we shall both be bridegrooms. Who is it to be? The Queen of England? I am sorry for her . . . though they say she is a fury herself. Ha . . . ha . . ."

"Do not laugh like that, Carlos. It is not to be the Queen of England."

"Juana . . . Juana . . . why do you look at me like that? Why do you look so sad and frightened?"

"Because, my darling, I have such bad news for you."

"For me? Oh! He is going to stop my marriage. He hates me. He hates me to be happy. He will keep Isabella from me. But I will run away. I will go to her. I will go to the King, her father, and tell him how they treat me here."

"No, Carlos, no. Your father has decided that . . . you are too young to marry, and . . ."

Carlos let out a howl which was like that of a wild animal. He ran to Juana and began beating her with his fists.

"Stop . . . stop!" she cried. "You have not heard, Carlos. Do you want me to tell you? I thought it better that you should hear from me."

He glared at her, and all his misery showed in his face.

"Isabella . . ." he muttered. "Isabella . . ."

"Yes. But I cannot tell you till you lie down."

His lips were twitching and there was foam at his mouth. But he allowed her to lead him to a couch, and there he lay while she knelt and took his hand. It was clammy and the pulse was erratic.

"Carlos, my Little One. I would give my life to spare you this. Your father . . . he is going to marry Isabella himself."

He did not speak. He just lay with eyes wide open; she thought he had not understood, and she began to pray: "Holy Virgin, help me to comfort him. Holy Mother, help him, because he needs your help so much . . ."

Now he was speaking. The words came through his clenched teeth;

but he did not pray. Juana felt her limbs go stiff with horror as she heard his words.

"Hate . . . hate . . . hate . . . I will kill him. This has decided it. I will kill him . . . with mine own hands . . ."

Then the tears rolled down his cheeks, and suddenly he turned on to his face and began to bite the cushions on the couch; strange noises came from his lips; his clenched fists were shaking; he twisted and turned, and as he rolled over she saw his face. There was blood on his chin, and his eyes were staring inhumanly.

He did not see her. He saw nothing but the pictures conjured up in his distorted mind. He had forgotten his love for Isabella in his hatred for his father.

Juana ran from the room. He was in one of those terrible fits which had afflicted Juana's own small brothers. And as she ran, calling for attendants, she could not shut out of her mind those words of the young Prince concerning his father:

"I will kill . . . kill him . . . with mine own hands!"

TWO

In The Palace of the Louvre, a frightened girl of fourteen was preparing herself for her marriage with the greatest monarch in the world.

She had wept so much that she could weep no more. She had confided her miseries to her young sister-in-law, Mary Stuart, herself a bride of less than a year. Mary was kind, for the two girls had been brought up together and were great friends, rivals in beauty and learning, and so happy until the news had come of this great honor which had fallen to Elisabeth.

"It is so different for you!" cried Elisabeth to Mary. "Such a marriage as yours could not but please all concerned. You married François, and you and François have loved each other ever since you came to live with us, and it is all as it was before, except that you are his wife; and when he is King of France you will be Queen. Your life is easy; you see whither it is leading. Whereas I must go away . . . right away from France to this land of Spain where they never laugh, and dance only in the most solemn manner. And I must marry an old man—nearly twenty years older than I. He is thirty-two, Mary. Think of that! And he has already had two wives. They say he is gloomy and that it is all prayers with him."

"But think, dear Elisabeth," said Mary. "You will be the most important Queen in the world . . . the Queen of Spain."

"I would rather be Queen of France than of any country in the world."

"But you will be Queen of Spain as soon as the ceremony is over. I can only be Queen of France if dear Papa dies, and that could do nothing but bring unhappiness to us all. And, Elisabeth, being Queen of France is not always so very pleasant. Think of Queen Catherine, your mother."

Elisabeth glanced over her shoulder. She was always afraid of talking about her mother, who would come so silently into a room, watching and listening, so that one turned and found her there. It was said that she had strange powers, and Elisabeth often felt that she knew what was being said even when she was not there.

"She is not here," said Mary now, following her gaze.

"No; but she might be."

Mary was very bold, conscious of that beauty which attracted all at court. She had often been careless before the Queen, showing a lack of respect which she would not have dared show Diane, Duchesse de Valentinois, the King's mistress, who ruled the court as Queen. Mary was careless, and Elisabeth feared that one day she would be sorry for behaving as she had toward Queen Catherine.

"Well," went on Mary, "you have seen how a Queen may be humiliated. It is Madame Diane de Poitiers—I beg her pardon, Duchesse de Valentinois—who is the real Queen of France. But they say that King Philip would not keep a mistress to humiliate his wife. You may be sure that the Queen of Spain will be treated with more respect than your *honored* mother, the Queen of France."

Elisabeth went to the window. "I hate it," she said. "All these people . . . all these foreigners . . . all the ceremonies and the preparation. Oh, Mary, how wonderful it would be if we were all young again without thought of marriage!"

"There are always thoughts of marriage with people like us."

"I mean if we were in the schoolroom. You remember? Vying with each other, trying to write better Latin verses than one another? And Papa's coming in to see how we were progressing? . . ."

"Coming in with Diane; and we all had to kiss her hand, do you remember, and she would fuss over us as though she were our mother?"

"I remember."

"And the Queen, your lady mother, would come in, and . . ."

"I remember that, too," said Elisabeth. "And once you called her a merchant's daughter. You should not have done that, Mary."

"But I did, and she is ..."

"I should not listen to you."

"Elisabeth, you are afraid of life. That is your weakness. You are afraid of your mother, and now you are afraid of Philip. You are beautiful—almost as beautiful as I am! Never fear. You can enjoy life at the court of Spain ... if you are wise."

"I wish I were as gay as you. But it is so easy to be gay when you are married to dear François and may spend the rest of your life here ... with Papa and all the family."

Elisabeth looked down on the gardens, where her young sister Margot was walking arm in arm with her special playmate, young Henry of Guise. Margot was only six, yet self-assured; they were like a pair of lovers, those two. François and his young brother Charles came into the gardens; they were looking for Mary, Elisabeth knew, for they both adored her.

"Oh, why cannot I stay here!" cried Elisabeth. "This is my home. This is where I belong. Mary, François and Charles are looking for you."

Mary came to the window and rapped on it; the boys looked up. Young Margot and Guise paid not the slightest attention; they were absorbed in each other.

"Go to them," said Elisabeth. "Do not let them come here. I wish to be by myself for a while."

Mary kissed her tenderly. "Do not fret so, little sister."

When Mary had gone, Elisabeth sat down and covered her face with her hands. She was trying so hard not to think of what was before her. She had been given Philip's picture. Such a cold face, she thought it; she did not know whether it was cruel or not. He had fair hair and blue eyes; and when the picture had been formally given to her she had had to kiss it.

Her father had said: "This is the greatest honor that could befall any Princess. The great Philip of Spain has chosen you for his wife." Oh, why had he not married the Queen of England? Why could she not have stayed just a little longer with her family? Her sister Claude had been married recently, and Claude was even younger than she was; but Claude had been married to the Duke of Lorraine, and that meant that she would not go right away from her home; she could often come and see them all. What comfort that was! But Elisabeth knew that once she had crossed the borders to that gloomy land of Spain and entered the household of her gloomy husband, she would never return.

"Holy Virgin," she prayed, "let something happen ... anything ... but let me stay with Mary, François, Charles, little Hercule, Margot, Papa, and Diane and ... and my mother ..."

Suddenly she knew that she was not alone in the room. Hastily she lowered her hands. Her mother had entered quietly, and was standing very still, leaning against the tapestry on the wall, watching her.

Elisabeth rose hastily. "Madame, I ... I did not hear you enter."

"Stay where you are, my child."

The flat features betrayed nothing; only the dark eyes seemed alive in that heavy face.

"So," went on Catherine de Medici, "you have been weeping and wailing and getting your sister-in-law to commiserate with you because you are to be the most important Queen in the world. That is so, is it not?"

How did she know such things? She knows everything, thought Elisabeth in a panic; she has some secret power which René or the Ruggieri brothers have given her.

"Mother ..." she began. "Madame ..."

"Yes, my child, you are sad because you must leave your home. My dear daughter, it is the fate of us all. I was no older than you when I left my home in Italy and came to France."

"Yes, but ..."

"But what?"

"That was to marry Papa."

Catherine gave that loud burst of laughter which was familiar to them all. "He was a stranger to me."

Elisabeth looked at her plump mother and thought how she would willingly change places with her, endure all the humiliations which any other woman would suffer—Catherine gave no signs of suffering them—from the dazzling Diane, who, although so much older than the King and the Queen, had had the King's devotion ever since he was a boy.

Elisabeth would willingly change places with anybody who had not to go to Spain to marry Philip.

"Yes, but . . ." faltered Elisabeth.

"I was as alarmed as you are. But you see, I became the Queen of France and the mother of you all, and one day, my daughter, you will laugh at your fears even as I do now at mine." Catherine came close to Elisabeth. "You will have much to occupy you in your new life. I shall write to you often and my letters will bring you something of myself. When you read them it will be as though I am speaking to you. You will remember that?"

Elisabeth tried to conquer the fear she had of her mother. She knew all the children had it—except young Henri, whom Catherine petted and adored. Even Margot, brazen and bold, trembled in the presence of her mother.

"You will be our little ambassadress at the court of King Philip, dearest child. You will not forget us all . . . your father and mother, your brothers and sisters."

"I shall never forget you," cried Elisabeth. "I shall long to be home with you."

"Bah! When you are Queen, you will be content with your lot. You are young and very pretty, and I doubt not that your husband will wish to please you. That will depend on you. It is for you to *make* him wish to please you."

Elisabeth wished her mother would not smile in that way. It frightened her even more than when her face was quite expressionless. The smile suggested distasteful things—caresses, love-making with a husband whom Elisabeth could only be happy in forgetting.

"There is a stepson, Elisabeth—Don Carlos, he who was to have been the bridegroom." Catherine laughed again. "Never mind. You have the better one. A king on the throne is worth many an heir to the same throne. For we know what is, but how do any of us know what may be? Now, child, this will be your first mission at your husband's court. You will arrange a match between your sister Margot and Don Carlos. That is what I wish you to do; and if you achieve it *I* shall be very proud of you. It will be almost as though I am there ... so you will not be lonely." She laughed again. "I shall write to you often. I shall give you the benefit of my advice and comfort. Dearest daughter, although you will be gone, we shall not really be parted. You believe that, do you not?"

"Yes, Madame."

Catherine put her cold lips against her daughter's forehead. Then she went silently from the room.

Elisabeth closed her eyes and began to pray for a miracle, something that could happen to prevent or even delay her journey to Spain.

She saw her father later. It was easier to talk to him although he was the King. It had always been thus. When he had come to the nursery, the little ones, unaware of his rank, had clambered over him, pulling his beard.

Now that beard was silver although he was only forty. He was a man slow of speech, a little taciturn in the company of adults, but at ease with children. He was Father first, King second, to his family.

She told him how she dreaded the ceremony, how she was afraid of the solemn Duke of Alba, who had come from Flanders to act as proxy for his master, since the Kings of Spain did not leave their country to bring home their brides; their brides came to them.

He was kind; he understood.

"It makes me sad to lose you," he said, "although I shall be proud of my little Queen of Spain."

"But to leave you all, Papa ... all my brothers and sisters and you ... dearest Papa ... you most of all."

He stroked her hair. "It is the fate of such as we are, dearest child," he said. "We all have to face it. Princes and princesses all have their marriages made for them."

"But, Papa, I cannot bear it. I cannot."

"Dearest, you will. We all do. In a little while you will be happy there, and Spain will be your home instead of France."

"But Spain is not France, and it is France I love."

"It is your home you love, Elisabeth; and Spain will be your home, for your home will be where your husband is. You must not cry. You must not have red eyes for the ceremony or the King your husband will hear of it and feel slighted. He might even cancel the arrangements!"

"Papa, do you think he would?"

"Elisabeth, if it were not this marriage it would be another."

"I have prayed, Papa, that something will happen so that I need not go."

"I said earnest prayers at the time of my own marriage."

"But you found happiness later."

"Great happiness, dearest child."

Then Diane came in and, smiling at the father and daughter, she lifted the hair from Elisabeth's hot face and kissed her; for Diane behaved as a mother to the royal children, and that was how they thought of their father's mistress.

She said: "The child is exhausted, and there are all the ceremonies before her! Come, Elisabeth, my dear one, you must go to bed and I will have a soothing draught made for you. I will bring it to you myself and sit with you until you are sleepy. When you are rested you will feel better. Will she not?"

"She will indeed," said Henri; and as he looked from his daughter to his mistress, it was as though he were telling Elisabeth that even when life seemed very cruel to princes and princesses, it sometimes was very kind to them in unexpected ways.

The dreaded day came nearer and nothing happened to prevent the marriage. Emmanuel Philibert, the Duke of Savoy, was also in Paris, for he had come to marry Elisabeth's Aunt Marguerite. With the two marriages the alliance between France and Spain would be very firm indeed, and England would be completely isolated, Elizabeth of England losing her two suitors by the marriages which were to take place in Paris that summer.

Little Elisabeth de Valois was formally betrothed to Philip by proxy in the great hall of the Louvre, and as she stood beside the Duke of Alba, with whom was the young Prince of Orange, who had accompanied Alba from the Netherlands, she felt that even Philip could not be more forbidding than his proxy. There was some small comfort in that.

The next day the actual ceremony was solemnized in Notre Dame to the delight of all except the bride, for the pomp and magnificence was equal to that which had enchanted Paris at the marriage of Mary Stuart and the Dauphin of France the year before.

Elisabeth clung to her father's hand as he led her from the Bishop's Palace to Notre Dame. Her dress was covered with beautiful pearls, her mantle was of blue velvet, and about her neck was hung a locket containing Philip's portrait; there was also the huge pear-shaped pearl—the most valuable of all Spain's crown jewels—a present from the bridegroom to the bride. She looked very small beside her glittering father, who whispered words of comfort to her as he acknowledged the applause of the onlookers. Behind her came her sister Claude to carry her train, with Mary Stuart, the Dauphine. This, thought Elisabeth, was one of the last occasions when she would be surrounded by the members of her beloved family. The Imperial crown which she must carry on her head weighed her down more by its significance than by the weight of gold and jewels.

Now she must stand beside the Duke of Alba, who was dressed in glittering cloth of gold, while the Cardinal of Bourbon proclaimed her the wife of the King of Spain.

The French, unlike the English, could outdo the Spaniards in courtesy and brilliance; and this they proceeded to do to the best of their ability. There was an inevitable undercurrent of uneasiness at such a time; the wedding had not increased the amity between the rival factions of France. The Catholic party, at the head of which were the Guises, was delighted, for the match was very much to their liking; the Protestant party, at the head of which were the Bourbons, was made uneasy by the new and close tie with Catholic Spain.

But, at the brilliant ceremonies that followed, the Guisards and the Bourbons veiled their antagonisms; and when, shortly afterward, the King's sister was married to the Duke of Savoy, the wedding celebrations in recognition of the double wedding must, all had declared, be doubly magnificent.

As each day passed, the little bride's uneasiness grew. Nightly she prayed for a miracle. She begged for a few more months, a few more days in France.

There were many interviews with her mother, when she was given instructions as to how she might bind Philip to her; she was continually told that she must remember that first she was a princess of France, and it was the interests of France and her family that she must further.

Ceremonies seemed endless. There were many jousts and tourneys, and always she, with the elder members of her family, must be present in a pavilion of honor to see Frenchmen tilt against Spaniards.

At length there came that day which she would never forget as long as she lived. How could such a day begin so ordinarily! There was nothing in the brilliant June sky to warn them all that this day would be different from any others spent in rejoicing. The crowds were as numerous as ever; the pavilion and dresses of men and women as glittering as was to be expected of the most brilliant court in the world.

The jousting was held close to the Bastille near the gate of St. Antoine. Elisabeth sat with her mother, her sister Claude, and that other bride, her aunt Marguerite. Above their heads the silken canopies kept off the rays of the sun. The crowd was expectant, for the King was to joust today.

Elisabeth was aware that her mother was uneasy. There was an affinity between them, and Elisabeth sometimes thought that she knew more about her mother than the others.

Catherine de Medici was known to be different from other women; no one could have borne as she did the constant humiliation of watching Diane take all the homage which was Catherine's by right; she had special powers which were given to her by her magicians; she was quiet, and only her children feared her. For, thought Elisabeth, we are the only ones who know the Queen of France.

When the King rode into the arena he was wearing, as he always did, the black-and-white colors of his mistress Diane. It was not this habitual slight which made Catherine uneasy; but there she sat, tense, not missing a single movement made by the King.

She was clearly relieved when the joust was over and the King emerged victorious. Elisabeth wondered afresh at her mother's love for her father. Not all the humiliation he inflicted on her could stifle that quiet, tense emotion. The King was the kindest person Elisabeth had ever known, yet she could not understand her mother's devotion; for although he was always courteous to his wife, he so clearly did not love her, and that was apparent in the very tone of his voice when he spoke to her. Perhaps he believed, as so many people did, that she had poisoned his elder brother, so that he might be King and she the Queen. Moreover, he loved Diane so much that nothing could prevent his showing it. Diane to him was his Queen. In spite of that, Catherine loved him.

Now the King was declaring that he wished to tilt again, and Catherine had half risen in her seat. She wanted, Elisabeth knew, to beg him not to. Too much exercise was bad for him. He had had an unpleasant attack of giddiness after a game of tennis only yesterday; and now he had jousted enough.

But the King was like a boy, as proudly he bore his mistress's colors. He declared that he was as fresh as when he had started; he would break one more lance before he retired from the field.

A young Franco-Scot came forward at his command—Montgomerie, the Sieur de L'Orge.

Catherine seemed to have communicated some of her uneasiness to this young man, for he begged the King to excuse him; but the King insisted.

It was all over in a few minutes. Had Catherine risen to protest before it happened? Elisabeth did not know.

Montgomerie's lance, striking the King on the gorget, had splintered, and one of the splinters had entered the King's eye. Henri fell to the ground, his face covered with blood.

Elisabeth was vaguely aware that her mother had risen and that on her face was an expression of dreadful understanding.

Elisabeth pressed her hands against her madly beating heart. She feared the worst of all tragedies had overtaken her. And so she had her wish. The journey was delayed. She was heartbroken during those last weeks in France.

The King must lie in state; he must be buried with the utmost ceremony.

Philip was impatient to receive his bride. The new King François and his lovely wife, Mary Stuart, were completely under the control of Mary's uncles, the Guises, which was a comforting thought for Philip; he had heard rumors that the character of the Dowager Queen Catherine was not quite what people had believed during her husband's lifetime. It was as though she was awakening, said his spies, and that her previous meekness had disguised her sinister character. There were some who had nicknamed her "Madame le Serpent," and the name seemed to fit. Philip realized that his young wife would be much under the influence of such a mother, and his demands that she should be sent to Spain became more and more insistent.

Catherine de Medici had many excuses ready. The trousseau of the Queen of Spain was not yet prepared, and she was sure the King of Spain would not wish his bride to arrive like a little commoner. There were innumerable negotiations; there was an enormous quantity of baggage which had to be transported over the Pyrenees; and the Dowager Queen thought it only right that Elisabeth should remain behind to attend the coronation of her young brother, François.

Philip was growing uneasy. He was a husband, yet no husband. The French were defying him; it seemed to him that the Flemings were defying him also.

At the assembly of the States-General in Ghent which he had recently attended, there had been many bold speeches. The Flemings resented the Spanish soldiers Philip had brought to their shores, and they said so. One man had said that it would now be the simplest matter to set up the Inquisition in the Netherlands, and as the Netherlands was a free country, it would have no hospitality to offer a foreign institution.

Philip had grown pale with anger at the mention of the Inquisition. "That is not merely a revolt against me," he said. "That is a revolt against God."

He did not trust Orange. He knew the Prince was negotiating a marriage with a daughter of one of the Protestant princes.

The Flemings were turning against him; he was on bad terms with his Uncle Ferdinand; and his young wife was held from him and was doubtless being instructed by that artful Italian woman how to act as a spy in his court.

Clearly something must be done. He would put down revolt in the Netherlands; he would return to Spain in order to discuss this with his ministers, and at the same time to receive his bride there.

The Prince of Orange himself was at Flushing to bid Philip farewell before he embarked. Philip looked coldly at the young man and said: "I am well aware that you are responsible for your countrymen's opposition to my wishes."

Orange replied: "The opposition to your wishes, Sire, can only reflect the feelings and the views of the people."

Philip turned impatiently away, muttering: "No, Orange; you cannot deceive me. You are to blame . . . with your heresy. You . . . and you alone."

Orange realized that Philip's utterance was tantamount to a declaration of war, and he was exultant. He determined in that moment to rescue the Netherlands from the yoke of Spain and all the cruelties of the Inquisition.

From the surrounding country, people were crowding into Valladolid; far beyond its walls the sound of tolling bells could be heard. This was no ordinary *fiesta*. It was a saint's day, one of the holidays of Holy Church; best clothes were worn, expressions of sobriety were worn like masks to hide excitement. Water-carriers, who sold cool drinks to thirsty travelers, did good business along the dusty road that day; all those who had stood aside to watch the royal procession enter the town were now eagerly pressing forward, anxious to secure a place well to the fore in the Plaza Mayor.

There was about to take place the greatest *auto-da-fé* any had ever witnessed. The King would be present; the Prince Don Carlos with his

Aunt Juana would sit in the state gallery; and more men and women would be burned alive—and many of them members of the nobility and the court itself—than had ever been burned on one occasion.

Who could resist such a spectacle? All those who witnessed it would talk of it for the rest of their lives. It would be more diverting even than the torturing of bulls. No wonder people were crowding into the town; no wonder men and women were trampled underfoot in their efforts to be first in the Plaza Mayor.

The terrible scene was set in the great square before the Church of St. Francis, and the Inquisitors were already seated on the sumptuously carpeted platform; and in the gallery were the members of the royal family with their attendants. Juana was heavily veiled, as she always was in public; Philip, his eyes aflame with fanaticism, presented a less cool facade to his subjects than usual; and Don Carlos, white-faced, magnificently dressed as he loved to be, was more deeply conscious of his father than of anyone else in the whole assembly.

Beside Philip sat his friends, Ruy Gomez da Silva, Gomez Suarez de Figueroa, and the Count of Feria. Ruy glanced covertly at Philip. What was he thinking? wondered Ruy. But he, who had lived so near to Philip for so many years, could guess. Philip was thinking of God's pleasure in the drama which was about to be enacted; he was thinking of the delight of God in maimed and tortured bodies, in the cries of agony.

Ruy shivered and turned his gaze upon the young Prince. Carlos was brooding. He was not thinking so much of the sights he was about to see; he was thinking of his father and the wife who would soon be coming to him.

As Secretary of State and chief adviser to the King, Ruy was fully conscious of the uneasy days which lay ahead. He would like to speak his mind to Philip concerning Carlos; he would like to explain to the King the thoughts which he could not suppress. He was deeply conscious of the Grand Inquisitor, Fernando Valdés, Cardinal-Archbishop of Seville, who was in charge of today's spectacle. There was not one person in the crowd who could look at that man unmoved, and Ruy was no exception. The reputation of the Cardinal-Archbishop was second only to that of Torquemada. Since he had been in command of the dread Inquisition, he had determined to increase its power, and this he had done with marked success. He had enlisted new spies; they were everywhere, listening to unwary conversations, tempting the careless to betray themselves. Under Valdés, new instruments of torture had been devised. He was the man whom Philip had appointed to stamp out heresy in Spain; for, said Philip—and Valdés echoed his words—how could they hope to free the rest of the world from the Devil unless Spain herself was beyond reproach?

There was now a deep silence over the square; then it seemed as though all the church bells in the town were tolling.

The doors of the great prison would now be opening. Ruy knew this, because he had witnessed similar ceremonies. Out of the gates of the prison a wretched procession would now be filing and at any moment it would be possible to see their vanguard.

He watched a black-eyed gypsy girl cross herself as she touched her rosary; his eyes strayed to the water-carrier in tattered rags. In the slant of the man's eyes Ruy recognized his Moorish ancestry. And beside that man was another, whose lips were moving in prayer; his features suggested Jewish blood. Had their ancestors taken part in such a spectacle—a more active part than these two would take? Perhaps *they* had been rich lords, rich merchants. Who could tell what one's descendants would come to when the Holy Inquisition's greedy claw seized a man and his property?

These were dangerous thoughts. As the King's closest friend, holding a high position in the country, he should not be thinking them.

Here came the troops, resplendent in their uniforms. Ruy fixed his eyes upon them because he did not wish to look beyond them. He was weak today, weak and fanciful. He was unnerved, not only by the sights he knew from experience he would have to witness, but by the mad hatred which he sensed in Carlos. He knew now that he was a lover of peace. He hated cruelty in any form. There was not a man or woman present who would not condemn such thoughts, coming at this time. He should confess those thoughts. Dare he? Certainly not. Whom could one trust? One's confessor today might be a familiar of the Inquisition tomorrow. Ruy might at times be a sentimental man, but he was a wise one. God alone should know his thoughts. God would punish him, if he deserved punishment. He was appalled suddenly to realize that for such thoughts he could be sentenced to join that group of men whom he did not wish to look upon. Another thought, swift as lightning, followed. The man beside him, the King and his friend, would not hesitate to destroy him if he knew what was passing through his mind.

What a fearful sight they presented!

"They are heretics. They are heretics!" Ruy repeated to himself. "Think of that. Heretics! Their sufferings may bring them salvation if they repent in time."

But he found no real peace in those words. He must therefore delude himself. He must catch the exultation which he sensed about him. The sun was hot, but the royal gallery was shaded by the hangings which shut out the burning heat. Ruy could smell death and decay in the air. The wounds of some of these men and women who stumbled behind the soldiers were turning gangrenous.

Ruy assured himself: They would die in any case very soon.

They came, stumbling on; some had to be carried in chairs because their legs had been broken on the wheel or on the *chevalet*; the arms of some hung helpless at their sides. Those without eyes had to be led. There were some who lacked ears and noses.

Is this necessary? Could we not offer them easier death?

Ruy answered his own questions. The Inquisition in its mercy gives these people a foretaste of Hell that they may repent in time and save themselves from an eternity of suffering.

He was happier now; he was guiding his thoughts into the right channels.

These victims who had once been men and women—very like the men and women in the square, very like the people on the platform—all wore the symbol of their shame: the hideous, loose-fitting *sanbenito* and caps made of pasteboard with grotesque devils painted upon them.

There were three types of this coarse woollen gown, and the spectators could see at a glance what fate was intended for the wearers. Among the mournful procession were some whose garments were simply marked with a red cross: they were guilty of the venial sins, and penance, imprisonment, and confiscation of goods was to be their punishment; after their sentences were pronounced they would be taken back to the gloomy prison of the Inquisition to expiate their sins. There were others whose garments displayed busts of human beings in the act of being consumed by long red flames which were pointing downward; this indicated that although their bodies would be burned they would not feel the flames since, as they had recanted, they should first be accorded the mercy of strangulation. The third type of garment displayed busts and heads in the midst of flames which pointed upward, fanned by mocking devils; these were the unrepentant heretics who were condemned to be burned alive.

"Repent and be reconciled!" chanted the monks who walked on either side of the yellow-clad figures. "Repent and be reconciled!"

Following the prisoners came the jailors and more monks, the magistrates and the important officials of the Inquisition on mules, the trappings of which were so gorgeous that for a few moments the eyes of the crowd were fixed upon them instead of on the miserable victims.

Philip's pale skin turned to coral as the sarcenet was held high. It was red—the color of blood—and embroidered with the heraldic arms of the Inquisition, the Papal arms and those of Ferdinand and Isabella.

The sermon of faith, preached that day by the Bishop of Zamora, was longer than usual; and after the sermon came that great moment when Philip endeared himself to his people as few other sovereigns ever had.

There was a great silence in the crowd as Valdés rose. He raised his hand, and all in the square—man, woman, and child—knelt and lifted their hands toward the skies as they chanted the Oath of Allegiance to the Holy Office. They would be faithful to the Holy Catholic Church and its Inquisition in life and in death; they would give their right eyes, their right hands in its service, and if necessary their lives.

And as they began to chant the Oath—which was not demanded of the King—Philip sprang suddenly to his feet; his Toledo blade flashed from its scabbard; and holding it before him, the King himself repeated with the people the Oath of Allegiance to the Inquisition.

When the chanting ceased and the people raised their eyes and saw their King standing there, his sword gleaming like silver, his pale face alight with fervor, there was a brief, awestruck silence before someone in the crowd shouted: "Long live the King! Long live Philip to reign over us!"

The tumult broke then; it lasted several minutes.

Ruy looked at Philip, standing beside him, the jeweled sword in his hands. He recognized the fanatic, and thought with love and pity of a small boy shivering and naked in the Cloister of St. Anne. Other pictures flashed in and out of Ruy's mind. It was inevitable, he thought. It had to be. Everything which has happened to him has led to this moment.

Carlos was watching his father, and hatred had complete possession of him. If he but had the strength to take that gleaming sword and plunge it into the heart of the man who had become the husband of Isabella!

"My Isabella!" muttered Carlos piteously. "Mine!"

His hatred was so strong that it set a haze before his eyes; he could not see the square; the black-clad monks and the figures in their yellow garments of shame and despair were blurred before his eyes. Ordinarily the scene would have delighted him. What could be more exciting than to watch so much suffering and to do so under a cloak of piety? God himself, according to the King and the Cardinal-Archbishop, was looking down upon them, flashing His scornful hatred at the miserable victims, applauding the spectators and officials and all those who had taken the Oath.

But there was only one man whose suffering could bring Carlos complete satisfaction. Those broken men and women meant no more to him than the rabbits he might roast alive for a little fun.

Into the *Quemadero*—the place of fire—that space in the center of the square where the stakes had been set up, came the victims, and among them were two men, recently well-known at court. Don Carlos de Seso, a noble Florentine, had been a great friend of the Emperor; he had settled in Valladolid and there had become interested in Lutheran doctrines. He believed that it was his duty, as he had discovered the truth, to teach it to others. He had been a rich man, and such as he were the favorite prey of the Inquisition. With him in the square was Domingo de Roxas, who had himself been a Dominican monk.

With startling suddenness, de Roxas, as he stood there, his body broken, his arms hanging impotent at his sides, raised his voice and began to preach to the multitude. It was some minutes before he could be stopped, and then only by the painful wooden gag which was screwed into his mouth.

But even more startling was that moment when de Seso, fixing his eyes on the central figure in the gallery and raising his voice so that all could hear, cried: "Philip! I speak to Philip the King!"

There was about this man a dignity which even his torture and the hideous yellow robe and pasteboard cap could not take from him.

Philip, almost involuntarily, rose to his feet, and thus they faced each other: the King of Spain, his black velvet doublet a-glitter with diamonds, and the wretched man de Seso, his face, through long incarceration in the airless dungeons of the Inquisition, as yellow as his *sanbenito*.

"Is it thus then, Philip," said de Seso, "that you allow your innocent subjects to be persecuted? Does it not fill you with shame to see our shame?"

Philip answered in ringing tones, for he had given his allegiance to the Inquisition, and in his eyes it was the work of God which he and his Inquisitors were doing on Earth:

"Shame? For you is the shame; for us is the glory. If you were my own son, I would fetch the wood to burn you. If my son had denied the true Faith as you have done, he should stand there with you."

The crowd cheered madly: "God bless great Philip! Long live Philip our King!"

It was some time before the ceremony could go on. This was a day which all those present would remember while they lived. They had seen great Philip take the Oath of Allegiance to the Inquisition, which no other sovereign had done. It was significant. Philip had proclaimed himself: Catholic first, King second. Those present had heard him, with his son beside him, declare that that same son should suffer in the *Quemadero* as any other, should he prove false to the Faith. What man could have greater love for the Faith than he who was ready to lay down the life of his son for it?

The names of the prisoners were being read aloud with the lists of their crimes; they were sentenced; some were led away to prison. Those who had recanted were strangled before they were bound to their stakes. And now the great moment had come. The fires were lighted and the screams of the living filled the air.

But to have seen the King with his shining sword was more memorable than even the sight of flames that swirled about broken bodies; to have heard him speak the Oath, more wonderful than listening to the screams of heretics and the triumphant shouts of the servants of God.

But Carlos could not take his eyes from his father's face; and Ruy, watching, could only think: The pity of it! The pity of it all!

A bitter wind was blowing as Elisabeth rode south. The journey was long, and she was thankful for that. With her rode her mother and the two Bourbon Princes—the Cardinal of Bourbon, who had officiated at the proxy marriage, and Antoine, the King of Navarre and Duke of Vendôme, who had married that Jeanne of Navarre whom Philip himself had once thought to marry.

No French lady could travel without an abundant supply of garments and, having been brought up in the French court, Elisabeth was very conscious of fashion. Mules, laden with her extravagant trousseau, traveled with the party, for her dresses must be of the French fashion, acknowledged to be the best in the world.

She wished she could recapture that excitement about her dresses which she had felt when she discussed them with Mary Stuart and even little Margot—who, though so young, was quite conscious of fashion—in the familiar apartments of the Louvre or at Blois.

At intervals along the road the peasants had come out to wave a sad farewell to the little Princess, to marvel at her beauty, and to wish her good luck in her married life.

At the town of Chatelleraut, Catherine de Medici gave her daughter a last embrace and uttered the final words of advice and warning.

Antoine, with some French nobles and the Spaniards who had met the party, continued to accompany Elisabeth.

It was a journey of a hundred accidents. The weather was bad and they must at times travel through sleet and snow; some of the baggage was mislaid and the French ladies were in a panic, thinking they might not have dresses fine enough in which to face the Spaniards. The French were closely guarding French honor and carefully watching for slights; and the Spaniards were even more jealous of their dignity.

When it was time for Elisabeth to be formally handed over and to say good-bye to Antoine, whom she loved, she felt herself unable to bear the parting.

When Antoine made his speech, in which he said that he had brought the Princess from the house of the greatest King in the world to be delivered to the most illustrious sovereign on Earth, she broke down and wept; whereupon the emotional Antoine so far forgot his dignity as to break off his ceremonial speech, take her in his arms, and try to comfort her.

All the noble Spaniards—the greatest in the land assembled to represent their King in this important ceremony—were shocked by such conduct. Their glances implied that the Queen would have to learn to behave differently now that she was in Spain.

The Duke of Infantado, head of the great Mendoza family, whose duty it had been to receive her at this stage on behalf of the King, reproved her as he led her away.

"I beg your Highness to remember," he said, "that you are now the Queen of Spain, and the Queen of Spain does not so condescend to the Duke of Vendôme—even though he may call himself the King of Navarre."

Elisabeth's grief subdued her fear. She said sharply: "The Duke of Infantado is greatly daring to speak thus to the Queen of Spain, who will say good-bye to those she loves in the manner of her own people, who do not seek to hide their genuine feelings if they wish to show them."

The Duke was taken aback, but she was so beautiful, so young, so appealing that she blunted the edge of his Spanish dignity; moreover, he realized that she was not the frivolous girl he had imagined her to be.

He could only bow his head and murmur: "I crave your Highness's pardon."

All along the road the Spaniards came out to see their new Queen. Her beauty enchanted them. She was typically French in poise and gesture, yet her features bore traces of her Italian ancestry.

She was calmer now that she had said good-bye to her relations. It was too late to hope for a miracle, and since the death of her father she had done with hoping for miracles. Her clothes were not only rich, they were becoming; and the Spaniards had never seen anything like them. She bowed and smiled at the people with French warmth which was so different from Spanish frigidity. She charmed these people as she rode among them. "Surely she is the most beautiful Queen in the world," they said.

She had long since learned to read the Castilian language, and now she rapidly taught herself to speak it, and if her accent was that of a Frenchwoman, it merely added to her fascinating qualities.

Even the old members of the Spanish nobility were won over by her manners. Even grim Alba himself was attracted by her.

One grows up, thought Elisabeth. One cannot cry when one has no tears left. This is the fate which befalls all princesses.

But she knew that the greatest trial had yet to come. Each day brought her nearer to it, and every little fracas between French and Spaniards prepared her for it. There was still the meeting with Philip—and after that the life with him—to be faced.

Philip was waiting for her at Guadalajara. Juana and Carlos were with him.

Carlos was in a state of extreme tension, though no one but Ruy and Juana seemed to be aware of this. Carlos would have heard the reports regarding the bride; she seemed to have enchanted all those who had come into contact with her, and, although she was not yet fifteen, she had appeared to make even the grim Alba behave like a young man in love.

"Guard my little one," muttered Juana. "I pray all the saints to guard him."

Ruy was thinking: Is Philip blind? Does he not realize the effect of this on one so unbalanced as Carlos?

He must be prepared to go to the defense of Philip, for anything might happen. In such a moment Carlos's mind might topple over into complete insanity. Ruy must be at hand to guard the King.

Philip seemed almost indifferent. He was worried about the Netherlands. The Prince of Orange was hatching evil plots; he knew it. His cousin Maximilian and his sister Maria were growing closer to the German princes; they must be watched. There was so much to occupy his mind, and he only had time to think that this Elisabeth of Valois would suit him because she was young and would bear him children. Marriage was a duty to be endured for the sake of his country.

He was facing a new phase of his career, and he was determined to be ready to meet it. He had said good-bye to Catherine Lenez; Isabel Osorio had gone into a convent, for she knew that, now he was the King, their life together was ended. All Isabel's children would be provided for by Philip, and later would have good posts in his household or in his armies. Philip could be trusted to do his duty.

He had already sent for his half-brother Juan, in order that he might fulfill the promise he had made to their father, and Juan was being brought up and educated with Carlos.

There was another boy who shared their lessons. This was Philip's cousin, Alexander Farnese, whom Philip had brought home with him from the Netherlands.

Alexander was the son of Margaret of Parma, who was herself one of the illegitimate daughters of the Emperor Charles. Charles had always made his children's welfare a concern of his, and he had married Margaret to Alessandro, the illegitimate son of Pope Clement. Alessandro, who had been known as the Nero of Florence, had, fortunately for Florence and Margaret, died a violent death a year after the marriage. After Margaret had been a widow for some years Charles found another bridegroom for her; but in her second marriage Margaret was hardly more fortunate than in her first, for now she was a woman and her new husband, Ottavio Farnese, was only twelve years old. The union was naturally not a very happy one, although it brought Margaret her son Alexander. Charles, aware of her capabilities and that character which was more masculine than feminine, bestowed on her the Governorship of the Netherlands, and this Philip had allowed her to retain.

He was considering now whether it might not be expedient to have the two sons of Maximilian and Maria brought to Spain, for the same reason as he had brought Alexander: ostensibly to be companions for Carlos, but actually as hostages for their parents' good behavior.

With so much to occupy his mind, and so many problems to be faced, it was small wonder that Philip had little thought to spare for his bride.

She was now riding into the town on a white palfrey; on one side of her was the Duke of Infantado and on the other the Cardinal of Burgos. In the streets the people were shouting their pleasure; and here, in the ducal palace, everything was in readiness, for the actual marriage ceremony must take place as soon as the bride arrived.

Philip stood on the dais. Carlos was beside him. How he fidgeted! Could not the boy show some dignity? There was Juana, looking more as though she were at a funeral than at a wedding. Philip was uneasy suddenly. Would Juana's melancholy lead to trouble one day? And here was Ruy, standing close to him—surely closer than was necessary—as though he were preparing to face a host of enemies rather than his sovereign's bride. Philip wanted to say: "My dear friend, there is no need for uneasiness. I feel none. I do not believe this Princess of France will be very formidable." Lightly he wondered how Ruy fared in his own married life with the stormy, one-eyed Ana.

Glancing at Carlos, Philip saw that his lips were moving. Hastily Philip turned away from his son.

What would the new Queen think of her stepson? She must surely congratulate herself when she contemplated what she had escaped. Whatever she thought of her own bridegroom, he would certainly seem preferable to Carlos.

Meanwhile, Carlos was saying to himself: "She is mine. This was to have been my wedding day. But he takes everything from me."

He did not know what he would do when she entered. Could she really be as beautiful as they said she was? When he saw her, he believed, he might be so jealous that his hatred of his father would compel him to kill him. He might try to seize Philip's sword and run it through his heart.

Those who had seen her had said of Isabella: "She is so attractive that no cavalier durst look at her for fear of losing his heart to her; and should the King see this it might cost a man his life!"

And she is mine! thought Carlos. Mine . . . not his.

Outside the procession had halted before the ducal palace and the doors were thrown wide open that the little Queen might enter.

She stepped into the hall, and she was the most beautiful creature Carlos had ever seen. She was far more charming than any picture could show.

Carlos, watching her as she was led to the spot where the King stood, wanted to shout: "Do not be afraid of him, Isabella!" He loved her the more because of that fear he sensed in her. "You are mine, Isabella, and together we will plan to kill him."

He was aware of a hand on his shoulder and, turning, he looked into the eyes of Ruy Gomez da Silva. Carlos quailed slightly, for he knew that he had betrayed to this man the burning hatred he felt for his father.

The King was now greeting the French Princess, and she was answering falteringly in Castilian.

Then Juana knelt and kissed the Princess's ermine-edged robe. Elisabeth smiled at her; she had pleasant smiles for all except Philip; for him she had only fearful glances.

Now it was Carlos's turn. He knelt. He kissed the edge of her robe; he lifted his eyes, alight with adoration, to her face; and all the time the hammer-beats of his heart were declaring: "She is mine. . . . mine!"

Her smile bewitched and maddened him; but almost immediately Philip had laid his hand on her arm and she was turning away that she might be presented to the members of his suite.

Carlos moved to his father. Now was the moment...now...here before them all.

The people would cry: "Philip is dead. Long live King Carlos!" This was to have been a marriage, and it will be the scene of murder. Never mind if the King is dead. Here is a new King. Never mind if the bride has lost her husband. Here is a new husband for her!

Again he felt the pressure on his shoulder. He turned sharply and looked up into the dark face of Ruy.

Words trembled on Carlos's lips. "How...dare you?"...But he would not speak them. He would not betray himself to his father's friend. This was not the time. It was not easy to murder a king. Careful planning was needed.

He felt calmer now—calm and sly.

The little bride was looking fearfully at Philip.

Philip said with a half-smile: "Why do you look at me so intently? Are you looking to see how many gray hairs I have?"

She grew pale and turned away. His unexpectedly cold voice had increased her fears.

Philip was unhappy; he was deeply conscious of having frightened her when his intention had been to set her at her ease.

He could not explain. The nobles and their ladies were coming forward to greet her.

Carlos continued to watch the King, but Ruy Gomez da Silva was constantly at the Prince's side.

The marriage ceremony had been performed; the feasting had begun. There must follow the tourneys, the bullfights; and, as ceremony demanded it, Philip must joust before his bride, an undertaking which did not please him, but, since he looked upon it as a duty, he would not shirk it.

As he sat by her side through ceremony after ceremony, he was wondering how he might set her at ease, how he could explain to her that she must not be afraid of him. He could not behave as the French, because he was a Spaniard; he knew that her people were volatile, expert at paying compliments, dancing, wearing fine clothes—everything, in fact, that he was not. But he wanted to explain to her that he would be kind, and all he would ask of her was that she should do her duty as his Queen.

It was when they were at last alone that he laid his hands on her shoulders, and, smiling down at her, said: "Do not be afraid of me. I want you to know that I am not the monster they represented me to be."

"They did not," she said.

"Then why be so afraid of me? Is it because I seem old to you?"

She was stung to truthfulness. "It might be so."

Then he smiled, and the tenderness of his smile succeeded in disarming her, for he was at his best when he was alone with women. "Then," he said, "remember this: because I am so much older than you are, I am more likely to have understanding and be more tender than a younger husband might be. Believe me, it is so."

She did not answer; she continued to tremble, wishing with all her heart that she were at home in the Louvre, and the sounds of Paris were outside instead of the loud rejoicing of the people of Guadalajara.

Philip took her hand and kissed it with tenderness. "Be of good cheer. I will show you that I am no monster. We had to marry because that was good for both our countries. I would like to disperse your fears. I would like to see you smile. I will show you how I long to please you. If you would rather that I did not disturb your rest this night, you have but to say so and . . . I will leave."

She found that she could no longer hold back her tears. She sat very still while they flowed down her cheeks. He stood looking at her in dismay; suddenly she raised her eyes to his.

"I crave your . . . your Majesty's pardon," she stammered. "They said . . . I thought . . . I had not expected you to be so kind . . . and it is that which makes me weep."

So life with His Most Catholic Majesty was not so frightening after all. She could not love him; he was too old and solemn; he was not even like the men of his own age whom she had known in her own country—men like Antoine and his brother the Prince of Condé; he was not like the great Duke of Guise. These men were gallant and charming, amusing and witty; they were always magnificently attired, playing the parts of romantic heroes as well as statesmen and soldiers. Philip was quite different, and it was hard to believe that he was more important than any of them. None would have thought it; the ceremonies in his honor seemed to bore him; he was so quiet, so dignified, so solemn. But for his kindness when they were alone he would have terrified her.

Yet if she was a little afraid of her husband, there was one other who frightened her even more, though a great distance separated them. It seemed to the young Queen of Spain that her mother was never really far away in spirit; Catherine de Medici seemed to be looking over her shoulder on those occasions when the little Queen committed some breach of Spanish etiquette. She seemed to be present even in the royal bed-chamber, admonishing her daughter so to charm this strange man that he would become her slave. The girl was continually mindful of her mother, and during those first months in Spain, although Catherine was far away, it seemed to Elisabeth that the bond between them did not grow less.

She could not forget those instructions she had received before she left home. She was to work for France; she was to tell her mother every little detail of what occurred; she must miss nothing and she must write with the utmost care, remembering that their letters might be intercepted.

Her mother's first command had been that she must win the young Don Carlos to her side. She must make him her friend, and when he was she must show him the pictures of little Margot which would be sent to her in due course; and she must sing Margot's praises to such an extent that the young Prince would be all eagerness to see her.

It was because of her mother that the Queen disregarded Spanish etiquette and sought out Carlos.

He was a strange boy, she knew. Ever since the marriage he had shut himself away, and she had heard that he had hardly spoken to anyone and would eat nothing. He had been coaxed and threatened, yet none knew what was wrong with him and he would not explain. He would open his door to no one but his two companions, his uncle Don Juan and his cousin Alexander Farnese.

The young bride of a few weeks could surely be forgiven if she made mistakes. In any case she did not greatly care if she were not. It was a lifetime habit to obey her mother and this she must continue to do.

So she chose a moment when she could slip away from her attendants unnoticed, and went along to those apartments which she knew belonged to her young stepson.

She entered an antechamber unperceived and quietly opening a door, she found herself in a schoolroom. A boy sat at a table. He was not Carlos, but a very handsome boy—handsome enough to be French, she thought. He stood up, and with a grace which might also have been French, bowed low.

Now she recognized him as Don Juan—her husband's young half-brother, who was a little younger than herself.

"Your gracious Majesty . . ." he began.

She answered in her charming Castilian. "Please . . . please . . . no ceremony. I should not be here, you know. Are you working?"

"Yes, your Majesty."

"And the Prince, my stepson?"

"He should be here, your Highness, but he has just left in a passion."

"In a passion?"

"He will not tell us what troubles him, but he is very angry."

"I would I could see him."

"He swears he will see no one, your Highness; but if that is a command . . ."

She laughed. "No . . . no. I would not command. I do not wish him to think that because I ask something he must obey me. I would rather he looked upon me as a friend."

A door opened and Carlos stood on the threshold. He said: "Isabella!"

She smiled at him and his heart began to hammer that mad litany: "Mine . . . Mine . . ."

She came toward him and her smile held all the charm of which he had dreamed. He knelt suddenly and kissed the hem of her robe; he remained on his knees looking up at her.

"I should not have come thus," she said. "But I wished to see you."

And still he continued to kneel and gaze up at her.

"You must tell me to go," she said, "if that is what you wish. You must forget that I am the Queen. I would not dream of . . . commanding you to receive me . . . if you did not wish to do so."

"Isabella," he said slowly, "you would but have to command and I should obey."

He rose to his feet, still looking at her, marveling at the beauty of her oval, childish face, the eyes that were deep-set and heavily lashed, the sweet, childish mouth. And her dress was beautiful. It was meant to be simple, but French simplicity was so much more becoming than Spanish grandeur.

He became aware of Juan, who was clearly marveling at the change in him, and he was angry that any should share this moment with him and Isabella.

He cried: "Begone! The Queen comes to visit *me*. You are dismissed."

Juan, good-natured, easy-going, indifferent to his nephew's whims, lifted a shoulder and, bowing to the Queen, retired. He wondered whether he ought to tell some responsible person that her Majesty was alone with the mad Prince.

"Carlos," she said, "I wish us to be friends. I think we should be, do you not? For we are of an age and . . . do you remember . . . they once intended us to marry?"

"Yes," he said, with smoldering passion. "I do indeed remember."

"Well, 'twas not to be, and so you are my stepson. But we are friends . . . the best of friends."

"You never had a friend like Carlos."

"I am glad to hear you say that. I thought you might not like me."

"How could that be?" he cried. "You are beautiful, Isabella."

"Isabella!" she repeated. "I must get used to that. It is always Isabella now. I was Elisabeth at home."

"Elisabeth is French, and you are Spanish now."

"Yes. I am Spanish now."

"Do you mind?"

Her face clouded a little. "It is hard . . . at first, but it is our lot. That is what my papa said. It was the fate of princes and princesses, he said, and although it was hard at first, sometimes we find great happiness."

Carlos was fascinated. He watched her lips as she talked; her pronunciation of the familiar words made them so attractively unfamiliar. He was so moved that he wanted to put his arms about her and weep.

He saw that there were tears in her eyes. In her frank French way, she explained, "It is because of my father. I always cry when I think of him."

"Did you not hate your father?"

"Hate him? How could I? He was the best father in the world." She saw the hatred in his face and she cried out in alarm: "Carlos! What is it? You look so fierce."

He could not yet tell her of the great passion in his life. He must not frighten her; perhaps she had not yet learned to hate Philip. Carlos was afraid that if he told her his thoughts he would frighten her, and if she were frightened she might run away.

"Nay," he said. "I am not fierce. I am happy because you came to see me."

"I thought I might offend you. You Spaniards stand on such ceremony, do you not? Oh, Carlos, I am glad you did not mind my coming to see you. I shall come again, Carlos, now that you and I are friends."

"I shall never forget that you wanted to see me, Isabella. I shall never forget that you came like this."

"You are so different, Carlos, from what I thought you would be. Then we *are* friends. Show me your books. Tell me how you live here. And I will tell you about France, shall I? That is if you wish to know."

"I wish to know all about you. I have learned to read French because I wished to speak to you. But I should be afraid to speak it."

"Oh, speak it, Carlos, speak it! You do not know how happy that would make me! How I long to hear it!"

"You would laugh."

"Only because I should be happy to hear it. Come then."

Carlos laughed and blushed and said in French with a very strong Castilian accent: "Isabella, I am happy you are come. Carlos bids you welcome to Spain."

And she did laugh, but so tenderly that he was happy. Then the tears came to her eyes and she said: "You learned that for me, Carlos. That is the nicest thing that has happened to me since I came to Spain."

Then she put her hands on his shoulders and bent her head, for she was taller than he was, and she kissed him first on his right cheek, then on his left. That moment, Carlos was sure, was the happiest in his life.

He was showing her his books, and she was telling him about the court of France when the door opened and Alexander Farnese and Juan looked in.

Neither the Queen nor the Prince noticed them; and the two boys shut the door and looked at each other in astonishment, as they tip-toed away.

What had happened to Don Carlos? they wondered.

The court was in despair.

The young Queen was dangerously ill. She had danced the night before as gaily as any, though many had noticed that she seemed unusually flushed. They had thought at the time that this was due to excitement, but the next morning there was no doubt that she was in a high fever.

The Queen was suffering from that dread disease, the smallpox.

She had felt too sick to rise from her bed that day. Philip, who had spent the morning with his councillors, heard the news as he left the council chamber.

"The Queen is ill, your Highness."

"Ill? Ill? But she was well last night."

"Yes, but, your Majesty, when her ladies went to attend her rising this morning, they were alarmed; they called the physicians. We fear the smallpox."

A sense of blank despair swept over Philip. He felt desolate. She had seemed to be a pleasant child, amusing with her foreign ways and very pleasing to the eye, but . . . just a child, a useful child who would cement French and Spanish friendship while she was young enough to give him the son he desired.

But was that all she meant to him? Now he thought of her piteous gratitude because he was not the monster she had expected; he was kind, she had said. Did she know that there were times when he had absented himself because he presumed that was what she wished? Did she realize that he, so utterly sensitive, having suffered marriage with an aging woman, could understand something of her dilemma? She was so charming; all agreed on that.

He knew in that moment, and the knowledge brought surprise with it, that if he lost her he would be a most unhappy man.

Could he be in love with this child? Was it possible? Surely he had done with emotional love affairs? So he had thought. He had dismissed Catherine Lenez; Isabel Osorio had retired to a convent. Now he was like that young man who had loved Maria Manoela. No, it could not be. He was sad because the charming creature was ill. He was merely disturbed because, if she died, he would have to make another marriage, and so much time would have been wasted and the bond with France slackened. He had decided there should be no emotional disturbances in his life. He was dedicated to God and his country.

But, more than anything, he wanted to see her.

As he made his way to her apartments he met the physicians.

"Your Majesty," they cried, "it would be unwise to go into her chamber now. We are certain. It is the smallpox."

"I should see her," he answered. "She will expect to see me. I must reassure her that everything shall be done . . ."

"Your Majesty . . . the pox is highly contagious. It would be against our advice that you enter the chamber."

He hesitated. They were right, of course; he was foolish and it was so rarely that he acted foolishly or even impulsively. What had happened to him when he had left the council chamber and had heard the news of her illness? He was unsure. He was so deeply disturbed.

But he must see her. She was so young and she would be afraid. He *must* reassure her as he had reassured her on their wedding night when she had been so terrified of facing marriage with the King of Spain. Poor little Princess, she had come through one ordeal and now must face another. The King of Spain or Death—which would be more terrifying to his little bride? Of course he must see her. He must reassure her. Remember, said his common sense, always at his elbow, you would jeopardize your life—that life which is devoted to the service of God and the country—you would sacrifice *that* to an emotional whim! It was folly. It was unworthy of Philip the King and God's partner here on Earth.

Still he walked on. The physicians were staring after him in consternation, but he paid no attention to them.

A wild figure came running along the corridor. It was his son. "Carlos!" he cried.

Carlos's face was blotched with weeping, and when Philip caught the boy by the arm he stared sullenly at his father.

"Where do you go?" asked Philip.

Carlos stammered: "She is ill. Isabella . . . She is dying. She will want to see me."

"You are mad. She has the pox. You dare not go to her."

"I will. She is sick and ill. She will wish to see *me*."

"You shall not go!" said Philip sternly. "The risk is too great. Do you not know that?"

"Do you think I care for risks? I care only that she is ill. And I am her friend."

"Go back to your apartments."

"I will not." Carlos scowled at his father. "Let me go. I will go to her."

"Carlos, calm yourself."

"You cannot forbid me . . . I . . . who am her friend."

"I am her husband," said Philip. He signed to two men-at-arms and bade them conduct Don Carlos back to his apartments and keep guard on him that he might not leave them.

Carlos, struggling, his heart filled with black hatred, was led away, while Philip opened the door and went into the sick-room.

She opened her eyes and smiled at him. He had sent everyone away. He wanted none to witness the emotional scene which he half feared might take place.

She was conscious enough to know what he risked by coming to her like this.

"You must go," she said.

"Isabella," he began almost shyly, "I wanted to tell you . . ."

She smiled, but her glance was vague; it was as though she looked beyond him to someone at the foot of her bed. So strong was the impression she gave him of seeing someone that he turned to look; but there was no one there.

"Isabella," he went on, "you must not die. You must not."

"No . . ." she whispered. "There is too much to do . . . for France."

"Isabella, look at me. I have come to see you."

Now her eyes were upon him. "You *must* not stay," she cried. "It may be death."

Nevertheless, he took her hand and kissed it.

"Do you know why I am here, Isabella?" he asked with passionate tenderness. "It is because I thought you would be the happier for seeing me."

"You must not . . . Oh, you must not. But you are kind to me . . . you are very kind."

"Please, Isabella, do all you can . . . to get well . . . not for France, but for me. And when you are well, little Isabella, we shall be happy . . . you and I!"

She did not seem to hear his words, and because of this he whispered: "Isabella, I believe I love you. I know I love you, little one."

There was consternation at the Louvre. Couriers were galloping between France and Spain.

Catherine de Medici was terrified that her daughter would die and that she herself would lose contact with Spain; she was also afraid that even if Elisabeth recovered she would be so ravaged by the disease that she would lose all claim to beauty. Catherine, herself being in no way attractive, attached great importance to the power of feminine beauty. That was why she had, at home in France, gathered about her a band of beauties, her *Escadron Volant*, to fascinate soldiers and statesmen whose secrets she wished to learn. She had hoped that her beautiful young daughter would so charm her husband that he would be ready to betray his state secrets to her; and that Elisabeth, like the dutiful daughter Catherine had brought her up to be, would pass on those secrets to her mother.

Catherine therefore sent for her magicians, René and the notorious brothers, Cosmo and Lorenzo Ruggieri; and with them she concocted lotions to preserve the skin. They decided that if the skin of a person suffering from smallpox were spread liberally with the white of eggs, disfigurement could be avoided. Accordingly she sent instructions to the French ladies of the young Queen's retinue, at the same time demanding a constant flow of news concerning her daughter's progress.

She had always been worried about Elisabeth's health. There were certain irregularities which she had kept secret and had insisted on Elisabeth's keeping secret, for she feared they indicated that her daughter—as she believed was the case with some of her other children—had inherited through her grandfather, François Premier, the ill effects of that disease of which he had died and which was called by the French *La Malade Anglaise.*

As soon as she knew that her daughter would recover, Catherine wrote to her: "Remember, my child, what I told you before you left. You know quite well how important it is that none should know what malady you may have. If your husband knew of it, he would never come near you . . ."

Although she felt so much better, the little Queen was very uneasy when she received that letter. Her attendants could not understand her grief. They held up mirrors before her that she might see her pretty face with the skin as clear as it had been before her illness.

"You must thank your mother for this," they said. "She sent so many lotions, but it was the egg remedy which saved your complexion."

But thoughts of her mother, they noticed, could do little to soothe the Queen.

She was naturally glad to be well again and to see that her skin was smooth and beautiful; but she could not forget how Philip, at great risk to himself, had visited her daily; and, she reasoned with herself, if it was true that she was affected by a very terrible hereditary disease, it seemed even more wicked not to tell him now than it had before.

When he came to her, sat by her couch, held her hand, and brought her presents of rich jewels and fruit, she wanted to tell him; but she dared not, because she still felt the influence of her mother in the room.

She dared not disobey her mother.

Now she was well again and there were celebrations to mark her recovery.

Philip seemed almost young, kissing and caressing her when they were alone together. Nor did she object to those caresses; she felt it was rather wonderful that he, the most powerful King in the world, so stern and cold to others, should be almost gay when he was alone with her, taking an interest, it seemed, in the dresses and jewels she wore.

There were so many dresses—all richly embroidered and cut in the French style; she wore a new one every day, for once she had worn them she liked to give them away, especially to the Spanish ladies, who were delighted to possess a French dress, particularly one which had belonged to the Queen.

But the suspicion that she might be diseased haunted her.

One day she said: "Philip, I do so much hope that I shall have a child, but sometimes I fear . . ."

"Dear little Isabella, why should you fear? You shall have every care in the world when the time comes."

But he was afraid as he said those words. He was a young man again in the bedroom of Maria Manoela; he was sitting by the bed of a young wife who was too near death to be conscious of his presence. He would be haunted all his life by a young bride whom he had loved briefly, and so tragically lost. It was alarming to think of this lovely young girl, facing the danger which had robbed him of Maria Manoela.

She saw the fear in his face and she said quickly: "Why are *you* afraid?"

He was silent, wondering how he could explain to her what she was beginning to mean to him. He could not say to her: "I had thought I was done with emotional entanglements. There were so many good reasons why we should marry and be content with our marriage; they are enough. I am dedicated to my destiny, and my greatest wish is that you should have a son; and if you fail in this and die in the attempt, why then, I must quickly get myself a new wife. Sons for Spain; an heir to take the place of Carlos. That is the very reason for our union."

Yet he was beginning to suffer as once before he had suffered. He was beginning to dread the time when she would bear their child.

She could not understand his thoughts.

"I . . . I did not mean," she said quickly, "that I was afraid of the *pain* of bearing a child. It was that . . . there might not be a child. Queens do not bear children as easily as commoners, it seems."

"Is that all you fear, Isabella?" he asked.

Briefly she hesitated. Then she said: "I am afraid . . . that I . . ." But she could not go on, because it seemed that her mother was there, forbidding her.

"I would not have you afraid of anything," he said gently.

"But it is my duty to have children, and if . . ."

"It is our duty," he said with a return of his solemn manner. "Let us hope that before long we shall have a child." He paused and said quickly: "You will not suffer in the ordeal more than I shall."

Then she made one of her pretty gestures. She threw her arms about him.

"You are so good to me . . ." she said. "You are so kind."

Her mother sent pictures from France. There was a beautiful one of Margot. The little girl, with her slanting, merry eyes and her gay little mouth with that expression of sauciness, was enchanting. There was also one of Catherine, her mother.

She read the accompanying letter:

"These pictures are for you, my dearest daughter. Show them to the

Prince, particularly the one of little Marguerite. Is it not charming? Little Margot grows irresistible. Everyone loves her. Do not forget what you have to do for your sister. If your husband were to die, you would be the most unfortunate woman in the world, for what would your position be? There would be a new Queen of Spain, the wife of Don Carlos. If that wife were your sister Margot, why then your position would be assured. So you *must* bring about this match . . ."

She must. Of course she must. And what fun it would be if Margot were there with her! She tried to imagine the high-spirited Margot—who had already announced her intention of marrying her dear friend Henry of Guise—in this court, married to Carlos. Henry of Guise was the most handsome boy she had ever seen. And Carlos? Well, she was fond of him because he was so gentle with her, and if he was in one of his passions, she alone could bring him out of it; but what would Margot think of him?

She went along to the apartments of Carlos, taking the pictures with her. She came and went as she liked now. She had dispensed with much of the ceremony which it behooved the Queen of Spain to use. No one seemed to mind. This was the enchanting Isabella, the favored one. Everyone loved her, including the King; and they could see no harm in anything she did. She was just a charming child for all that she was the Queen of Spain.

"Carlos," she cried. "I am here."

He was with his companions, Alexander and Juan. They all stood up to greet her, and she joined them at the table. They sat around it like four children, only there was a look of passionate yearning in the eyes of Carlos which was unchildlike.

"I have brought some pictures to show Carlos."

She put it in that way because she knew it would please him that the pictures were mainly for him to see. *He* must be the one she came to visit. If he thought she came to see any of the others, he would not reprove *her*, but he would sink into deep melancholy. She could, with a word, make him happy or sad. And she must please him; it was her duty to please him; those were her mother's instructions.

So now she produced the pictures.

"They have just come. Look! There are two of them."

"I am to see them," said Carlos, elbowing the others away. "Isabella brought them for me, did not your Highness?"

"I brought them for you to see, Carlos. But the others may look if they wish. Which do you like better, Carlos? Tell me first and then I will tell you who they are."

He was so happy to have Isabella there, so happy to be near her. He smiled first at her, to let her know that she was more interesting to him than any picture could be.

He said: "Ah, this *chiquita* . . . she is beautiful."

"She is indeed. She is my sister; and the elder lady is my mother."

"I do not like so well your mother," said Carlos.

"No; indeed you would not, for she would seem so old to you."

"And fat," said Carlos. "But the little one is so pretty."

Juan asked her name.

"It is Marguerite, but my brother Charles nicknamed her Margot. She is the gayest creature I ever knew. How I wish she were here!"

"I wish I could bring her to you, if that would please you," said Carlos wistfully.

"Mayhap she could come on a visit?" suggested Alexander.

"It is a long journey," said Isabella. "I wonder how she would like it here."

"You are sad," Carlos put in.

"Only when I think of those at home in France. There were so many of us. François, who is now the King, and Charles, Henri, Claude, Margot, and little Hercule . . ."

"Well," said Juan, "now you have Carlos, Alexander, and Juan."

She smiled and kissed them in turn. It was astonishing to them, but they knew it was the way of the French.

Carlos could not bear to see her kiss the others; he put his arms about her and clung to her as long as he dared.

She showed the pictures to Philip, interrupting him while he was busy with his dispatches from all over the Empire.

There was bad news from Flanders. He knew that Orange was organizing a revolt.

He was sitting deep in thought, when she appeared—an enchanting vision in her Parisian dress, her black hair dressed in a new style. How could he help but be delighted to see her? It was so much more pleasant to contemplate her than the treacherous Orange.

"But I am interrupting," she said. "I came to show you the pictures which have arrived from Paris."

"Everything that is charming would seem to come from Paris," he said. "I pray you, let me see the pictures."

She showed him the one of her mother first. The plump, inscrutable face looked back at him.

"And the other is my little sister. This is beautiful. Is she not charming? Do you like this picture, Philip?"

"Very much."

"I wish you could see Margot." She looked at him wistfully. "Oh, Philip, how _I_ wish that I could see her."

She sat, rather timidly, it was true, upon his knee. The French were so demonstrative, but he understood. She was going to ask some favor. It was a little childish of her, but then he loved her childishness. And this was a habit they would have taught her in the French court.

He looked at her quizzically yet indulgently, and she went on: "Carlos will have to have a wife. He grows old. Philip . . . would it not be wonderful if he could marry my sister Marguerite?"

Now it was all quite clear. So Madame le Serpent had set his own wife to cajole him. Catherine had made one of her daughters Queen of Spain, and she wished to make sure that the Queen who followed should be a daughter of hers. Catherine clearly set great store by Spanish friendship; but the woman was not so clever as she rated herself. Did she think he was a besotted fool to be persuaded on matters of state policy even by the most charming of wives?

He drew Isabella toward him and put his arm about her; and as he did so he looked at the plump, flat face of the woman in the picture.

He was thinking: Yes, Madame, you sent me your daughter and I made her my wife. From now on she shall be my wife entirely and cease to be your obedient daughter. If she is to act the spy and agent, it is better that she should act so for her husband than for her mother.

And he decided that he would mold her; he would make her completely his. He had won her friendship and affection with his gentleness; before long he would win her passionate devotion; then she would be free from her mother's influence.

At length he answered: "My dearest, we must not think of marriage for Carlos at this stage. He does not enjoy good health; and I do not intend to allow him to marry until his health has greatly improved. If and when such a time should come, I will choose a wife for him. Until then, let us not think of his marrying." Seeing her disappointment, he smiled wryly. "Why," he went on, "your little sister looks so gay. The Louvre is the place for her. Do not brood on the marriages of others; think only of ours, which we are discovering to be a good one, are we not?"

"Yes, Philip, but . . ."

"Isabella," he interrupted, "your mother writes often to you, does she not?"

"Why, yes, indeed."

"You never show me her letters."

"N . . . no. Was it your wish that I should?"

He saw the panic in her eyes and marveled at the power of a woman who could arouse it at such great distance. "Only if you wished to show them to me," he said.

"I . . . I would, of course, do so if you wished it."

He took her hand and kissed it tenderly. "There are times when I think you are afraid of your mother. Are you, my dear?"

"Afraid of her . . . but I love her. I love all my family."

"Perhaps it is possible to love and fear. I would not have you afraid. There is nothing to fear. Why should the Queen of Spain fear the Queen Mother of France? Tell me that."

"I do not know. But she is my mother and we always had to do what she wished."

"Or be beaten? Tell me, did she beat you often?"

"There were times."

He laughed, and permitted himself to show a little of the tenderness that surged through him. He held her fast against him and said: "No one shall beat you anymore, my Isabella. There is no need to fear anyone, particularly those who are far away and cannot reach you. If they should ask you to do what you do not wish to do, then you must refuse. And if you should be afraid—why, here is the King of Spain to defend you."

He laughed, and his laughter was always pleasant to hear, because it was so rare; so she laughed with him.

"Then you will promise me not to be afraid anymore; and if you are, you will tell me all about it?"

"Yes," she said with only the faintest trace of hesitancy. "I will."

"Then take your pictures, and when I have finished with these papers I will join you. Perhaps we will ride together. Or shall I show you my new pictures and tapestries? Anything that you wish."

"I should like to ride," she said.

She picked up her pictures and went from the room. She was a little relieved, for he was right. It *was* rather silly to be frightened of someone living hundreds of miles away, when the most powerful monarch in the world was your husband who had sworn to protect you.

What Philip did not understand was—and how could she explain this?—that, while it was true she was afraid of her mother, she was also afraid of him.

With the passing weeks Philip's love intensified. He had never been so happy, in spite of the troubles in his dominions. He felt young again. He faced the extraordinary fact that he was in love, even as he had been in the days of his first marriage with the pretty little Maria Manoela.

But how much better this could be. Maria Manoela, charming as she was, had been an uneducated girl compared with Isabella. Isabella was young, it was true; she was very gay—with her French attendants; she loved fine clothes and jewels, but that was because she was French.

She would mature. He remembered how he had thought thus of Maria Manoela. One day he would be able to explain his feelings to Isabella. Had he not assured himself that this would be the case with

Maria Manoela? And when he had told her, it had been too late; she was by that time deaf to his eloquent explanations. But what had happened in the case of Maria Manoela would not happen with Isabella. History did not repeat itself as neatly as that.

No! He had loved his first wife and lost her; he had hated his second marriage; he had suffered enough. And now he had come to the third, why should he not enjoy perfect happiness? He would. In time she would return his passionate love, but he must wait for that day. He must be patient; he felt that if only he could override that absurd fear she had of him, all would be well. He knew that there were times when she forgot he was the King of Spain; she forgot the stories she had heard of him and was spontaneously happy. Well, it would come. He could feel confident in the future.

In the meantime there was Carlos to disturb his peace. If only Carlos had never been born, or had died at birth, what a lot of trouble would have been avoided!

One day when he and Isabella had been riding together and returned to the palace, Philip discovered that Carlos was about to cause him even more anxiety than he had so far.

Isabella had retired to her room when the Prince's tutor presented himself to Philip. The tutor was distraught.

There had been a particularly painful scene that morning. The Prince had looked from his window and seen the King and Queen riding out with their attendants; he had then seemed to go quite mad, and, picking up a knife, had rushed at the nearest person—who happened to be this tutor.

"Sire, but for Don Juan and Don Alexander, I doubt I should have been here now to tell this to your Majesty."

"Where is he now?" asked Philip.

"He fell into a fit almost immediately, your Majesty. He lashed out with feet and fists; but afterward grew calm and, as is usual after such experiences, he lay quiet and still, speaking to no one."

"What caused the trouble?"

"We have no idea, your Highness."

But the man had some idea. Philip saw it in his face. He was on the point of demanding an explanation, but thought better of it, and decided to see his son for himself.

He went along to Carlos's apartments and there dismissed everyone. Carlos, white and shaken after the fit, stared sullenly at his father.

"Why do you come here?" he snarled. "To taunt me?"

"Carlos, I came to ask you what is the meaning of this outburst. I know you cannot control your actions when you are in such a state, but it is your own passion which brings on these unfortunate lapses."

"You know!" cried Carlos. "You know, do you not? I saw you. You know that she would have come to see *me* this morning. You knew it, and that is why you took her away from me. Was she not to have married *me*? She was mine . . . *mine* . . . and *you* took her. You took her from me. I had her picture and I learned to speak French for her. She was mine and you knew it, and you hated me. You wanted to hurt me as you always have. I love Isabella . . . and you have taken her from me."

Philip stared in horror at his son.

Now he understood the horrible truth. Carlos was mad enough to fancy he was in love with Isabella.

What horror could not grow out of such a situation, when a semi-maniac such as Carlos was involved? Who knew what tragedy lay ahead of them?

Prompt action was needed as it never had been needed before.

Philip turned and hurried from the room.

Within an hour he had decided that Don Carlos was not being educated in accordance with his rank. He was to leave Toledo at once for Alcala del Henares, that he might have the benefit of the best teachers at the University there.

Don Juan and Don Alexander should accompany him, and there should not be a day's delay.

Those were the King's commands.

*P*hilip was afraid, for Isabella was very ill, and he had a horror of childbirth.

He must think of those days which had followed the death of his first wife, and he could not rid himself of the superstitious fear that in love he was doomed to frustration. First Maria Manoela had died. Was it now to be Isabella?

Very little else seemed of any real importance to him now. His troops had suffered a great defeat at Tunis, and it seemed as if the Turks' hold on the Mediterranean was becoming firmer. Here was a blow against the Faith itself. The Infidel was encroaching on Europe; and no Spaniard, remembering the tragic history of his country, could feel complacent. The Netherlands were clearly preparing to break into open revolt. Yet Philip could think of nothing but Isabella.

In the first months of her pregnancy he had had a silver chair made for her so that she might not tire herself by walking. In it she had been carried everywhere. He had to face the truth; for all her vivacity, she was not strong and she seemed to droop and fade like a flower in the heat of the sun.

Then had come the miscarriage. There was to be no child, and Isabella's life was in danger.

He went to her bedchamber and sat by her bed. Day and night he stayed there, hoping that she would open her eyes and smile at him.

At times it seemed almost unbearably like that other occasion. But this was different. She was not going to die, and eventually she began to recover. She was very thin and her black hair seemed too heavy for her little head to carry; she wore it loose about her shoulders, for to have it piled on her head tired her so.

His only pleasure at that time was in arranging for her convalescence. He himself decided how she should rest, what she should eat. The women about her marveled, for the King of Spain had become a more devoted nurse than any of them.

The Queen was aware of this, and sometimes she would look at Philip with anxious puzzled eyes. One day she said to him: "It is a sad thing when a Queen cannot bear her husband sons."

"You are a child yourself," answered Philip. "And I am not old. There are many years left to us, for which I daily thank God."

"What if I should *never* bear a child?"

"My dear, you must not say such things. Of course you will. I know you will."

"It may be that I shall not."

"We will not think of such a thing."

"Is it not better to face facts, Philip?"

"You have become solemn during your illness, Isabella."

"Nay. This thought has been with me often. The King of England put away his wives because they could not bear him sons."

"He cut off the head of one because he wanted another woman. Have no fear, Isabella. I am not the King of England."

"But you are the King of Spain; and the King of Spain needs sons even as did the King of England."

"I have one son."

"Carlos!"

"Oh, I admit I should like to have others . . . yours and mine, my dear. That I should like more than anything. But it will happen yet. Shall we lose heart because of one failure?"

"Philip, there is something you must know. You should have known before."

"Well, Isabella?"

"The King of England could not get sons, and some say it was because his body was diseased. He suffered from *La Malade Anglaise*, some say."

"I have heard that."

"My grandfather suffered from that same disease. He died of it."

"What are you trying to tell me?"

"Perhaps I am not the right wife for you."

Her eyes were blank; he could not read the thoughts behind them. Did some part of her long for escape? Words came to his lips—tender and pleading. But all he said was: "You are. Of course you are. You are my wife. Is that not enough?"

She would not look at him. She said slowly: "But if I cannot give you sons . . . if I should be unable to give you sons . . ."

"Have no fear. If God wishes us to have sons we shall have them. Everything that happens to us is due to the will of God."

"Philip, I am glad that you know of the rumors concerning my grandfather."

"I have always known of them."

She was thinking that her own brother Charles was wild, even as Carlos was wild, that François, the young King, suffered from many infirmities. It was God's law that the children should suffer even unto the third and fourth generation for the sins of such fathers. If she was doomed to suffer for her grandfather's excesses, she must accept God's will as Philip would.

She was comforted and relieved because he knew of these things. There he sat, at her bedside, and she was aware of the warmth of his feelings beneath that cold surface. During her illness she had been perpetually conscious of his devotion.

He was a strange man, but he was good to her. She was more fond of him than she had ever been before; she put out her hand and he took it. She thought: If I were not afraid of him I could love him.

She was grateful; he had helped her escape from the fear which had dominated her childhood. She was no longer afraid of her mother, because she was under the protection of the man who would dominate her life from now on, and whom she might one day love.

There was bad news of Carlos. When was news of Carlos ever good?

Messengers came to Philip, who was staying in the Valladolid Palace at that time. He had been enjoying a certain peaceful contentment. He felt that he would soon subdue the Netherlands, and had started work on that great monastery, the Escorial, which, when he had witnessed the desecration of St. Quentin, he had vowed to build. He intended to fill it with the art treasures which his father had taught him to love and revere, and when he was there he would live quietly as a monk. His father had repudiated his crown when he retired to the monastic life. But Philip intended to combine the two. He would spend half his time in fasting and in prayer that he might the better rule his country.

Isabella's health had improved considerably; her high-spirited temperament helped her. She was herself once more, and Philip felt that he had been foolish to have suffered so acutely. She was surely stronger than Maria Manoela had been. Soon there would be children born to them, and if he had a son—a healthy and intelligent boy—he would disinherit Carlos. He had discussed this possibility with Ruy, whose opinion it was that the disinheriting of Carlos—providing the Council agreed to it—could only be of advantage to Spain.

Ruy was grave when he talked of Carlos. He was fully aware of the Prince's feelings for the Queen, and that knowledge Philip knew, disturbed him deeply.

Such were Philip's thoughts when the news was brought to him.

"There has been an accident, your Majesty," said the messenger from Alcala. "The Prince lies nigh to death."

Ruy was with Philip at the time. Philip could not help but be aware of the sudden tension in his friend. Was it hope?

Philip betrayed nothing of his feelings, and the messenger hurried on. "It was a few nights ago, your Highness. The night was very dark and the Prince, hurrying down a staircase in his establishment, slipped and fell from top to bottom. He received injuries to his head and spine . . . terrible injuries Highness."

"You came straight to me?" said Philip.

"Yes, your Highness."

"And it is some days since the accident," said Ruy. "We know not what may have happened in the meantime."

"I shall leave at once for Alcala," said Philip.

Ruy rode beside him when they left. Philip knew that Ruy regarded the accident in the light of a blessing. Carlos was no good to Spain, no good to Philip; therefore, Ruy's thoughts would run, it is well to be rid of him.

Philip knew, even as Ruy did, that while Carlos lived he would give trouble to all, and in particular to his father. Ruy worshipped logic, but Philip worshipped duty. However painful that duty, Philip would follow it. Ruy would have delayed on the journey so that the best physicians, who were with the court, might not reach Carlos in good time; but Philip saw nothing but the need to save his son, whatever misery that might bring to himself or to Carlos.

With all urgency, the court proceeded to Alcala.

Now the whole of Spain was in mourning. The heir to the throne was dying, wailed the people. They forgot the stories they had heard of his conduct. Don Carlos was the hero now. There were lamentations. There were pilgrimages to the shrines of the saints. Many sought to win Philip's favor by having themselves publicly scourged in the hope, they said, of calling the saints' attention to their sorrow, but actually in the hope of calling the King's attention to their loyalty to the crown.

At Alcala Philip found Carlos in a very low state. He did not recognize his father, and this many thought to be fortunate for it was generally believed that excitement at this time would surely kill the Prince.

Dr. Olivares, the greatest physician in the world, whom Philip had brought with him from Valladolid, examined Carlos, and his verdict was that Carlos would die if nothing was done to save him; there was, he believed, a faint hope that the operation of trepanning might do this. If the King gave his permission for the operation, Dr. Olivares would see that it was carried out with all speed.

With Isabella and Ruy beside him, and his courtiers and statesmen about him, Philip waited for the news; and as he looked at the faces of those gathered about him, he fancied that only in Isabella's did he see any expression of real grief.

Why should she care for the fate of this lame epileptic who was a source of anxiety to all those who came into contact with him? Why, of all these people, should Isabella be the only one who sincerely prayed for the recovery of Carlos?

Philip could not shut out of his mind the memory of a distorted face, of eyes which stared madly into his while a harsh voice cried: "She is mine . . . mine!"

How could he be jealous of a poor, half-mad creature like Carlos?

At length Olivares presented himself to the King, and one look at the doctor's face was enough to tell everyone present that the operation had been successful.

But although Carlos had not died during the operation its results were far from satisfactory. The Prince's head swelled to twice its usual size so that his eyes were completely buried in his flesh and he could not see. A rash broke out on his skin and he suffered agony.

He was in constant delirium, calling perpetually for Isabella; but when she went to him he did not know her. He shouted threats against someone, but as he mentioned no name, those about him could only guess at whom the threats were directed.

Philip prayed for guidance. Isabella knew that he was thinking what a blessing it would be if Carlos died, and she knew that he was fighting against such thoughts. To Philip, duty was all-important, and she was aware that if he believed it was his duty to go into the sickroom, put a cushion over Carlos's face, and suffocate him, he would not hesitate to do so.

Was he wondering even now whether he might hint to the doctors that the moment had come to rid Spain of Carlos?

Her fear of this strange man who was her husband was growing. She would never be able to forget the fanatical light which had shone in his eyes when he had talked to her of the work of the Inquisition. She was dreading the day—for she knew that as Queen of Spain she could not escape it—when she would have to attend an *auto-da-fé*. She recalled with horror the executions her mother had forced her to witness at Amboise. She was a good Catholic, but cruelty horrified her. She could not look on calmly while men and women were tortured, no matter what they believed. Now it seemed to her that she had escaped her mother's tyranny for that of another. The last months had made a woman of a frivolous girl, and as that woman was a tender-hearted one, she could not love a man who thought it righteous and godly to torture men and women, even though he had been to her the kindest of husbands. She was becoming complicated, whereas she had been simple; she wanted to escape, but she knew not how.

Philip decided that it was his duty to do everything in his power to save his son's life.

He explained to Isabella that in the Monastery of Jesu Maria were buried the bones of the Blessed Diego, a Franciscan lay brother, who had led a life of sanctity and was said to work miracles.

"It is years since he died," said Philip, "but his memory has never faded. If he saves the life of my son he shall be canonized."

"Let us pray to him," said Isabella.

"We will do more. I will have his bones dug up, and they shall be brought to Carlos and laid upon him."

Philip's indecision was past. He had found the solution to his tormenting problem. If Carlos was saved through the intercession of the Blessed Diego, he would know that he, Philip, and Spain were not yet to be relieved of their burden.

Carlos was tossing on his bed. Don Andrea Basilo and Dr. Olivares, the King's most worthy physicians, stood by his bedside.

Carlos was moaning in agony. The terrible swelling of his face made him unrecognizable.

Philip arrived in the sick-room, and with him were two monks from the Monastery of Jesu Maria. They carried a box in which were the bones of the Blessed Diego.

Philip said: "We will place them about the body of my son. Then we will kneel and pray to the saint to intercede for us. He is noted for his sympathy for the sick. Doubtless his intercession will succeed."

So the bones of the long-dead monk were placed about Carlos, and some pieces of the cerecloth, in which the body had been wrapped, were scraped off the bones and laid on Carlos's face.

Carlos screamed. "What is this, then? You have come to kill me, I smell death. I smell decay. Is death here then?"

"We have brought the bones of the Blessed Diego," said Olivares.

"You have brought death. I smell it. It fills the room. You have brought death to me. It is my father who has done this because he longs for my death."

Dr. Olivares bent over the bed. "We are striving to save your life," he said. "Pray with us. We have here the bones of the Blessed Diego, and to him we are directing our prayers. The King and the Queen are praying for you now. They pray for a miracle."

"The Queen . . ." said Carlos in a whisper.

"Pray, your Highness. Pray to the Blessed Diego."

Carlos was delirious. He dreamed that he saw a monk rise from his tomb, his body wrapped in cerecloth.

"You will recover, Carlos," said the Holy Man.

In Carlos's delirium, the cerecloth fell away from the body of the monk; and now it was clothed in a dress of the becoming French style, and the dress covered not the old bones, but the beautiful young body of Isabella.

"*I* am praying for you," she said. "Carlos, *I* wish you to be well."

When at last the delirium faded the swelling in his head began to subside. People in the palace and in the town and in all the country were saying: "Here is another miracle of the Blessed Diego."

Carlos had recovered physically, but his mental sickness had taken a more violent turn. Yet he could not be kept at Alcala indefinitely; he was old enough now to take his place at court, and this the people would expect of him. So he came to Madrid where he had for company Don Juan, Alexander Farnese, and his two cousins, the sons of Maximilian and Maria of Austria, who were to be brought up at the Spanish court.

These lively, intelligent young people might have been excellent company for a normal boy; but poor Carlos was far from normal. He was sullen for days on end; he refused to eat for long periods, so that all feared he would starve to death; then he would decide to eat, and make himself ill because he would not do so in moderation. He would rise from his bed in the middle of the night and demand boiled capon; he would lash his attendants with a whip which he kept handy for the purpose, until the food was brought to him. All his attendants longed to be removed from his service, with the exception of his half-brother, Garcia Osorio, who seemed able to soothe him better than anyone else. This boy, perhaps out of gratitude to Philip, had made the Prince his special charge, and would show the utmost tact in dealing with him. Carlos was relying more and more on his half-brother; he tolerated him because, although he was handsome and of lively intelligence, he was illegitimate, and that pleased Carlos, as it gave him a sense of superiority. Young Garcia was of great value in the household, since he could manage Carlos better than anyone except the Queen; and the King had ordered that the Queen should see her stepson but rarely.

It was a matter of continual grievance to Carlos that Isabella was kept from him.

Sometimes he would get together a band of young men—the most dissolute he could find—and they would roam the streets of Madrid, insulting women, pulling off their cloaks, forcing them against walls, and mishandling them. Rape was rarely committed, for Carlos forbade this; this fact set in circulation rumors that he was impotent, which in its turn enraged Carlos. But he did nothing to prove it was not, which supported the belief.

The whole world now knew that the heir of Spain was at least unbalanced. Yet many sought his hand. Catherine de Medici still wanted him for Margot, and sent urgent letters to the Queen of Spain. There was talk of his marrying his Aunt Juana, and Philip himself was not against this. It was said that Carlos and Juana would have made a strange pair—she with her melancholy madness, he with his wild insanity. Philip's sister Maria and her husband Maximilian were very eager to secure him for their daughter Anne. They wrote to him and professed great affection for him.

Carlos liked to imagine himself as a husband—either of Margot or

Anne. A favorite game of his was to imagine himself procuring horses and riding to France, where Catherine de Medici would receive him and marry him to her daughter Margot, or riding to Austria where he would be fêted by his Uncle Max and Aunt Maria, and married to his cousin Anne.

But there was one who remained for him the most desirable in the world, the mere mention of whose name could soften his ugliest moods and bring him back to comparative sanity. That was Isabella— his father's wife.

Although Isabella continued to wear her beautiful dresses and give them away with the utmost extravagance, she could no longer delight in these things. At times she felt homesick for France; but at others she felt she no longer had a part in what was happening in her old home. Margot's letters were gay and inconsequential; they were all about Margot's own adventures and the people who admired her, what she wore, what journeys she made, and how Henry of Guise grew more handsome than ever. But when Isabella thought of her native land nowadays, it was of terrible conflicts between Catholics and Huguenots. There had been such quarrels in the days of her youth, but it was only now, when she was living close to the mighty shadow of the Inquisition, that they seemed to have such horrible significance. The people she had known and loved were involved in wars against each other. There were the Guises against the Prince of Condé and Coligny. There was Jeanne of Navarre, whom she had known so well and with whose little son she had played, in terrible strife with her husband, Antoine, that kinsman with whom she had parted so piteously when she had been brought to Spain. And all these conflicts had their roots in religion. It was incongruous. Christians were supposed to love each other; yet these Christians were fighting . . . killing each other.

She was at length obliged to attend an *auto-da-fé*. She did not know how she would endure that ordeal. The memory of the hot square would live in her mind forever; she would never, she feared, forget the grim Inquisitors, the pomp of the royal gallery, the victims in their yellow garments dragging their tortured bodies to the stakes.

I am a Catholic, she told herself. I know the Catholic Faith to be the only true Faith, but I cannot bear to see these people suffer so. And when I see them I care not that they are heretics. I only want to save them. I find myself caring for nothing ... not for God, not for religion if God and religion demand of us such action.

She felt a hatred toward the land of her adoption because it was the home of torture. She shrank with revulsion from the man who sat beside her in the royal gallery, his eyes intent, the fervor lighting his face. She wanted to cry out in protest when the people shouted with glee and the agonized screams of men and women filled the air while the flames licked their already mutilated bodies.

She wanted to live in a world of kindness and fun—not torture and misery.

One day Madame Clermont, one of the French ladies who had accompanied her into Spain, came to her and intimated that she had something important to say.

When they were alone, Madame Clermont could scarcely speak, she was so excited.

"Your Majesty, I have discovered a Frenchman in distress."

"What is this?" asked Isabella indulgently, for poor Clermont was of a romantic nature and was constantly bewailing the lack of those adventures which had seemed to come about so naturally in France.

"He had an accident in the street close to one of the inns there ... which was fortunate for him. It might have been on the mountain roads, and then Monsieur Dimanche would have said good-bye to this life."

"You are incoherent, Clermont. Who is this Dimanche, and what is this all about?"

"It is very mysterious, dear Majesty; and that is what makes it so exciting. No one seems to know who he is or what his mission; and he, poor man, is too far gone in delirium to speak much sense. But he is handsome—very handsome—and he is a Frenchman. Spanish innkeepers are a grasping breed. Do you know, Highness, they do not wish to keep him in their miserable inn, for fear he should be unable to pay his bill? They do not like foreigners, they say. And that is a slight to your Majesty! They have put him in a barn close by; and he, poor man, is very sick indeed."

"What is he doing here, I wonder?" said Isabella.

"That we shall doubtless discover later; but knowing how interested your Majesty is in our own countrymen, and women, I guessed you would not care to know that one of them was lodged in a barn, and a sick man at that!"

"Indeed I do not," said Isabella. "It is most inhospitable."

"One of the palace serving-women has a comfortable lodging not far from the inn—nor from the palace. If it should be your Majesty's wish that this man be taken there, she is willing to have him, and to care for him until he has recovered."

"Let it be done," said Isabella. "I will send one of my own doctors to him. I should not like a Frenchman to return to France with tales of the ill-treatment he received in Spain."

So the mysterious Frenchman was removed from the barn to the lodging of the serving-woman; and it was some days before Isabella knew what an important problem he was to bring into her life.

For the next day or so Isabella thought no more of the Frenchman. It was her custom to interest herself in her fellow countrymen, and if any visited Spain to do all in her power to see that their stay was enjoyable. It was not the first time she had helped people in distress. She herself would pay the servant in whose house Dimanche was lodged; she would reward her doctor for his services to the man. It appeared to her at that time that there the affair of Dimanche ended.

It was Clermont who brought the news to her—excitable Clermont who looked for drama and romance in everyday life. Drama had certainly been found among the papers of Monsieur Dimanche and, Clermont assured the Queen, in the few words he had let slip in his semi-conscious state.

Clermont begged to be alone with the Queen and, when she was absolutely sure that they would not be overheard, divulged what she had discovered.

"Dearest Highness, I do not know how to tell you. Dimanche is in the service of Spain."

"A Frenchman . . . in the service of Spain!"

"What I have found out, Highness, is horrible. And I do not know what to do. I remember them so well . . . as you do . . . the Queen and her little son. That brightest of boys . . ."

"Clermont, Clermont, what do you mean? Of whom are you speaking?"

"The Queen of Navarre and her son young Henry. There is a conspiracy—and this Dimanche is one of those who will carry it out—to ride to Pau in Navarre, where the Queen is at this time with her son, to kidnap them and bring them here to Spain . . . to . . . the Inquisition."

Isabella could not speak. The memories were too vivid. She was back in that hideous square; she was watching the shambling figures in their yellow robes. Their faces had been indistinct; perhaps she had not had the courage to look at their faces; perhaps she did not want those to haunt her all the days of her life. But now there would be faces . . . the faces of the Queen of Navarre—dear Aunt Jeanne—and little Henry, the rough young Béarnais of whom, in spite of his crudeness, they had all been so fond.

A plot had been discovered through this accident to one of the conspirators, a plot to take honest, noble Jeanne and torture her and burn her alive—and perhaps her little son with her. And Fate had brought this to the knowledge of the Queen of Spain.

"Highness," cried Clermont, "what shall we do? What can we do?"

Isabella did not speak. She could only hear the chanting voices, taking the terrible Oath; she saw the man beside her—the man she had married—his eyes aflame, his sword in his hand, swearing to serve the Inquisition, to torture and murder—yes, murder—Jeanne of Navarre because she was a heretic.

At length her voice sounded in her ears, firm and ringing, so that she did not recognize it. "It must not be."

"No!" cried Clermont excitedly. "No, your Highness. It must not be. But what can we do?"

What could she do—she the little Queen, the petted darling? Could she go to Philip and beg him not to do this thing? It would be useless, for she would not be pleading with the indulgent husband; it was that man with the eyes of flame and the sword in his hand who had decided the fate of Jeanne of Navarre.

It would be so easy to weep, to shudder, to try to forget. She had been her mother's creature, now she was Philip's.

But she would not be. She was herself—Isabella, kinswoman of the noble Jeanne; for noble she was, heretic though she might be.

So she said again: "It must not be." And then: "It shall not be."

She was going to fight this evil. She was going to pit her wits against Philip, against the Inquisition. She did not care what happened to her. She was going to do everything in her power to save Jeanne.

How?

It was not impossible. The chief conspirator was for the time being a victim of his accident. It would, she gathered, be some days before he could set about his diabolical work.

She said: "We have a few days' start of him."

"Yes, Highness. But what shall we do?"

"It is simple. We must see that she is warned."

"How?"

"By sending a messenger into Navarre."

"Dearest lady, this is dangerous. Can *you* send such a messenger?"

"I have my servants."

"They are the servants of his Majesty."

Isabella was silent, and Clermont, her face suddenly very grave, went on: "If you do this, you are working against the King your husband."

Isabella answered: "I know it." Her young face hardened suddenly with resolution. "And I will do it," she said.

She was no one's creature now. She was indeed herself; and so should it be to the end of her days.

But who could help her? Whom could she trust?

There was one who would do all in his power to please her, one who would keep her secret from Philip.

She had begun to realize how loyal all these people of the court were to their King. There was only one of them who would go against him.

Don Juan, Alexander, Garcia, the young Austrian Princes, Ruy, and all the courtiers and statesmen could not be trusted. She knew that if she told them of her need they might agree to help her or not, but they would all consider it their duty to lay their knowledge before the King.

If she asked one of her grooms to take a message to Navarre, how could she be sure that he would obey her in what must surely be done in disobedience to the King? Surely, they would reason, if she wished to send a message to her kinswoman she should not have to do it in secret unless it was against the wishes of the King.

There was one alternative, and however unwise it might be she must take it. She must warn Jeanne.

Carlos had lately been collecting horses. She knew that he had been making wild plans to escape from Spain to France or Austria, taking with him one or two of his attendants, whom he believed he could trust. He was constantly sending away horses from his stables and bring-ing in new ones. There were a few men who would be faithful to the Prince, for even if they did not love and respect him, they believed that he would one day come to the throne.

Yes, Carlos had it in his power to help her now; and there was no one else whom she could trust.

She sought him out and told him that she wished to speak to him privately; she asked if he would take a walk with her in the gardens.

When they were safe from eavesdroppers, she said: "Carlos, I want your help. I need it badly."

Carlos was delighted.

"I will do anything," he assured her. "You have but to ask me."

"I must have horses and riders. Perhaps two horses and two trusty men. You will not betray me, Carlos?"

"Dearest Isabella, they could torture me on the *chevalet* and I would never betray you."

"I knew it, Carlos. God bless you. You are my friend."

"You never had a truer friend, Isabella."

"Then promise you will be calm, for we need calmness."

"I will be calm. Look at me, Isabella. See how calm I am."

"Yes, Carlos, I see. I should not burden you with this, but I can trust no one else. The King must not know."

Now Carlos was eager. He had a secret with Isabella, and Philip was shut out. This was one of his happiest dreams come true.

"I have to get a message to my aunt, the Queen of Navarre. She must be warned to leave Navarre at once and ride to Paris, and she must take her son with her, for there is a plan to capture her and hand her to the Inquisition."

Carlos's eyes gleamed. "My father plans that," he said. "He is angry because the French do not fight the Huguenots as he would have them do. Isabella, shall we fight with the Huguenots? Are we heretics, then?"

"Nay, Carlos. It is not that. We are good Catholics. But she is my dear kinswoman and I cannot bear to think of them torturing her. It makes me so unhappy. Perhaps I am a bad Catholic, but when I see strangers hurt I become desperately unhappy, and I would rather die myself than see my aunt taken. I would risk God's displeasure if need be."

"We will defy them all, Isabella."

"Carlos, you have the horses. Will you help me to get a message to her?"

"At once. Oh, Isabella, thank you . . . thank you for making me so happy. We will send two riders and each shall take a different route. I would I could go myself . . . Then you would see what I would do for you."

"I see it now, Carlos."

"I can send riders whom none will miss. I . . . I . . . You see . . ." He began to laugh suddenly and wildly.

"Carlos," she begged, "do not laugh like that. You will spoil every-thing. Be calm and clever as you have been."

He was silent at once. "I will be calm and clever. And I will be happy because in this we are together . . . you and I, Isabella . . . against Philip."

She shivered, and, gripping her arms, he looked up into her face and cried: "I am happy . . . happy . . . happy, Isabella. I am happy tonight."

He looked sane now, and almost handsome. She wanted to weep, not only for his madness, but for that other madness which made men delight in torturing each other.

FOUR

*T*he memory of the part she played in saving Jeanne from the Inquisition never left Isabella. It was one of the most momentous things she had ever done, and marked a turning point in her life.

Philip never discovered the part she had played in foiling his plans. He knew that Jeanne had been warned of his intentions in time to enable her to escape, with her son, out of Navarre into the heart of France and safety. Isabella often wondered what his reactions would have been to her deception. There were times when she felt a little remorse, but she only had to recall the cruelty of the *auto-da-fé* to justify her actions; and she never doubted for a moment that if she were presented with a similar situation she would meet it in the same way.

Her feelings toward Philip had necessarily changed. How could she love a man who had been ready to send a noble woman like Jeanne—or any person, man or woman for that matter—to the flames? It was merely because Jeanne, a woman whom she had known and loved, was involved that this had been brought home to her. Even in his tenderest moments she would think: If *I* became a heretic, he would condemn me to the flames.

If that was piety she preferred human frailty.

He cares more for his soul than anything on Earth—*his* soul. He thinks he is doing his duty in a manner which will please God and win him eternal bliss. Is that noble? Is that selfless? Is it according to Christ?

She wished she could be young and frivolous again. She wished—more than ever since she had betrayed him—that she could give him a son. It seemed that was not to be. There had been another pregnancy which had ended in failure.

She sought to please him as much as she could. She would not spare herself. She made the long and arduous journey to Bayonne, as his deputy, with the Duke of Alba, that she might meet her mother and her brother Charles, who was now King of France, for a conference on the borders of France and Spain.

What joy it was to see young Charles again, yet how sadly he reminded her of Carlos, with his hysteria and his moods of strangeness. He was still devoted to her and so happy in their reunion.

When she met her mother, she knew how she had grown up, for Catherine no longer had the power to disturb her. Truly she had escaped from Catherine; one day she would escape from Philip.

Catherine showed her awareness of that escape, saying: "You have become a Spaniard!" There was bitter disappointment in her words; she knew well enough that her eldest daughter was no longer her thrall.

I am no more Spaniard than French, thought the young Queen: I am myself.

However, she followed Philip's instructions in trying to persuade her mother to adopt a more Catholic policy in France; but she knew that Philip meant her inclusion in the mission to be merely a sign of his love for her, and to give her the pleasure of seeing her family. It was Alba and Catherine who paced the long galleries in endless converse, and discussed the future policies of France and Spain.

After she returned to Spain she became pregnant once more, and this time her child lived. Alas!, it was a daughter, and she named her Isabel Clara Eugenie. This child delighted her, but she was not released from the responsibility of giving Philip a son.

How tender was Philip at that time, superintending arrangements himself, making sure that everything should be done for the sake of his little Queen, seeming mutely to plead with her to give him that love which he needed from her and which she could not give! What could he do to please her? That was what he seemed to ask. And how could she answer: By not being Philip; by being just the kind and tender person you are to me without that grim shadow who is always beside you—

Philip the fanatic, Philip the murderer of men and women, Philip the man who would have tortured Jeanne of Navarre and sat in the royal gallery with Queen Isabella beside him while that noble body was burned at the stake. How could she say that to him? And if she did, how could he change? He was Philip, the man his father, his Spanish upbringing, and life itself had made him.

Carlos was restive. He was a man now, and he considered it was ridiculous of his father to treat him as though he were a boy—and he the Prince of Spain.

His conduct became more riotous. If Isabella had been allowed to visit him more frequently he would have been quieter. But his father prevented those visits. Isabella herself would have come. Had she not come to him when she needed help? He wanted to shout that through the streets of Valladolid and Madrid. But he must not. It was a secret between them.

Many thoughts chased each other confusedly through his troubled mind.

Together they had saved the heretic Jeanne of Navarre. That pleased him, and because of it he would always have a fondness for heretics. He wanted to be a soldier like Alba, winning victories, and with all the people welcoming him when he returned from the wars. In his dreams he rode at the head of a cavalcade, and everyone was shouting for the conquering hero, Don Carlos, instead of the Duke of Alba.

He wanted to be a statesman like Ruy Gomez da Silva, bland and wise, always calm. He wanted to be King, but not like Philip—quiet, morose, who did not know how to enjoy himself. It was time such as he were out of the way.

In his saner moments he liked to know what was happening in the dominions to which he was heir. Since the trouble in the Netherlands, Philip had talked of going there himself to subdue his unruly subjects.

"I wish I could go!" cried Carlos. "I understand heretics."

Now he began to talk of heretics with some affection. Why, he demanded, should they not be allowed to have their own thoughts? Why could they not have their own way of worshipping God? Why not?

Why not? Carlos would scream at his attendants. Why could they not answer? Why not indeed? Should they disagree with Don Carlos and face his unaccountable wrath, or alternatively run the risk of incurring the displeasure of the dread Inquisition?

Carlos knew what he wanted now. He wanted to go to the Netherlands. He wanted to be the Governor. He shouted his desire to all who cared to listen. He spoke continually of his sympathy with the people of the Netherlands, and at length a deputation came from that country asking that the Prince should be the new Governor.

Philip was exasperated. He visited his son.

"You cannot go to the Netherlands," he said coldly. "You do not know how to conduct yourself here. How could you hope to govern others when you cannot control yourself?"

Carlos's fury broke loose. He screamed his defiance. Then suddenly he stopped and, remembering how he and Isabella had outwitted this man, a slow smile touched his lips.

He spoke clearly and coherently. "You hate me, do you not? You know that I wish to go to the Netherlands and that the Flemings wish to have me there; but you refuse my request and theirs. You do this because you hate me. You frustrate me, and I know why. It is because of Isabella."

"You talk nonsense," said Philip.

"Do I? Do I, your gracious Majesty!" He laughed. He was thinking of her standing before him, appealing to him so beautifully. "Carlos . . . you are the only one I can trust to help me . . ." And together they had worked against this Philip. They had saved the life of the Queen of Navarre . . . he and Isabella. Small wonder that he loved all heretics. The Queen of Navarre was a heretic, and she had brought him close to Isabella . . . and Isabella loved him. She had come to him that they might work together against Philip.

He spoke quietly then, as though to himself: "She was mine, and you took her from me, but do not think it will always be thus. You are old . . . and she is young . . . and I am young, and I shall always be between you . . . because she is mine . . . mine . . ."

Philip turned abruptly and left him. His son was quite mad, but what an unhealthy situation was this! Carlos and . . . Isabella! It made him shudder. Carlos did not see himself as others saw him.

Yet Philip was deeply disturbed. He knew that Isabella did not really love him as he wished to be loved. He was fully aware of the restraint between them. He wanted the love of Isabella—the complete love of Isabella—more than he had ever wanted anything in his life.

Carlos . . . between them! That was ridiculous! But it was a disturbing thought.

After that visit from his father, Carlos's fury broke out more wildly than ever. He began to seek opportunities of offending the most important men.

The Inquisitor-General, Cardinal Espinosa, had banished an actor from Madrid. Carlos discovered this and, because he was beginning to hate all men in authority, he declared that the banished man was his favorite actor, and he wanted to know what right a priest had to oppose the son of the King. At the very first opportunity he sought out the Cardinal and, in the presence of the officials of the church and the court, he taxed him with deliberately seeking to oppose and annoy the Prince.

The Cardinal defended himself in as dignified a manner as possible, but Carlos was out for revenge and blood. He drew his sword, shouting: "Miserable priest who dares oppose a prince! Miserable torturer of heretics!"

None dared strike the Prince, but it was essential to save the Cardinal, and his friends, ranging themselves about him, hustled him from the room, leaving Carlos foaming at the lips, waving his sword and flashing his wild eyes menacingly at those who remained. Garcia Osorio was fortunately present and managed to soothe him.

But the great Cardinal Espinosa could not allow such an attack on his dignity as well as his person to pass without protest. He presented himself to Philip.

Philip was full of remorse and, as was so often the case when his subjects brought complaints of his son, the interview ended with the Cardinal's kneeling before the King and swearing to endure even the insults of the Prince for the sake of Philip.

One night Carlos tried to throw one of his servants out of a window because he did not obey his summons quickly enough. On another occasion when riding he pursued Don Garcia de Toledo, the brother of the great Duke of Alba, with his riding whip. Don Garcia had no alternative but to fly before him for fear that he might be forced into an affray in which the Prince might suffer.

It was becoming increasingly clear that Carlos was now nothing less that a violent madman.

Isabella was again pregnant, and Philip therefore decided that he would not go in person to the Netherlands. There was one whom he could trust and whom his Council agreed would be the very man to put down revolt in that troublesome country—a man of ruthless methods, of great personal courage, a fervent Catholic—the great Duke of Alba himself.

When the news of the Duke's appointment was brought to Carlos he fell into a mood of melancholy and would eat nothing for three days. He was growing very thin through lack of food, and when his frenzies were on him they would exhaust him.

He would lie in his bed and refuse to see anyone, and as he lay there he would talk to himself of death and hate, blood and murder.

Alba, ready to leave for the Netherlands, had occasion to visit the Prince, and when he saw him Carlos completely lost control.

He came out of his silent melancholy and shouted: "Who are you who dares to come here and mock me? How dare you take the governorship of the Netherlands when you know that it belongs to me?"

Alba, seeing the condition of the Prince, sought to placate him. "Your Highness is too precious to his Majesty to be exposed to the dangers of the Netherlands."

"Do you suggest that I am a coward, sir?"

"Indeed not, your Highness. We know you long to go and fight Spain's battles. It is solely . . ."

"You know that, and you consent to go in my place! You take from me that which is mine?"

"Your Highness, as heir to the throne . . ."

"Ah! Remember it, villain!" Carlos, laughing horribly, showed Alba the dagger he had been hiding in his sleeve. "This is for you, sir. This is for you, Lord Duke. We will send the corpse of a noble Duke to the Netherlands . . . that we will!"

Carlos's maniacal laughter rang out as he lunged at the Duke; but Alba was ready; he caught Carlos's arm and twisted it so that the dagger fell to the ground.

Carlos, impotent to continue his attack, screamed, and attendants came running in.

"Take this man. Set him in irons. Bring me a sword and I will pierce him to the heart. I will kill him . . . kill him . . ."

He glared at the cold face of the Duke, and he hated him in that moment almost as much as he hated his father.

Alba said contemptuously: "Take him. Give him some soothing medicine. His Highness is very excited this day."

Then, almost throwing the Prince into the arms of his attendants, he strode from the apartment.

Isabella was aware of the rapidly increasing tension between father and son.

She longed to comfort Carlos, but she was again pregnant, and each successive pregnancy left her less able to contend with the next.

She was praying urgently for a son.

Ruy, whom she looked upon as one of her greatest friends, knew of her anxiety. She was aware that he shared it. He, more than anyone, seemed to fear the growing menace of Carlos.

Once he said to her: "If your Majesty should have a son, he would be the heir to the throne."

"And Carlos?" she asked.

"The Council has agreed that in such circumstances Carlos would be declared unfit."

"Poor Carlos. He would never forgive me."

Ruy answered: "Carlos would forgive your Majesty anything."

She was startled. Was he warning her, this good kind friend who seemed to see further than anyone else? Was he suggesting that Carlos was in love with her! She could not accept that. He was her friend; she was sorry for him; but that he should think of himself in the role of lover was incongruous.

Ruy said: "Sometimes I wonder what would happen if by some terrible mischance Philip should die and the crown pass to Carlos. Spain would be as Rome under Caligula."

"I see," she said, "that I must have a son . . . if not now . . . later."

"Your Highness will. I beg of you not to be too anxious."

But the child which was born to her, though healthy, was a girl.

"There is plenty of time," said Philip and Ruy and all those to whom the birth of a male child was so important.

Then Carlos demanded their attention.

After the birth of her daughter, Isabella's convalescence was a long one. She was subject to headaches and fits of dizziness; she had grown pale and thin. Yet such was her beauty that, although she had changed from the dazzling young girl who had first come to Spain nearly ten years ago, she was still possessed of great charm. If her eyes were less bright, her hair less lustrous, there was in her countenance an expression of such sweetness that those about her loved her more than they had when she had been a sparkling young girl.

In spite of her ill-health, she was still determined to give Philip a son.

Carlos was mad and must never be allowed to rule Spain. She traced this new and greater wildness in him to their adventure together when she had asked his help for Jeanne of Navarre, for again and again he would refer to his sympathy with heretics, and continually he spoke of her, the Queen.

Her secret weighed heavily upon her; she was remorseful, yet she knew that, could she have that time over again, she would act in exactly the same way.

Philip, absorbed in state duties, moodily occupied with thoughts of Carlos, did not notice the sad preoccupation of Isabella. Always with him she was the charming and obedient wife; and although he knew that he did not possess her passionate devotion, for which he longed, he still believed that one day it might be his.

Isabella spent much time at Pastrana in the Palace of the Prince and Princess of Eboli. She found great comfort in the companionship of Ruy and his wife. Ruy, in particular, understood something of the conflict within her and he knew that it concerned Carlos.

On one occasion he reminded her of the conversation they had had before the birth of her daughter. He knew, and the Princess his wife knew, that it would be unsafe for her to bear more children.

"This problem will have to be faced by Philip and the Council," Ruy said to her. "Carlos cannot rule; but you and the King have two daughters. It may well be that Isabel Clara Eugenie will make as great a Queen as her forbear, the great Isabella."

"What would Carlos feel if he were replaced by a girl?" she asked.

Ruy said: "Your Majesty must forgive my forwardness. If I speak to you as a father, that is because I am old enough to fill that role and because of my great regard for you. Let your task be to comfort Philip, to preserve your strength for this great work. You have given him two daughters. Let that suffice."

She gave him her sweetest smile.

"I thank you, my Prince, for your advice, but I would not take it if I could. Very soon I hope my son will be born."

Both Ruy and his wife were sad to hear this news that once again she was to have a child.

𝒞arlos had decided to wait no longer. His father hated him. He had been born for one purpose, and he was now going to fulfill it. He was going to kill his father.

It had been such a wonderful dream: to raise the dagger and thrust it into the black velvet doublet, to watch the dull red stain on black velvet and diamonds, to see the pale eyes glaze in anguish—but not before Philip had looked into the face of the murderer and known him for his son.

Afterward he would ride away—perhaps to France, perhaps to Austria. But he would not long stay away from Spain; he would come back . . . for Isabella.

He kept his secret, planning cunningly. It would have to be a moment when he was alone with his father, for there must be none to protect Philip. He, Carlos, would be subdued; he would mislead Philip.

"Father," he would say, "I will reform. I swear I will."

And when Philip came close to lay a hand on his shoulder, to speak of his pleasure in his son's calmness—then would come the quick uplift of the arm, the deep thrust, and blood . . . blood . . . the blood of Philip.

He had arranged for horses which would carry him away from the palace. He had told Juan and Garcia that he would need horses; he had ordered both of them to procure horses for him.

The idea of confession occurred to him. He had taken great pleasure in the confessional, for when he confessed it was as though he lived through exciting experiences again.

He did not intend to confess his plan to murder, but there was that about Fray Diego de Chaves which drew his innermost thoughts from him.

When he said: "What have you to confess this day, my son?" Carlos's hot tongue licked his lips. He was obsessed with the great sin of patricide, but in the solemnity of the confessional box he was suddenly afraid. He was going to commit murder, but he told himself that it was a judicial murder. He was going to do something which, all his life, he had longed to do. But he wanted absolution. He did not want to burn in hell for committing a murder which was no ordinary murder.

So he would demand absolution, and this poor priest would not dare deny him, nor would he dare betray him.

He said: "I am going to kill a man, and I wish for absolution."

"My son! You plan murder and you ask forgiveness! You know that cannot be."

"It must be!" screamed Carlos. "It must be."

"Murder, my son, is a mortal sin. You plan to commit it, and ask for absolution beforehand. Think what you say."

"It is possible. I am the Prince."

"Sir, there is One higher than all the princes of this world."

"Then He will forgive me when He knows what a wicked man I intend to kill."

Fray Diego prayed that he would be able to deal adequately with this new phase of madness. He said: "What plot is this? I must know before I can grant absolution."

"It is a person of very high rank whom I shall kill."

"It would be necessary for me to know the name of this person and any of those who plot with you."

"None plot with me. I plot alone. Come, man. Grant absolution or I will run my sword through your miserable body."

"I must know the name of this person of high rank."

"You shall. His name is Philip, and he is King of Spain!"

The excitement was too much for Carlos; he fell to the ground in a fit.

The priest called for help and dispatched a messenger to the King.

Carlos was in his apartments. He was sullen, would speak to no one, and all that day he had eaten nothing. He could not remember what he had said to the priest.

He lay on his bed. Beneath the coverlet he had hidden two swords. They were naked, ready for use. Beneath his pillow were two loaded pistols. He was trembling with excitement. But what had he said to the priest?

He heard voices in the antechamber. With one hand he grasped a sword; with his chin he felt for the pistols.

The door opened unceremoniously and several men entered the room. Among them Carlos recognized the Count of Feria.

He struggled up. "How dare you break in on me thus!" he cried. "Why do you come? Men-at-arms . . . here! The Prince commands you. Arrest these intruders."

There were several men about his bed then, and with a sudden movement Feria had stepped forward and stripped off the coverlet.

Before Carlos could cry out, he had seized the two swords. Carlos's hands went at once to the pistols, but one of the men was quicker than he was. He seized the Prince's wrists while another took the pistols from under his pillow.

"How . . . dare you!" sobbed Carlos. "You forget . . . I am the son of the King."

At that moment there was a brief hush as Philip himself entered the chamber. He stood at the end of the bed, and in the candlelight father and son gazed at each other. Carlos thought he had never seen such a cruel face, never looked into such cold eyes. He was very frightened; for he knew that at last he had gone too far.

"What . . . what does your Majesty want?" he stammered.

"Close all doors," said Philip.

This was done, and now Carlos saw that the room was filled with men and that the Count of Feria had taken up his stand on the King's right hand.

Carlos was trembling. He knew that the doom which he had always dreaded was upon him.

The King did not speak to his son. He addressed the assembly. "I place the Prince, Don Carlos, in your hands," he said. "Guard him well. Do nothing that he commands without first consulting me. Keep him a close prisoner."

"Why?" cried Carlos. "What have I done? I have not killed you. I have been betrayed. You cannot treat me thus . . . You cannot."

"I have nothing more to say," answered Philip; and he turned away.

Carlos knelt on the bed. "Father," he pleaded. "I beg of you . . . do not make me a prisoner. Let me go free. I shall kill myself if I am a prisoner."

"Only madmen kill themselves," said Philip sternly.

"I am not mad. I am only sad . . . sad and desperately unhappy. I always have been. Nobody loves me except . . . except . . . But those who love me are kept from me. But that does not alter their love. I am there . . . whether you wish it or not. I am there between you. I am young, King Philip, and you are old. I shall kill somebody . . . even if it is myself . . ."

Philip was at the door. He had made up his mind how he would act, and the councillors of state had agreed with his actions. The matter was finished.

Windows were fastened; doors were locked; and guards placed inside and outside the apartment.

Don Carlos was indeed his father's prisoner.

Carlos lived in his own dark world, lying on his bed for days, speaking to no one, rising in sudden frenzy and throwing himself against the walls of his room, refusing to eat for days at a time, then demanding a feast and eating so ravenously that he was ill.

What was to become of Carlos?

While Carlos lived there could be no peace of mind for Philip. The Prince was well guarded, but escape from a prison such as his was not impossible. What if he found his way to Philip and committed the crime he had planned? What if, Philip dead, he called himself King of Spain? Who could deny his right to the title?

Philip thought: I, who would give my life to my country, have given it a monster.

To whom could he speak of such a matter? To Isabella? She was frail, wraithlike; he trembled to look at her. She seemed aloof from him; he wondered what rumors she had heard.

"Philip," she said, "could I not see Carlos?"

"Indeed not."

"I might help him. He was fond of me."

"I know it," said Philip grimly.

"What will become of Carlos?"

He did not answer. He knew she read certain thoughts which came into his mind, for her dark eyes grew darker with horror.

She wanted to cry: "Philip, you could not do *that*. You could not murder your own son." She remembered what he had said at the *auto-da-fé* in Valladolid. She heard it repeated many times. "If my son were a heretic, I would carry the wood and light the fire at his feet." But he could not murder his own son.

She could not speak her thoughts aloud, for outwardly he had made a Spaniard of her.

There was nothing they could say to one another. Carlos was between them.

Philip was closeted with Espinosa, the Inquisitor-General. Isabella believed they talked of Carlos.

She began to think of the excuses he would make: "Carlos spoke as a heretic, and those who speak as heretics are condemned to death."

But not your own son, Philip! she wanted to cry. Not your own son!

Philip was closeted with Ruy.

And she knew that they all planned to rid themselves of Carlos.

They were alone in their bedchamber—the King and the Queen—but it seemed to them both that there was another there, a shadowy third. He would not let them rest. Both were thinking of him and his demoniacal laughter. The madness of him! thought Philip. The pity of him! thought Isabella.

Philip began to pace up and down. He had a decision to make. He must do this thing. But how could he? He is my own son, he mused. Then it seemed to him that he heard the stern voice of righteousness, of God perhaps: "What if your conscience *is* burdened with murder? What is your conscience compared with the good of Spain?"

He was in an agony of indecision. There were so many thoughts in his mind. He longed to rid himself of Carlos. He feared Carlos; and ridiculous as it seemed, Carlos *was* between him and Isabella.

What was she thinking as she lay there watching him? Of Carlos? She knew his thoughts. She must know the purpose of those secret meetings with Ruy and the Cardinal. She knew that the destruction of Carlos was being planned.

He could not speak of it. He was deeply conscious of that quality in him which did not allow frankness. Moreover she had set herself apart from him. Yet her eyes were pleading with him now. You cannot kill Carlos, Philip, they said. You cannot kill your own son.

And why should she plead? What was the meaning of Carlos's secret smile? Only Isabella could calm Carlos. Only Isabella was fond of him. Was there some secret between them?

Why had Carlos looked so cunning... so pleased... so certain when he had said: "I shall always be between you!"

"Philip," said Isabella, "you are tired and you have much on your mind."

"So much," he answered. "So many decisions to make."

He longed to put his arms about her, to beg her to help him. He wanted to explain his feelings for his son, his disgust of him, the humiliation he suffered on his account, and above all that faint—and he was sure unfounded—jealousy.

But how could he talk of such things to Isabella? All through the night the agony of indecision continued.

Dr. Olivares sought out the King. He must speak to him in private.

"Your Highness, the Prince of Eboli has spoken to me concerning Don Carlos."

"How do you find my son?"

"Sire, he is sick—very sick of the mind."

"And of the body?"

"It is astonishing how he remains as well as he does in that respect. Your Highness, the Prince of Eboli has told me it is your Majesty's wish that a certain medicine should be given to Don Carlos."

"If the Prince of Eboli told you that, you may take it as a command from me."

"Then I crave your Majesty's pardon for the interruption. I did not care to administer such a medicine except at the express command of your Highness."

"I have decided," said Philip coolly, "that this medicine will be beneficial."

"I understand your Highness."

Dr. Olivares bowed and glided away.

Isabella said: "Why did Dr. Olivares come to see you this day? Has he news of the Prince?"

"Yes," said Philip.

"He is better?" she asked eagerly.

"He will never be better. It is for us to hope that he will not be worse."

Isabella, looking at her husband, saw in his face a calmness which, she knew, came from his having reached a solution to a problem which had given him much anxiety. She came to him and slipped her arm through his; it was a gesture from the old days when she had been more demonstrative in her affection.

"Philip," she said, "you seem at peace. I am glad."

Then he turned to her and gravely kissed her brow.

"Isabella," he said, "let us pray as we have never prayed before. Let us implore God that this time it may be a son."

Isabella felt suddenly cold as she looked into the inscrutable face of her husband.

Carlos was in a docile mood. He took the broth which had been specially prepared for him; but after drinking it he became very weak and could only lie still and speak in whispers.

He seemed not to know where he was, to be living in the past, calling himself the Little One, and asking for his locket.

His attendants sent for his Confessor.

Philip was called to him. He gave no sign of the emotion within him. He stood at one end of the bed, and as Carlos opened his eyes and looked at his father a faint smile touched the Prince's lips.

Carlos *knew*. In those seconds his eyes told his father that he knew. There was no hatred now; he knew that soon he would have left this world in which his father had all that he, Carlos, had most desired: Dignity, the respect of men, and . . . Isabella.

Carlos tried to speak, but the death rattle was in his throat. His smile said: "I was to have killed you, and I made you kill me instead. You think you are the victor, Philip. But are you? You know, as I know, that it shall be as I said: I shall always be between you and Isabella."

And for a moment, as he looked into the cold blue eyes, he saw Philip flinch, and he knew that in death the victory belonged to Carlos.

He had made a murderer of the man he hated; he had made him a murderer of his own son.

Isabella now knew that she would never give Philip the son for which they had fervently prayed. She was dying in the attempt to do so.

She had mourned Carlos deeply; she knew that his tragedy was interwoven with her own. She was weary of this harsh world in which she lived. From the Netherlands came terrible stories of the suffering under the cruelty of Alba . . . in the name of Spain. Her beloved France was torn in agony with its wars of religion. She did not wish to live amid such cruelty.

She had escaped from her mother, but she could never escape from Philip. She had been right to fear him as she had when she had first heard she was to marry him. Whenever he was near her now she saw him, not as Philip the King and tender husband, but as Philip the murderer of his own son.

She thought: If I had been a heretic, he would have carried the wood; he would have lighted it at my feet.

Always about him was an aura of horror. She could never think of that Philip who had been kind to her without seeing his other self, the gloomy fanatic, the man who had sought to bring Jeanne to the stake, the man who had taken his sword in his hand and sworn to serve the cruel Inquisition, who had sat tense and exultant while the bodies of men and women were burned in the flames, and the screams of martyrs rose to Heaven. Carlos was indeed between them, for she could never see her husband but as the man who had murdered his own son.

Yet she was sorry for him, this strange, frustrated man.

Now that her end was near she wanted to say to him: "Philip, you are failing to realize your dreams and the failure comes from yourself. Show kindness and tolerance to the Flemings and you will beat Orange yet."

Kindness! Tolerance! But he had determined to set up the Inquisition all over the world; he believed the Inquisition to be an instrument of God. There was no kindness and tolerance there.

"Philip, Philip!" she wanted to cry. "How mistaken you are! You did not dream impossible dreams. You might have won the world and I might have loved you as you wished to be loved. With kindness and toleration the world could have been happy under your domination. I might have loved the man you could have been. But you do not understand, and the failure to make your dreams realities is due to yourself."

But how could she say such things? And how could he ever understand them?

Her daughter was born to live but a few hours.

Philip sat by her bed. He knew that she was slipping away from him.

"Isabella!" he cried. "Come back to me. We will be happy yet."

She smiled sadly. "It is too late, Philip," she whispered. "Oh, do not grieve for me. You see me well on the way out of this unhappy world into a better one."

"Isabella . . . Isabella . . . there is so much I have to tell you . . . so much I have to say. Life for us will be better yet."

But he knew that he had lost her; and it seemed to him that he heard the mocking laughter of the son whom he had murdered.

A
FAVORITE
OF THE
QUEEN

*I*t was hot, even for *August*; the foul odors from the river, carrying the threat of pestilence, hung in the sullen air that sultry day; but the crowds who were assembling on Tower Hill were oblivious of discomfort. Traders had left their shops or stalls in Candlewick Street, East Chepe, and the Poultry; horse-dealers were coming from Smithfield Square; the goldsmiths from Lombard Street, the mercers of Chepeside had deserted their houses, realizing that there could be little business at such a time. Apprentices, risking a whipping, crept out after their masters, determined to see what could be seen on Tower Hill that day.

Laughing and jesting they came. All men and women believed that the hardships of Henry VII's reign were behind them and the days of plenty were at hand. No more cruel taxes would be wrung from them; no more fines; no more impositions. The old miser King was dead and in his place was a bonny golden boy who laughed loudly, who jested and made sport, and loved to show himself to the citizens of London.

It was he who had provided this day's pleasure for them; and it clearly indicated what they might expect of him.

"God bless King Hal!' they cried. "See how he pleases his people! He is the one for us."

The cheers for the King mingled with the jeers for the traitors. Some apprentices had made two effigies which they held high above the crowd, to be mocked and pelted with refuse.

"Death to them! Death to the extortioners! Death to the misers, and long life to King Harry!"

Jostling, cursing, laughing, they surged about the hill. At the summit, close to the scaffold, members of the nobility were gathered. The bell of St. Peter ad Vincula had begun to toll.

At the edge of the crowd, not venturing into it, stood a boy. He was pale, soberly dressed, and was staring, mournful and bewildered, at the weather-washed walls of the great fortress which seemed to stand on guard like a stone giant. So grim, so cruel did it seem to the boy, that he turned his gaze from it to the green banks where the starry loose-strife flowers were blooming. He remembered a day—long ago it seemed to him now—when he had taken his little brother to the river's edge to pick flowers. He remembered how they had strolled along, arms full of blossoms. The flower of the water betony was like the helmet a soldier would wear, and he was reminded that soldiers would soon be coming out of the great prison, and with them would be the men who were to die on Tower Hill that day.

"Death to the traitors!" shouted a man near him. "Death to the tax-gatherers! Death to Dudley and Empson!"

The little boy felt the blood rush to his face, for his name was John Dudley, and his father was one of those who would shortly lay their heads upon the block.

He would not look, this little John. He dared not. Why had he come? He knew not. Was it because he had hoped to see a miracle? His father had seemed to him the cleverest man in England; and not only did he seem so to John, but to others, for Edmund Dudley, a humble lawyer, had become chief adviser to the King. But kings die, and often favors die with them; and a friend to one king may be a traitor to another; and if that king is desirous of winning his people's love, and those people demand a man's head as a symbol of *his* love—then that head is given.

He was standing up there now, the father of the boy. Little John stared at the ground, but he knew what was happening, for he heard the shouts of the people. Then there was silence. He looked up at the sky; he looked at the river; but he dared not look at the scaffold.

His father was speaking. The well-remembered voice rose and fell, but the boy did not hear what he said.

Then all was silent again until there came a shuddering gasp from the crowd. John now knew that he was fatherless.

He stood, helpless and bewildered, not knowing whether to turn shuddering away or to run forward and look with the crowd at his father's blood.

Now the executioner would be holding up his father's head, for he heard the cry: "Here is the head of a traitor!"

He wondered why he did not cry. He felt that he never would cry again. The shouting people, the gray fortress, the sullen river—they seemed so indifferent to the plight of one more orphan.

Such a short while ago he had been John Dudley, eldest son of a king's favorite minister, with a brilliant future before him. Now he was John Dudley—orphan, penniless—the son of a man whom the King had called a traitor.

He felt a hand on his shoulder. "John," said a voice, "you should not be here."

Turning, he saw standing beside him a man whom he knew well, a man whom he had looked upon in the light of an uncle, one of his father's great friends in the days of his prosperity—Sir Richard Guildford.

"I . . . wished to come," said John haltingly.

"I guessed it," said Sir Richard. " 'Twas a brave thing to do, John." He looked at the boy quizzically. "And not to shed a tear!"

He slipped his arm through that of the boy and began to lead him away.

"It is better for you not to be here, John," he said.

"What would they do to me?" asked the boy. "What would they do if they knew I was his son?"

"They'd not harm you, a boy of . . . how old is it?"

"Nine years, sir."

"Nine years! 'Tis young to be left alone and helpless . . . and your mother with two others."

"They will take all we have . . ."

Sir Richard nodded. "But 'twas not done for the love of your father's possessions. It was done to please the people. Who knows . . ." He looked at the boy shrewdly, but stopped short.

"Did the people so hate my father then?" asked the boy incredulously.

"Kings must have scapegoats, my boy. When a king does what his subjects do not like, that is the fault of his statesmen; it is only when he pleases them that the credit is his. It is the late King against whom the people cry out. Your father and Sir Richard Empson are the scapegoats."

The boy clenched his fists. "To be a scapegoat! I like that not. I would be a man . . . and a ruler."

Then suddenly he began to cry, and the man, walking beside him, helplessly watched the tears roll down his cheeks.

Sir Richard understood. It was natural that the boy should cry. He did not speak for some seconds, then he said: "This day you shall come home with me. Nay, do not concern yourself. I have seen your mother. I have told her that I would find you and take you to my home."

They had now reached the river's edge where a barge was waiting; and as they went slowly up the river, the sobs which shook the young body became less frequent.

At length they alighted, and mounted the privy steps which led to the lawns before Sir Richard's home.

As they entered the mansion, and crossed the great hall, Sir Richard called: "Jane! Where are you, my child?"

A girl, slightly younger than John, appeared in the gallery and looked down on the hall.

"I have a playmate for you, Jane. Come here."

Jane came solemnly down the great staircase.

"It is John," she said; and the boy, looking into her face and seeing the tear stains on her cheeks, knew that she too had wept for his father, and was comforted.

"He has suffered much this day, Jane," said Sir Richard. "We must take care of him."

Jane stood beside the boy and slipped her hand into his.

Sir Richard watched them. Let the boy forget the shouts of the mob on Tower Hill in the company of little Jane. He was safe with Jane.

As Sir Richard Guildford watched John Dudley grow away from his tragedy in the months that followed, he recognized in him that strength of character which had been Edmund Dudley's. He was excited by the boy, sensing in him latent ambition, the will to succeed, the passionate desire to bring back honor to the Dudley name. Sir Richard could look with pleasure upon the growing friendship between his daughter and this boy; and nothing less than having John in his own house and bringing him up as his son would satisfy him.

It was not difficult to arrange this, for Sir Edmund's widow and her children were forced to look to relations and friends for help, and Lady Dudley was only too glad that Sir Richard had taken this interest in her son.

It was Sir Richard's custom to talk to the boy, to nourish that ambition which he knew was in him; and one day, as they walked in the City to Fleet Lane and over Fleet Bridge and on to Ficquets Fields, Sir Richard talked of John's father.

"Your father was a great man, John. When he was your age, his position was little better than your own."

"Nay sir," said John. "It is true that my father was the son of a small farmer, and himself but a lawyer, yet he was descended from the Lords Dudley; and I am the son of a man who is called a traitor."

Sir Richard snapped his fingers. "The connection with the Lords Dudley was never proved," he said, "and I doubt it existed outside your father's imagination."

The boy flushed hotly at that, but Sir Richard went on: "Oh, it was clever enough. Dudley needed aristocratic ancestors, but he found them for himself. No doubt he made good use of them. But between ourselves, John, there is more credit due to a man when he has had to climb from the valley to the top of the mountain than when he starts near the top."

John was silent and Sir Richard continued: "Just for ourselves we will see Sir Edmund Dudley as the son of a farmer, himself a lawyer, yet such a master of his profession that the King sought his aid and through him and his friend Empson, ruled England."

The boy's eyes had begun to shine. "The son of a farmer merely— and he one of those who ruled England!"

"What should that teach you? Just this: No matter how lowly you may be, there is no limit—*no* limit—to the heights to which you may climb. Think of the King. Dare he look too far back? Is it not true that his Tudor ancestor was the son of a groom, and a bastard? Think, boy, think! This is treason and I'll whisper it. Dudley or Tudor? Is one better than the other? Remember it. Always remember it. Your father had great ambition. It may be now that he looks down from Heaven on you . . . his eldest son. It may be that he asks himself: What will my son do in this world? Will he rise as I did? Will he learn from my mistakes? Has he the fire within him which will make him a great man? John, I doubt not that your father looks down from Heaven upon you and prays and hopes."

John did not forget those words. He was determined to be as great a man as his father.

In the games he played, he was always the leader. Already he was Jane's hero. Sir Richard was pleased as he watched the growing affection between John Dudley and Jane Guildford.

Sir Richard's position at Court had brought him into contact with the King, who was as yet a careless boy in love with pleasure, yet a boy with an awakening conscience. Sir Richard thought that the King's conscience might play its part in the future of his young protégé.

Henry still frowned at the name of Dudley. He was well aware that the execution of his father's favorite and adviser had been carried out for the sake of his, Henry's, popularity. Henry had not yet come to terms with his conscience. It could not yet persuade him, as it would later, that Dudley and Empson had deserved their fate, so the very mention of the name Dudley brought discomfort to him. But when Sir Richard subtly begged royal permission to ask the Parliament for the repeal of the attainder against the Dudleys, Henry was almost eager to give that permission.

Let the boy inherit his father's wealth. The King did not want it; he had that vast accumulation of riches, which his own father had amassed through his thrifty reign, to squander. Yes, let the attainder be repealed. Let the son of Edmund Dudley have his father's riches. The King could then feel happier when the names of Dudley and Empson were mentioned; he could put aside the thought that those two men had been executed to placate the people from whom much of his father's wealth had been extorted.

The first step was therefore taken. John was no longer penniless. He was a rich *parti* for young Jane; although he could not yet go to Court.

Sir Richard came home full of excitement. "See what I have done for you, John!" he cried. "Now it will be your turn."

"Yes, now it is my turn," said the solemn boy.

Jane watched them gravely, wondering what this was all about. But there was no need to explain such matters to Jane. She was happy because her father was happy; and she saw in John that deep brooding concentration which she respected although she could not share it.

As they went out to the stables together she said: "Something good has happened, has it not?"

He nodded but he said no more then for he did not wish the grooms to hear.

As they rode across the clover-starred meadows, he said: "I am no longer without means. My father's fortune is to be returned to my family."

"John . . . does it mean you will go away?"

He smiled at the fear in her eyes. "If I went away, I should come back. You know, do you not, Jane, that when we are old enough we are to marry?"

"Yes, John," she answered.

"You will be happy then, Jane. So shall I!"

He was sure of her contentment—as sure as he was that one day he would be a leader of men. It did not occur to her that this might be arrogance on his part; if he was arrogant, then, in her eyes, arrogance was a virtue.

As they cantered across the fields she was thinking of their future, of their marriage and the children they would have.

He too was thinking of the future, but not of his life with Jane. Jane's love was something he took for granted. The thunder of horses' hooves seemed to say to him "Dudley—Tudor!"

Read all of the Tudor novels in historical order published by Three Rivers Press

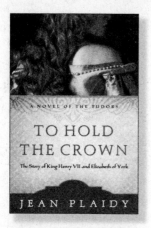

To Hold the Crown
The Story of King Henry VII and Elizabeth of York

1

Katherine of Aragon
The Story of a Spanish Princess and an English Queen

2

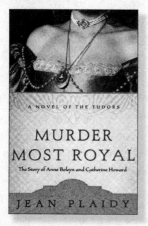

Murder Most Royal
The Story of Anne Boleyn and Catherine Howard

3

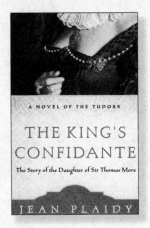

The King's Confidante
The Story of the Daughter
of Sir Thomas More

More previously published as
St. Thomas's Eve

4

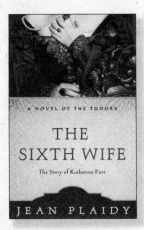

The Sixth Wife
The Story of Katherine Parr

5

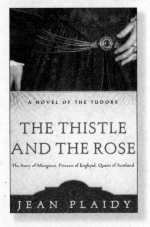

The Thistle and the Rose
The Story of Margaret, Princess
of England, Queen of Scotland

6

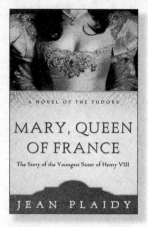

Mary, Queen of France
The Story of the Youngest Sister
of Henry VIII

7

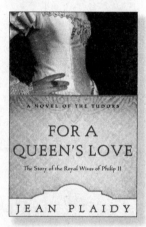

For a Queen's Love
The Stories of the Royal Wives
of Philip II

previously published as
The Spanish Bridegroom

AVAILABLE IN SPRING '10

8

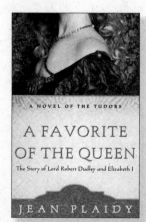

A Favorite of the Queen
The Story of Lord Robert Dudley
and Elizabeth I

previously published as
Gay Lord Robert

9